GUERNICA

GUERNICA

A Novel

Dave Boling

PICADOR

First published 2008 by Bloomsbury USA, New York

First published in Great Britain 2008 by Picador

This edition published 2010 by Picador
an imprint of Pan Macmillan, a division of Macmillan Publishers Limited
Pan Macmillan, 20 New Wharf Road, London N1 9RR
Basingstoke and Oxford
Associated companies throughout the world
www.panmacmillan.com

ISBN 978-0-330-54413-9

1 3 5 7 9 8 6 4 2

A CIP catalogue record for this book is available
from the British Library.

Printed and bound in the UK by
CPI Mackays, Chatham ME5 8TD

Visit **www.picador.com** to read more about all our books
and to buy them. You will also find features, author interviews and
news of any author events, and you can sign up for e-newsletters
so that you're always first to hear about our new releases.

For the victims of Guernica . . .
and all the Guernicas that followed

Guernica is the happiest town in the world . . . governed by an assembly of countrymen who meet under an oak tree and always reach the fairest decisions.

—Jean-Jacques Rousseau

Guernica was . . . an experimental horror.

—Winston Churchill, *The Gathering Storm*

The painting which I am presently working on will be called *Guernica*. By means of it, I express my abhorrence of the race that has sunk Spain in an ocean of pain and death.

—Pablo Picasso

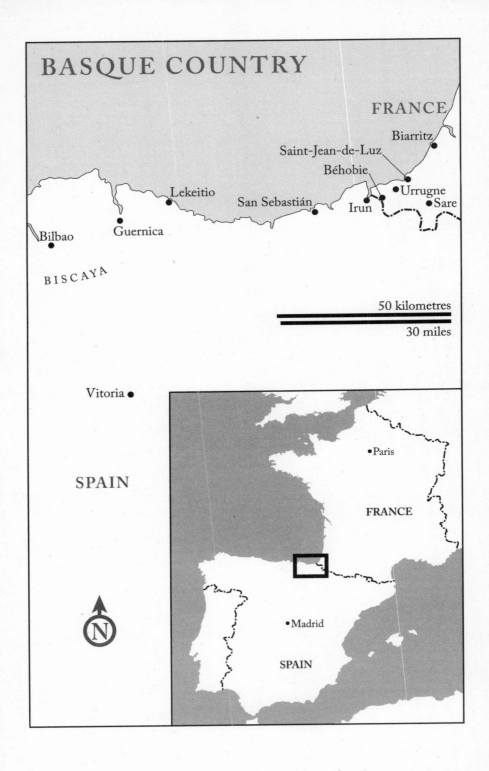

BASQUE COUNTRY

FRANCE

Biarritz

Saint-Jean-de-Luz

Béhobie

Urrugne

Lekeitio

San Sebastián

Sare

Irun

Bilbao

Guernica

BISCAYA

50 kilometres

30 miles

Vitoria

SPAIN

Paris

FRANCE

Madrid

SPAIN

N

PROLOGUE
(Guernica, 1939)

Justo Ansotegui returns to the market now to hear the language and to buy soap. He places bars in scattered dishes where he can catch their scent during the day, although they fail to mask the odours of the livestock that have lived in his house for generations. As he sits in the evening, he'll idly lift a bar to his nose. He strokes his moustache with one so the scent will linger in the coarse black hairs that droop past his upper lip and conceal his expressions. The many times when he awakens in the night, he touches a bar at his bedside and then smells his fingers, hoping the fragrance will invite certain memories into his dreams.

Alaia Aldecoa, the village soap-maker, explains that the bars are blended with sheep's milk and scented with an ingredient she keeps secret, but Justo is not interested in how they are made, only how they make him feel.

'*Kaixo*, Alaia, it's Justo,' he says, approaching her booth on market day.

She accepts his unnecessary introduction. She has known him for years, and besides, his scent has preceded him. From the pocket of his braced woollen trousers, now drooping at the waist, he extracts a slippery coin. It carries a pleasant smell, as it's coated with residue from a soap bar he keeps in there, too.

'I would like a bar of the Miren blend,' he says.

The soap-maker pinches a smile at the sound of the name 'Miren', and, as she does every week, she has two bars set aside in a separate wrapper for Justo. She sells that blend to no one else. As always, she rejects his payment, and he places the coin back in his pocket. She devotes time each week to trying to imagine something she might say that would brighten his day, but once again she has nothing but soap to give him.

It's Monday afternoon, the traditional shopping day, but the new market isn't crowded. Business resumed reluctantly in the past three years, and the market is now some distance east of the old site, closer to the river. It's smaller because traffic is scant and money scarce, and so many people are gone. Since much of the trade is restricted by government control and rationing, market day is now about things other than just buying and selling.

As he moves from Alaia's booth on the edge of the marketplace, Justo listens to the clacking of the gathered *amumak*, like a clutch of hens, trading their only abundant currency: gossip. In earlier times the grandmothers would negotiate the purchase of beef tongue and shoulders of lamb, and the mild green peppers they would dust with garlic and fry in olive oil. And they would sniff at the colourful garlands of chorizo sausages hanging from the butcher's booth. The spicy links would be browned in an iron frying pan along with eggs, which would absorb their rusty juices and pungent taste. Scent tentacles from the stove could lure a family to the table without conscious assent. The flavour would cause the little ones to gather at Amuma's lap and exhale into her face the garlicky breath of joy.

There's no haste for them at the market now; there is so little to choose from. So they painstakingly examine every vegetable and heft each precious egg.

'These are too small,' one says, triggering a flurry of critiques from the others.

'These vegetables are not fresh.'

'I would never serve this to my family.'

'Are we buying today, ladies, or just fondling?' the vendor asks.

They scoff in unison but are reluctant to replace the produce. It's easier to deem the food unacceptable than admit they cannot afford it. Even in good times the elderly women were particular about such matters, since cooking defined them. More than the collection, inflation and distribution of gossip, their mission is to feed. Ageing may change many things, but it can't diminish their skills in the kitchen. And to improve as a cook is a way to annex emotional territory within a family. But with so little food now there is no medium for their art. And the hunger that once chewed at them like a mean dog now seems more like an annoying house-guest who simply refuses to leave.

Justo passes their gathering. They gesture and pause, then resume chattering and bobbing, energized by a new topic. They will peck at the particulars of Justo's life until another subject causes them to blink and move on. Communication is an illusion anyway, since all speak at once.

The bells of Santa María toll the hour, and many turn their heads to look up into the cloudless sky.

Under the blue-striped canvas awnings of the *taberna*, older men play *mus*, a four-man insult contest waged around a deck of cards.

'Come, play, Justo, I will need a new partner once this one smothers under the mountain of shit he's been using for brains,' an old friend calls, sparking rebukes from the other players. Successively all four grumble, '*Mus!*' and it is unanimous that the inadequate cards they've been given should be tossed in. If all players agree, the hands are scrapped and re-dealt with fresh starts and new opportunities for all.

'The world could learn much from this game,' a relieved player says.

Justo declines the offer to play, which is only a courtesy anyway. Of the numerous activities denied a man with one arm, Justo has found that forgoing *mus* is among the smaller sacrifices.

So they proceed with the tics and gestures used to signal to their partners, acts that are not only allowed but encouraged. The creative Basques decided that cheating could be prevented by declaring it a legal part of the game. Accordingly, if one never recognizes the existence of a border, then carrying goods across it is not smuggling, merely nocturnal commerce. And if a race believes it has always lived in its own nation, then protecting its imaginary boundaries is a matter of patriotism, not separatism.

A wink of the right eye to a *mus* partner reveals a bit of information and a tongue-waggle supplies another, but when the tricks fall badly, one speculates that his partner uses his farm animals for unconventional recreation.

'God, I wish I still had sheep – for that reason or any other,' the partner answers, laughing off the insult.

Justo produces a one-note laugh and the sound surprises him. Vagrant threads of humour arise at times. Some still try, at least. On the blackboard *taberna* menu behind them, in small letters beneath the list of offerings and their prices, is a note highlighted only by a snowflake asterisk: if you're drinking to forget, please pay in advance.

'Stay, Justo, please stay,' one implores. 'I may need the services of Guernica's strongest man to pull my foot from my partner's arse.' It's another courtesy comment to Justo, whose renowned physical strength has not been publicly demonstrated for some time.

'No merciful God would have put on His earth so many Fascists or such ignorant partners,' one player says, his voice lowered. Justo scans the area to see if anyone takes offence at the statement.

He has not come to the market for cards or levity. Once the most visible of the town's characters, he now passes odd hours adrift in the streets and alleys. He watches, overhears discussions of the news of the town, and disappears.

The *amumak* cluck, 'Of course he might be, you know, disturbed, like his father, considering everything . . .'

'Oh, yes, he might be, considering . . .'

'I think he is . . . yes . . . who wouldn't be?'

Justo has heard the whispers and is not bothered by being thought

4

mad. It might even be a good thing these days. People ask fewer questions.

On a bench of land to the west, the symbolic oak of Guernica stands rigid and undisturbed. The residents tell and retell the stories of ancestors gathering beneath the oak tree since the Dark Ages to make laws or plan the defence of the land from invaders. Somehow, the rebels and Germans didn't damage the tree, though little else escaped their influence.

Across the market, there are no displays of the red, white, and green Ikurriña because the flag is banned in public. There are no pelota games, as there used to be, because the fronton has not been rebuilt. There are no dances at the plaza in the evenings after market day because dancing the *jota* or *aurresku* in public could lead to arrest.

Justo doesn't consider these realities anymore since they no longer apply to him. He's beyond punishment. Conspicuous in his boasts and bluster for so many years, Justo mostly listens now. If the Guardia Civil officers are occupied elsewhere, the market is the best place to hear the language. Since Miguel left, Justo has only the company of a hogget and a few suspicious chickens at home, and they offer such predictable conversation. In truth, they visit him as much as Miguel had in the final weeks before he withdrew into the mountains in a search for . . . something.

So Justo comes to listen. The language always has been the most important act of separation anyway, as the bond is to the words more than to the land. Since nothing on maps reflects their existence, the extent of their 'country' is the range of their language. But like the dances, the flag, and the celebrations, the words are banned, making a prayer whispered in Basque as illegal as a call to arms in the public square.

Justo's brother Xabier, the academic priest, told him that the Basque race has gone unassimilated by invaders because of the isolation of their stony coast and encircling mountains. But Justo joked in return that they have survived by being incoherent to all others. It is a unique defence.

5

Even the sounds of the market have changed. The *mus* players throw their pasteboard cards to the table so hard and fast that it sounds like clapping, but then they pause to watch over their shoulders for the guards in their tricorne hats and green capes. And the *amumak* in their black shifts and scarves – rolling boulders of women – are unafraid of any man bearing arms or condemnations. But their nattering has a lower tone, as there are fewer to have to talk above.

The locals now shuffle between booths as an accordion player squeezes out a waltz from under a drooping canopy that muffles the notes, making it sound as if the music is coming from the distance, or from the past. Many move as if they're wading through a heavy pointlessness – trying, like the *amumak* with the vegetables, to hold on to things that are no longer theirs. To laugh at cards and profit from business feels like an insult to those who can no longer laugh and profit. To them, the decay of will is an act of consideration. They buy what they must and return home.

According to the old Basques, everything that has a name exists. But Justo would argue that things now exist that are beyond description, which imagination cannot conceive: the explosions, the smell of things aflame, the sight of oxen and men mixed into gory Minotaurs among the rubble. They existed yet are unspeakable.

At the market now, tinkers sell used copper pots with silver scars from solder repairs, and farmers cover their tables with patchy bouquets of bunched greens and small pyramids of potatoes. Alaia Aldecoa again sells her soaps that smell of the nearby meadows. Commerce, the pulse of normal existence, slowly and respectfully returns on these Mondays.

Justo Ansotegui extracts a scented coin from his pocket and buys two potatoes as an excuse to hear another voice. For a moment, he listens to the language, to the rhythm of the phrases and their melancholy inflections. But there are no words for the things they have seen.

PART 1
(1893–1933)

CHAPTER I

Baby Xabier cried from his cradle, and when Angeles didn't stir, Pascual Ansotegui touched a match to the oil lamp on the wall and retrieved the newborn for his feed.

'*Kuttuna*, it's time,' he whispered, careful not to disturb their sons sleeping in the next room. But within a moment, his scream shook Justo and little Josepe from their beds. In the smoky lamplight, Pascual saw Angeles's sheet-white face and a dark stain on the bedding.

Justo and Josepe scrambled into their parents' room and found baby Xabier wailing on the floor. Justo picked up his little brother and returned him to the cradle. Josepe fought to pull himself onto the bed to be with his mother but only managed to claw the bloody blanket towards his face. Justo pulled him back and whispered to him. The three stood at the bedside as a corrosive grief began to hollow out Pascual Ansotegui.

Angeles had presented him a succession of three robust sons in a span of four years. Almost from the moment she recovered from the delivery of one, she was once again carrying the next. The men in the village laughed at Pascual's appetites, and he took a dash of pride in their jokes. Good-natured, accommodating, and fertile as the estuarial plain on which they lived, Angeles gave birth without complications. But a few days after the uneventful appearance of her third son, she simply failed to awaken. Pascual was left with two children, a newborn, and a harness of guilt.

The boys grew together in a hyperactive litter, teasing and challenging and wrestling one another from predawn awakenings until their nightly collapse, often not in their beds but sprawled at odd angles wherever their energy randomly expired. The increasingly absent Pascual kept them fed, a minimal challenge on a thriving farm, but they otherwise operated on their own initiative and imagination. Four males now lived at Errotabarri, the Ansotegui family farm, with no maternal or feminine influence past the few reminders of Angeles Ansotegui's brief life, a comb and brush set on her dresser, a few dresses in the cupboard, and a ruffled floral-print apron that Pascual Ansotegui now wore while cooking.

As Pascual withdrew, physically and emotionally, the boys gradually took over the farm. Even young boys understand that chickens need feed and eggs must be collected, so they completed these tasks without recognizing them as work. Even young boys understand that stock need food for the winter, so they learned to swing the scythe through the musky grass and fork the hay high against the tall spindle that supported the stack.

When one of them came across a rotten egg, it became ammunition for an ambush of an unsuspecting brother. They dived together into the cut grass before collecting it. They hid in the haystacks before spreading them for the stock. They rode the cows bareback before they milked them. Piles of wood were forts before they became fuel for the hearth. Every task was a contest: who could throw the pitchfork furthest? Who could run fastest to the well? Who could carry the most water?

Because each action was a competition or game, there was rarely a division of labour; the three shared each job and moved in unison to the next. Virtual orphans, they were nonetheless content, and the farm operated in a surprisingly efficient atmosphere of playful mayhem. But at times even the instincts of farm boys could not lead them to anticipate threats to stock or crops. For three boys easily distracted by the ballistic possibilities of rancid eggs, surprises arose.

Had Pascual Ansotegui been conscious of the passing of the seasons, he would have reminded his sons that the ewes about to lamb in the spring needed the protection of the shed. But in the first warm afternoons of spring, the shed was merely a wall for young boys playing pelota. When Xabier clumsily sent the ball onto the roof and it wedged between cracked tiles, Justo retrieved the ladder and scaled the slanted shed, placing one foot dramatically on the peak, as if he had reached the summit of Mount Oiz. Josepe sensed in his posture the potential for a new game.

'How about you can stay up there until one of us hits you with sheep shit?' he said, having retrieved several dried pieces.

As he took aim at his brother, Josepe spotted a sliver of darkness banking in tight circles above the hillside. 'Justo, Justo, an eagle – are there lambs out there?' he screamed.

'Get the gun!' Justo yelled, leaping down onto a bale and rolling off onto his feet.

Pascual Ansotegui's rifle was old before the turn of the century and the boys had never seen it fired. At thirteen, Justo was as strong as some of the men in the village, but Pascual had never taught him how to shoot. Josepe could hardly lift the iron weapon off the pegs in the shed. He dragged it to his brother with both hands at the end of the barrel, the butt bouncing along the ground.

Justo took it from him, raised it to his shoulder, and waved the heavy barrel in the direction of the diving eagle. Xabier knelt in front of him and grabbed the stock with both hands, trying to buttress his big brother's hold.

'Shoot him, Justo!' Josepe screamed. 'Shoot him!'

With the rifle butt inches from his shoulder, Justo pulled the trigger. The cartridge exploded in the barrel, and the recoil thrust Justo to the ground, bleeding from the side of his head. Xabier flattened out beside him, screaming from the noise. The shot did not even startle the eagle, which was now applying a lethal clench of its talons into the neck of a tiny, still-wet lamb.

With Justo and Xabier down, Josepe charged. Before he could

reach it, the eagle extended its wings, hammered them several times into the ground, and lifted off on a downhill swoop just over Josepe's head.

Justo fought his way uphill to Josepe. Xabier, crying to the point of breathlessness, face freckled with his brother's blood, ran in sprints and tumbles to a neighbour's house for help.

'Look for other newborns, and let's get the ewes into the shed!' Justo shouted, regaining control. They saw no other lambs that were vulnerable, and they both herded the oblivious mother ewe, still dragging birth tissue, into the shed.

The neighbours held Xabier to calm him. But what did he expect them to do? Where was his father, after all? 'Boys your age shouldn't deal with these matters and certainly shouldn't be firing rifles; it's a good thing none of our stock was harmed,' they said. He couldn't hear them over the painful ringing of his ears but read rejection in their faces.

'Well . . . fine!' Xabier yelled, breaking away to rejoin his brothers.

The shaken boys gathered in the shed and clutched the ewe, which was bothered not by the loss of its offspring, a development it had already forgotten, but by the fierce embraces of these boys, one of whom was bleeding all over her wool.

When Pascual Ansotegui returned that evening, the boys stood in a line at the door, in descending order of age, and Justo briefed his father on the events. Pascual nodded. Justo and Josepe accepted his minimal response. Xabier, though, flared with indignation.

'Where were you?' he yelled, a spindle-thin nine-year-old in third-hand overalls stained with blood.

Pascual stared without comment.

Xabier repeated the question.

'I was gone,' the father said.

'I know you were gone; you're always gone,' Xabier said. 'We'd get along just as well if you never came back.'

Pascual tilted his head, as if this would bring his youngest into clearer focus. He then turned away, pulled the floral apron from its peg on the hearth, and began to make dinner.

Justo knew early that he, as the eldest, would someday assume sole control of Errotabarri, and his siblings understood that they would inevitably find work elsewhere. If inequitable to the younger children, the pattern assured survival of the *baserri* culture. Justo Ansotegui would claim his birthright and become the latest in the chain of stewards of the land that extended back to times when their ancestors painted animals onto walls in the nearby Santimamiñe caves.

Bequeathing the farm to the eldest carried no guarantees. He who inherits the farm may never leave to discover other opportunities, to go to sea, perhaps, or to a city like Bilbao. But to run the *baserri* was to shepherd the family trust, Justo believed. Still, he expected a period of apprenticeship to learn. For another year or so after the lamb's slaughter, Pascual Ansotegui unenthusiastically attended mass each morning, mouthing the responses. He returned to church to pray in silence again in the evening, wandering unseen in between. Eventually, he stopped attending mass, and one day he drifted off.

It took several days before Justo realized his father had gone missing. He alerted the neighbours, and small groups searched the hillsides. When no evidence of death or life surfaced, the boys assumed that he had been swallowed up by a crevice or a sinkhole, or that he just forgot to stop wandering.

Although the boys loved and missed their father, their affection for him was more out of habit than true sentiment. They noticed little difference in his absence: they still performed the same chores and played the same games. Justo was now in charge.

'Here, this is yours now,' Josepe said to him, handing him the ruffled apron.

'*Eskerrik asko,*' Justo said, thanking his brother. He lifted the strap over his head and tied the worn sash behind his back in solemn ceremony. 'Wash your hands for dinner.'

He had the family *baserri* to run. He was fifteen.

When they were very young, the boys learned the history of Guernica and of Errotabarri. They learned it from their father, before he drifted off, and from the people of the town who were proud of their heritage. From medieval times, Guernica was a crossroads of the old Roman way and the fish and wine route that wound through the hills inland from the sea. Intersecting them both was the pilgrims' route to Santiago de Compostela. For centuries, representatives of the region met under the Guernica oak to shape laws that outlawed torture and unwarranted arrest, and granted unprecedented privileges to women. Although aligned with the Kingdom of Castile, they maintained their own legal system and demanded that the series of Castilian monarchs from the time of Ferdinand and Isabella come and stand, in person, beneath the oak of Guernica and swear to protect the Basque laws. Because the economy of the region hadn't evolved under the feudal system, the Basques owned their own land and were never divided into sovereigns and serfs, merely farmers, fishermen, and craftsmen, free and independent of any overlord.

A *baserri* in Biscaya often came to have a name, which sometimes served as a surname for those living there, as if the land and the home were the real ancestors. The home, after all, would outlive the inhabitants and maybe even the family name. They presumed that a well-structured building, like family relationships, genuine love, and one's reputation, would be timeless if protected and properly maintained.

At the time Justo Ansotegui assumed control of Errotabarri, a thorny hedgerow outlined the lower perimeter of the farm, and a platoon of poplars flanked the northern, windward edge. Crops were cultivated on the southern side of the house, bordered by several rows of fruit trees. Pastureland spread above the home, rising to a patchy stand of burly oaks, cypress, and waxy blue-grey eucalyptus. The trees thinned out just beneath a granite outcrop that marked the upper border of the property.

The house resembled others near Guernica. It required the boys to annually whitewash the stucco sides above a stone-and-mortar base and to re-stain the oxblood wooden window frames and shutters. Each stone-silled window accommodated decorative boxes of geraniums, providing dashes of red across both levels and all aspects.

Even as a young single man, Justo sustained these floral touches that had been important to his mother.

As with many a *baserri* on a hillside, the house was wedged into the slope. The lower floor, with wide double doors on the downhill side, housed the stock in the winter months. The upper floor, with a ground-level door on the uphill side, was home to the family. Housing cows and sheep in the same building protected the animals from the cold, and they returned the favour by warming the upper level with their rising body heat.

Inside, a large central room held the kitchen, dining, and living areas, with rough-cut oak columns supporting exposed quarter-sawn rafters. The hearth extended inward from a corner of the kitchen. Maize was nailed to the beams to dry, and herbs for cooking and medicine cured in the warmth above the hearth. Interwoven vines of red peppers hung from the column closest to the kitchen, next to the dangling links of chorizo that lent a heavy garlic scent to the room.

An unknown ancestor had carved the *lauburu* into the lintel above the main door. This four-headed symbol of their race, like a spinning clover leaf, bracketed their lives, appearing on everything from cradles to tombstones.

Each former master of the land inadvertently bequeathed items to Justo. He still stacked hay on tall wooden spikes that had been carved generations before. And the iron shears he used in the shed had snipped wool from sheep dead a century. Some of the smaller items offered wordless mysteries from the edge of the mantel; there was a small bronze horse with its head reared high and an iron coin bearing unknown symbols.

During Justo's proprietorship, the apron was likewise memorialized, draped from a nail in the mantel. And before he would pass, the mantel would also support a length of plaited human hair so dark that it absorbed light.

Swatting the rump of a reluctant donkey to keep it grinding up the steep trail, Pablo Picasso chuckled when he considered how his friends in Paris would react to the vision of him in such a position. That he would think of them now, here in the Pyrenees, was a symptom of the problem. There had been too much getting in the way of his art in Paris. And this mountain trail to Gósol, with the lovely Fernande on a donkey beside him, was his path away from all that.

It had been all too much talk of art. And when they talked, their art rose from their heads, not their guts, and their paintings went back and forth like day-old conversations.

He didn't need Paris now; he needed Spain. He needed the people and the heat and the unshakeable feeling of belonging.

Fernande would sit for him now and wouldn't talk about his painting. She knew better. He had come back to Spain for a short break, come to this quiet town in the mountains, to tear art to pieces, to make it something it hadn't been, or perhaps something it had been long before. This was a place he could *feel* art. It came up at him from the dirt and radiated down in waves from the sun. It was time to shatter art and reshape it, as one might do with bright pieces of broken glass.

Justo promised his brothers this: no one would work harder. But even as he made that vow, he conceded to himself that he knew very little of the business of operating a farm. So he began making social visits to neighbours, slipping into the conversations questions about the timing of planting certain crops or tending fruit trees and managing stock. Most neighbours were sympathetic, but they had little time to worry about somebody else's farm – unless they had a daughter who happened to be his age. Most would consider Justo something well short of handsome, but this boy nonetheless owned his own *baserri*.

Justo enquired of the neighbouring Mendozabels how he might establish hives for bees that would pollinate his fruit trees and provide honey. Mrs Mendozabel informed him that they would be delighted to help him, that in fact they should all visit over 'a full dinner, which you surely don't get much of at Errotabarri, not the kind that our Magdalena makes every night.' Justo arrived in his work clothes, consumed dinner without conversation beyond that of the *baserri*, and took little note of Magdalena in her white Sunday dress and the 'special pie' she baked for him. He was too busy for Magdalena and all the rest of the Magdalenas who were successively dressed, powdered, and trotted out for his inspection. The dinners were pleasant, though, the information helpful, and yes, it was true, he didn't bake pies at Errotabarri.

Small farms could not be considered flourishing businesses, but few noticed the poverty on the hillside above Guernica. Families were fed, and whatever was left over was carted to market or traded for those goods they could not produce themselves. Justo envied the neighbours who enjoyed an abundance of help from children. By comparison, he faced a manpower shortage. Josepe and Xabier helped, but they were less invested in the jobs now. Justo rose in the darkness, worked without break through the day, and fell asleep shortly after eating whatever it was he bothered to toss into a pot that night. Josepe never complained of the food; Xabier did so only once.

Justo discovered a few tricks but never cut corners on work that would affect the land or animals, only himself. He did not sew or mend clothing and never washed his or his brothers' garments, he told them, because they would only get dirty again. If his brothers wanted to clean themselves, he did not complain, as long as the work had been done.

'You look nice this morning,' one charitable woman commented to Justo when the three boys showed up to Mass at least partially groomed.

'Yes,' Xabier cracked. 'But our scarecrows are bare today.'

And so Justo spent no time arranging for his own comforts, and he gave no thought to entertainment or diversion.

At times in the field, hypnotized by the rhythmic swinging of the scythe through the grass, he discovered that he had been talking to himself aloud. He would look around to be certain Josepe or Xabier had not come upon him silently and heard his words. In these moments he realized his problem. He was lonely. The jobs that had been so exciting in the presence of his brothers had become mere labour.

The only break he allowed himself came on feast days, when he would finish his work in the morning and then walk into town to take part in the competitions, the tug-of-war, the wood chopping, the stone lifting. He won many of them because of his imposing power. And because these exposures to people were so rare, he attempted to share with everyone all the jokes and examples of strength that went unappreciated during his seclusion at Errotabarri. If he became out-rageous and self-inflated, it was entertainingly so, and those in the town anticipated his visits and cheered his many victories. For some-one so lonely at home, the attention felt like the first warm day of spring.

At one of these outings he met a girl from Lumo who had come downhill to join the dancers. Her name was Mariangeles Oñati, and she caused Justo Ansotegui to re-evaluate his approach to personal hygiene and self-imposed solitude.

Josepe Ansotegui smelled the Bay of Biscay long before he could see it. Having walked the serpentine mountain road north from Guernica for two days, past the caves and the jagged marble quarry and beyond the well-tended farms, he descended steadily in the dir-ection of the breeze that carried the briny musk of low tide. When he arrived at the Lekeitio harbour in the softening dusk, clusters of women in aprons and scarves were pulling small fish from nets along the quay. They chatted and sang in pleasant harmony.

Josepe scanned the boats moored along the perimeter of the harbour wall, looking for crews still at work. The first man he approached about a job responded with a laugh and a shake of the head. The second told him that fishermen came from fishing families, and farm boys were meant to be farmers, as was life's order.

'My older brother took over the family *baserri*, so I thought I'd give fishing a try,' he explained. 'I was told there was always work to be had on the boats.'

'I've got some work,' a man on the adjacent boat shouted. 'Let's see if you can lift this crate.'

With great strain, Josepe hoisted an overflowing crate of fish to his knees, then up to his waist, and off-loaded it to the dock. He looked back with a sense of triumph.

'Yes, you're strong enough,' the fisherman said. 'No, I don't have any work for you – but thanks anyway.'

In the stern of a boat closest to the harbour mouth, a fisherman stood alone scanning the sky. '*Zori*,' the man said of his skyward focus when Josepe approached. 'The old fishermen looked for *zori*, for omens, by reading which way the birds were flying.'

'And are the birds saying anything special this evening?' Josepe asked, glancing at a squadron of gulls that bickered above the harbour.

'I think they're saying they're hungry; they're circling the processors, waiting to dispose of our messes.'

The two shook hands.

'I'm Josepe Ansotegui of Guernica, I'm almost seventeen years old, and the only fishing I've done is in a stream with a string and a pin,' the boy said. 'But I'm told I'm smart, and I'm looking for work.'

'Did you catch anything with your string and pin?'

'I caught a fat trout once, yes,' Josepe offered proudly.

'Did you gut and clean the fat trout?'

'Yes, I did.'

'That's all you need to know about fishing right now; you're hired,' Alberto Barinaga said. 'We'll worry about your intelligence later.'

Barinaga, owner of the *Zaldun*, welcomed Josepe on board and into his home. Perhaps he had foreseen a productive relationship in the flight of the birds. In time, Barinaga became impressed by Josepe's stories of growing up in a pack of playful boys following his mother's death, and he admired his strength and his attitude. But mostly he came to appreciate his dedication to learning the business of fishing. In daily tutorials, while he scrubbed the gunwales or repaired the nets, or while at the family's dinner table, Josepe absorbed the encyclopedia of maritime lore and culture the veteran captain presented.

'We chased the bowhead whales and the cod to the shores of the Americas,' Barinaga preached at dinner. 'The *Santa María* was one of our caravels, and Columbus had a Basque navigator and crew.'

'That is why he ended up in the Americas instead of the Indies,' his eldest daughter, Felicia, needled.

'Magellan had our navigators, too,' the captain continued. 'Some have suggested that we are so good on the waters because our race began on the lost island of Atlantis.'

He paused for effect, nodding his head as he buttered a thick slice of bread. 'It is a possibility that I would not discount.'

Josepe, in turn, learned of his *patroia* from the gossipy crews of other boats. Barinaga was much admired among the family of fishermen. On several occasions, his seamanship allowed the *Zaldun* to arrive in time to rescue foundering boats and endangered crews. Josepe pulled in the lessons with both hands. He learned the songs of the sailors and joined in the singing as they repaired fraying nets on the days when rough seas sentenced them to work ashore.

Josepe repaid Alberto Barinaga's hospitality by having sex nearly every night with his daughter Felicia in the bedroom directly beneath her sleeping parents.

When Xabier returned from school one afternoon and rushed to help his brother turn hay to dry with the long trident forks, Justo noticed scratches and purple welts across the backs of his hands.

'What happened to you?'

'I gave an answer in Basque,' Xabier said.

Justo hadn't been to school for years, but he remembered the teachers who belittled them at every opportunity and used a ruler or a willow branch to swat students who spoke Basque instead of Spanish in class.

'I'll take care of this.'

At the age of eighteen, shirtless beneath unwashed overalls, Justo went to school the next morning. Once the class was seated, save for Xabier, Justo approached the teacher, a bespectacled Spaniard with a marigold boutonnière.

At the front of the classroom, Justo lifted Xabier's raked hand towards the teacher and said two words.

'Never again,' Justo said in Basque.

The teacher responded with a showy bluff, expecting the young farm boy to be daunted. '*Vete!*' he demanded in Spanish, pointing towards the door. The teacher paused. He turned to the class and saw every student focused on the showdown. '*Vete!*' the teacher repeated, chin raised.

Justo struck so quickly the teacher was helpless, grabbing the extended arm and pulling it down between the teacher's legs. Spinning around the bent-over teacher, Justo took the wrist with his other hand and lifted it so that the teacher straddled his own arm. In the span of a second, the teacher went from imperiously pointing towards the door to being bent in half, with his arm between his legs and pulled up tightly against his scrotum.

Justo's grip on the teacher's wrist tightened as he lifted his arm even higher, causing the teacher to rise onto his toes to reduce the pressure on his groin. The teacher groaned. Students sat in stunned silence.

Justo bent and looked around at the teacher's sweaty face and said two words. 'Never again.'

Justo lifted him higher for an instant, then released his grip. The teacher dropped to the floor.

The first colourful instalment of Justo Ansotegui's legend passed from student to parents that afternoon, and every father relayed it to friends that evening at the *taberna*. The teacher did not appear the next morning or the following one, and he was replaced. When Justo next appeared in town, several men he didn't know stepped from shopfronts and clapped their hands in approval. Justo smiled back and winked.

Xabier never needed his big brother's assistance to get good marks. Not nearly as physical as his brother, Xabier instead felt himself grow stronger with every bit of information he committed to memory. He had no property and few possessions, but these facts were his: history, mathematics, grammar. So he assumed the role of dutiful student. If he had to act as if he was accepting of these Spanish teachers' politics, he could easily pretend. By sixteen, he had consumed everything the teachers offered.

The next move was Justo's, and he proposed it with typical bluntness at dinner.

'You know, Xabier, you're not much help around here, and I may want to get married someday; have you ever thought about going into the seminary, maybe in Bilbao?'

Xabier was as devout as any boy, and he certainly had done nothing that would serve as an obstacle to joining the clergy; he simply had never considered it. He admired the parish priest but had never sought to emulate him. But it would be a way to continue learning.

'Priests live comfortably; they're respected in town,' Justo continued. 'Besides, you've got no hope with women anyway.'

Xabier was not insulted, as he assumed Justo was right on that account. But Justo was his brother, not his father, and who was he to tell him what to do? He was about to question Justo's authority when his brother made a final point.

'Mother would have liked it.'

The issue spurred all-night introspection. And when he rose at dawn, Xabier was reasonably certain it was a good idea. He informed Justo – with reservations.

'I thought there might be something more dramatic about a big decision like this. I thought priests felt some calling, that they heard some kind of heavenly voices.'

Justo, his muscled shoulders and arms extending from his ruffled apron, scooped eggs from a pan onto Xabier's plate.

'You did hear a voice,' he said. 'Mine.'

CHAPTER 2

Justo Ansotegui's reputation rose uphill to the village of Lumo. There, Mariangeles Oñati heard that he was a defender of causes, a wit, and a wag, although some suggested he was an overeager curator of his own mythology. Most often she'd heard that he was the one to watch during the strength events on feast days. One friend claimed that he had carried an ox into town across his shoulders and then celebrated the feat by throwing the beast across the Oka River.

'Yes,' Justo said when asked of the story. 'But it was only a small ox, and downhill most of the way into town. And the wind was with me when I threw it.'

Mariangeles came to dance at one of the festivals with her five sisters. She also decided it was time to watch the men's competitions, which she usually avoided.

The largest young man standing beside a debarked log at the start of the wood-chopping event joked with the gathering as he removed his boots and sad grey stockings. Going barefooted seemed to Mariangeles a foolhardy act for one who would be flailing an axe so near his feet.

'After all these years of competitions, I still have nine toes,' he said, proudly wiggling the four remaining appendages on one of his bare feet. 'But this is my only pair of boots and I can't afford to damage them.'

The man bent at the waist and tore into the pine log between his feet. Halfway through, he hopped a hundred and eighty degrees to work on the other side. The log split beneath him well before any others in the competition. Justo was seated, nine toes intact, replacing his socks and boots before the runner-up broke through his log.

In the wine-drinking event, Justo was less impressive. Unpractised in the use of the *bota*, he sprayed wine over much of his face. After coughing and spitting, he took what was left in his bag and squirted shots into the mouths of grateful friends, who had turned up their open mouths as if awaiting the sacrament.

But in the *txingas* event, Justo was unmatched. The 'farmer's walk' tested strength and endurance as the competitor carried 110lb weights in each hand up and back along a measured course until they dropped. The collapse for most competitors followed a customary pattern. On the second lap, the knees began to bend dramatically – sometimes in both directions; on the third, the shoulders pulled the spine down into a dangerous curve; and finally, gravity yanked the weights and the man to the turf.

Mariangeles stood near the starting point when Justo was called. He grasped the ring handles of the weights, his face straining as if he'd never get them off the ground. It was false drama for the audience, because he then easily hoisted them and unleashed a proud *irrintzi*, the traditional mountain cry, rising in pitch to a shriek with quickening ululations.

Justo marched without struggle, his back rigid. The back is the trunk of the tree, he reasoned, the arms merely the branches. Past the marks where others had fallen in exhaustion, Justo Ansotegui nodded to the crowd, gesturing at little ones who would praise him to future grandchildren.

'Doesn't it hurt?' a young boy asked as he passed.

'Of course, how do you think my arms got so long?' Justo volleyed, and at that moment, he straightened his arms against his sides, a move that caused the sleeves of his shirt to ride up, making his arms appear to grow in length by a third.

The boy gasped and howled along with the crowd.

Justo's weakening arrived so gradually no one could notice. Already the winner by several lengths, he chose not to further delay the inevitable and set the weights gently at his feet.

It so happened that Mariangeles discovered the need to visit acquaintances near the finishing line after Justo's competition. And who could have imagined that a friend would say something so humorous, just as Justo walked past, that she found herself unleashing her most feminine wind-chime laughter, which caused Justo to turn in her direction? And because it had all been so amusing, it was natural that she still would be locked in her broadest smile – the one that gave greatest depth to her dimples – when Justo looked her way.

Justo glanced and walked on.

'Unnnh,' Mariangeles muttered. This must be the most arrogant man in Guernica, she thought.

Behind the scenes, Mariangeles quickly arranged to present the prize, a lamb, to the winner of the *txingas* event.

'Congratulations,' she said to Justo in front of the crowd. She handed him the lamb and moved in for the ceremonial kiss on his cheek. She took a close look at his jagged, misshapen right ear, retreated slightly, and came in for a kiss on the other cheek.

'Thank you,' Justo said, and announced to the crowd, 'I am going to fill the valley with my flock from winning these events.'

Justo waved and accepted congratulations as he worked through the crowd, lamb peeking out from inside the bib of his overalls. Mariangeles skirted the gathering so that Justo would have to pass her again.

'Would you like to dance?' she asked.

Justo stopped. He looked down at himself, in his soiled overalls. He looked back at her.

'We can find somebody to hold your lamb.'

She took the leggy lamb from him and hugged it to her face.

'Did somebody tell you to do this?' Justo asked.

'No, I just thought you might like to dance, if you're not too worn out from all the chopping and lifting.'

But they didn't dance. They sat and talked as the lamb gambolled around them and returned to 'nurse' on Mariangeles's finger whenever she placed a bent knuckle near its mouth. Her sisters watched them, and on the walk home, they unanimously voted against her seeing this boy.

Yes, she agreed, he was not the most handsome of her suitors. He was almost frighteningly powerful, and he was missing the outer curl of his right ear. And for all his bombast in front of the crowd, he had been without confidence when they were alone beneath the tree.

'He's homely,' a sister said.

'He has character,' Mariangeles argued.

'He's ugly,' a less generous sister offered.

'He has his own *baserri*,' Mariangeles's mother commented from behind the group of girls.

Her mother's frankness stilled the warm adrenaline that had driven her since she introduced herself to Justo, and even her walking slowed from the weight of its significance. Was that at the root of her interest in this man? She was almost twenty, the eldest in a family of six girls and a lone brother who was nine. Her father had injured both legs in a fall at the farm, leaving him weakened and affixed to his wooden rocking chair like sagging upholstery. Did she flirt with Justo because the time had come for her to move on? She returned home in silence as her sisters debated his many inadequacies.

Others interested in Mariangeles presented flowers or sweets when they arrived at her home and then sought private time with her. Justo arrived empty-handed but wearing his work clothes. He gave her mother a vigorous handshake, patted the father on his shoulder, and asked a question that instantly won over Mrs Oñati and the sisters: 'What can I do around here to help?'

'To help?' the mother asked.

'Help – heavy lifting, woodcutting, repairs . . . whatever is the hardest for you ladies.'

Mariangeles's mother sat down and composed a short list. Justo looked it over and nodded.

'Come on, Mari, put on your work clothes and we'll be done with this before dinner.' When Mariangeles went in the sisters' sleeping area to change into older clothes, her mother followed.

'You know, you learn more about a person by working beside them for an hour than you can in a year of courting,' her mother said.

After an afternoon of work, they sat together for a relaxed meal, with everyone feeling as if Justo was already part of the family. The sisters, who now would not have to repair the roof of their lambing shed, agreed that Justo was a more appealing prospect than they first thought. Not handsome, to be sure, but a good catch. And looks, well, they're not everything.

A month later, at the next community fair, Mariangeles stood in the first row alongside the *txingas* course. Justo went through his pre-competition theatrics, padding back and forth along the path a few times, before stopping in the middle of the grounds, taking a sharp left turn, and walking directly towards Mariangeles.

He collected the handles of both weights in his massive left hand, barely needing to lean into a counterbalance, and with his right hand retrieved a gold band from his trouser pocket.

'Will you marry me?' he asked the stunned Mariangeles.

'Yes, of course.' They kissed. He reapportioned the weights and went back to the competition. As Justo walked, a man overseeing the event skittishly approached and walked beside him.

'Justo, you went off the path, you're disqualified,' the judge informed him.

Justo continued past the mark of the winner, just to show he could have done it anyway, and rejoined his future bride, apologizing for not adding another lamb to their flock.

Justo was right; seminary studies suited Xabier, who displayed exceptional recall of facts and details. But more relevant to his future, he showed a trustworthy manner that inspired people's confidence.

As he eased from secular studies towards the strictly clerical, and as he became familiar with the tasks expected of a priest, he grew more certain this was his calling. Many seminarians question the personal costs, but Xabier had no need to reconcile himself on that issue. His most critical self-examination instead involved the soul-baring question of whether he had the ability to truly help those who would approach him in their time of greatest need.

His gravest frustration came from the unstable connection he detected at times between holy protocol and simple human existence, as he discovered that sometimes doctrine failed to apply to daily reality. So many of a priest's hours with parishioners, he discovered, involved the mind-numbing coddling of insecure adults and constructing reassurances built on vaporous faith. He had no doubts of his deep belief; he was more sure of that than ever. But how could he use it to benefit others?

He was instructed to advise people that deaths and hardships are tests. And when people dared ask for reasons and proof, he was to lay down the cleric's ultimate trump card: 'God works in mysterious ways.' Xabier decided that if he ever heard himself use that phrase, which amounted to taking an easy way out, he would give up the cloth and become a fisherman with Josepe. So he tested himself alone at night, fabricating ghastly scenarios in which he was confronted by troubled faces begging for answers.

An imaginary grieving mother beneath a black lace veil looks up from her baby's grave and asks, 'How could a caring God let this illness take my child?'

Xabier decided he would embrace her and whisper his belief in her ear. 'I truly don't know how it could happen, but I . . . I . . . believe she is in His arms right now, where she feels no more pain, where she is whole and she is happy. And she is still in all of our hearts and can never be taken from there.' He would hold the woman then and listen to her sobs and absorb her tears with his shoulder until she was ready to withdraw, no matter how long it took.

A bent and toothless woman, wedged against a wall and smelling of sepsis, raises a gnarled hand and asks, 'Where is God's mercy for the poor?'

In his vision, Xabier would sit on the ground beside her. 'Do you have family anywhere who can help?' If she answered yes, he would find them and urge them to take custody of her health. If she answered no, then he would become her family. 'Come with me, sister, and we will find a place for you.' She would be poor, but she would be cared for.

A large man with an indistinct shape and hidden face asks him from a dark corner, 'Is avenging a grievous wrong a sin?'

Xabier would say, 'If it is a matter of pride, deny yourself; if it is a matter of honour and true belief, then ask, "What is the cost of this honour?" I believe you'll find your own answer.'

Xabier knew he had romanticized himself as compellingly noble in these imagined situations (as well as slightly taller and considerably more handsome), but when he repeatedly arrived at compassionate responses, he felt certain there was nothing else he could do with his life that would have an equal impact. He also realized that his answers frequently had little or nothing to do with faith, religion, doctrine, catechism, or papal decree.

CHAPTER 3

The midwives convened at Errotabarri devoted as much attention to Justo Ansotegui as to his wife, Mariangeles, whose imminent delivery was already being ably managed by her mother and five sisters.

Relegated to the main room, the surplus caretakers brewed cups of hot tea from mint and sorrel leaves for Justo. They applied cool, moist cloths to the back of his neck, while others rubbed the meaty webbing between his thumb and first finger. It had no curative value, but he didn't know that and it kept him distracted. All had theories on the care and handling of distraught first-time fathers. But their main function was to keep him focused while, in the bedroom, Mariangeles did all the work. Two of the midwives had attended to Justo's mother, Angeles, and in other rooms they whispered sad recollections. 'Poor thing. No wonder the father here is so upset. He saw her, don't you know?'

It had been not quite a year since Justo Ansotegui and Mariangeles Oñati had married. They were imperfectly matched in some ways, but they were mutually respectful and so enamoured of being married to each other that they thought of little else. They delighted in assuming their roles – dutiful husband, loving wife – as much as they enjoyed defying them. He acted the prankster husband (putting a lamb under the covers of the bed one night) and she the playful wife (riding cows, leaping wildly into the haystacks from the shed roof).

Farming and marriage progressed smoothly, and it was an ideal environment for the production of balanced and happy children. Yet that was the source of their first disagreement.

Mariangeles never doubted that Justo would protect her, care for her, keep her fed and safe, and give her a house filled with strong, healthy children. Coming from a large, mostly happy family, Mariangeles had envisioned a similar life for herself. But when her prolonged delivery extended more than a day, leaving Justo limp from imagined possibilities, he made his first demand.

'That's it; no more,' he said when baby Miren was three days old.

'No more what?'

'Babies.'

Mariangeles was nursing and still raw from the delivery and the lack of sleep, and she was not prepared for a debate.

'This is the one thing that puts you at risk,' Justo said. 'I don't want you to go through this ten times, or five times . . . or even twice. Maybe you can survive it, but I never will.'

'Justo, my mother had no troubles, and I'm sure I won't, either,' Mariangeles offered.

'Yes, your mother had no troubles,' he said, raising his voice. 'And mine didn't either until she died in that bed.'

They passed a day drifting separately inside Errotabarri without speaking.

They met at the cradle when baby Miren awoke from a nap. Justo handed her to Mariangeles, who lay back on the bed to nurse. For the first time, he told her the details of standing on that spot, seeing his mother, seeing baby Xabier wailing on the floor, seeing his father drift towards a vanishing point. Mariangeles extended the arm that was not holding their baby. She pulled Justo close, and he joined her on the bed, leaning his head on her shoulder.

Manfred von Richthofen awoke congested. The cold and misty weather didn't help, as a strong easterly wind carried a chilly bite. His allergies compounded the problem, attacking him as they did every spring. He took medication to clear the congestion. After all, it wouldn't do to have the Red Baron, who had just claimed kills seventy-nine and eighty the previous evening, going around with the sniffles.

Aggressive and deadly in the cockpit, the Red Baron was nonetheless admired for his chivalry, a carry-over from the nineteenth-century mores that guided his caste of Prussian noblemen. Stories told of him writing letters of sincere regret and condolences to the widows of victims. One wounded British pilot was shepherded by von Richthofen to a German base to be taken prisoner. On his second day in the field hospital, the English pilot received half a dozen cigars, a present from the Red Baron.

His 'Flying Circus' had recently added another von Richthofen. In addition to his brother Lothar, a veteran ace with his own renown, von Richthofen now also commanded his young cousin, Wolfram von Richthofen. Although new to flying, Wolfram was given a precious Fokker triplane.

'If we come across the Lords, circle above the action,' the Red Baron told his cousin, using his pet name for British airmen. 'Watch and learn.' Veterans told new pilots that they could fly above the skirmishes and not be targeted; it was how young pilots on both sides eased into combat.

Royal Air Force planes from the aerodrome in Bertangles, near the Somme River in northern France, spotted nine Fokker triplanes and engaged. As the combatants met and separated into lethal pairs, the Red Baron circled behind a British Sopwith Camel and opened fire, but his guns jammed. Above him, Wolfram von Richthofen strayed too close to the action, and an eager young enemy pilot could not resist the target. Seeing his cousin's peril, the Red Baron disengaged from his dogfight to drive off the British attacker, who veered wildly up the Somme canal.

Perhaps unable to free his weapons, perhaps sluggish from the medication he'd taken, the Red Baron failed to score the kill. The normally omniscient von Richthofen also did not notice a Camel rallying from behind and diving steeply in his direction. At little more than a hundred yards from von Richthofen's flame-red Fokker, the RAF pilot opened fire. The wounded Red Baron broke off into a climbing bank to his right.

Whether struck by shots from the plane or by rifle fire from nearby Allied ground forces, the Red Baron received a mortal wound. He managed to land the Fokker in a paddock near the St Collette brickworks. British and Australian soldiers raced to the plane as von Richthofen shed his goggles and tossed them over the side of the cockpit. He turned off the engine to reduce the chances of a fire. When the soldiers arrived, the famed Red Baron looked at them with resignation and uttered his final word.

'*Kaput.*'

Of course they heard their daughter Felicia slipping into Josepe Ansotegui's room every night, and they recognized the sounds of frantic young lovers' failed attempts at stealth. Moans muffled by pillows can be confused with no other sound. Alberto Barinaga and his wife acknowledged that Felicia was nearing her eighteenth birthday, and Josepe was a good young man, so they were intentionally indifferent to their couplings, and they did a passable job of voicing surprise when the two announced their plans to be married.

Every crew in Lekeitio attended the ceremony. At Josepe's side were his brothers, Justo and Xabier, both wearing starched white shirts that Justo purchased for the occasion.

The brothers posed for a photograph afterwards: Felicia was seated in her wedding dress, with Josepe standing behind her, hand on her shoulder, and Justo and Xabier at her flanks. The protocol demanded serious looks for such pictures, but the three brothers all flashed the Ansotegui smile, which left their eyes little more than dark slits.

'Watch the birdie,' the photographer said, pinching the fingers of his right hand against his thumb to get their attention. It was their first picture.

Several years later, the flu pandemic killed Alberto Barinaga. After having served his apprenticeship eagerly, Josepe Ansotegui took over Barinaga's boat, which did not automatically assure his acceptance by the collection of strong-willed fishermen. His eventual consideration as *patroia* of *patroiak* was a gesture of respect for Ansotegui's farm-bred willingness to work as hard as any crewman while on board and for his level-headedness and vision in matters of their community.

Although among the youngest captains, he proved many times that he was concerned with the well-being of the collective. But Josepe would freely acknowledge that he did not have the background in the fishing business that most other *patroiak* enjoyed. He found that he did not have to go far to divine a deep reservoir of sound counsel, merely across narrow Arranegi Street, in fact, to the home of José María Navarro.

Navarro was the *patroia* of the *Egun On* ('Good Morning' – an uplifting name for early rising fishermen). Navarro had fished since he was a boy with his father, who had fished since he was a boy with his father, in an uninterrupted skein of genetic filament stretching back before anyone could imagine. When Josepe was called upon for any administrative purpose requiring knowledge beyond his ken, he'd consult with José María Navarro aboard the *Egun On* or slip across the street in the evening with a bottle of wine.

José María never sought greater responsibilities in the community. Ansotegui was welcome to shoulder the task of being the leader of the fleet, as Navarro had enough to keep him busy, specifically the development of his two sons and a pair of younger daughters.

Eduardo was the family firecracker and comically called 'Dodo' by his brother, Miguel, when he was learning to speak. The two daughters, Araitz and Irantzu, arrived in the second wave.

While Josepe Ansotegui and José María Navarro melded complementary strengths to guide the community, their wives, Felicia Ansotegui and Estrella Navarro, grew as close as sisters. The husbands fabricated a pair of pulleys anchored into the first-floor window frames that allowed Felicia and Estrella to hang and retrieve laundry on adjacent lines above the street and talk to each other through the hall windows as they worked. They chatted about the children, about their husbands, about the news of the town.

'Oh, I have to start boiling the beans for this evening,' one would say, and the other would agree that it was indeed time to start boiling her beans as well. They would finish one job and then meet in the street to go to the market, where one might see some nice corn or cabbage and both would purchase the same produce. Off to daily Mass, they sat side by side in the same pew for each service. In tandem, holding each other's arm, they stopped in the square to visit other mothers. When one spoke, the other bobbed her head in perpetual assent. They were like twins connected by laundry line. And on breezy days, the Ansotegui and Navarro bed sheets and shirts and trousers and skirts fluttered together like colourful pennants.

CHAPTER 4

The animals living in Errotabarri's basement rarely disturbed their upstairs neighbours. The wood fire in the hearth, with its tiny explosions of scented pitch pockets, and the sausages and peppers drying in the kitchen mostly covered any smells that might drift up from the lower level. That didn't stop Justo from operatically scapegoating the livestock whenever he committed an indiscretion of the bowels.

'Vulgar cows!' he'd shout, looking down at the floor.

'Vulgar cow, indeed,' Mariangeles countered each time, causing them both to laugh as if it were the first time they'd shared the exchange.

Miren found the shared-housing arrangement comforting. She grew close to the animals, helping milk the cows in the morning and evening, leaning her head into their warm, fat sides and telling them about her day, elaborating whenever one would turn its head to express specific interest.

At night, the sounds of the animals' low groans and rustling in the straw rose through the floorboards, providing soothing background sounds. And as she slipped into sleep, she sometimes confused the rumbling flatulence of grass-fed cattle with a storm thundering in the mountains. They were peaceful beasts who were partners in the enterprise that was Errotabarri.

When sleep wouldn't come, she often slipped to the floor in the dark and whispered to the animals through fissures in the planks. The sheep, placid in all circumstances, were oblivious to her overtures and never considered the importance of messages being sent from above. They slept in fluffy clusters and could not be roused by a soft human voice.

Cows, though, were sociably curious. Miren would call lightly to them, sometimes mimicking their gentle moo-eh, and one directly below would tilt its head, allowing a huge brown eye to peer up at the source of the disembodied voice. Had it been their nature to reflect and expand, these could have been the genesis moments of bovine religious movements.

Sometimes she'd whisper her secrets to these friends, feeling the relief that comes from saying words aloud, even if only to beasts. She'd speak the name of the boy she liked at the moment or confess her hopes and doubts. The cows were generous with their attention, their upturned eyes sensitive and somehow understanding. They seemed to say, 'Go ahead, dear, I'm listening.' In the warm months, when the stock grazed and slept in the upper pasture, Miren missed their company and for weeks would have trouble falling asleep without their muffled lullabies.

For a time, Justo kept donkeys, breeding and selling the yearlings at the market. When the mares foaled, Mariangeles and Miren would midwife the process. The birthing was frightening, but the foals, in their leggy romps, so frisky and clumsy, delighted Miren. They entered the world as a fuzzy collection of outsize ears and trembling legs, and Miren could not help but constantly kiss their soft-whiskered muzzles and stroke their bristle-brush manes.

She loved their vigour and the way their ungainly sprints implied aspirations beyond life as a mere donkey. When weeks old, they would nurse in the paddocks and suddenly, as if jolted by unseen lightning, let loose with their little honk-and-whistle bray and dash in tumbling circles around their mothers. With imaginations faster than their legs, they splayed and rolled and reared and kicked, falling flat and rising without shame to race in circles again, perhaps recalling a connection to distant ancestors that branched off to become Arab stallions. And following a lap or two of frivolity, they suddenly would stop and return to their mothers' milk, fuelling for the next imaginary race upon the sands of some great forgotten dunes.

Their performances would entertain Miren for hours, so she always claimed donkey care as her own job. She once asked her father if a foal could stay in her room at night and sleep in her bed. He did not reject the idea because the animal needed to be with its mother and it would be frightened in such a situation. Instead, knowing his daughter's own energetic disposition, he kidded her that she would keep the poor thing awake with her attentions, and everybody knows that a little donkey, an *astokilo*, needs its rest. That made sense to Miren, and in her natural concern over the foal's welfare, she conceded that it would be against sound judgement.

The only truly offensive part of sharing her home with domestic beasts came in the coldest months, when her father butchered chickens on the ground floor rather than fight the weather while doing the job outside. The decapitation was noisy and the chicken died without dignity. Blood was everywhere.

A neighbour's boy who sometimes helped her father with the process delighted in gathering up an amputated chicken foot and clasping the exposed tendon to maniacally manipulate the foot as he chased young Miren. She knew these were only the severed feet of chickens, but she still would race out into the cold to escape. Those nights, she'd awaken, shaken by dreams of clenching talons. She would roll over, hear the comforting sound of a cow pissing pro-digiously downstairs, and float gently back to sleep.

Picasso spotted the young woman through the windows of the Galeries Lafayette on Boulevard Haussmann and prowled outside the grand department store until the attractive light-haired shopper exited. He rushed to her side before she could cross the street.

'Mademoiselle, you have an interesting face; I would like to paint your portrait,' he offered, tossing out an invitation that rarely failed. 'I have a feeling that we will accomplish great things together.'

She examined the man with the wild sweep of thinning hair and dark eyes, who had not actually bothered to introduce himself before promising a productive future relationship. He sensed her initial reluctance and, as if it would explain everything, added, 'I am Picasso.'

Marie-Thérèse Walter was a blonde seventeen-year-old, and she agreed to model for the artist. To celebrate her arrival at the age of majority the next year, they consummated their relationship. Marie-Thérèse would become the face of many paintings, and her gracious and placid nature came through as tincture to the art. Hers would become a mournful face in his most famous painting.

Dodo Navarro named his game the Loop. Miguel had no interest in the competition, but it was difficult to reject a challenge by a big brother. And it ultimately gave him an early victory, a sense of peace in the water, and an understanding of Lekeitio harbour that would one day preserve his freedom.

When Dodo and Miguel were in their early teens, the Loop was strictly a circling of the harbour. They swam across the harbour mouth, scrambled up the steps of the lower breakwater, and sprinted through the dangerous gauntlet of flying hooks cast by sport fishermen on the pier. With Dodo teasing Miguel with every stride, they raced through the clusters of families socializing at Independence Plaza, hit full speed in the stretch up the wharf, curved around the net boxes and fish carts at the north corner near the fish processors, and made the final sprint back down the high breakwater. The first to dive back into the sea, completing the loop, won.

Dodo, more mature and stronger, dominated the early races. Miguel accused him of cheating from time to time because Dodo often altered the path or shaved corners. 'The only rules are to do what it takes to win, little brother,' Dodo responded. But when Dodo hurdled a pram in the plaza to gain an edge and their father was lectured that afternoon at the wharf by an agitated *amuma*, Dodo was made to apologize. He quickly invented a new course. The next route was solely a test of swimming to San Nicolas Island, which rose outside the gates of the harbour like a humpback whale frozen in mid-breach.

'I only have one question,' Miguel said. 'Why do you get to choose?'

'Because I'm the oldest; I get to lead the way. That's how it is. If you want to race with your sisters, you get to set the route.'

'I don't even want to race with you,' Miguel admitted.

Named for the patron saint of sailors, San Nicolas Island was covered in slender pines, tangled wind-thrown timber, and feathery sea grasses. From the harbour mouth, the island was almost a quarter-mile swim and was protected by a brisk tidal current and the white, corrugated surf.

The island, in conspiracy with the surging and retracting tide, held a secret that hinted of magic. With a tidal variance of at least a dozen feet most of the year, the island had two personalities. For all but two slivers of time of each day, San Nicolas was as protected as any coastal island. It could be visited by boat or by a strong swimmer, but its rocky perimeter discouraged even those incursions. At lowest tide, however, the sea withdrew to reveal an umbilical pathway that snaked from Isuntza Beach all the way to the southernmost point. For little more than an hour twice a day, the island could be accessed via a slippery concrete trail that seemed an invitation to explore an otherwise guarded and forbidden place. If this hour coincided with a summer sunset bleeding across the hills behind town, as a sea-scented breeze caused the grasses to whisper, the atmosphere of romance often overcame young couples who had ventured to the island for privacy.

While the island seduced them to settle in and become familiar, the sea served as an intolerant chaperone. If the pair became too absorbed in their dalliance, the path would submerge again, and they would have the option of swimming to shore or spending a cold night surrounded by the judgemental sea, with no excuse to offer their parents besides the obvious.

Even in their early teens, Miguel stood as tall as Dodo and was slimmer, with stringy muscles operating the lengthy levers of his arms and legs. Miguel could reach the island and be on the inward leg of the swim before Dodo touched the island rocks. When Dodo finally joined his brother back on the breakwater, he generally congratulated Miguel by shoving him back in the water, a gesture that Miguel considered meaningless since he had already proven he could swim and, in fact, do so much better than his brother.

Once Dodo tried to gain an advantage by swimming to the island and racing back along the briefly exposed walkway to the beach, but his bare feet slipped on the mossy surface, sending him flying into the water, with his head missing the concrete by mere inches. He'd been certain the ploy would work and scheduled that race to coincide exactly with the lowest tide, the timetable of which was implanted in the mind of every fisherman's son.

Miren fretted over God's opinion. As deeply as she loved to dance, to do so in a convent, in front of the cloistered sisters, seemed an unwarranted risk. She worried that it might appear as a mark against her in some future heavenly accounting session.

'Are you certain they want us to dance inside the convent?' Miren asked her mother for the third time that morning.

'Sister Terese invited us,' Mariangeles Ansotegui answered. 'She wouldn't have asked if it was forbidden.'

Terese, Mariangeles's cousin, was a sister of standing at the Santa Clara convent, situated behind the Casa de Junta parliament house and the Guernica oak on the hill behind the market. Among her fondest memories from the secular world were those of her cousin dancing. Terese had danced with her in groups, and although she knew the steps and followed the beat, she could never keep up with Mariangeles, who seemed a part of the music. Her talents had not faded with time, and it was a gift of grace that was passed to her daughter, Miren.

Sister Terese felt that an afternoon watching local folk dance would be an acceptable diversion from the monastic ritual of the convent. Besides, she had not seen Miren, now fourteen, for many months.

'Couldn't you dance alone?' Miren pressed her mother as they neared the outer gates.

'Don't be silly. Do you think God can't see you dance everywhere else? There's hardly a time during the day when you're not dancing. When don't you dance? In your sleep?'

'No, I dance in my dreams. I dance best in my dreams.'

'Well, if God hasn't minded so far, then I don't think the sisters will, either.'

They wore the traditional outfits: black velvet waistcoats and satin aprons over long-sleeved white blouses, their scarlet satin skirts lined with horizontal black stripes at the hem. Their hair was channelled back by cinched white scarves; the laces of their peasant slippers wound over white stockings up their calves and were tied below the knees, accentuating their lean lines.

Sister Terese led them through the outer courtyard and into a large, empty anteroom in the main building. Along the inner wall, a grated double door sent light into the sisters' dining quarters. Through the arabesque wrought-iron gate, Miren could see vague dark figures, a cluster of mute, ominous shadows, motionless as stalagmites. She had danced at festivals before the entire village; she had danced without anxiety in front of drunks and strangers and amid the glares of young men. But to spin her skirts for the brides of Jesus was another issue.

When Marie-Luis, one of Mariangeles's sisters, who was accompanying the dancers on the accordion, eased open the bellows and pressed the first spirited notes, Miren thought nothing of her audience or the consequences. If St Peter called for an accounting someday, she'd dance a *jota* for him and let him judge for himself.

Miren and Mariangeles began spinning in mirrored orbits, doing triple kicks and turns, side kicks and turns, arms upraised and fingers snapping. With each spin, their skirts rose outward only to gather tightly when they stopped and reversed, creating swirling eddies of red satin.

Between dances, Miren noticed that a girl, perhaps her own age, had entered the far end of the room through a side door. Dressed in a workman's shirt and a peasant skirt, with an apron ornamented by random stains, the girl began moving when the music resumed. She didn't spin or kick or snap her fingers but weaved sensuously in one spot. She was neither nun nor novitiate, but she was also no one Miren had seen in school or in the village.

After several dances, Sister Terese signalled to Marie-Luis that one more would be sufficient. For the first time, Miren focused on the figures behind the grated archway. When her spins brought them into her scope of vision, Miren detected motion behind the screen. The sisters were no longer ominous black shadows but flashes of movement, arms upraised in dance. Sister Terese had not told her about this. Yes, they were nuns, fully devout and willing to renounce pleasure to abide by their covenant of hardship. But they also were Basques, and when a *jota* was played on an accordion, they were compelled to whirl in their habits, wimples fluttering, snapping their fingers in time.

With that vision, Miren felt absolved; she wasn't offending the sisters, she was performing in front of fellow dancers. She told her mother she'd happily dance at the convent as often as they were asked. Miren was particularly eager for the next performance and was determined to learn more of the curious girl swaying to her own rhythms in the corner of the room.

The fish attacked as Miguel slept. Giant mackerel splayed their jaws wide in his face and sprayed jets of caustic, fetid slime. Ghosts of slaughtered sea creatures visited in exaggerated and distorted forms. Octopuses with dozens of adhesive tentacles clutched and then engulfed him with their huge soft heads, and he would awaken to find himself wound tightly in his blankets, head buried in his pillow.

He never actually said the words to his family, but Miguel Navarro despised fish, live or spectral.

It was impossible for him to return to sleep after these attacks, always knowing that within a short time he would have to leave his bed and face a reality that was only marginally less grotesque than his nightmares. More troubling to him than the smell rising from the hold, where hundreds of fish slithered in their mutual slime, were the undulating waters that unsettled him the moment the *Egun On* sailed past San Nicolas Island, only minutes outside the Lekeitio harbour walls.

On rough days, as the boat rose to the crest of each wave, Miguel was thrust off his heels for an instant of weightlessness, only to be cast back down with knee-buckling force when the boat bottomed into a trough. Most fishermen learn to absorb the motion with their legs, like riders on horseback, and for several hours after they return to land they walk in a bobbing fashion, compensating for a motion that the ground does not make. It never came to Miguel, though, and within the first half hour on the boat, he would lean over the transom and repeatedly bow, like a pump handle, to disgorge his breakfast into the turbulent Bay of Biscay.

'Don't look at the waves or the deck,' his father told him. 'Keep your eyes on the horizon.'

But the horizon danced and tilted on gimbals.

'Pray to St Erasmus,' Dodo said, having tried to help his brother by asking the priest for the name of the patron saint of those with stomach disorders.

'St Erasmus, please help me,' Miguel often started, but sometimes he could not finish that brief prayer before having to race to the stern. Miguel's lone relief from suffering came from the lemon drops his father gave him. They didn't stop him vomiting, but they gave his bile a more tolerable citrus flavour as it surged towards the sea.

Miguel felt a distressing sameness to it all. When he looked at his father's hands, with the trails of white burns from lines and nets, and red scars from knife slips, and barnacle-like patches dried on the skin from the salt winds, he doubted that any physical feature revealed more about a person's work than did the hands of a fisherman.

To be so disturbed by it all left him feeling like a traitor to his name and his race.

'No such thing as a seasick Basque,' Dodo would say. 'That's like a brave Spaniard or an intelligent Portuguese – doesn't happen.'

Miguel was proud of his family's heritage as seamen, his father's daily dedication, and Dodo's ability to work without tiring, without freezing, without regurgitating, all the while singing and joking and playing practical jokes on everybody else on the boat.

Even his mother's connection to the business inspired him. At two o'clock each morning, the town weatherman would scan the darkened horizon and sniff the winds to decide if the seas would be fair enough to safely send the fishing fleet to work. Sometimes a small committee of retired fishermen would convene to offer opinions. They had little upon which to base their forecasts other than the time of year, the clouds, and whatever meteorological value came from licking one's finger and holding it pensively to the wind. When a consensus was reached, it was passed to the callers, who would trundle through the damp darkness to the residences of the crews and sing out, 'In the name of God, arise!'

Miguel's mother, Estrella Navarro, was a caller. Her strong voice bounced off the house fronts and the pavements of the lanes, which were so narrow that only three could walk abreast. Her 'arise' was sung in a pleasant vibrato that inspired awakening. Miguel was often conscious before the call anyway, disentangling from the octopus in his bed.

It was hardly a secret that Miguel was not destined for a future as a sea captain. One morning the contractions of his stomach hit with such force he was unable to reach the gunwale in time. To vomit on his father's deck would be an unforgivable violation. Miguel had no choice but to yank the beret from his head and fill it. He struggled across the deck and heaved the ballooning hat overboard. It floated

45

away like a menacing black jellyfish. It would be a long time before he would wear a beret again.

José Antonio Aguirre confessed a few pedestrian sins to Father Xabier Ansotegui, a junior priest at the Basilica de Begoña in Bilbao. But before the priest could mete out the Hail Marys, Aguirre opened a discourse on Spain's political volatility.

'Primo de Rivera's henchmen in the Guardia Civil have too much latitude; they're vigilantes more than a national police force in some areas, and they've hated and pressured us for decades,' the man said. 'And at this rate, there will never be rights for workers or for women, and certainly not for the Basques. God help you if you're a working Basque woman.'

'I think I'm supposed to give the lectures in here,' Xabier said, peering through the lattice. 'Who are you?'

Aguirre introduced himself, and Father Xabier recognized the name. A former football star from a family of Bilbaino chocolate-makers, Aguirre was mayor of nearby Getxo and was rumoured to be the leading candidate for president if the Basques ever gained independence.

'I'm sorry, I get worked up,' Aguirre said.

Xabier conceded that was one of his own shortcomings.

When Aguirre discovered that the priest was from Guernica, he launched into high oratory fit for a political speech. 'More than four centuries ago, Basques held a congress beneath the tree of Guernica,' Aguirre said, too loudly for the confessional. 'They declared that all Basques were equally noble before the law without exception. And any law, whether by king or court, should be disregarded if it ran contrary to liberty—'

'Yes, I know,' the priest interrupted. 'Do you have any more sins we need to discuss?'

He did not, but for half an hour, they talked about labour problems, social issues, the dictates of the Church, the alcohol content of holy wine, the best eating places on either side of the

Nervión River, and poetry. Aguirre was a friend of the local poet/journalist Lauaxeta; Father Xabier was an admirer of the Andalusian poet/playwright Federico García Lorca. Through the grating, Aguirre quoted Lauaxeta from memory, and Xabier volleyed a Lorca line about the poet who wants 'to press his ear to the sleeping girl and understand the Morse code of her heart.'

'Yes, but he's not Basque, so it's sadly inferior,' Aguirre said.

'You sound like my brother,' said Xabier, which led to a discussion of Justo and farming and the phenomenon of elder siblings and the influence of birth order. When Aguirre finally exited, having talked his way out of penance, the elderly woman waiting for the confessional shook her head in scorn, imagining the sins he must have committed to be in there that long.

Miguel loved the ritual of being a fisherman even if he barely tolerated the practice. He even enjoyed the pre-dawn walk to mass at Santa María de la Asunción, across the brick cobbles slippery with the night dew that seeped up from the harbour.

A sense of peace calmed him when he stepped through the main door of the centuries-old church. The wooden floors answered their steps with a groan in the dialect of the deck planks of their boat. The Navarro crew gathered in the front of the church near a small side altar dominated by the likeness of San Miguel subduing a fearsome sea serpent. To his left the archangel Rafael proudly held a large fish like a trophy. The Navarros considered it a daily reminder of their goals: to catch bigger fish and hope that divinities controlled any threats that might rise up from the seas. Piety was no guarantee, but before leaving every morning, Miguel bowed to San Miguel, visited the sign of the cross upon his chest, kissed his thumbnail, and pointed to the heavens.

On the short walk across the square to the harbour each morning, Dodo proudly farted as if it were performance art, but the others were always too sleepy to protest. In the dark, even the chatty gulls slept, abed on their communal perch near the peak of San Nicolas Island.

But there were enough sounds without them as the rigging groaned against the moorings and the fenders of the boats uttered rubbery squeaks when men stepped aboard and altered the attitude of the beam.

From various parts of the harbour, in primitive, wordless communication, came the coughs of the fishermen. Years of dank mornings and days at sea inflamed their respiratory systems. Each cough was distinctive, and without looking up from his work in the predawn chill, Miguel could recognize who was aboard the various crafts by their bronchial signature.

With the physical work of net preparation resting with his sons, José María Navarro would sit on a gunwale breathing deeply of his final cigarette before casting off. Each inhalation caused the tip to brighten and cast a red glow across the terrain of his face. The light of the embers showed his eyes clenched in pleasure and left dark shadows in the lines radiating from the corners of his eyes, like the wakes of tiny boats, carved deep by the years of staring into the sun that skipped off the water.

As lines were cast off, Miguel already could hear the plangent waves. And past the breakwater he saw them crest and curl and die white against the seaward rocks of the island. The *Egun On* slipped out of the harbour, leaving a ripple that spread and vanished as they headed into the still-dark sea. At this point, a surging tide of dread started rising in the slender passage at the back of Miguel's throat.

CHAPTER 5

When Miren Ansotegui asked about the girl at the convent, Sister Terese recounted the heartrending history of Alaia Aldecoa's blindness and abandonment by her parents. She did so with a motive.

'She has a sense of independence,' Sister Terese said. 'She has so many questions that she's afraid to ask us. We hope to find someone to take her outside to see how well she could do in town. We're happy to have her, and she can stay forever if she wants, but we think she would rather live out there.'

The sisters intentionally didn't indoctrinate Alaia to their lifestyle. If she were called to it, that would be fine, but they didn't push. She was sequestered because of others' neglect, not her own choice. They were renunciates, she the renounced. They taught her soap-making as a potential vocation, and they helped her manage an impressive degree of mobility. Having been raised inside a simple, walled compound, Alaia had little need for guidance other than her walking stick. With this experience in an enclosed environment, she developed a sense for detecting obstacles and hazards that would carry over outside the convent.

'Would it be all right if I took her into town?' Miren asked. Sister Terese had hoped for exactly that offer without wanting to impose.

What Alaia discovered in the first moments outside was that Miren Ansotegui was more of a challenge than the unknown open spaces. Outside the walls, Alaia spoke at the same deliberate pace with which she walked. Miren was the opposite, skipping, spinning, gesturing, and tossing out possibilities at a withering rate.

'First, we'll go to the market and get some fruit,' Miren said. 'The apples are wonderful now.'

'I would . . . ' Alaia said.

'And then we can go to the houses of some of my friends, so you can meet them. And then we can stop at the cafe to have some lunch. And then we can go to the town square.'

'. . . like that,' Alaia continued.

'Maybe I can find somebody with an accordion and I could teach you some of our dances.'

Alaia stepped back from Miren, as if distance could protect her from the avalanche of words. She might go months without having to absorb so much language at the convent, and she had never needed to sort through so many options. Yes, it was exciting, but goodness, enough.

Alaia's slight retreat caused Miren to speak louder.

'And then we can go to my house for dinner,' she added. 'And you could meet my family. And you could spend the night in my room.'

'Miren,' Alaia broke in, 'I'm not deaf.'

Guernica embraced Alaia Aldecoa. It didn't hurt that she was towed in the wake of Miren Ansotegui, the graceful young dancer who happened to be the daughter of the town's renowned strongman and the much-admired Mariangeles Oñati. Their curiosity over Alaia's condition quickly gave way to admiration as they watched her open to others and adapt and compensate for her disability. She seemed so fearless, to walk around like that. After the two girls left a shop or cafe, those within often tested themselves with the voluntary onset of blindness, closing their eyes for a few steps before stubbing their toes or scraping their shins on furniture, or giving in to the urge to peek through eye slits. What a shame, they agreed, and such a pretty girl, too. Didn't she already show womanly bulges in that sackcloth dress with the rope sash?

Miren touted Alaia as 'the most unique person in Guernica' and bragged about her new friend as if she was a possession. Rather than being offended at being treated as a new pet, Alaia thrived on the exposure, and before long she was able to negotiate the market and several places in town without holding Miren's arm, using only the walking stick the sisters had carved for her. When the sisters heard of the success of her outings, they felt as if they'd helped nurse an orphaned animal to health and were about to release it back into its own habitat.

On her early outings, Alaia found Miren to be as frenetic as the sisters were restrained and Miren's hyperactivity to be as far from her personal rhythms as were the sisters' meditations and prayer. She had gone from the company of slumbering lambs to guidance by a playful sheepdog puppy. After sensing Alaia withdraw a few times, Miren recognized her new friend's need for a slower pace and softer voice, and their trips became more relaxed. Still, Alaia could sense Miren's spirit vibrating at a pitch she could almost hear from a distance, humming like the sisters at vespers.

Not a heartbeat separated Justo Ansotegui's pious 'Amen' to the pre-meal grace from the start of his detailed personal biography for the sake of his daughter's new friend.

'Let me explain myself to you, child,' he said as he made the first forceful incisions into the bread.

Mariangeles and Miren groaned in chorus.

'I am well known to be the strongest man in Guernica, and I suspect most women would agree that I am the most handsome man in the Pays Basque, too.'

'Papa!'

'Justo!'

'Wait, women, it is only considerate that she understand the importance of this occasion,' he said. 'But she must promise not to inform the sisters of my appeal, or the convent would be emptied by morning and Errotabarri would be crowded with those in black habits gathered to praise my manly form.'

'Justo, that's sacrilege!'

'Papa, that's disgusting!'

'Alaia, pay no attention to this man,' Mariangeles said as she brought another dish of vegetables to the table. 'If he is the most anything in the country, it is the most boastful.'

'Come here, woman, let me smell those hands,' Justo said to Mariangeles.

Justo buried his face in her palms and inhaled, finally pulling away as if intoxicated.

'I love the smell of a woman who has just cut celery,' he declared.

Alaia sorted through every smell that arrived as Mariangeles ferried plates to the table. She tried to memorize the flavours of the meal, the lamb with mint sauce, the bread coated in farm-churned butter, the beans, the paprika-dusted potatoes, the mild asparagus and peppers soaked in olive oil and garlic. And for dessert, she devoured the sweet flan that several times wobbled off her spoon before she could track it down.

Mariangeles delighted in Alaia's joy of food. It was one of the things that always appealed to her about Justo, too. Even his belching seemed a compliment.

'Alaia, dear, you are welcome here for dinner any time,' Mariangeles said.

'Yes, you must come back,' Justo said, thoughtfully combing the evidence of dinner from his moustache. 'I have many feats of strength to tell you about.'

'Papa!'

'Justo!'

Alaia was not offended. It was this meal, in fact, that most convinced her that she would move out of the convent as soon as possible. That lamb. That mint sauce. Those vegetables. Butter. More butter, please. And that flan, oh, dear God, that flan. Did the sisters know of flan? How could anyone renounce flan?

When Miren rose to lead Alaia towards her room, Justo stood and gathered them both close, one beneath each powerful arm. He squeezed them and clenched his hands together behind their backs and rocked them in rhythm. Miren squirmed as any daughter would, but Alaia squeezed in a matching response.

'We will be disappointed if you don't come back often to have more of this food and friendship,' Justo said, kissing Alaia on the crown of her head. 'My little one here needs the company of others besides her boastful father and her cows and little donkeys.'

'Alaia, may I present my dearest friend, Floradora,' Miren said, placing in Alaia's hands the rag doll that had shared her bed since she was a baby.

'She has shiny brunette hair . . .'

(Brown yarn.)

'. . . a graceful neck . . .'

(Stretched thin from nightly hugging.)

'. . . a shapely body . . .'

(Rags inside a stocking.)

'. . . lovely skin . . .'

(Wool petted smooth.)

'. . . a nice smile . . .'

(Red paint.)

'. . . and beautiful dark eyes.'

(Black beads.)

Alaia touched the beads.

They rested in her bed end to end, Miren with her head propped on the headboard and Alaia angled upon a pillow against the footboard. A small grilled brazier filled with coals taken from the kitchen hearth warmed the room and released a wispy plume of incense to collect among the beams. Miren wanted to learn of blindness and Alaia of sight; Miren, feelings, Alaia, visions; Miren, sound, Alaia, colours; Miren, the solitude of the orphanage, Alaia, the comfort of all things familial.

'What is the worst part of being blind?' Miren asked.

'Having to try to tell people what it's like.'

'Do you have better hearing than us?'

'What?'

'Do you – oh . . . do you have a better sense of smell?'

'Yes, and your feet are horrible,' said Alaia, leaning over Miren's toes.

'Do you see light at all?'

'Not really, some shadows.'

'Does it seem dark all day?'

'I don't really know dark from light.'

'Are you angry that you can't see?'

'Not angry, really. I'm happy I can do most other things.'

'How did you lose your sight?'

'The sisters told me that I was born too early, and that was probably the reason. I was not yet developed. My eyes are not the only part that does not work. I also don't get the monthly visits that the sisters told me of.'

Miren: 'Lucky you.'

Alaia: 'The sisters tell me it means that I can't have little ones.'

Miren: 'Oh, no. I'm sorry. That's something I know I want, but I'm afraid of it. My *amuma* died after having a baby.'

The girls talked through much of the night. Alaia could never tell the sisters of the boundaries she felt at the convent, how she imagined she was living inside a box. But she could share that with Miren. She couldn't ask the sisters how she looked, whether she was beautiful, but she could ask Miren. She couldn't tell the sisters how wonderful it felt being in the town and meeting people, and knowing that her blindness made her special to them. That might cause them to have doubts about the decision they made to relinquish the warmth of others. She knew that when people met her, she would not be forgotten. But she couldn't say that to the sisters because it might make them feel as if they had been forgotten once they went behind the walls.

And then they wrestled. Pillows were hurled and blankets flew.

'Hey, that's not fair . . . you've got to close your eyes,' Alaia said.

And Miren did, out of fairness.

The wrestling was a welcome connection to them both, an excuse to feel another body like theirs but not theirs; to judge themselves against another by touch, size, weight, strength; to feel the softness of another's hair and skin. Two young girls could not just reach and touch each other in this way, but in the guise of playfulness, all was appropriate. Alaia started by grabbing a nearby foot and shaking it, and Miren tentatively joined in after it was clear that wrestling with a blind girl was not only tolerated but appreciated.

As they calmed, Alaia became absorbed by Miren's quilt, feeling the varied textures of the cloth squares, the wool, the linen, the cotton, and one of velvet, all held together with tufted yarn knots. She slept under a plain woollen blanket at the convent.

Nearing sleep, Miren asked, 'What's it like not having a family?'

Alaia didn't answer for so long that Miren assumed she hadn't heard. As Miren started to doze, she answered softly, 'Nobody touches you.'

When Alaia readied to be returned to the convent in the morning, Miren placed Floradora in her hands.

'She's yours now,' she said solemnly. 'You need her company more than I do.'

Alaia hugged the doll and touched her face.

That morning Miren had removed the beads, leaving only horizontal stitching where the eyes had been.

The waitress was in her early forties and out of the practical range of their affections, but her prominence in the foredeck attracted the younger, flirtatious members of the crews to the Seaman's Cafe in Lekeitio. Unseasoned at romantic nuance, they peppered her with suggestive references and were dealt rejection with a playful ridicule that was a part of the game. It served as courting practice as they tested tactics they could use when the target was an actual marriageable female. But most were more familiar with casting wide nets than the subtle use of baits.

'I could make you the happiest waitress in Lekeitio,' Dodo said.

55

'What, would you leave a tip?'

Dodo winked and pursed his lips as for a kiss.

'You, my friend, smell too much like my husband,' she said. 'And you are far too eager. Women can smell desperation – even on a fisherman.'

She turned and fingered the back of Miguel's hair. 'But you, the quiet one, you will break many hearts in time.'

Dodo groaned loudly, punching his brother's shoulder, envious of the comment.

'You,' she said to Dodo, 'would be wise to learn from this one.'

Miguel flushed with embarrassment, an emotion he knew was unknown to Dodo.

'She's just kidding me to make you jealous,' Miguel said.

Dodo laughed at his naive brother.

'These are not the waters for finding women, Miguel,' Dodo rationalized.

Miguel had witnessed Dodo's brief and doleful history with the girls of Lekeitio. He was playful as a puppy until he began breathing fire with his politics. His emotional elasticity wore down relationships quickly.

The waitress returned with a basket of bread, putting a conciliatory hand on Dodo's shoulder. Misreading the gesture – which was typical of him – he returned it with an arm around her hips. She slapped his hand with enough force to cause others to turn. Dodo laughed overly loud to imply it had all been a joke. But the message was received.

Rebuked, Dodo moved on to his second-favourite topic, the politics of Spain, and lectured his younger brother on the varied platforms of the Socialists and Republicans and Fascists and Anarchists.

Miguel listened as he ate, while Dodo used his fork mostly for gesturing, especially when repeating reports of conflicts that were growing more lethal around Spain.

'There was no news of it in the papers, but I heard of this from a crew from the south,' Dodo said between bites. 'The Guardia fired into a crowd of demonstrating land workers in Extremadura. They killed a man and wounded two women, and the rest of the crowd surrounded them and killed the guards with stones and knives. Can you imagine?'

No, Miguel hadn't heard of it, and he wondered if such a thing could be true. Dodo might say anything to emphasize his point.

'It happened again at a protest, a peaceful protest, in Arnedo,' Dodo said. 'Guards killed four women and a baby, and wounded thirty people who were just standing there watching.'

'Why wouldn't we hear something about it?' Miguel asked.

'Because they don't want you to hear, that's why. People are afraid to talk. Afraid it will happen to them. Which is exactly why we have to be ready.'

The waitress, standing behind Dodo, listened to his stories. She shook her head slowly and said to Miguel, 'Don't listen to him, dear, he won't be so angry when he finds a girl.'

Had there been a reason for the citizens of Guernica to hold a referendum on the most popular person in the village, Miren Ansotegui would have won easily. She was only sixteen, but she seemed to encourage people to take part in her youth rather than give them reason to be jealous of it. She reminded them how life looked before it became so complicated.

It was more than the way she floated through the streets of town, so lean and loose-limbed, her black plait a pendulum swinging from one hip to the other with each stride. More appealing was her knack for disarming people, for drawing them near, as if initiating them into her own club of the unrelentingly well intended. There was no trick to it beyond good nature. As she spread warm greetings to everyone she passed, she uncannily enquired about that single portion of their lives that made them most proud. She always opened a gate to somewhere they each wished to go. And then she listened.

'Do you have any more of those incredible peppers, Mr Aldape?' she would ask the old man with a vegetable cart. 'I couldn't stop eating them the last time we had them. They were the best peppers I've ever had.'

Or she would buzz into the Aranas' dress shop with 'Mrs Arana, I saw your granddaughter the other day at the market and she must be the most beautiful baby I've ever seen; is she walking yet?' It allowed them to brag about themselves without the stain of immodesty. She had asked the question, for heaven's sake, and it would be rude to contradict her or decline to elaborate. As Miren hurried on to further encounters in town, her path of courteous enquiries left a wake of goodwill. Charmed acquaintances felt better than they did before she appeared and were eager for her quick return. There was much more about them, after all, that she would want to hear.

She might mention the particulars of an event in support of whatever was her charitable cause at the moment. If Miren Ansotegui was going to be there, it would be entertaining, and it was guaranteed that many others would be likewise ensnared by her plans. Their involvement would allow them to recount their munificence the following day in the cafes and *tabernas*, and also, they presumed, would place them on the unofficial list of Contributors to Miren's Causes.

When Aitor Arriola's house burned to the stone after an ember from the hearth blew into the kindling pile, neighbours were helpful in getting his family back on its feet. But because of the burns Aitor suffered while trying to fight the blaze, his attempts at reconstruction would be delayed past the onset of bad weather in the fall.

Seeking out every unmarried gentleman in town, regardless of age, Miren promised them a special dance at the next *erromeria* if they would work one hour helping the Arriolas. She charmed commitments out of nearly a dozen men aged fifteen to seventy-five. As they arrived with their tools, Miren showily pencilled their names on a list, making them promise to attend the dance on Sunday evening to be thanked and rewarded. Although some arrived sheepishly, every man who helped rebuild the house turned up to redeem the promise. Those who were not dancers claimed they had just come to be friendly, even if they had not been to an *erromeria* in years. And a number of them were dragged out to dance by Miren, who patiently taught them the simplest box-step waltz.

Mrs Arana, who found Miren's civic flitting uplifting as she moved from shop to shop and friend to friend, labelled her *tximeleta* – the Butterfly. It was an image Miren shed at a late-summer dance practice.

Her group of a dozen young girl dancers gathered in a small square behind a cafe to practise for an upcoming performance. Friends of the dancers sat on benches beneath the plane trees or at the several tables under the striped awning that covered the back patio of the cafe and provided a pocket of relief on the warm evening. Miren had parked her friend Alaia Aldecoa on a chair on the patio and ordered her a glass of cold cider.

The group rehearsed the hoop dance, which required the girls to weave at increasing speed, tapping one another's bamboo hoops with greater force as they tightened the intricate steps. Alaia frequently rose to sway in place when the music played, but this evening she appeared to drift away from a man at the cafe who was talking to her. Miren did not recognize him and approached them both during a pause.

'Is there a problem, Alaia?'

'I just asked this young lady if she wanted to dance with me,' the man said, turning his head towards Alaia.

Miren looked at Alaia, who seemed uncomfortable, having edged further away.

'Did she tell you she didn't want to dance?'

'That's what she said.'

'This is my friend, sir, and if you haven't noticed, she happens to have lost her sight.'

'I don't see anything wrong with her.'

Miren fought against her anger and smiled to douse the tension. 'Sir, you may have enjoyed too much wine, so I'm sure you want to move on now, don't you?'

'Look, little one, she's big enough to take care of herself.'

Miren's artificial smile vanished. Inadvertently trained for this by her dance practices, she struck at the table with her hoop, causing the man to jump.

'Hey!' he shouted, rising from his chair.

Miren recoiled and struck again so quickly that the bamboo whistled in the air. But she didn't touch him with the decorative weapon. She slammed the bamboo on the table in front of him, then on the table leg, then on the back of his chair, then on the awning support just behind his head. Hit after hit, with the bamboo cracking like rifle fire, she repeated this circuit of strikes around the man as he cowered, seeking to reduce his surface area. Given the energy of her attack, Miren could have peeled his skin off if she struck him.

'Call the Guardia!' he yelled when Miren backed away.

'What will I tell them?' the cafe owner asked. 'That a slip of a girl frightened you with a dance implement?'

'I don't care what you tell them, something needs to be done.'

'I will do you a favour, friend, since I take it you are not from here. I will tell you this: her father is Justo Ansotegui, the strongest man in Guernica, who would happily gut you with his bare hands if he heard any word of this.'

The cafe owner handed the flustered man a tea towel to wipe the sweat from his face. When he spun and left, towel to his head, the rest of the stunned dance troupe broke into *irrintzi* screams and cheers. As the dancers gathered around them and expressed their awe at her bravery, Miren felt the sickening drain of adrenaline after a conflict. She was embarrassed that she could not have found a better solution. She should have been cleverer, she told herself. She did not speak to her father of the incident, afraid that he would seek out the man and dismember him. But word of her outburst became the news of the town by the next morning.

If anything, the community loved Miren Ansotegui even more thereafter, with one difference: she was not called the Butterfly with such frequency.

CHAPTER 6

José María Navarro occasionally imposed on his friend Josepe Ansotegui for personal advice. In this case, it regarded his youngest son, Miguel. 'He is sick on the boat every day,' he told Ansotegui as they walked the wharf after mooring one afternoon.

'I know, the crew make bets on how much time it will take every morning before they see him barking at the sea. But Dodo threatens them if he hears anybody make fun of him.'

'He won't give up, Josepe. I know he would feel like he's letting me down. If we don't find something else for him, he'll stay on this boat, being sick every day for the rest of his life. But if I force him off, he might never forgive me for the insult.'

'I heard Alegria at the shipwright's was looking for an apprentice,' Ansotegui said. 'Would Miguel be happier building boats?'

Navarro laughed at the obvious answer. 'Oh, yes, but knowing him, he'd be afraid it would disappoint me. And I suppose I'm worried it's going to sound like I want to be rid of him.'

'Just mention to him that you've heard of the job; if he wants it, he'll let you know. I'll put in a word to Alegria for him.'

As Estrella Navarro began clearing the dishes after an evening of general table talk, José María mentioned to his wife that Alegria was looking for an apprentice.

Miguel overheard. 'Would a shipwright's apprentice have to go to sea?' he asked.

'No, never, if he chose not to. There might be some time on board doing finishing work in the harbour.'

'I want that job!' Miguel shouted, standing quickly, with both arms in the air as if he'd been pardoned from a prison sentence. 'If you feel all right about it. If you can get along without me. *Patroia*, to tell you the truth, fishing makes me sick.'

Although he hadn't built anything in his life, Miguel was suited to the job. Within a year, he was not only fully competent but had developed an affinity for the process. He enjoyed the trips into the hillside forests to cut and mill the mountain oak, and he relished finding ways to shape wood to his purpose. He began adding his own touches, flourishes that might not be called for in the design but gave distinction to the product.

He carved esses onto the end of rails or gunwales and used veneers of alder and ash to create decorative inlays of compass roses in the wood near the helm. These extras became the signature of his work. The men in the boats were of a serious nature, but considering the hours they spent on the craft, a small bit of style was well appreciated.

Soon captains were ordering the kinds of Miguel's handiwork they had seen on other boats. In addition, Miguel brought his deeply ingrained daily timetable to the shipwright's shop. He still attended the fishermen's mass at four o'clock every morning, sitting with his father and brother, and only tacked off course when they reached the harbour. Instead of continuing on board with them, he headed down the wharf to the shop to begin working on the boats hours before his colleagues arrived. Building boats meant staying connected to the fishing business, he reminded his father. His hands were still involved in shaping the family legacy.

A friend of Miren's told her of a cabin that might be perfect for Alaia, located in a rill at the edge of town on the lower border of old man Zubiri's *baserri*. Having been unused for years, the place was simple, not much more than a shepherd's cottage. The shingle roof had grown thick with moss in its peaty location under a cluster of alders.

At first, it was hard to separate it from the forest because branches had grown down into the organic roof thatch, as if the trees were trying to embrace the little house.

When Miren neared the cabin, a gentle but overgrown path beside the stream led her directly to the front door. There, at the bottom of a glade, there would be only two directions for Alaia to consider: uphill and downhill. To go upward would lead to the adjacent meadow, where Alaia might have access to plants and herbs for her soaps; to go downhill, with the stream at one side, would funnel her directly to town and the market.

Miren talked Zubiri into letting Alaia have it without rent in exchange for soaps. It had been unused for some time, Miren pointed out, and as a widower whose children had long departed, Zubiri didn't need the space. In fact, he would benefit, Miren promised, because they would make repairs and improvements to his property. Miren took on the cleaning and refitting, with the help of half a dozen men from town. The path was cleared, and the sagging front steps were rebuilt with a solid handrail. Mariangeles donated a quilt with a lace border she had sewn, and Justo used the oxcart to carry a winter's worth of firewood. He stacked the pieces just outside Alaia's back door on the north side of the house, where it also would insulate against winter winds that would sluice down the notched terrain.

Mariangeles arranged a few small pieces of cookware above the hearth, and Miren spaced Alaia's pots and jars and equipment in an orderly array on the table that would be used as her soap-making bench. In a day, Miren walked Alaia around the one-room house and took her into the fields and down into town several times to reinforce her mental landscape. She also spent the first night in the cabin with Alaia, hoping to ease whatever anxiety she might feel after having slept nearly every night of her life inside convent walls. It was peaceful there as the small stream created soothing background sounds. And as the fire warmed the cabin, the moss on the roof gave off a rich organic smell.

'I never could have done this without you, Miren,' Alaia said the next morning.

Miren hugged her. 'I'm so happy for you. I'll visit every day.'

'Miren . . .'

'Yes?'

'Please don't,' Alaia said. 'I'll never be on my own if you're taking care of me all the time. I know how you are. We're dear friends, but I really can do this.'

'But I want . . .' Miren started to argue, but the sound of two words – 'I want' – stopped her. 'You're right, that's how I am. You tell me what I can do and I'll trust that you're in control of everything else. You'll do fine. But I'll check in, and we'll meet in town all the time. Zubiri is just up the hill, and Josu Letemendi, a boy our age, lives at the *baserri* across the stream. I'm sure they'll be happy to peek in on you.'

José María Navarro scored the sign of the cross into the crust of the bread. His sons, Eduardo and Miguel, and his wife, Estrella, crossed themselves with precise strokes. The two youngest, their daughters Araitz and Irantzu, paused their jousting with forks for the very serious business of the blessing. Along the axis of the cross, José María carved the round loaf into halves and then into thick slices. The first piece he removed, plated, and placed on the edge of the hearth.

'To calm the stormy seas,' he said, observing a traditional seaman's gesture.

Eduardo accepted the platter, placed one slice on his plate next to the fillet of sea bream, and slipped another into his shirt pocket. 'In case I have need to calm the stormy stomach later,' he announced. 'You should take an extra for later, too, Miguel.'

'Mass is at midnight,' Estrella said. 'And I warn you not to arrive in a condition that will embarrass us. We worked hard to build our name, and at least one of you seems unaware of the need to preserve it.'

'*Corpus Christi . . . sanguis Christi*,' Dodo offered with exaggerated piety. 'We will only drink to pre-sanctify the event.'

'*Et spiritus sancti*,' added Miguel, crossing himself again and peering up from his mock prayer to see if his mother was about to slap him across the head. She had cuffed him on the left side of his crown so frequently, he claimed, that it was the reason for a stubborn cowlick there.

'Well, if you see Olentzero out there, please send him to our house with something sweet,' she said, referring to the 'Christmas coal man' – Josepe Ansotegui – who was carried throughout town in a basket, tossing treats to the little ones.

'And where will this pre-sanctification take place?' José María asked.

'Bar Guria . . . we're going to work on the harmonies for tonight's hymns,' Dodo said.

'Watch your language,' José María warned.

It was not a counsel against profanity; it was a reminder to be cautious with whom they spoke Basque – a jailable offence depending on the mood of the Guardia Civil at the moment.

'*Dominus vobiscum*,' Dodo replied.

The wind from the sea fluted through the narrow walkways of the fishermen's quarters with a chilling whistle. Pulling their jackets tightly around them, Eduardo and Miguel walked towards the procession that accompanied Olentzero beneath the coloured lights along the wharf. A quartet of strong men hoisted a basket chair upon their shoulders and carried the beloved Olentzero from house to house. A collection of carol singers and children clustered tightly, drawing closer for warmth as they stopped to sing and toss small trinkets and sweets.

'Olentzero, we hope you are carrying a *bota* on this cold night,' Eduardo shouted at his friend. 'You'll scare the little ones if you arrive frozen solid.'

'Maybe you'll be able to bring more for me if I fall short; with so many good little ones to see, it will be a long night,' the jolly coal man said, lowering his voice and nodding his head towards the rear of the pack of followers. 'You'll notice our special helpers tonight.'

At the perimeter of the gathering was a pair of armed Guardia Civil officers loitering behind the revellers.

'One of our singers already has been kindly asked to observe tonight's festivities from behind bars,' Olentzero said.

The wine fuelled Eduardo Navarro's outrage. The customary discussions at Bar Guria were of women and exaggerated tales of sexual adventures. But as two tables of *mus* players offered energetic damnations of their opponents and their partners, and others dined on *pintxoak* and laughed over their wine, Dodo was hardly filled with the seasonal spirit of peace and fellowship.

'Iker Anduiza is in jail tonight,' Dodo protested, loudly enough to cause his tablemates to dip their heads. 'Domingo Laca was taken away last week after some neighbour reported him for teaching our history to schoolchildren.'

His friends Enrique and José Luis Elizalde had heard Dodo's railings for many hours on the wharf and in the bars. They talked of the Second Republic and the hopes of renewed freedoms, perhaps even nationhood. But they knew that most expression was still subject to the whims of whichever demagogue had strong-armed his way into a position of local influence.

'We've driven off better than these,' Dodo preached. 'They've jailed us for hanging our flag. What's next? Lopping off our *pelotas* to keep us from breeding more little Basques? Is that when we'll fight them off? We were ruling ourselves when they were still swallowing the limp chorizos of the Moors.'

'Fine, Dodo, but let's not fight the war tonight,' Miguel urged.

The thought of backing away offended Dodo. 'Why not? I know you care, too. How can you be so tolerant?'

'I see what's right,' Miguel said in a low, firm tone. 'I see what's right, and I agree. But what's right for me doesn't include prison just now. What's right seems like keeping ourselves going until we can make this go away.'

'You're hiding, little brother. You're not facing the truth.'

'Dodo, I'm facing it; I'm just not fighting it before Mass.'

They locked on to each other's eyes, Miguel detecting his brother's dangerous fervours, Dodo sensing a puzzling inner peace. They nodded in silent truce, and Dodo gave his brother a conciliatory slap on the shoulder.

'Let's get some air and have a *cheesh*,' Dodo said. 'Maybe we can find a guard in need of watering.'

The numbing wind that tumbled in with the waves did little to sober the unsteady Dodo, and it was still several hours before they were to meet at the church of Santa María de la Asunción for mass. 'Eat that bread you brought, Dodo,' Miguel said. 'It will shut your mouth for a few minutes.'

But Dodo did not eat the bread, instead using his mouth to begin singing a song about fishermen leaving early in the morning to sail far away. He sang in Basque. Miguel put his arm around him to try to quiet him. 'Yes, Dodo, it is very quiet next to the pier, and there is a pretty white boat floating on the water.'

From an alley next to the town hall stepped two Guardia Civil officers with rifles, uniformed in their green capes, with their patent-leather caps reflecting the festive lamps connecting the trees of the square. Miguel instantly clasped a hand across his brother's mouth.

'Merry Christmas,' Miguel said with feigned holiday cheer.

The Guardias inflated their chests and clenched their faces. Enrique and José Luis pulled the two Navarro brothers back out onto the street before Dodo could further confront them. The two guards strutted off.

'You should stay and learn the beauty of the Basque songs,' Dodo shouted after them. 'Or are you too busy sneaking off to probe each other's *culos*?'

Dodo said the word in Spanish, to be certain they understood.

67

'Dodo, stop,' Miguel urged.

'No, I want to talk politics with these . . . gentlemen.'

The square had filled with those early to Mass, or out to visit friends, or on their way to the *tabernas* for celebration. The procession around Olentzero, too, had grown larger.

The two Guardias turned and looked at Dodo from a distance of several yards. Dodo leaned in their direction, pulling against Miguel's grasp, puckered his lips dramatically, and blew them a kiss. Groups of villagers laughing aloud, safe in their numbers, forced the officers to return and save face.

The smaller guard stepped forward and jabbed a rifle into Dodo's chest.

'Get over here, García,' he called to his partner. 'We've got a subversive.'

Dodo had told his friends his feelings about the Guardia so often that they could have joined him in the recitation: they are those not intelligent enough to clean fish, those not dignified enough to shovel manure, those for whom a rifle serves in place of the fundamental male organ.

He cleared his throat to begin voicing the screed for the Guardias.

'Stop . . . now,' the shorter guard said, elevating the rifle from Dodo's chest to his face. 'I will count to three.'

'Oh, that's it; I wondered what the qualifications were to join the Guardia Civil,' Dodo sneered. 'Now I know; it is the capacity to count to three. Let's hear you, now, one . . . two . . .'

Miguel moved to step between the two, and the shorter Guardia, sensing a threat, pivoted the rifle butt to catch him on the jaw. He dropped instantly, but as the Guardia paused, Dodo wrenched the rifle from his hands and struck him exactly as he had done to Miguel. The taller Guardia lifted his weapon towards Dodo but froze in place at the sight of his bloodied compatriot. Fully confronted by indecisiveness, the taller guard chose not to fire his weapon, instead blowing his whistle for reinforcements. Behind him, Miguel struggled back to kneeling and lunged at the guard, knocking him to the ground.

Instinctively, the brothers scrambled and separated. Miguel slumped between buildings and slipped into the shadows of the huge church. Dodo, unhurt and able to simply outrun the Guardias, headed brazenly across the square. The crowd that had gathered around Olentzero parted for a moment and then swallowed him up.

By the time the half-dozen Guardias had collected, their mettle dimmed by the sight of their fellow's blood freezing in rectangular patterns around the cobbles, Dodo was already being carried off in a basket, wearing the hat and jacket of the jolly coal man Olentzero. Josepe Ansotegui, now clothed in another's borrowed coat, had surrendered his disguise to allow Dodo's escape.

The Guardias splintered in pairs to search for the criminals, two up towards the centre of town, two down towards Isuntza Beach, and two around the wharf. Even though he had been knocked into semi-consciousness, Miguel recognized the time and tide. After sneaking behind the church and gaining distance from the Guardias, he recovered his breath and merely strolled away from the threat.

The tidal current had reversed from its low point a short time earlier, allowing him to keep his feet dry for the entire walk out to San Nicolas Island. The inflow submerged his path almost the minute he reached the southern edge. From a leeward rock, he watched the frenzy in the plaza. The Guardia had set up posts near the entrance and exits of the church and examined all who attended Mass. Even with the wind blowing icy needles and the arthritic groaning of the frozen pines, Miguel could hear the organ playing in the distance and hymns being sung.

'Merry Christmas,' he mumbled to himself, spitting blood and pulling from a pocket the slice of bread that Dodo had forced upon him. He had to break the bread into small pieces to wedge it between his tender jaws. He shivered through the frigid night in a three-sided notch in the rocks covered with gull dung. Shortly before dawn, the *Egun On* arrived on the seaward side of the island, blocked from view of the land, and picked up the suffering Miguel. Onboard were his father and a surprisingly cheerful Dodo, pleased to have drawn blood in the skirmish. They had deduced Miguel's whereabouts and apologized for not being able to retrieve him earlier.

The frigid trip to St-Jean-de-Luz on the nearby French coast didn't calm Dodo, who was excited to explore mischief in the old pirate town. Even inside the protected harbour there, flexing waves caused the *Egun On* to bounce against the fenders as Dodo accepted a wobbling embrace from his father and then his younger brother.

'Try to stay out of trouble,' José María Navarro said as he handed Dodo a small envelope.

'Keep it, *patroia*, I will be fine,' Dodo protested, looking down at his father's scarred hands.

'I know you will, but you'll need to get settled here and find work.'

Miguel thought of jokes about wine being more expensive and women being more demanding in France, but his mouth was swollen and talking was painful; his vomiting on the trip to St-Jean had ripped open cuts on the inside of his mouth. He was too angry to joke.

Dodo stepped up onto the dock and, turning to wave goodbye, saw his brother's critical look.

'Miguel . . . I'm sorry,' Dodo said sincerely, but then pointed to his brother with a grin. 'I wouldn't doubt if I've done you a favour. You're going inland now; you were never meant to be on the water.'

Miguel, for the first time, added up the consequences: he would leave his home, lose his good job, and have to move to a strange town, always keeping watch over his shoulder in case the Guardia was around.

'Thanks,' he said with as little movement of his mouth as possible, 'appreciate it.'

José María Navarro piloted the *Egun On* back out to sea. 'I must have set a fine example of fishing as a way of life,' he said. 'It looks like neither of you will be on board with me for a while.'

Miguel didn't answer, patting his father on the shoulder and then hugging him with one arm from the side as both looked out over the bow.

By evening, the *patroia* had ferried his son as far as possible up the estuary. Miguel disembarked at a high-tide pier, and although he knew he was on firm ground, the earth still bounced and dodged beneath him with every step.

PART 2
(1933–1935)

CHAPTER 7

Dearest Miren,

I hope you are all well, and you and your mother have been keeping my big brother in his place. A bear of a man like him tricking your mother into marriage is one of the great acts of deception.

I wanted to tell you of a friend who is moving to Guernica. His name is Miguel Navarro, and I have known his family for many years. You may remember him from your visits to Lekeitio when you were much younger. He is one of the boys who lived across the street in the family of my friend José María Navarro. I have already contacted Mendiola in Guernica, and he has the need for a helper in his carpentry shop. A change in locations will be good for Miguel. He is a fine young man.

I'm hoping you will meet Miguel and can help him settle in there. I'm sending this letter to you rather than your father because I fear Justo would end up scaring the boy. I can trust you to help him make friends and meet people if you get the chance. Miguel is about your age, or a little older, perhaps twenty, and my daughters have assured me that it is not a chore to have to look at him.

Thank you, Miren.

Love to your beautiful mother and that big brother of mine.

Osaba Josepe

Finally absorbing the importance of Alaia's message – that becoming a pest is not charitable – Miren fought her instincts to bring food and help with cooking and cleaning and all those jobs she was certain were easier for a sighted person. A protocol evolved: she visited Alaia's cabin only when invited or by prearrangement. But they saw each other every Monday at the market as Miren jumped in with making change and packing soaps when business was brisk. She also served as Alaia's unofficial ambassador, telling everyone in town of the wonders of her products. They ate together one night each week, usually at Errotabarri, where Mariangeles cooked her specialities and Justo entertained with his stories, always happy to perform before a larger audience. And once a week Miren cooked at Alaia's, baking and preparing some items that would keep for meals later in the week. Within this unspoken arrangement Alaia grew increasingly independent.

One Monday at the market, Alaia invited Miren to come to her cabin.

'Is there a surprise?' Miren asked when she arrived.

'Yes, I am giving you a present . . . your own soap,' Alaia said, handing her a stack of yellow-green bars separated with waxed paper. Miren inhaled and was enthralled.

'I love it; what's in it?'

'Miren . . . it's a secret.'

'It's like no soap I've smelled . . . it's like . . . what . . . Errotabarri?'

'That's what I was looking for.'

'This is so different.'

'It is,' Alaia said. 'I wanted something that said "Miren". I tried combinations of things, and this was the one I settled on. The older women like the florals, the jasmines and lilacs; the younger women like the citruses or the mixtures, oats and honey or almonds and strawberries . . . not as powerful, but they still smell like soap.'

Miren inhaled the scent again.

'Don't keep it a secret; what is it? I promise I wouldn't tell anyone about my soap.'

'I'll give you some hints,' Alaia said, enjoying the game. 'It's made with a little oil extract so that it will serve as a lotion, too, and keep your skin soft and moist.'

'There's more.'

'Yes, that's the secret. I heard about it from a wise man once.'

'I can't wait to try it out.'

'There's a pot of water that I warmed; strip off your blouse and give it a try,' Alaia said.

'Alaia!'

'Miren, I'm blind, you couldn't have more privacy in the convent. Besides, you don't have anything that I don't have . . . except for eyes.'

'Well, I'll tell you, I've actually got less than you've got, if you have to know the truth.'

Illogically self-conscious, Miren turned and tentatively removed her blouse and soaped her torso. She breathed in the fresh fragrance, splash-rinsed herself, dried herself with a towel near the sink, and replaced her blouse.

'Oh, I love this, thank you so much,' she said. 'How could you know this would be so perfect for me?'

'Because when I smelled it, I thought of you.'

'I've never heard of anything so thoughtful,' she said, hugging her friend. 'Now when I come near you, you'll be able to identify me by my smell.'

'Miren, I can usually hear you chattering with people long before I can smell you.'

'But now when you hear those people talking to me, I'm sure they'll be saying, "Oh, there goes Miren Ansotegui – doesn't that girl smell nice?"'

They hugged once more and Miren, without thinking, began tidying up Alaia's worktable.

'Miren . . . stop it.'

'I'm sorry.' Miren put down the mixing bowls Alaia had been using. 'I have a question for you, and feel free to tell me no if you are uncomfortable with it: would you mind if I shared some of the new soap with my mother? I think she would love it, too.'

Mariangeles did love the soap. And so did her husband, Justo.

The Guardia Civil may have dispossessed Miguel Navarro in Lekeitio, but it did him the service of creating a job opening for him in Guernica. Raimondo Guerricabeitia, assistant carpenter in the shop of Teodoro Mendiola, was stolen off by armed guards one day on his walk home from work. No explanations were given to his family; he simply did not arrive home that evening. Without the formalities of charges or a trial, the Guardia planted Guerricabeitia in a prison. Was he a criminal? A revolutionary? Or did a neighbour betray him with a false claim to the Guardia?

While not uncommon in other areas of the Pays Basque, such an abduction was still rare at the time in Guernica, where the Guardia mostly tolerated cultural displays and acted incursively only on tips. All that Mendiola knew was that Raimondo was a serviceable carpenter who gave no outward indications of political leanings. But someone may have said something, someone with a grudge. And he was gone as if erased.

When Josepe Ansotegui sent to Mendiola a young shipbuilder in need of quick employment, the timing worked for all concerned. Josepe was delighted when he heard that he was actually filling a manpower void. Raimondo, though, was experienced and well past the apprentice stage. Mendiola ran a small but well-established business. His helper usually felled the trees and milled the timber with a rip saw and planer, while Mendiola constructed the furniture, cabinets, and hardwood flooring. The felling of the soft pines and cypress used for cabinets and inexpensive furniture was simple, but dealing with the old-growth oaks required greater exertion. At the least, the young man who delivered himself for work looked healthy and fit enough for the challenges of handling the obstinate hardwoods.

'The recommendation of Josepe Ansotegui is enough for me,' Mendiola said when Miguel arrived. 'I've known him and his brothers, Justo and Xabier, for a long time. Justo is filled with pride and hot air, and Xabier is filled with the Holy Ghost. Josepe's word – now that, that is solid as oak. And Josepe tells me you are a fine shipbuilder from a good family. That is all I need to hear.'

Mendiola anticipated a period of unprofitable adjustment. But that was not the case, not even in the first days. Miguel's experience at the shipwright's in Lekeitio translated well to his new duties. He had worked with quarter-sawn oak when building ships; he was acquainted and comfortable with the planing and joining and finishing of wood.

The construction of boats is a marriage of utility to function, with the conservation of space and weight being key. There was little need for ornamentation or the fashioning of the wood into pleasing and comforting forms. Making furniture was about little else. But the young man impressed his new boss with his indefatigability and, as an unexpected bonus, with his creativity.

Mendiola, hands darkened to sepia by years of applying stain, started Miguel's lessons with the construction of a traditional Basque oak chest, with heavy hinges and an ornate flap lock. After a look at the plan for the standard measurements, Miguel confidently set about building it.

'It won't look like a boat, will it?' Mendiola needled.

'No, but it might turn into a very attractive bait box,' Miguel answered.

When Miguel returned to the shop with sturdy oak timbers one day in the first week, Mendiola commented on their size and potential for larger furniture pieces.

'I thought you'd like it,' Miguel said. 'I know I'm new here, but I found this huge oak with a little fence around it next to that assembly building, and I thought I should go ahead and cut it rather than go all the way up into the mountains looking for timber. People made a fuss, but I got it down anyway.'

Mendiola stuttered in panic before grasping Miguel's joke. He elaborated on the story in each of the *tabernas* he visited that night, commenting that he was sure he was going to enjoy working with the new man.

After mere weeks, Miguel stopped reading the printed designs for the furniture and began creating works of his own vision.

'Where did you get the idea for the lines of this?' Mendiola asked Miguel after he finished a chair that had an appealing bend to the back supports.

'When I was felling the tree,' he said.

To Miguel, an arching branch might ask to be the arms for a rocking chair, and stout bole wood sought to become the central pedestal for a dining table. The cypress, with its delicate, persistent scent, called out to be a drawer for clothes or the lining of a chest. The wood also seemed to speak to those who purchased the furniture. Miguel would incise a delicately curved notch in the arms of a chair that invited hands to rest there, or he would rout a bevel on a tabletop that insisted that all who passed must drag their hands across the edge.

Mendiola found his net income rising because of Miguel's growing clientele. In turn, Miguel discovered a job that suited him even better than shipbuilding. He could be productive, creative, and expressive, and be gratified that his work would last long after he was gone. He inhaled the smells of fresh wood chips and sawdust and varnishes and stains, not fish. And the ground had finally stopped rolling beneath him.

The *txistulari*, playing his small black flute with his left hand while beating his tabor with the right, created more sounds than seemed possible for one person. The woman on the accordion joined in, especially for the *jotas*, along with a boy who finger-drummed a tambourine. They provided music, without stop, all afternoon and evening at the Sunday *erromeria*, attracting nearly everyone in town.

Families arrived together and danced, sometimes three or four generations at a time. Grandfathers executed the steps they'd mastered sixty years earlier as little ones squealed in their arms. Old quilts and canvas tarpaulins made a bright patchwork across the grounds around the dance area, where families lounged and ate sandwiches of chorizo and thinly sliced beef tongue. Some dozed beneath trees after too much wine. Others played *mus* or whist at small tables, or just enjoyed the spectacle of the spinning dancers.

The *erromeria* served as an outdoor crucible for the selecting and melding of future mates. It was Sunday; all had been to Mass, taken communion, and been freshly absolved, guaranteeing this to be a wholesome family oriented environment where the inquisitive and bored could scrutinize the courting pairs.

Miren Ansotegui rarely stood still long enough for young men to attach themselves. She joined the choreographed folk dances with her group of friends and then broke off to share dances with a random succession of males and females, whoever happened to orbit her sphere at the moment. But she did rest on occasion, now that she was old enough to refresh herself with the wine kept near the tables under the shade of the canopy.

Mendiola urged Miguel to attend the function as a way to meet the villagers who were their customers. Mendiola accompanied the musicians on the slow waltzes with an old cross-cut saw that quivered with his mournful bow strokes. Miguel enjoyed the music and the flowing current of the dancers but found his attention quickly fixed on a young woman with a thick plait that extended past the V of her white scarf and whipped behind her as she spun. She was elegant and moved with a grace that caused him to stare without realizing it.

After several dances in the encroaching twilight, Miren retreated towards the cafe canopies where Miguel sat. At the moment she passed his table, a lamp on a nearby post was lit, and to Miguel it seemed to illuminate only her face. He moved involuntarily. Without offering his name or asking hers, he waved to the girl to catch her attention.

'Can you come here?' he said, surprising himself with how much he sounded like his brother Dodo. 'Sit down.'

He fell in love several times each day without making an effort, but the sight of her unsettled him like mornings at sea. When the warm-honey lamp glow fell across her face, he was stunned.

She turned, paused, and took a quick inventory. She saw the typical Basque face, varnished by work in the sun; the typical teeth, made to seem whiter in contrast to the burnt-olive face; the typical hair, black and fiercely independent; the typical body, powerful but lean, with ropy muscles knotted by hauling nets or wrestling stubborn rams. He did not wear a beret, but yes, he was acceptable.

'Why not?' she answered – agreeable, but without any eagerness that could be misinterpreted. Her posture on the edge of the chair signalled that the length of her stay would depend on his powers to charm.

Miguel read the signs and sensed the pressure.

'You have the most beautiful eyes I've ever seen,' he said without prologue.

She squinted sceptically, then opened her eyes wide and sarcastically fluttered her lashes like frightened butterflies. 'Oh?'

'You have . . . the eyes . . . of a Gypsy fortune-teller.'

She groaned. 'And what do you know of Gypsy fortune-tellers?'

'Are you sure you are ready to hear of such things?' he asked, buying time for a story to come together in his mind. He was distracted from the task by Miren's wide, dark eyes under her raven-wing brows, and also her delicious scent.

'Yes, tell me now or I leave.' Miren slipped further towards the edge of the chair.

'Fine, then,' he said, turning his chair around so he could fold his forearms across the back. 'I was a fisherman in Lekeitio when I met her.'

'A Gypsy?'

'Yes, her name was . . . Vanka . . . and she worked in a *taberna* at the harbour.'

Miren's face softened but did not surrender a smile. 'Vanka?'

'I visited her every night after the boats came in and the catch was cleaned. We grew to be – ' dramatic inhalation – 'deeply in love.'

'And she was beautiful, this . . . Vanka.'

'Oh, yes, but not nearly as beautiful as you, although she had huge, dark, mysterious eyes . . . much like yours.'

Lashes fluttered again. *Proceed.*

'Her parents were killed in a Gypsy tribal feud—'

'A tribal feud . . . the worst kind.'

'Yes, and as a poor orphan, she found her way to the harbour and to the *taberna* owned by an uncle and aunt.'

'They were Basque and she was Gypsy?'

'Yes, they were related through a long-past marriage.'

'And it was your duty to help the orphaned girl feel welcome.'

'I am a gentleman, after all.' Slight bow of the head.

'Of course. Did you first wave at her and tell her to sit down without a proper introduction?'

'No. Your eyes are beautiful, as I said, but your ears may be weak; I told you, she worked there, she served me dinners.' Miguel said this with a smile, to assure her he was not insulting her ears, which appeared to be both functional and lovely. 'And after an appropriate time, we began seeing each other, and our relationship grew and grew until we were to be wed.'

'But you would not be here now, talking to me, if you and your beautiful Vonda—'

'Vanka.'

'Vanka. You would not be here without your dark-eyed Gypsy if this great love had not encountered some problems.'

'True . . . for some reason, although she was a Gypsy and supposedly gifted in such things, she would never look into my palm to tell my future—'

'Did you consider that she might not want to touch someone who handled fish all day?'

'—until the night before we were to be wed . . .'

He leaned closer, took the girl's hand, and lightly dragged a fingertip across the tender valley of her palm.

'By a candle's light at her uncle's *taberna*, she finally looked into my palm. She was silent for a moment, but her huge, dark Gypsy eyes grew wet, and a single heavy tear dropped into my hand.'

He hesitated, allowing the image to ripen, and also because he simply did not want to release her hand.

'She said that I was destined to find great love with a beautiful, dark-eyed girl . . . but that girl was not to be her. Then she ran from the *taberna* and I never saw her again,' he said, sadly triumphant. 'This is what I know of Gypsy fortune-tellers, and what I know of the secrets in their beautiful eyes.'

Miren pulled back her hand. 'That is pure nonsense, of course, but it is a good story. And living with my father, I'm a fair judge of such things.'

She stood and announced, 'Stay here, I'll get us some wine.'

Miguel turned his chair around and leaned back with his hands behind his head. Vanka? God in heaven . . . Vanka? Where did that come from?

Before Miguel could finish congratulating himself, the girl returned with a piece of waxed paper stacked with *barquillo* biscuits and a small carafe of wine.

'Thank you, these are just like Vanka used to bring me,' he joked, causing her to wince. 'Are you from Guernica?'

'Errotabarri, a *baserri* on the hill above the town,' she said, pointing in the direction of home. 'I am Miren Ansotegui.'

Miren Ansotegui? Ansotegui? A relative of Josepe, no doubt, he thought. He wondered if he had met her when they were much younger, thinking he would have remembered this girl.

'Can you tell me the truth long enough to give me your name?' she asked.

'I am Miguel Navarro, freshly arrived from Lekeitio. I just started working with Mr Mendiola. Learning carpentry.'

They both took bites of the soft, rich biscuits and sips of wine, regrouping, strategizing, and wondering if they had said the right things, wondering what they could possibly say next. Miren knew one thing that she wouldn't tell him: her walk in his direction that evening was not a coincidence.

At the wheel of his powerful and commodious Hispano-Suiza, Picasso motored from Paris along the coast towards Spain. With his mistress Marie-Thérèse told to await his return, the artist was accompanied by his wife Olga and their son Paulo. He passed through the Basque Country, stopping at St-Jean-de-Luz before crossing the Bidassoa River and once again entering Spain at Irun.

'I know many Basques,' he told his son, now fifteen. 'Nobody works harder or is more dedicated to his family. We used to say, "Straight and tall, there goes the Basque." The ones I know could be stubborn and suspicious, but to have a Basque as a friend is something you can count on for a lifetime.'

At San Sebastián, Picasso and his family dined at the Café Madrid, where he was buttonholed by supporters of the rightist movement in the Spanish government. To add the noted Picasso to their list of allies would be worth a great deal to them, they said. They stated it as a reference to his renown and influence, but they would not have been offended if he also wished to donate some of what was reputed to be a considerable fortune.

They cared only for the good of Spain, they stressed, for returning it to its state of glory. They were the best means to that end. They could make Spain what it had been, they promised. They could make it a nation of which Picasso would be proud. He would want to return there to live.

Picasso enjoyed the meal in the scenic coastal city but declined the political overtures. He was an artist who wanted nothing of politics. Art was about other things. Politics, he told them, bored him more than any other talk.

The matter was dropped, but the trip was one Picasso would remember until his death; it was the last time he would visit Spain.

Dodo had never had to work so hard to get into a bar fight. But that's how these French Basques were, he'd heard, soft and submissive. They hadn't been hardened by years of Spanish oppression.

When he lived in Lekeitio, Dodo had a great deal of casual contact with French Basques, as the crews from Lekeitio or Bermeo or San Sebastián often met those from St-Jean-de-Luz or Biarritz at sea. As much as they ignored the border on land, there was even less of a boundary on the water.

He had been told that they were sympathetic and helpful to their cousins from Spain if the personal costs were not too great. And he loved hearing the stories of St-Jean's history of privateering and smuggling; he appreciated a town where profitable lawlessness was a source of great civic pride. But his acclimatization to his new home did not go smoothly. He objected to the French reverence for degenerate royalty, as half the town of St-Jean-de-Luz was named after Louis XIV because he happened to be married there almost three hundred years earlier.

While eating and drinking in a musty fishermen's haunt next to the quay in Place Louis XIV, Dodo felt compelled to stand and enliven the evening by sharing a few of his thoughts with the locals.

'Real Basques would never name anything after a king,' he announced. 'To real Basques, every man is his own king.'

This was met with a chorus of indecipherable shouts, and a few hard crusts were thrown in his direction. He turned and scowled when one bounced off the back of his head.

'Do we need a Spaniard telling us how to act?' one called from the far end of the bar.

'Whoever called me a Spaniard must die now, of course,' Dodo said into the crowd, spitting slightly when he pronounced 'Spaniard'.

All laughed.

'It's natural that the Spanish would want to at least try to control our provinces; we have great riches in ore and timber and industry. The French have no reason to covet this place, since you are famed only for your pastries. They are very good pastries, I grant you, but not really worthy of an armed invasion.'

All laughed again.

'It is obvious that you have all gone soft, since nobody here is man enough to rise and fight me.'

More laughs arose.

'Stand up and fight . . . somebody . . . anybody.'

More bread flew in his direction.

Frustrated but reassured of his superiority, Dodo returned to his table. His plate was empty. Someone had eaten his fish.

'Hey . . .'

Conscious of being watched, he swallowed back his ale in a long gulp and slammed the mug down on the table.

This, too, struck the bar's patrons as extremely humorous.

Dodo rose to leave, hoping there was enough of a path to the door that he'd be able to swagger out.

'*Arrête, monsieur!*' the barman shouted. 'Payment.'

Dodo reached into his pocket and found it empty. He tried the other pocket. Empty. He must have misplaced his money.

'I'll be back with money,' Dodo said. 'You can trust a *real* Basque.'

As promised, he returned within an hour with payment for the fish and ale. He had calmed down, sobered somewhat, and was greeted by cheers when he entered the bar. Three men who had thrown bread at him invited Dodo to join them at their table.

'Thank you for the fish,' the tallest said, licking his lips. 'It was delicious.'

Dodo nodded and smirked.

'Thank you for the money that I found,' said another, not removing the pipe from his mouth, 'sitting there in your pocket.'

'When did all this happen?'

'While you were telling us how weak and soft we are,' the tall man said.

Dodo ordered a bottle of wine for them all, and they talked without hostility of life on both sides of the border.

'That you would stand and offer to fight everybody in the bar told us something about you,' the tall one said.

'That I'm stupid?' Dodo asked.

'No, that we *are* different,' the tall one said. 'None of us would have challenged every man in the place. I would just warn you that because we choose not to fight you does not mean we are incapable.'

He reached below the table and pulled from his boot a silver knife that looked to Dodo like a small pirate sword. He pointed it at Dodo's navel and ran it upward through the air in front of his chest in a motion that mimed the gutting of a fish.

'What you need to ask yourself, when you deal with those who wish you harm, or with the Guardia or the gendarmes, is this: is it more profitable to bloody their nose or to steal their wallet? I think you would be surprised to find more satisfaction and less risk in stealing from them. Besides, it makes them feel foolish and leaves them with even less dignity.'

'I like that,' Dodo admitted. 'I think I can learn a few things from you.'

'More wine, monsieur.'

'So, do I get my money back?' Dodo asked his new friends.

The one with the pipe shook his head. 'That, *mon ami*, is the cost of the first lesson.'

The tall one introduced himself as Jean-Claude Artola. 'My friend with the pipe here is Jean-Philippe, and this *petit homme* we call J.P.; his name is Jean-Philippe also, but it would be confusing for us to have to call them both Jean-Philippe all the time.'

The three would give him more lessons, as they agreed that Dodo, with his connections with fishermen on the Spanish side, might be valuable to their unofficial international commerce. But he would have to be examined by the leader of their group.

'There is someone else you need to meet, but not just yet,' Jean-Claude said. 'After a few trial runs in the mountains, if you have what it takes, you'll have to pass her inspection.'

'Her?'

Artola smiled and nodded. Dodo thanked them with handshakes and then exaggerated hugs before leaving, shortly before dawn.

'I'd like to thank you for not eating my fish or stealing my money,'

Dodo said to the small man, J.P., who had said little during the evening.

The three laughed again, harder this time.

'Where's the joke this time?' Dodo asked.

'While you were standing up to fight,' Artola explained, 'our little friend here pissed in your ale.'

CHAPTER 8

The women jabbed their sticks at the ground as if hoeing weeds from a row of vegetables. Miguel had never seen anyone work the fields with the grace of these costumed dancers, though. Of the dozen women, he watched only Miren, although one older dancer shared her easy elegance.

A lone man, exaggeratedly intoxicated, entered this dance from off to the side of the courtyard. He carried a large flour sack on his back. As he stumbled about, the hard-working women set upon him in choreographed redress, scolding him and pounding at his sack with their sticks. Even in dance, the image of the avenging Basque matriarch was reinforced.

Miren alone was the focus of the next dance, and cheers rose when she gathered a glass off a nearby table, filled it with wine, and placed it in the middle of the dance area. To a quickening beat, she stepped lightly on all sides of the glass. Without looking down, she stepped over it and beside it, side to side, front to back, barely missing it as her feet wove an intricate pattern. The breadth of her skirts at all times impeded her vision of the glass, making her avoidance of it an act of unfathomable precision. Then, impossibly, she rose and seemed to hover before gently landing atop the glass, one slipper on each side of the lip. And she was off again, levitating, flitting on each side, and then once more leaped back onto the glass, alighting softly with bent knees.

Miguel was stunned to watch a girl so feathery and deft that she could dance on the lip of a wineglass. It was not stemmed crystal or a delicate flute, but it was nonetheless glass, and she danced so joyfully atop it, oblivious to the possibility that it could shatter beneath her. She not only didn't break the glass but didn't spill a drop of wine, either.

A final leap, on and off, coincided with the last bar of music, and a greater cheer echoed across the courtyard. Accepting the applause with a deep curtsy, Miren retrieved the wineglass and drained the deep-red contents in a single gulp. She saluted the cheering crowd with the empty glass and licked her lips in theatrical enjoyment of the wine.

Miguel closed his eyes and reminded himself to breathe.

The night had cooled and the dancers broke off into smaller groups for a frenetic *jota*, joined by villagers of all ages. Miren approached Miguel at his table, bringing with her the lovely older dancer who led the troupe.

'How could you possibly dance on a glass?' Miguel asked before she could speak.

'Well, first you have to get a very strong wine,' Miren said.

'Actually, it's supposed to be a man's dance, but none of our boys can do it,' the woman said. 'We went through a lot of glasses and blood before we learned that.'

Miren gestured formally to the woman. '*Ama*, this is Miguel Navarro from Lekeitio, a friend of Osaba Josepe's. Miguel, this is my mother, Mariangeles Ansotegui.'

'This is your mother?' Miguel asked without subtlety, snapping his head back.

'*Bai, bai, bai*, I hear that all the time, I'm proud to admit,' Miren said, hugging her mother as they giggled like sisters.

'Ah, and you're the young man so experienced in the ways of the Gypsies,' Mariangeles teased.

Miguel bowed his head into his hands, feigning more embarrassment than he truly felt. He was gratified, in fact, to learn that he'd made enough of an impression on Miren that she had mentioned him to her mother.

'Well,' said Mariangeles, 'I don't have to be a Gypsy fortune-teller to see some dancing in your future. Let's see what he can do with those large feet of his, Miren.'

Miren grasped his hand to lead him to dance. But Miguel sank leaden into his seat, not budging even as she tugged.

'Come on, Miguel, it's time to dance.'

'I am afraid I didn't learn much dancing on the fishing boat,' he said.

'What did you learn on that boat?'

'How to vomit lemon drops.'

Miren paused and sent a curious gaze to her mother. It was not worth pursuing now. She tapped at his thigh with her 'hoe', as if to shepherd him onto his feet.

'Better seen as clumsy than perceived a coward,' she warned.

'Better perceived clumsy than proven an oaf.'

'Everyone can dance,' Miren said. '*Any*one can dance.'

'I would hate to prove you wrong . . . I don't know the steps.'

'You don't have to know steps; can you snap?' Miren asked, clicking her fingers as she rolled her hands above her head with a flamenco flair.

'Snap? Like an angry crab,' Miguel said, snapping slowly but loudly.

'Can you kick?'

'Like an angry mule.'

'Can you jump?'

'Like . . . er . . . whatever animal is very good at jumping.'

'And are you Basque?'

'Although I do not wear a beret anymore, yes, I am Basque.'

'Then you can dance,' she announced with certainty.

In this assumption, she was vastly mistaken.

As a dancer, Miguel Navarro was energetic, enthusiastic, and so flamboyantly inept he attracted a crowd. He had attended the feast-day celebrations with everyone else in Lekeitio and, at times when they were not proscribed by the Guardia, was exposed to many of the folk dances. While his brother, Dodo, had learned to execute a few basic steps, Miguel never connected the music to the moves or managed to translate the steps into dance. He was well coordinated and artistic in other manners, yet it was possible that he was even worse at dancing than he was at fishing.

But if Miren Ansotegui, the most fluid dancer he'd ever seen, saw fit to invite him to be a partner, who was he to reject her? So he rose, walked to the centre of the courtyard, and began moving as if he was on the rolling deck of a fishing boat. He snapped out of time, and he kicked like a palsied goat. Several of his leaps ended in scrambling sprawls from which he bounced back up as if they were not only fully intended but a product of considerable practice and creativity.

'My, that was graceful,' Miren jabbed.

'I've seen no one else attempt that step,' Miguel responded.

'True enough.'

With one high kick to belatedly mirror Miren's move, he caught the hem of her skirt and lifted it so high she had to push it down to maintain modesty. Another time, he stumbled into her and buckled the knee of her supporting leg, causing them both to tumble.

Dance was serious to her, but she still enjoyed Miguel's enthusiastic performance. It was endearingly pathetic, and besides, he had warned her.

'You dance like a little donkey trying to run,' she laughed, recalling her favourite animals on the *baserri*. 'That's you, *astokilo*, the little donkey.'

'I'm trying,' Miguel said, bending over with his hands on his knees, inhaling loudly. 'Do you think I'm ready for the wineglass?'

'Only if you're going to drink from it.'

José Antonio Aguirre brought rage with him into the confessional. He carried a page of type a reporter friend had brought him from the newspaper. The story was from Madrid, regarding the establishment of the Falange Party.

'You'll never believe this,' Aguirre started.

'What about the forgive-me-fathers?' Xabier asked.

'No time.'

'No time for confession?'

'Listen,' Aguirre said, tilting the paper so he could catch more light through the latticework. ' "José Antonio Primo de Rivera, son of the former dictator Miguel Primo de Rivera, proudly proclaimed this a step on the path towards the brand of totalitarianism established by Italian dictator Benito Mussolini." '

'Oh, no, he wants to be Mussolini?' Xabier groaned. 'The world really needs another Mussolini.'

' "The urgent collective task of all Spaniards is to strengthen, elevate, and aggrandize the nation. All individual, group, or class interests must be subordinated without question to the accomplishment of this task",' Aguirre read.

'Questioners will be shot,' Xabier mocked in an authoritarian voice.

' "Spain is an indivisible destiny. All separatism is a crime we shall not forgive"—'

'Basques and Catalans will be shot,' Xabier announced.

' "Ours will be a totalitarian state. The system of political parties will be resolutely abolished"—'

'Voters will be shot.'

' "A rigorous discipline will prevent any attempt to poison or split the Spanish people, or to incite them to go against the destiny of the Fatherland"—'

'Fathers will be shot.'

' "We reject the capitalist system, which disregards the needs of the people, dehumanizes private property, and transforms the workers into shapeless masses that are prone to misery and despair"—'

'Shapeless masses will be shot.'

' "Our movement integrates the Catholic spirit, which has been traditionally glorious and predominant in Spain, into the recon-struction of the nation." '

Aguirre and Xabier looked at each other and shook their heads, unable to come up with a clever rejoinder.

They were Catholic, sitting in a confessional inside a basilica, and they wondered how the Fascists could announce plans to suppress practically everybody in the country but still revere the 'Catholic spirit'.

The course of young love in a village rarely strayed from well-trodden paths. A couple might dance together a time or two at that first *erromeria*. And if the chemistry continued to bubble for both, they would dance exclusively with that partner at the next *erromeria*, and on the third week, each would join with the other's family at a table or on a blanket to share wine and food, opening themselves for interrogation.

It was not as if the community had failed to watch their every movement in every dance prior to this. By the third week, there had been subtle enquiries made about the boy or girl; thorough exam-inations of their families had been completed.

The progress along this road of courtship could be hurried if 'accidental' meetings took place during the week in the village. Such was the case when Miguel convinced Mendiola that he needed to be in town at midday to deliver a repaired chair, and Miren informed her mother that she needed to be in town at midday to purchase yarn. Both executed the promised tasks, and no one could suspect anything beyond happenstance if both, while on important errands, reached a cafe on a pavement shortly before noon.

After her customary greetings to everyone in the cafe, Miren assumed a seat at a table facing the street. She ordered her coffee, which was served along with a small dish of olives. She nodded at all who passed and breathed in the air of car exhaust as if it were perfumed.

'I had to be in town to get some yarn, and a coffee sounded so

95

good to me,' she informed the waiter. Having declared her purpose for stopping, she was pointedly surprised by the appearance of Miguel.

'How nice to see you,' she said, looking around. 'Here's a free seat.'

'Thank you. Some coffee might taste good about now.'

Behind their backs, the waiter smirked at their failed artifice. Miguel sat at the next table, also facing the street. By looking in opposite directions whenever someone passed, the two further cemented their relationship through shared conspiracy. To have made plans to meet again in town was a mutual investment. To be at the cafe together made them accomplices; it pulled them together in a pact against absolute honesty.

'You have met my mother—' Miren started, talking from the side of her mouth as she looked forward.

'I have, and she is a delightful person,' Miguel interjected. 'But I can only imagine what she had to say about my dancing performance.'

'She said that she has never seen anything like it. She wondered if your Gypsy had put a curse on you.'

'Oh, good, she thinks I'm cursed.'

'She was joking. She liked you very much.'

Sensing they'd be there all afternoon at this pace, Miren surrendered the charade and turned fully to face Miguel.

'Since you made such a good impression on my mother, I would like you to come to Errotabarri . . . to meet my father.'

'You make it sound as if that will be a chore that I won't enjoy,' Miguel said, turning to look her in the eyes.

'No, no, it won't necessarily be bad. It's just that he is well known in Guernica. He's probably the strongest man in town . . . maybe a little overpowering in some ways . . . at times loud . . . and some people might say frightening, although I've never actually seen him harm anyone.'

Miguel thought through the possibilities. The lengthening quiet concerned Miren, who feared she had driven him off.

'The thing about it is that I'm his only daughter, his only child, and he is bound to be a little protective of me.'

'I would expect nothing less,' Miguel said, opening his palms. 'I would not admire a man who was not protective of his daughter. That is his job in life. They obviously have raised you to be a good person. You are the best reflection of them.'

Good, Miren thought, he has honourable instincts. But goodness, could he be ready for Father? Should I warn him? Should I prepare him? Should I trust Mother to exert her leverage to keep Father from chasing him off? Yes, that's the best course of action: to implore Mother to control Father. But is there any hope that it will be enough?

Miguel had met forceful men before, and he felt up to the meeting. Miren was worth it.

Miren stepped into Errotabarri and before she could put down her sack of yarn, her mother asked how her meeting with Miguel had gone.

'What meeting?'

'Mrs Jausoro stopped by already.'

'It wasn't a *meeting*. What did she have to say? Did she say we were having a *meeting*?'

Mariangeles bent slightly at the waist and slouched her neck to cause her back to hunch up before assuming a quavering voice to replicate the old woman's dramatic report:

'I had to tell you that I saw Miren in town, at a cafe, having coffee with the new young man who has come from the fishing family in Lekeitio, who doesn't wear a beret, but who does such good work at the shop of Teodoro Mendiola. Yes, he's handsome of course, but that fades, and they were sitting side by side in daylight on the main street, and they had olives, too, don't you know? No, they didn't touch, but since they were trying to act as if they weren't up to something, it meant they surely were up to something, and a mother, you know, needs to hear these things because one can never be too

97

careful when a daughter is of a certain age and a handsome man, although that fades, comes from a strange town where God only knows what kind of breeding he has.'

'He just happened to pass and decided that he wanted some coffee,' Miren said in a higher-than-normal pitch, subconsciously trying to reassume the sound of an innocent little girl incapable of guile. As had the waiter at the cafe, Mariangeles rolled back her eyes.

'*Ama*, I want him to meet Papa.'

Mariangeles began laughing and continued to the point that Miren looked as if she was ready to cry.

'*Ama*, please, can't you talk to Papa? Can't you make him promise to be nice and not chase him away?'

'You really like this boy, don't you?' Mariangeles asked.

'I really do, yes.'

'Then why do you want him to die?'

'How was your coffee with Miren Ansotegui?' Mendiola asked the moment Miguel stepped into the shop.

Miguel groaned. 'This town . . .'

'Somebody came into the shop and told me about it already,' Mendiola said.

'Of course they did. We just happened to meet at the cafe and coffee sounded good. That's all it was. Coffee at the cafe. We talked a little. We did not even sit at the same table.'

'It obviously fooled everyone,' Mendiola said. 'Son, do you know what Justo Ansotegui will do to you if you act dishonourably with his daughter?'

'I won't act dishonourably with his daughter; I enjoy her company and I'm serious about getting to know her,' he protested. But his curiosity overcame his eagerness to put the subject to rest. 'All right, what would he do?'

'He is the strongest man in Biscaya; he could snap you over his knee like . . . a dowel rod,' Mendiola said, as he was holding a slender dowel rod in his hands at the time. He considered breaking it for effect, but it had taken half an hour to mill it to specifications, so he just bent it slightly.

Miguel understood the message anyway.

The wine weighed more than Dodo expected as he hoisted six bottles of champagne in a pack on his back and another four in a sling pouch hanging from his shoulder.

'I should get twice the pay,' Dodo argued when arrangements were made for him to carry the wine through a mountain pass to meet a compatriot at a *venta* on the other side of the Spanish border. 'I have to carry it uphill.'

If nothing else, Dodo looked the part, in a woollen sweater and trousers, with a shepherd's waistcoat and rope-soled espadrilles, all beneath his beret. He carried the smugglers' beloved *makila* walking stick, carved from the medlar tree, with a horn handle and a spiked tip that could double as a weapon.

Jean-Claude Artola had taken him along on two jobs in the mountains, and Dodo had deemed himself ready to join the silent fraternity. This would be an easy first solo mission for Dodo, and the load was not as heavy as many that were carried.

At sunset, he crossed the valley and slipped into a pine forest until he found the stream he was to follow on the early part of his journey. He walked through patches of evening light that made the fallen yellow leaves glow like a path of gold. Yes, he thought, this is the way to make a living. There is romance in this, even in the name the smugglers use, the '*travailleurs de la nuit*' – the workers of the night.

By dark, he reached the branch of a smaller stream that would lead him to the higher boulder fields, the tree line, and then to the meeting point at the pass. The small rill then branched, and after a mile the water disappeared under tight brush cover. This, he discovered, was not the way. He retraced his steps, looking for the proper path towards the shoulder of the ridge that he could follow upward. Two exhausting hours later, thick wild-rose brush encircled him, snagging his trousers, pulling at his espadrilles, and several times snatching off his beret. There was no stream, no path, and certainly no light. There was no direction, either; he often was uncertain if he was going up or down.

One route that looked promising left him battling brush higher than his head. The packs had doubled their weight and his sweat had soaked through his sweater and was matting the wool on his waistcoat. Adhesive webs clutched at his face and neck, making him certain that giant spiders were walking on his flesh and were ready to bite his eyes and crawl into his ears and lay eggs. If he hated anything worse than the Spanish, it was spiders. As he walked, he clawed at the air in front of him with both hands, trying to break down their elastic strands. For the first time in his life, his anus itched, from the stress, he imagined, and all that damned French cheese.

He should have reached the pass long ago, but he was not prepared to give up. Retreat is impossible, anyway, when you have no idea where you are. He feared that he was circling, covering the same ground. So he picked a direction and committed himself to staying with it regardless of the impediments, and within half an hour he had worked himself to the edge of the boulder field.

Now he was sure he could pick up speed. Within five steps, he cracked his shin on a jagged outcrop. He felt the cold air and moisture on his leg, but it was too dark to examine the damage. Wait, I have twenty matches, he thought, I'll light one every ten or fifteen paces and work my way to an opening. Each match burned only a few seconds, though, and it caused the subsequent darkness to seem even blacker.

Then he heard a squeaking that sounded like the rats he used to chase out of the net boxes on the wharf. But there were so many, and they were in the air all around him, some striking the felt nib at the top of his beret. Oh, God, he thought; he hated bats even more than spiders and Spaniards. He swung at them blindly, trying to keep them off his head, once connecting with one so well that he could feel the fur and diaphanous wings. He sat, lit a match, and saw thousands of the flying devils dipping and swooping above him in thick black sheets. He would light no more matches.

'I can do this,' he said out loud. 'I've been in trouble before. I am a Navarro.'

His pep talk caused him to pick up speed, unwise in a hillside of saw-toothed granite, unstable scree, and gaping sinkholes. He slipped but caught himself and gave up elevation to go around a large outcrop towards a flatter meadow. Feeling each step with his toes, he made better time through the open places. But when he touched something soft with his canvas espadrille, and it felt alive, he withdrew half a step and struck a match.

The sudden light awakened a cluster of sleeping bears.

'*Jesus, God, shit!*' he screamed as he was knocked down by the startled beasts.

'*Jesus, God, shit!*'

His heart pounded through his ribs. He waved his *makila* as if he was a swordsman, hitting none of them but jabbing himself in the leg, cutting through his trousers. He could feel blood leaking into his shoe. And it was not a hard rock he had fallen on but his backpack filled with bottles.

He lit a match; yes, he was bleeding.

He lit another; good God, those weren't bears, but some kind of small, furry horses that had regrouped and bedded down again only yards from him.

'Don't come near me,' he warned them through the darkness.

He lit another; yes, the crunch he had heard and the smell of wine meant what he thought it did. Still seated, he carefully picked through the broken glass in his pouch, finding most of the bottles shattered.

'Shit and derision,' he mumbled.

Dodo removed the pack from his back and sat where he had fallen. Only a few of the bottles were undamaged. He unwound the wire restrainer on the top of an unbroken bottle from his pouch, and with his scraped thumbs he worked the cork off. The badly shaken bottle spat it far into the darkness with a 'bop' that could have been heard for miles.

Halfway through the first bottle, he decided that pouring alcohol on the cut on his leg would sterilize it. Much of the other wine had already soaked through his clothing anyway, making it stick to his body. The sweet, fruity smell only attracted the bats in greater numbers. There was no point in flailing at them now.

He was well into a second bottle before he passed out on the rocky talus, leaving the bats free to gather on him, lick up as much champagne as they pleased, and try to fly home drunk before dawn.

CHAPTER 9

'Sit, sit, my new friend; welcome to Errotabarri.' Justo gave the boy a reprieve; he didn't offer to shake his hand, a gesture he generally used to measure the breaking point of a man's finger bones. Instead, he issued a double-armed hug that was gentle enough that Miguel was allowed to continue breathing, but firm enough that Miguel sensed that he had escaped a vice that had been only partially constricted.

That went well.

But Miguel was forced to ask himself: How did this man sire such a daughter? He was not taller than Miguel, but he was as thick as the bole of a burled oak. His feral brows hung over his eyes like a pair of awnings, and the moustache that hyphenated his face was prodigious in three dimensions. The serrated edge of his right ear protruded from under his beret. Those who told Miguel that Justo looked like a cross between a Catalonian bull and a cave bear had not exaggerated.

'You are taken by my good looks, I see,' Justo said.

Miguel uttered a dry-mouthed laugh and looked towards Miren.

'Since I can see you are curious, my new friend, I will tell you about this ear of mine,' Justo said. 'It was gnawed off in a battle with a wolf in the mountains when I was young.' He lifted his beret and turned his head towards Miguel for better viewing.

'Ha . . . that was his final morsel. I made him spit it back out with his dying gasp. I wanted to sew it back on, but he had chewed on it a while and it would not have been as attractive as it is now had I sewn it back on.'

Miguel glanced at Miren again; she nodded and tilted her head, silently saying, 'Yes, yes, I know; be strong.'

Justo's strategy was now clear; this was not to be about physical intimidation. Mariangeles had stressed to him how much this meant to their daughter, and Justo gave his word that he would not assault the boy. No promises were made about frightening him.

'Since your background is on the boats and you are newly arrived in the hills, you will want to hear how we do certain things,' Justo continued. 'I must tell you first, before we eat, before we strengthen our friendship with food and wine, of one of our customs here on the *baserri*. It involves our stock.'

Mariangeles, unsure of his specific intent but certain it was ominous, placed a warning hand on her husband's furry forearm, her nails ready to puncture and drain blood if necessary.

'We have some sheep, not many, but enough to keep us busy. The ewes we want for breeding and shearing; one or two of the strongest rams we save intact for their services. But the other young males that we raise only for their meat need not bother us with their interest in breeding.'

Mariangeles tightened her grip.

'So we relieve them of their *pelotas*, you understand?' His laughter shook the furniture as he shaped his hands into cups, as if holding suspended objects.

Mariangeles squeezed.

'Some use a blade for the purpose, but it can slip and destroy other parts, and sometimes it causes nasty infections,' Justo said, ignoring his wife's silent pressure. 'Some of us, the elders in our business, have found that there's less bleeding if we just remove the *pelotas* by biting them off.'

Miguel gasped involuntarily; the women groaned – they had heard of the revolting process. But did he have to say it? Mariangeles withdrew her futile grasp. No point now.

'It is a story,' Justo finished, 'that you might want to keep in mind as you start to court my only daughter.'

Miguel redistributed his food on the plate. The main course was lamb, and Miguel wondered grimly if Justo had chewed this meat already. Mariangeles and Miren managed to sustain limited conversation but struggled to draw from Miguel stories of his background. Justo, though, filled the air with word torrents, and when he saw that Miguel had hardly touched the meat, he asked if the boy was familiar with eating anything that did not swim in the sea. When Miguel confessed to a mild appetite at the moment, Justo speared the meat off his plate and devoured it. 'Can't let food go to waste,' he announced.

'Let me now tell you of my sainted mother,' Justo said, starting a family history of his mother's death and his father's consumptive grief, all so extreme that it did not demand his gift for embellishment.

'The love my father had for my mother will stand through time as a monument to dedication and devotion,' he concluded with pride. 'So great was his capacity for love that he died of a broken heart when it was lost.'

Justo paused as if awaiting applause.

'But what about you boys?' Miguel asked without thinking.

'We grew into men, proud of his example.'

Miguel shook his head.

'What, Miguel?' Miren asked.

'Nothing.'

'What, Miguel?' Mariangeles echoed.

'That is a very sad story.'

But Justo now insisted. 'Say it, boy.'

'I would never be disrespectful,' he said directly to Justo, lowering his head in a signal of obeisance. 'But I think if your mother had the chance, I don't believe she would have said, "Your grief shows the depth of your love." I think she would have said, "Take good care of our boys. You have to love them for both of us now."'

'Careful, boy,' Justo said.

The fire popped, and Miguel flinched. It was the only sound in the room for what seemed like minutes. Justo never took his eyes off Miguel. Trying to at least alter the force of the stare, Miguel continued.

'I'm sure he loved your mother deeply, but I think it was selfish to ignore the boys. You lost two parents instead of one. Your father should be alive. He should be at this table right now. I should be able to meet him, a man who fought through his loss and still was there for his sons. I would admire him.'

Justo chewed on his moustache and all at the table sat in silent suspense. No one had ever talked to him this way. Full minutes later, he stood and walked around the table towards Miguel, who now anticipated strangulation. But he extended his hand. Miguel took it, and Justo encircled him, gently this time.

'Josepe said you were a good man,' Justo said. 'He was right. At least you're brave. You've given me some things to think about. You're welcome here in our home.'

'Why don't you two go for a walk; it's a nice evening,' Mariangeles said to Miren and Miguel.

Outside, Miren pulled him close. She was thunderstruck by affection and felt flushed, as if she had too much blood and not enough oxygen. Without thought, they kissed, barely touching lips.

She executed a quick *jota* step, a spin, and joined him at his side for the most enjoyable walk of her life.

The house was caked with dung from the small animals and birds that had taken up residence since its last owner moved to Bilbao without bothering to fix the broken windows. It was fusty with mildew and mould from a rug that had been soaked with rain beneath a cracked roof tile. The boards beneath the rug were warped like waves.

And Miguel could not have been happier. The grim condition made the house affordable and also gave him an excuse to rebuild it to his own specifications. Now he could strip it back to the studs and make it his own.

Of equal importance, it featured a small adjoining shed with large split doors opening to the west that he could turn into his own woodworking shop. After spending each day at Mendiola's, Miguel worked through much of the night on his new home. Within a month he had replaced the damaged floorboards with polished oak, constructed pine cabinets with etched doors, and had fabricated hardwood cornices and skirting boards to affix after he had patched and repainted the walls.

Miren begged to help with the renovation, and the two conspired to paint the interior on a day when Miguel was free from Mendiola. This was not a simple act. A young woman seen going into a man's house could fuel market gossip for months.

Miguel's house was on the edge of town and was among the last residences just inside the ring of farms that spread outside the core. After taking a roundabout path through town and executing patient surveillance, Miren determined it was safe. She immediately deemed the house cosy and had no trouble visualizing herself in permanent residence – stirring a pot over the hearth . . . mending Miguel's clothes . . . sweeping the floors . . . slipping into the bedroom.

A shirtless Miguel was lathing a table leg in the work shed when Miren arrived, and he was covered in fine wood chips.

'Welcome . . . what do you think?'

She forced herself to look around.

'I think Papa would kill me if he knew I came here.'

'He wouldn't kill you. He'd kill me,' Miguel corrected her. 'Ready to work?'

'I am indeed, sir.' She saluted.

Miren had dressed for duty, wearing a rag scarf, a full apron, and layered work shirts so she could dispose of the outer one if it became flecked with paint. But within minutes she was mottled with goldenrod freckles from paint spattering off the stiff bristles of her brush.

Miguel suggested he should do the high portions, with his greater range from the ladder, and she could paint the lower portions and the trim as high as she could reach. They arrived at an effective technique and were cautious to softly blend their brushstrokes where their work overlapped. Since her area was smaller and more easily reached, she stretched out ahead of Miguel and his ladder and took a break after almost an hour of work.

As they worked, they sneaked looks at one another when they thought they wouldn't be noticed. But they often were caught peeking, triggering embarrassed smiles. She liked to watch his hands as he worked; they had attracted her since he'd held hers that first night. They were powerful, and she wanted to trace with her fingers the path of the veins that rode over the muscles. Those hands let him create beautiful furniture that might last for centuries. It was a kind of power she admired.

Caught looking for the third time as Miren bent to replenish her brush, Miguel abandoned coyness.

'I'm sorry, I can't stop,' he confessed.

She smiled but didn't answer.

'Of course, all Basque women are beautiful,' he said to break a silence that had grown awkward.

'Is that widely known?'

'The sailors of Lekeitio have travelled the seas of the world, and they could never find more beautiful women.'

'How do you know they didn't discover more beautiful women and just never told anyone?'

'They always returned home.'

She rested her brush and walked closer in a swaying rhythm that forced Miguel to close his eyes.

'So, you're telling me that I'm just one of the many, then?' she said. 'Just another Basque girl.'

'No . . . no . . . no, if there is a woman more beautiful than you, then I would have heard stories of her. There would be songs about her, or poems.'

'Why don't you write a poem for me, then?'

'I've already created new forms of dance in your honour,' he said, returning to humour.

'True, but a girl loves a poem,' she said, applying pressure.

Confused now, Miguel surrendered control. The motion of those few steps, her smile, and those damned dark eyes. Those had been trouble from the start. He had spent several weeks now imagining the possibilities with her. He closed his eyes again, feeling seasick.

'This is probably not a poem; I never studied those things, so I don't know,' Miguel said. 'But I know what I want to do. Whenever you're with me, I want to make you feel like you do when you're dancing.'

Their hug was so firm that his sweat moistened her apron. Without permission, one of her legs wrapped itself around Miguel's calf, pulling her hips into his. And there they stood, breathing each other's breath.

'Would you share this house with me?' Miguel asked. 'Live your life with me?'

'Nothing would make me happier.'

'I love you,' he said. 'I truly love you.'

'I love you, too.'

They were quiet, standing and breathing.

'What do you think your father will say when I ask for permission?' Miguel asked softly as they pulled back to look at each other.

' "*Ala Jinko!* No man is good enough for my little one," ' she said in a surprising baritone. ' "The only man worthy of her is me, and I'm already taken." '

'But will he allow it?'

'Miguel Navarro, I don't care what he says; we're getting married.'

Justo belched so forcefully that the overhang of his moustache fluttered. 'Wretched cow,' he said, gesturing towards the ground floor.

'Justo, that works only when the animals are here. It's summer and they're out in the pasture.'

'In that case, please excuse me. But if it is not the fault of the cow, then it is yours. You forced me to eat too much.'

Mariangeles had been to the market that afternoon and purchased several hake fillets, which she fried with light egg batter. The fishermen of Lekeitio or Elantxobe sometimes brought a fresh catch to Guernica to sell or trade for farmers' vegetables or mutton. Justo had devoured all but the small piece that Mariangeles had set aside for herself.

'I am gluttonous only to remind you that you are appreciated,' Justo said. 'And so that you know that you are the finest cook in the Pays Basque.'

'Thank you, I will never complain of hearing too much on that topic,' she said.

'I'll take care of these,' he said, collecting the dishes.

'Justo,' she said, waiting until he turned to face her before continuing, 'I am proud of the way you reacted to Miren's news; I hoped you would be understanding.'

'Actually, Mari, I'm delighted with it. Miguel is a man as foolish as any his age, but he's a match for our daughter. She could find no better. I showed good judgement in not killing him.'

Mariangeles laughed. 'They make a handsome couple.'

'They will make fine grandchildren for us.'

'More than one? You won't mind more than one?' Mariangeles was surprised by the use of the plural as it regarded grandchildren.

'I don't mind; I hope they have a dozen. I hope they fill the town with their beautiful babies.'

Justo held out his arms, as if to invite his wife to bear witness to his open-mindedness.

'Good for you.'

He removed the apron from a peg, tied the sash, and began scraping leftovers into a bucket for the benefit of their last thinning pig.

'Thank you,' she said. 'Then I'll go into town and help Marie-Luis with that music project she's been working on.'

'Your sister can make magic with that accordion,' Justo said, dancing a passable two-step to remembered music. 'But this is the third time you've spent the evening with Marie-Luis. If I didn't know you were already married to the most coveted man in Biscaya, I might be suspicious that you were stepping out on me.'

'You are very certain of yourself.'

'And why not?'

Mariangeles took her bag and a jacket in case of evening chill.

'Dear one . . . ' Justo said softly. 'Remember, you hold my heart in your little hands.'

'I'm merely performing a charitable deed.'

Justo re-inflated. 'A-ha – as I thought. It would be a foolish woman who would consider inferior stock when she has Justo Ansotegui at home.'

He flexed his right bicep in a show of strength diminished by his dainty floral apron and the pig bucket.

'Mari . . . be careful this time.'

'Careful?'

'Yes, you hurt yourself the last time.'

Ah, yes, that's right, she thought; she'd told him that she had stepped in a hole on the walk home that night.

Miren, returning from a dress fitting, caught her mother hurrying out of the house.

'How's Papa taking this?' she asked.

'He's surprising me, actually. We just talked about it, and he's very pleased with your judgement. He believes it is a good reflection on him.'

'Where are you off to in such a hurry?'

'To see Marie-Luis.'

'Mama, is there more we need to do to the house before the wedding, with all the family coming in?'

'I think we might have time to paint a few of the walls inside,' Mariangeles said. 'I'm thinking about something brighter, like the colour that Miguel chose for his house.'

Miren nodded, then realized the implications of her mother's statement.

Mariangeles read her daughter's vacant look.

'Miren . . . the paint was all over you that day you came back from Alaia's. I know you weren't painting her cabin; where else would you have gone? I'm not judging; I trust you and I trust Miguel. But people in town are not so generous. Be careful – and be patient. And do a better job of cleaning off the paint next time. I'm very sure your father would not like the colour as much as I do.'

Miren Ansotegui needed to bring together two of the most important people in her life for many reasons, but above all else was the pride she took in both of them. If things progressed as she hoped, Alaia and Miguel would be close to her for the rest of her life, and she imagined the three of them ageing together. If they were jealous about each other, or if some animosity arose, it would be difficult for her to reconcile them.

She prepared both, telling Miguel of Alaia's challenges and needs and prompting him to carefully avoid all the verbal misstatements she had made, although Alaia never seemed offended. And she was cautious about telling Alaia how handsome she thought Miguel was, not wanting to make her friend feel left out or somehow thrown over. Yes, she confessed, she planned to marry him, but that didn't mean it would affect her relationship with her best friend, her sister.

'I want you to love her and I want her to love you,' Miren instructed Miguel.

'I know I love the way she makes you smell,' Miguel said.

'I mean it; she's a very special person and a very special friend,' Miren said. 'She has made me more understanding of people. She made me more understanding of the things others have to deal with. I can't believe the strength she has, how brave she is; imagine what it must be like.'

'If she's that important to you, she's that important to me. Is there anything I can do for her? Anything around her house? Repairs? Firewood?'

'I don't think so; she is very independent.'

'Maybe make her some furniture.'

'Oh, *asto*, that would be wonderful, maybe a nice chest for her things.'

'Does she need help getting here?' Miguel asked.

Miren explained her talents at navigation and the landmarks she would use to find her way to their meeting at the cafe. Now that Miren and Miguel were engaged, being together and even somewhat affectionate in public was acceptable.

Alaia arrived at the cafe, discreetly using her cane to probe the door for obstructions or steps. She entered and stood in the doorway, knowing that Miren would be watching and would come and guide her to their table. They hugged and kissed each other on both cheeks as always, and Miren led her to where Miguel had risen.

Miren was right, she was striking: shapely, with light brown hair and skin the colour of cypress heartwood. Had Miguel not known Alaia was blind, he could not have detected a problem that made her different from any lovely young woman merely walking with her eyes closed. She moved slowly, but that only gave her a dreamlike quality, he thought. And when Alaia and Miren walked arm in arm, they seemed not to diminish the impact of each other's appearance, as two attractive women might.

Miguel moved close upon introduction to give her a kiss on the cheek and then pulled her into a hug. Miguel whispered to her, and they embraced with greater energy. Miren sucked in her breath in shock.

'Oh, Miguel, you're so strong,' Alaia announced.

'Oh, Alaia, I've dreamed of a woman like you,' Miguel volleyed.

Miguel noted Miren's startled expression.

'Yes, we got her,' he said to Alaia. 'You should see the look on her face.'

Each mock lover assumed that Miren had prepared the other on how important it was that they hit it off well. Both had been amused by her concerns.

'You two . . . I was ready to jump in and break it up.'

'You threatened us that we had to get along; we thought this would make you happy,' Alaia said.

They hugged politely once more, as a legitimate greeting.

'I expected you to smell like Miren,' Miguel said.

'That kind is only for her. That's the Miren blend.'

'Alaia, remind me to get some more for my mother,' Miren asked. 'You won't believe this, but my father is using it now, too. He said it reminds him of my mother during the day. It doesn't actually suit him, but it's an improvement over what we were used to when he rarely even bothered to bathe. He's always saying, "Ah, that Alaia; that girl has powers." '

'I think as long as we keep it in the family it will be fine. Miguel, I haven't heard, have you met her father?'

'Yes. It was a very interesting evening.'

'You weren't frightened off?'

'At least not for now,' Miguel said. 'But I'm staying alert.'

They chatted over the afternoon meal, and by the time they'd finished telling stories, and Alaia and Miguel had shared every amusing anecdote they could remember about the girl they both loved, Miren was able to relax. No, it didn't appear there would be problems between Miguel and Alaia.

CHAPTER 10

José María Navarro moored the *Egun On* at a high-tide pier near Guernica and boarded his gleeful lading: a love-flushed son spliced to his luminous prospective bride. Miguel led Miren aboard, holding her hand for balance, and they made the voyage without losing contact at any point; there was always a steadying hand on a shoulder or around a waist. It wasn't until he sighted the seaward crest of San Nicolas Island, with its white belt of breaking waves, that Miguel realized that he had been so busy introducing Miren, bragging about her to his father, and pointing out features of the boat that he had completed the trip without growing nauseous.

'Goodness, young lady, you're as pretty as your mother,' Josepe Ansotegui announced when Miren and Miguel entered her uncle's home, not more than five paces across the street from where Miguel grew up.

'Now, that is the nicest compliment I could ever get,' Miren said, hugging her uncle.

'It's true; you're lovely, and our friend Miguel is a fortunate man,' Josepe said. 'Tell us, has your mother grown sick of that brother of mine yet?'

'She's hiding it well.'

The Navarros hosted a meal that evening for both families. At dinner, in respect of grace, José María and Josepe simultaneously removed their berets, revealing identical colouring: creased brown necks, wind-ruddy cheeks, and an abrupt line of stark white scalp above their ears – created by the unvarying positioning of their berets – which looked like snow above the tree line in the high Pyrenees.

Many toasts of wine were raised, and afterwards, Miguel sought to make an introduction of Miren through town, starting at the cafes and *tabernas* along the wharf. The couple drew people to them. No one had seen Miguel since he left Lekeitio; all asked about his current activities and praised his fortune in landing a bride.

Many sought to replay their account of his final night in Lekeitio, an encounter Miguel had never shared with Miren. She tactfully distanced herself from these conversations, talking about small matters with the girls in the group while inconspicuously keeping an ear turned towards Miguel's responses. Miguel quickly discouraged such talk, not knowing who could hear, or even who among this group might be willing to report his return to the Guardia Civil, who would be delighted to give him their own brand of homecoming welcome.

Miguel was then probed on the whereabouts of Dodo: 'Don't know, haven't heard from him; maybe he's gone to America to herd sheep.' It had become a common practice for fishermen to move to the mountains of the American West. His neighbour, Estebe Murelaga, wrote to many of them from Idaho. He knew nothing of sheep but had already saved enough money to start his own flock. Of course, no one believed Miguel's feigned ignorance; he and Dodo had been too close for him not to know where he had gone. But no one pressed him.

When Miguel and Miren completed their stroll of the wharf, they kissed in the empty street, under the lamps that used to illuminate Miguel's pre-dawn walks to Mass. He asked her to go to her uncle's first-floor hall window before she went to bed. When she arrived, Miguel was already in the opposite window of his house, reaching out, thrusting and retracting the laundry line.

'So, there are things about your past that you have forgotten to inform me of,' Miren said.

'There are a few, yes, but only because I didn't think you'd be interested.'

'That the man I'm about to marry has a taste for lawlessness – yes, that's something that might have interested me.'

'Trust me, it was not the great drama that everyone wants to make of it.'

Inadvertently, they each pulled the line in their direction when they listened.

'Should I know, though, if somebody was hurt?' she asked.

'Yes, somebody was hurt. Although it was nobody important, and I didn't come out of it that well, either.' Miguel wiggled his jaw with his hand.

'Could you still be in trouble?'

'Maybe.'

'Could they throw you in prison?'

'They throw anybody in prison these days.'

'But you?'

'It depends how good their memories are.'

'Should we get out of town?'

'Tomorrow will be soon enough; I think we're safe.'

'Is anyone safe?'

'If they haven't tracked us down by now I think we're fine.'

'Us? I may assume that you were involved with the mythical brother Dodo?'

'Yes, you may.'

'And I may assume that it was this mythical brother who started the trouble and you somehow got tangled up in it?'

'I'll take responsibility for myself, so don't assume too much.'

'When will I get to meet this mythical brother?'

'That, *kuttuna*, I don't know.'

'And will I like this Dodo?'

'You will be amused. I know that he will like you a great deal.'

'Oh, how can you be so sure?'

'Because he will likely try to steal you from me.'

'*Asto*, that will never happen.'

'Good, I wouldn't want to have to get violent with my own brother. He is already too willing to get into scrapes.'

The shuttling of words and rope ceased for a moment as a heavy woman huffed along in a halting gait up the small street beneath them. She looked up at them as she passed, smiled, shook her head side to side over the follies of youth, and trod along towards home. Miren dipped her head to the side so that her plait swung around her shoulder and settled in front of her. She removed the red ribbon from the bottom of the plait, kissed it, tied it to the line, and sent it over to Miguel to hold for the night.

'I know it's silly, but you can keep this tonight,' Miren said. 'I love you.'

'Good night.' Miguel put the ribbon in his pocket. 'I love you, too.'

Come October, they'd be married, and these two families would be connected by means more substantial than a laundry line.

Working alone at the upper edge of the oak habitat, Miguel felled timber through the morning and early afternoon, and with his borrowed mule skidded the logs back downhill to the small sawmill at the end of the day. Lately he found himself pausing more, though not from fatigue, because the logging had made him stronger and better conditioned. The stringy muscles that made him such an effortless swimmer were now knotted from sawing and logging oak trees. No, his breaks from work now were caused by a persistent inclination to take an inventory.

Encircled by the oaks, Miguel listened to the squirrels, who spoke only consonants, clacking their series of high-pitched hiccups. From the rocks came the soft, comforting gargle of doves, always in pairs, peaceful and mutually attentive. They had only the one muffled song, but it was a ballad that he found soothing.

The early autumn haze of woodsmoke in the valley generally softened the sun in the morning until the midday breezes swept the air clean. Higher, he could see how the mountains overlapped and were tinted a progression of green to blue to grey to ghostly in the distance. From the mountainside, he saw cotton fluffs of sheep speckle the felt meadows. Haystacks spread shadows in the afternoon light, and the roof tiles of the houses reflected like the scales of a red mullet.

In the marshlands by the estuary, flights of storks flashed their stark-white wings while banking in unison to alight. He had always bragged of Lekeitio as beautiful, but there the eye was treated to either the sea or the shore, with none of the subtle mood changes of these mountains. Yes, there was San Nicolas Island and the beautiful beaches next to the harbour. But fishermen rarely spend time relaxing on a beach; it feels too much like being on the threshold of work.

Scanning the terrain, Miguel flushed at the memory of the first time he brought Miren to this hillside. Moments before sunset, she stood in a patch of spiky rosebay willowherb blooms, her hair taken by the breeze just as the plants dipped and bowed. He closed his eyes to fix the image in his mind. When he looked at her again, she held a flower in her hands and was smiling back at him as if she had read his mind. He always suspected she had that power.

The mule whiffled, causing Miguel to refocus. He thought of his brother. Could Dodo attend the wedding? Anything could happen with him. But it would be unwise for him to visit now. Miguel snorted a laugh, imagining him being chased down the church aisle by Guardia officers, ducking between pews, hiding in confessionals.

But what a surprise I have for my father, Miguel thought: I'm now an eager fisherman.

Earlier in the summer, Justo had taken Miguel into the mountains nearby 'to have a talk'. Miguel feared it would be a lecture about another distasteful tradition of the *baserritarrak*. When they dipped into a glade shaded by alders and poplars, Justo pulled from his pocket some light fishing line and a sack of grubs he had gathered from the ploughed garden.

'What's this all about?' Miguel asked.

'I am going to teach the fisherman to fish,' Justo announced.

With line pitched and retrieved by hand, they floated the fat grubs across the stream. In a pool dammed by a wind-throw alder, they attracted thick, firm trout. With each catch, Justo shouted so fiercely the sound tumbled across the hillside. In those moments, through all the hair and the moustache and bombast, Miguel could see exactly who Justo had been as a boy. Mimicking his technique at another pool downstream, Miguel soon had half a dozen trout pulled up on the bank as well. Each time they landed a fish, they unleashed screams of success.

Justo cut an alder branch and weaved the switch through the gills and mouths of the trout as a stringer to carry them back to Errotabarri.

'One question,' Miguel said. 'Do we clean these fish with a knife or do we have to start chewing their guts out?'

Justo let loose his loudest shriek of the day.

'You can use a knife, son. But I am glad to know that you listen to my stories.'

Miguel realized that this was Justo's first use of the word 'son' while speaking to him.

'You have to tell me now, Justo, considering I'm marrying your daughter and I've treated her honourably, and hopefully have earned your trust . . . do you really chew the balls off sheep?'

Belly laughs again. 'Are you insane, boy?' Justo said. 'I tried it one time because I heard the old-timers talk about it and I thought I should just see if it worked. But it was disgusting. Imagine it. Why would anybody in the world want to put their mouth down there? And if you think the ram is just going to stand there and allow someone to bite off his balls, you are very much mistaken.'

Miguel cringed at the image.

'Josepe was trying to hold him by his horns and Xabier had his back legs, and when I got anywhere near down there, that ram was kicking and squealing. Those old-timers must have taken honing stones to their teeth, too, because I had to gnaw for five minutes to get just one of them off. I came away looking like I'd been in a knife fight, and Josepe and Xabier couldn't breathe for all their laughing. They had been cheering for the ram all the while. I used a knife to do the second one, and you've never seen a ram so happy to have a pelota removed that way.'

Miguel, himself out of breath from laughing at Justo's story, used his shirt sleeve to wipe his eyes. 'And you say you don't lie about these things.'

'I never said anything about lying; I told you that I don't exaggerate,' Justo said. 'I'll bet I've told you that ten thousand times.'

Both grinned as they headed off down to the valley, each holding an end of the branch.

'It makes a good story, though, does it not?'

'It's not one I will forget soon.'

The mule whiffled once more, causing Miguel to suspend his recollection. He was taken by a warm emotion that felt like nostalgia, except it regarded events yet to happen. He imagined so many years ahead, working at his craft, being married to Miren, raising a family here. He looked across the valley again; there was time for one more drink from his water bottle before skidding the logs down to the mill.

Aguirre hurried between the parallel rows of trees in front of the Basilica de Begoña, cigarette smoke trailing him as if from a train's engine. He slipped into the rectory after midnight, looking for wine and a priest's confidence, finding Father Xabier rehearsing and polishing his Sunday presentation.

Xabier poured Madeira.

'Here, I brought you something,' Aguirre said, sliding a book across the table. It was by his favourite poet, Lauaxeta.

'*New Directions*,' Xabier said, reading the title. 'I hope it's a map to better times.'

They touched glasses.

'I doubt it,' Aguirre said. 'That's why I'm here.'

'What? Is there more Madrid can do after cancelling our elections and revoking our tax rights, and—'

'It's a miners' revolt in Asturias,' Aguirre interrupted. 'They brought in Franco to end it. He did.'

Xabier leaned in, inviting elaboration.

'Torture and executions . . . killing men and women in the town whether they were strikers or not.'

'Were they Socialists – the strikers?'

'I suppose,' Aguirre said. 'Socialists, Anarchists, reds . . . probably just a lot of workers sick of their conditions.'

'I follow this. I try to study the politics. And I get these regular updates from you. But I'm having a harder time sorting through who's responsible for anything anymore. I get more and more parishioners wanting me to explain it to them every day. But I'm helpless.'

Aguirre nodded, finished his wine, and tried to simplify it for his friend. He started several times, halted, and finally admitted: 'Father, I'm not sure I even understand everything that's happening. Either we don't get the news, or it's been twisted in the telling. And it all seems to change from week to week, region to region. The alliances shift, parties change their names, and I'm confused all over again. I can only imagine what it's like for the farmer out in the country or the worker down in the mine.'

'I'm afraid that's not very comforting,' Xabier said.

'All I know for certain is that everywhere else on the Continent where there's been a power struggle like this, it's made it easier for the Fascists to take over.'

A brace of tan oxen, cloaked in sheepskin shawls, with flower garlands threaded around their horns, led the procession. Neck bells ringing as they stepped in unison, they pulled a two-wheeled cart bearing Miren's dowry and possessions. Copper pots clanged as the cart rumbled across the cobbles. A wood-and-leather bellows, attached by one handle, made small syncopated exhalations whenever the cart bounced. A large crucifix destined for the bedroom wall was propped reverentially in one corner, with a heavy rosary draped around its vertical axis like a necklace on a scarecrow.

Players of the *txistu*, drum, and tambourine followed, adding musical form to the rising clatter. The procession followed in pairs, not unlike the oxen: Miren and Miguel, her parents, his parents, family members, and then friends, with each woman carrying a wicker basket of presents or flowers.

Given the increasing difficulty of the times, the gifts were mostly handmade or home-grown, sometimes as ornate as heirloom embroidery, sometimes as simple as a fresh skein of wool newly spun and dyed a pleasing colour.

Miguel would not be able to recall much of Father Xabier's wedding Mass and nuptial readings, as he was focused almost entirely on Miren. Mrs Arana had made her dress of white satin, with pearl beads decorating the tailored Basque bodice that accentuated Miren's slender waist. At the lowest point of the bodice in the back, just before it gave way to the spreading skirts, Mrs Arana had embroidered a small silver butterfly, in honour of the nickname she had given Miren. Miguel saw the butterfly, and his mind was continually drawn to it.

With his brother Dodo unavailable for duty, Miguel enlisted his father to be his witness, a position he proudly filled for several reasons: he could not have been happier for his son, but he also delighted in assisting the witness for the bride, Alaia Aldecoa, down the aisle to the altar. For weeks, Mariangeles and Miren had taken Alaia to Arana's, where they selected fabric, executed repeated fittings, and constructed her first tailored garment. It, too, had a tight waist, on the theme of Miren's dress, but it was an autumn rust colour, and it served to flatter Alaia's lighter hair and generous figure.

Father Xabier's message included personal references to Miren and a tribute to the powerful marriage bond between Justo and Mariangeles that had shaped her. Xabier smiled at them as he spoke; Justo grinned beneath his moustache.

'Sending him to the seminary was worth it for this moment if no other,' Justo whispered to Mariangeles.

Miren, a month from her twentieth birthday, had as much trouble as Miguel focusing on the proceedings. At one point, when protocol caused the assembly to rise, she glanced back at her parents. Her mother, beautiful, happy, and immaculately dressed, leaned into her scrubbed but rumpled father. Without Justo noticing, Mariangeles reached behind him, curled his collar back down into place, and lightly pulled the tail of his coat so it would be more comfortable for him when he once again sat. In that moment, Miren saw the kind of wife she wished to be. It was not instilled in her by the Mass or the vows or Father Xabier's incantations; she wanted to care so much for her husband, even after more than two decades of marriage, that she would still attend to his upturned collar and crumpled jacket. She wanted that concern to be second nature. That was the vow she made to herself at the altar that day.

The first dance at the wedding party did not involve the bride and groom but was a man's dance executed in honour of the couple. Domingo Abaitua, one of the dancers in Miren's old group, stepped forward and bowed before the newly-weds as others cleared the dance area. Straightening, he removed his beret with a flourish and sent it sailing towards the couple. Music began and he executed a series of spins and kicks that grew higher and faster as the gathering cheered louder with each. He finished with a deep bow to the couple and vacated the floor.

Miren held her groom at arm's length. She'd worried about this for weeks. Against slight resistance, Miguel pulled her tight, encircling her with his right arm. Four notes were struck, and on the next beat, Miguel confidently stepped forward with his left foot, catching Miren unprepared. He had brought his feet together to conclude his first three waltz steps before she caught up to him. Her smile slackened in shock as Miguel used firm pressure from his right hand on her lower back to guide her into the turns. Gliding through spirals inside a circle, they flowed across the floor. He counted his steps aloud, but he could dance.

'How? When?' Miren could barely form the questions. 'Who?'

Miguel ignored them, content to grin at her amazement. And answering would have disrupted his counting.

Moving in unison, they were alone. They didn't hear the cheers of their families and barely noticed when the music finished, coasting gently to a stop rather than ending abruptly. How long had they danced? Had they ever not been dancing?

Without the benefit of a running start, and despite the constrictions of dress and decorum, Miren leaped onto Miguel, her arms clasped behind his neck, and kissed him on the mouth with a force that whip-lashed his neck. She threw her head back, her veil dipping to the floor, and unleashed an *irrintzi* scream. After the first shriek, Justo joined her, as did Josepe and Father Xabier, and then the rest of the guests.

When the first notes of a *jota* were played, Miguel prised his bride loose and withdrew a few steps to give them space.

'What?' Miren stood motionless.

Kicks, spins, snaps. If Miguel's *jota* performance was more studied than natural, it was notable for its absence of bruising and bloodshed. Miren joined him, as did a grinning Mariangeles.

'Where did we get this dancer who looks so much like my new husband?' Miren asked her mother.

'It was a slow process,' Mariangeles answered.

'*Kuttuna*, your kind and patient and fearless mother has been giving me lessons for months,' Miguel said, slightly out of breath.

'Mother . . . you must be . . . the world's greatest . . . dance teacher,' Miren said between spins.

'He asked me so sincerely, there was no way I could refuse,' Mariangeles said. 'And he tried so hard. I had to lie to your father to protect the secret.'

Miguel pulled his mother-in-law into a tight hug. 'Thank you,' he whispered into her ear, inhaling the same scent as his wife's. That soap. 'Sorry about all the damage to your feet.'

'It was worth it,' Mariangeles said, standing back to let them dance again.

'Any other surprises for me, *astokilo*?' Miren asked when they started another waltz.

'I hope there will be many.'

Miguel pulled back slightly to look in her eyes.

'I have something I'd better say since I believe we should build our marriage on nothing but truth.'

Miren stilled.

'I have to confess, I never really knew a Gypsy fortune-teller named Vanka.'

'You fool!' she shrieked, giving him a pretend slap on the head. 'I would be rid of you now,' she said, grabbing his arm, 'if you weren't such a fine dancer.'

With his parents dancing and Miren bouncing between friends and meeting her obligation to dance with every man in attendance, Miguel joined the brothers of his father-in-law.

As Miren danced with Simone, the chorizo-maker, who was redolent of garlic, and then with Aitor, the corpulent baker, Miguel could not stop watching her.

Josepe and Father Xabier lifted their wineglasses towards Miguel.

'*Osasuna*,' they toasted.

'*Osasuna*,' he said.

'You are a lucky man, Miguel,' Josepe said.

'I know that, my friend,' Miguel responded, still focused on his bride's movements. 'Could you have ever foreseen in all those years as your neighbour that I would one day join your family?'

'I think it's wonderful; she couldn't have found a better husband,' Josepe said. 'And so, neighbour, now that you are officially part of the family, do you want to know all the old secrets? Ask us anything. Father Xabier here is used to answering questions, so there's not much he hasn't heard.'

'Oh, you would not believe the things I hear in that box . . .'

'Does Justo confess to you?' Miguel asked, wondering for the first time if he would be obliged to start taking his confessions to the uncle of his wife.

'Justo does not come to me officially, no,' Xabier said. 'I'm certain he worries that I might issue undue penance because he once held my head underwater in the stock trough.'

'Go ahead, Miguel, ask,' Josepe said.

'All right, here is what I need to know,' Miguel pressed. 'I believe he likes me and we have a good relationship. He calls me "son", which I take as a good sign. Should I still be in fear for my life?'

His concern amused both brothers.

'If you promise not to pass this along to our brother, I'll tell you the secret to Justo Ansotegui,' Xabier said. 'He's no different from everybody else. Everyone is driven by what they want most. Work out what that is, and you have the answer to who that person is. Most of the time it's obvious, but all of us are usually too concerned about the things *we* want to ever stop and look at anybody else's motives.'

Miguel nodded, if only to hurry Xabier past the philosophy.

'We can see what makes you happy; you haven't taken your eyes off your bride since you sat down, even when you've tried to look us in the eye. You've found what you want, whether you knew it was what you wanted all along or not.'

Miguel nodded. He had been accurately diagnosed. 'How does this apply to Justo? You were going to tell me the great secret.'

Xabier took another drink of wine before starting. 'When our father died, Justo took it as his duty to become the father. To little ones, the father is the biggest and cleverest and strongest, the man in control of all situations. Most people grow up to learn that their parents are just people with the same weaknesses we all have. Justo never got the chance to see that. In some ways, he's still fifteen, trying to live up to his image of what a father is supposed to be. After a while, he felt he could be everybody's father . . . father of the whole town.'

Miguel nodded; it made sense. 'I'll admit that I am much less threatened by him now than I was at first. But I still don't want to anger a man who killed a wolf with his bare hands.'

Josepe and Xabier squinted in unison. 'What wolf?'

'The wolf,' Miguel said. 'The one that chewed his ear off.'

Miguel joined his four fingers and snapped them against his thumb in the vicinity of his right ear, pantomiming the jaws of a vicious wolf. 'You know . . . the wolf.'

'Wolf . . . there was no wolf!' Josepe shouted. 'Justo lost that part of his ear when he was young and tried to shoot down an eagle with a rusted-out rifle. The thing exploded on him and jammed the stock back into his head. He's been without that part of his ear for more than thirty years.'

'A wolf, eh?' Father Xabier said, flashing a priestly scowl. 'He'll need at least ten Our Fathers to work his way out of a lie like that.'

Miguel was in parts relieved and saddened by the debunking of a classic Justo Ansotegui myth.

'Did he kill the eagle, at least?'

'No,' Josepe said solemnly. 'It came out of nowhere and there was nothing he could do. We were all so little.'

Josepe and Xabier smiled at each other, thinking, That's Justo. It was just a story, of course, but both were certain that if a wolf actually had attacked Justo, he might very easily have throttled it with his bare hands, even as it chewed off part of his ear. It may have been fiction only because the situation never arose.

José María Navarro waited for a moment when his son was neither dancing nor talking to his new relatives to pull him aside and express his happiness and his pride. He also had news from France.

'Eduardo sends his love and his great jealousy over your fine catch of a wife,' the father said. 'I told him about Miren, how she is Josepe's niece and what a perfect match she is for you.'

Miguel smiled at the mention of Dodo. 'Was there any chance he could have come to the wedding?'

'No, none,' the father said. 'He wanted to, and he knew how important it was to you, but you would be surprised to know that he has learned to become cautious in many matters. He sends word to me occasionally through fishermen from St-Jean, or at times he's on a boat that we meet at sea.'

'So he's fishing?'

'No, he is staying active in the mountains,' José María said. 'But we sometimes make arrangements to meet and he comes out on the boat of some friends he's made in France.'

'In the mountains? Is he farming, herding sheep?' Miguel asked incredulously. 'That doesn't sound like Dodo.'

'No, not herding sheep.' José María leaned in close. 'He's in with a group of smugglers.'

Miguel laughed so loudly the sound rose above the music, and many turned in his direction. His father gave him a sharp, tight-lipped shush.

'Fine,' Miguel said in a lowered voice. 'But that's perfect for Dodo; I'm sure he is having a wonderful time and he's very good at it, if he can keep himself from taunting too many border guards.'

'Well, it sounds as if he's at least being smart enough to keep himself unseen. This is a dangerous business, and some of his friends have been captured and thrown in prison. If he got caught and they connected his identity to that business at home, it might lead to a bad outcome.'

'I'm stunned to hear that he's being cautious or careful about anything. How long will that last?'

'That, I don't know,' José María said. 'But he'd better behave himself.'

'Why now? Why now more than any time in the past?'

José María whispered into his son's ear: 'Because now Josepe and I are helping him.'

By the time the newly-weds reached their home, friends had unloaded the oxcart and decorated the interior with strands of chorizos and peppers. It would help the young couple sustain themselves without having to leave the house for a week or so as they got their marriage off to an amicable commencement. On the table was a present from Miguel's mother, a clear glass canister filled with lemon drops.

Miguel and Miren stepped inside, overtaken by weariness, stopping to kiss without even closing the door. The jokers who unloaded the presents had piled many of them on the bed.

Miguel picked up one to show Miren.

'My father must have done this.' It was a carved fishing boat, with *Egun On* painted on the stern. 'I'm going to put it on our mantel, to start our own collection of special things.'

'*Asto!*' she said, noticing the dark oak chest at the foot of their bed. On the top was inlaid a *lauburu* of light poplar, and beneath that was a routed pair of interlocking Ms.

'Your gift,' he said. They grew more intent on clearing the bed, and they doused the lamp before undressing.

They had known each other for almost a year and had been convinced of the genuineness of their affection, but they had never translated those feelings into the physical, always withdrawing by mutual unspoken decision. Neither had experience, but it wasn't important. In this moment, it was their nature that was most meaningful: his was to be patient and attentive to detail, hers to be giving and agreeable. He was a craftsman; she was an artist. They were inexhaustibly tender and fully transparent. He was power, she was grace. He solid; she liquid. Then both liquid.

PART 3
(1935–1937)

CHAPTER 11

Walking slowly through the small hillside meadow above her home, Alaia Aldecoa used her gifted nose to determine which of the flowering herbs had reached the point of readiness and which would supply the perfect scent to the soaps that she made and sold every Monday afternoon at the market. The lavenders and heathers she favoured matured at different times and at various elevations and compass positions. Like the people in the village, the herbs lived out their individual preferences, some seeking exposure and others darker places, with flowers attuned to the light and shadows and the length of the day.

The process took time and particular caution at first, but by now, Alaia could negotiate the terrain by smell alone. With her fingers, she tested the turgidity of the stem and bloom to judge the moisture content and the levels of nectar or sap and scent. She exchanged soaps for a small sack of oats from one neighbour, wood-ash lye from the charcoal-burner up the valley, and fresh strawberries and even certain vegetables from another farmer. And she was able to use the blooms of the lilacs and flowering osiers and dogwoods in her own garden. She catalogued their locations in her head, along with the recipes for her product varieties, some constructed on the creamy foundation of Pyrenean sheep milk she received, in exchange for bartered services, from a widowed farmer who lived nearby.

She charged so little for her soaps at the market that some who came from outside the valley wondered how she could manage. It would be insulting, though, to suggest to her that she should raise her prices. So customers usually made no comment as they bought soap squares for themselves and filled their sacks with bars to sell to their neighbours at home at double the price.

For Alaia, the income was secondary to the approval from the customers, who raved over her soap's smoothness and scent, so soothing and so reminiscent of the hillsides. Some women went on in detail about how it softened that rough skin on their elbows, or how effectively it scoured the stench of fish or field off husbands. Visitors who went inside her cottage were struck by the intoxicating mixture of scents. Adding those to the constant mumble and hum of the adjacent stream, Alaia Aldecoa's cabin exerted a powerful effect.

As she started to roll mint leaves between her fingers at her table, a visitor arrived, knocking lightly.

'*Bai*,' she said, and he opened the door tentatively and peeked inside. When he saw that she had not made an effort to turn away from her work, he knocked louder.

'*Bai*,' she said again softly, still focused on her table.

He rapped once more, even louder.

'Come in.'

She knew who it was without turning. He paused, taking in the outline of her dress and the storm-cloud hair that made her one of the most provocative women in the valley. Still facing away from the door, continuing to work with the materials at the table, Alaia pointed towards her bed.

The man sat and removed his shoes, then his shirt, and then his trousers. Alaia fingered a small leaf of the fragrant mint and placed it in her mouth, just under her tongue, and approached him now. The man took in the sun-reddened cheeks and poppy lips, and was unfazed by the darkened lids of her closed eyes. Instead, he saw the shape and hair of the mythical *lamiak* who taunted men from the mountain caves. He smelled the clusters of flowers and heard the tumbling hum of the stream, and he was overcome by their sensory collusion. She bent to offer her lips, and he shivered when he tasted the wet mint in her mouth.

Alaia Aldecoa, blind since birth, raised in a convent of sequestered sisters, served the village in a capacity far more personal and intimate than that of soap-maker. It was unlikely anybody was more talented or better suited to their calling.

Picasso fell to his knees at the feet of Marie-Thérèse and theatrically promised to divorce Olga. Marie-Thérèse was pregnant. But bureaucracy soon diverted his romantic intent. French codes, he discovered, required he evenly divide his holdings with Olga, which meant the surrender of hundreds of paintings of incalculable value. Yes, to live with passion and be ruled by love is life's only way, he preached, but in this case, love's price might be unreasonably dear.

Talk of divorce was dropped. Olga left him for good, and Marie-Thérèse swelled through the hot summer before giving birth to a daughter, María de la Concepción, whom they called Maya.

Picasso grew dark under the weight of the conflicts in what he later called the worst time of his life, and he gave up painting for most of the year. Instead, he wrote poetry, and he converted his pain into a large etching. He created women looking out an elevated window, a wounded horse, and a minotaur advancing on a young girl, who fearlessly faced the danger with an outstretched arm holding a candle.

He titled it *Minotauromachy* (Minotaur Battle); the characters were some he would save as trademark symbols, and the theme would be converted for future works. As usual, critics tried to decode his message, most assuming it was another ode to the perpetually tormented soul of Spain. In her critique, Gertrude Stein agreed that it was an homage to his native country, because Picasso simply 'can never empty himself of being Spanish'.

*

Mendiola knew that losing Miguel would hurt his business. Despite the depressed economy, his shop had grown more profitable. So it was not entirely out of his concern for Miguel's well-being that Teodoro Mendiola gave his friend warnings about starting his own business at home.

'People who work at home get bored,' Mendiola told him. 'They feel as if they're always at work but never get out of the house. Within a year the wife will be sick of the man and he'll wish he had a place to go to get away during the day.'

Miguel listened but did not expect that would be the case.

'Have you seen Miren?' he asked.

For a newly-wed man with such a wife, the time away from the workbench was unlamented. As it developed, each of Miguel's trips in from the shop to the house felt like a surprise party.

'I'm thirsty, dear.' They kiss.

'I need to wash my hands, *kuttuna*.' They embrace.

'Isn't it about time for lunch?' Urgent coupling bent over the table, disrupting her preparation of the midday meal.

Miren occasionally interrupted him in the shop, too, with equally contrived motives. '*Asto*, can you come in and reach this for me?' Each small task carried a tariff of at least one lingering kiss and an immodest grasp by one or the other.

Mendiola was correct in one regard: Miguel's mind, while at work, was often consumed by the image of Miren. But what distracted him also inspired him. He created finer products, with greater detail and polish and with lines that were subtly sensuous.

As he lathed table legs, he thought of her slender ankles and dancer's calves. As he bevelled the corner of a tabletop, it assumed the shape of her naked shoulder. He envisaged the crease between the lean muscles of her outer thighs when he configured a piece of edging. Armrests of chairs became her arms, tapering to the end, with the wrist dipping into a gracefully curved hand. And as he rubbed in the stain and polish, he thought of massaging her neck, and then her back, down the beaded moulding of her spine, down past the decoratively countersunk sacral dimples, down to the sculpted behind, with flesh the colour of clear varnished pine. Tenon and mortise, he thought.

The scent of the shop was that of fresh-milled cypress and wood adhesives. And, in time, surrounded by a mound of feathery sawdust on the floor, amid a musk cloud of varnish fumes, Miguel would slow and refocus, and realize that the piece was finished. It was beautiful and effortless.

Time for lunch, dear. Are you ready?

Unaware that Miguel had discovered in carpentry an element of eroticism, Miren occasionally was surprised by her husband's readiness when he left the shop. She would admit, too, that she found her mind wandering while kneading dough or washing vegetables. And when Miguel arrived with a specific intent, she was equally eager.

There was no element of surrender to this, as she had been led to believe from overheard conversations among older women. Yes, she was modest, but she was lustful, too; yes, he was lustful, but he was also respectful. And her natural playfulness found interesting avenues as she surprised him with the occasional tender bite or a single light fingernail scrape down the length of his spine, or, as he sometimes kissed her stomach, she would nip the end of his nose between her thumb and forefinger as mothers do to young ones when pretending to steal their noses.

Coming in from one project, Miguel found Miren making bread. The early afternoon sun from the southern window in the kitchen caused her to once again give off light. And the smell of the leavening dough was yeasty in the room. He walked lightly on his toes behind her. He slipped his hands onto her waist, eased her back against his hips, and immersed his face in her fragrant hair, inhaling deeply, spellbound.

'Oh, God . . . your smell,' he said.

'Oh, God, *your* smell,' she countered.

'That soap from Alaia is wonderful.'

'Yes, Miguel, you should use some.'

She turned inside the radius of his arms, flicked a heavy dusting of flour onto his sweating face, and dabbed a finger beneath each ear as if to apply a cologne. She pulled back to look at him so that they met only at the hips.

'Look at all the flour you wasted,' she said. 'Flour is hard to come by these days, and valuable.'

'Fine, then I will give it back. I'll give it to you here – ' he touched his floury lips lightly to the side of her neck – 'and here,' he said, touching them to the other side of her neck.

At the soft hollow between ascending cords at the base of her neck, he paused.

'Oh, yes,' she said. 'The recipe calls for more there.'

She leaned back to allow greater access, and the bread was left to rise on its own.

They always talked of personal things in the close time afterwards. Miguel told her of fishing and of his family and of growing up in Lekeitio, and how he had hoped there was a Miren somewhere for him. Miren told him about dancing and about her parents and about life on the *baserri*, and how she had no idea there would be a Miguel for her in the world. When conversation lapsed, he might race naked to the kitchen and retrieve a piece of bread or an apple that they would share, all so much more delicious now. There was no senseless modesty anymore, as he would hand Miren the food and stand at the edge of the bed, proudly male.

And one afternoon Miren made an observation Miguel found curious.

'I don't know if it's possible to tell such things, but I feel like we just started a baby,' she said, rolling to face him.

Miguel hoped that would be the case, as a family would further dovetail their lives.

'I've never heard a woman say anything about this,' Miren said. 'I should ask my mother if she had any idea when this happened to her.'

'Please don't, *kuttuna*, I don't want her thinking about us doing this.' In his mind, though, Miguel began shaping plans for the construction of a cradle.

Amaya Mezo hummed in a gentle contralto no matter how many hours she might be in the fields with her husband Roberto. It made the baby girl carried in the sling across her chest sleep as if she was in a rocking cradle soothed by tender lullabies. Amaya's cargo was Gracianna, her seventh child, five months old. Amaya never minded getting back in the fields to help Roberto, even in the dusty heat of the summer or when the windblown grass chaff bit into their faces and adhered to their sweat. Roberto told her many times that her songs made the work less tiring. It sounded to him like the calling of a bird.

The Mezos' *baserri*, Etxegure, was larger than the neighbouring Errotabarri. And in good times, the Mezos had more stock, along with an apple orchard that produced fruit for eating and for cider. Of course, the Ansoteguis had only one child, and she was now gone with her husband.

Amaya Mezo didn't think about the increasing hardships, as she was lost in her song and the rhythmic thrust of the two-pronged *laia* into the soil and the sun on her back and the sleeping sighs of the baby against her chest. But Roberto then made a sound she'd never heard.

Two uniformed Guardia Civil officers had snatched the unsuspecting Roberto, who struggled and was subdued by a rifle butt to the lower abdomen. He had fallen, and the two guards, each pulling at a flailing arm, had lifted him to a standing position.

'Amaya, run!' Roberto yelled. 'Get Justo.'

But she knew there was no time to fetch the neighbour; this was up to her. She raced at the guardsmen, child bouncing in her sling, brandishing her sharpened *laia* as if it was a jousting stick. Sensing her willingness to run them through, the guards pulled down their rifles and cocked the bolts, one levelled at Roberto's head and the other at Amaya's chest.

'One more step and we'll kill you both,' one said with a paralysing calmness.

Amaya stopped as if she had reached the end of a tether, frozen by the sight of the rifle at Roberto's head.

The baby screamed.

'What has he done?' Amaya asked. 'He's just a farmer.'

The guardsmen said nothing. With the point of a rifle, one guard guided Roberto towards the road while the other walked backward, his weapon never varying off a line that led directly to Amaya's chest. And they were gone.

With Mariangeles's help, Amaya spent every day seeking information at the Guardia offices. In a month, she was told that Roberto had been accused by 'concerned citizens' of selling produce without going through the appropriate ration accounting. When she asked when the trial would be conducted, when the accusers could be confronted, she was told that such formalities were not necessary in these difficult times.

' "Concerned citizens"?' Justo asked Mariangeles that night. 'Is that what it has come to now? People turning on each other? I'm going to see if I can find the person who did this.'

'I don't know what happened, Justo,' she said. 'I only know that he had no chance, and Amaya is going to have problems without him. All those children. The troubles are coming here now, too, aren't they? I don't want you doing anything foolish. Let's just try to be clever.'

Dark humour spread from man to man through Guernica's streets and cafes. Women refused to take part, perhaps because of higher sensitivity and delicate taste, or perhaps greater strength. Mendiola told Miguel that he knew times were hard because even the cats were looking over their shoulders as they slunk about the streets.

Coffee now consisted of recycled grounds with no sugar; bread was coarse and black, and meat was an almost forgotten delicacy. Those who still had pigs slaughtered them at night and then hid the meat to avoid being caught with unrationed pork. Those who had cached sacks of wheat broke into locked mills by night to grind whatever small amount of flour they could, risking arrest for making bread. Others started eating their maize, and some were said to have stolen oats out of horses' feed bags in town, as the provender for stock was becoming a staple for humans.

Miguel spent many days in the forests felling timber and learned which mushrooms were edible. He carried a sack to hold them. He still tried to fish in the stream for the small trout to bolster their sparse diet. Many of the streams were fished out, though. He thought of the thousands of fish he had pulled in during his days in Lekeitio and wondered how he could have found the process so distasteful. He thought of a grilled bream fillet and of the delicious *bacalao*.

One day he spotted a grouse in a patch of brush on a hillside and quietly dropped his saw. Never taking his eyes off the prey, he felt the ground for a stone and crept towards the oblivious bird. Ten yards, five yards . . . He rose and flung the stone, hitting the bird perfectly. He thrust both hands into the air and shouted. He could not believe it, but almost immediately he felt a sense of guilt that the stalking and killing had been so bereft of sport. But the bird was plump, and he brought it home along with some mushrooms. Miren rushed to Errotabarri to invite her parents for dinner. Mariangeles had been preparing a potato-and-leek soup and brought it along to add to the feast.

'Justo asked that we start without him and said he would be along as soon as he finished some work,' Mariangeles said when she arrived.

'What's he doing that's so important that he would miss a dinner of fresh game?' Miguel asked.

'He doesn't want me to say anything about this, but since Roberto Mezo was arrested, he's been spending several hours every day trying to help Amaya and her family,' Mariangeles said as she hoisted her pot of soup onto the table, careful not to spill any. 'There's no way she could make it without his helping with some of the harder jobs. Justo just tries to get up earlier and get his work done faster at home so he can help her family after that.'

Miren tended the bird at the hearth and Miguel sliced the

mushrooms and mixed them with some wild greens he had collected.

'Amaya tries to get Justo to bring home a few eggs or some grain every now and then as payment, but he refuses,' Mariangeles added. 'That would help, but they have so little, we couldn't take anything from them.'

As they sat and finished their prayer, Justo arrived, his face and clothes dirty and his customary boisterousness markedly subdued. Even his moustache seemed to droop.

'Did somebody mention a fat bird?' Justo asked.

Miguel carved the sign of the cross in the loaf and then sliced pieces off those axes, taking the first one and placing it on the mantel 'to calm the stormy seas'. Justo protested that this was no time to observe traditions that wasted food, especially since they were many miles from the sea.

Even the mannerly Mariangeles and Miren moaned as they ate the juicy bird covered with salt and herbs. And for a time, grateful eating was the only sound at the table.

'Papa.'

'Yes, *kuttuna*.'

'It's a good thing you are doing, helping the Mezos.'

Justo looked at Mariangeles, the informant.

'They need help; besides, I was losing a little of my strength, so a bit more work is good for me,' he kidded. 'I would wager she did not tell you who has been over there every day helping with the little ones and doing most of the cleaning and the housework, did she?'

Miren smiled at her mother, who shrugged in admission.

'Did they ever hear what happened to Roberto?' Miguel asked.

'Apparently there are more rats in town than the ones that are being captured and cooked,' Justo said.

'One of us?' Miren asked. 'How could people do that to their neighbours?'

'This sort of thing changes people – some, at least,' Justo said. 'You put too many chickens in the same pen, without food, and you'll see it. They'll peck each other to death.'

They chewed quietly.

'Character comes easy when the belly is full,' Justo added. 'It gets harder now. And could get harder still.'

It was the first healthy meal the four had eaten in some time, but the conversation left them unsatisfied, and Justo and Mariangeles departed with brief hugs and thanks soon after the dishes were cleared. Both were already exhausted, and they were now in the habit of going to sleep as soon as darkness came.

Early the following evening, as Justo finished his work at Errotabarri and headed to the Mezos', Miren and Miguel arrived to join him. Without explanation, they each took a scythe and began sweeping through the tall grasses and spreading it to dry.

'Thank you,' Justo said to Miguel.

'It's nothing; I don't want to lose my strength in my old age, either.'

Amaya Mezo, having prepared dinner for her children, left the kitchen without eating more than a few nibbles so she could join the trio in the field. As she gathered and spread hay, she began humming. Her three helpers picked up their pace. To them, it sounded like the song of a bird, carefree and at peace.

CHAPTER 12

Most of them never had much anyway, so it wasn't the poverty that so upset those in town. Some weren't even troubled by the rash of break-ins and stealing from businesses, as hunger nibbled away at people's principles. Many understood it, recognized it as human nature, and had considered it themselves in dark moments. It was only food, and the damage generally was small, a broken window or doorjamb.

But something more menacing filled the atmosphere now, an uncertainty that crackled in the air, in the suspicion on the streets that caused people to look down rather than ahead, and in the night that announced itself with the sound of bolts snapping shut.

To Miguel, it seemed as if many were pulling themselves in tighter, to become smaller, impenetrable. He saw those types every day, although they did not want to be seen. He talked to them every day, but they did not want to respond. They looked up as if they had been in a cloud of thought, coughed a quick greeting, and hurried off in search of a place to disappear.

Others had not changed; they hailed him on the street and made jokes about their circumstances, and asked of his business and wife.

'Until people start eating furniture, business will be slow,' Miguel joked each time to save himself the energy of thinking up new responses.

He had been able to stay reasonably busy with small speciality orders: a chest as a gift for some other newly-weds, a few cabinets and dressers . . . mostly fine finished work for those in town who still had a little money and cared for things that would last into better times.

As Miren's belly started to swell, Miguel began construction of the cradle. His slender wife approached pregnancy as she did all other endeavours, unsparingly and with an energy that infected those around her. Her lean dancer's figure began to fill out early, and after years of joking at her own expense about certain inadequacies, she loved how her blouses stretched tightly across the front. If pregnancy rendered some women too ill or uneasy to be intimate, it had an opposite effect on Miren, who became increasingly libidinous.

After the cradle was built, Miguel painted a fish leaping from the water at the head. At the foot, he painted a woman dancer, hands raised and a leg elevated in mid-kick.

'And when the baby is born and we see if it is a boy or girl, I will rout its name across the headboard,' Miguel told Miren one night.

'I wouldn't do that,' she answered.

'Why? It will become an heirloom for his family, then.'

'Because, dear, I don't want you to have to keep making different cradles for each of the many babies we will have.'

Miguel hadn't thought beyond the first. He had been so engaged in the process, so overtaken by having a child with Miren, that he hadn't considered later additions. Since she mentioned it, he liked the idea.

'Fine,' he said, running his hand through his hair and then clenching the back of his neck. 'How about if I just carve "Navarro" on the headboard? That should keep us covered for as many as we need.'

He expected fatherhood to alter his life, adding responsibilities and certain restrictions. But he could not envision it having an effect on his carpentry business. After baby Catalina was born, Miguel found himself veering away from his typical projects to spend time building things for her, starting with toys and furniture and progressing to things she couldn't possibly use for years.

Finished with her cradle, Miguel added a high chair so that she would someday be able to sit with them at the table. He then built a small set of chairs and a table for her to use when she invited little friends for imaginary tea. He constructed a hobbyhorse on wheels that she could push around, except he chose to fashion a ram instead of a horse. He took a sun-bleached ram's skull with a set of rounded horns that he had seen at Errotabarri, painted the bone a dark colour so that it would be less frightening, blunted the horn tips for safety, and attached it to the frame of the toy.

Mendiola always chided Miguel for the sin of overbuilding, saying his projects were created to a shipwright's tolerance. Partly as a joke for Mendiola, Miguel designed Catalina's pram in the shape of a boat. The sides were clinker-built of oak, and the exposed upper edges were capped like gunwales and joined at the pointed prow. Miguel liked the theme of the little 'craft' and was able to show Mendiola how easily it could be pushed with its oversized wheels.

'And this hood can be pulled down for storms at sea, correct?'

'There might be some foul-weather walking involved some days, sure,' Miguel answered. 'Why not build it to last? Who knows how many children are going to end up using it?'

'And if flooding becomes a problem, Catalina could go for a boat ride instead of a stroll, right?'

'And fish while she's doing it,' Miguel said.

Soon there was little room to walk through the clutter of furniture in their house. Miren viewed each piece as a family treasure and marvelled at her husband's skills but pointed out the impracticality of storing so much children's furniture. When she mentioned the surplus to other young mothers she knew, some expressed interest in buying what Miguel had already made or ordering similar pieces for their children.

His business evolved as demand for cabinets and chests and chairs and tables diminished, but the requests for children's furniture kept him busy. His added touch of routing the family name into each crib or cradle increased interest and allowed him to charge higher prices, as these now were being valued as long-term family possessions. Miguel had to tactfully deny this feature for some patrons. When Cruz Arguinchona asked for a cradle for his baby, Miguel had to break the surname into two parts on the headpiece, which Cruz understood and appreciated. But when Coro Cengotitabengoa ordered a cradle, Miguel told her he would have to carve the name across the headboard, footboard, and both side pieces.

They settled on a nice wood inlay of a *lauburu*.

Before Catalina was a month old, Miren could scarcely recall a time when she had not been a mother. At night, Catalina would whimper or cry only a few notes before either parent would rise. Miguel often would go to the cradle next to their bed, retrieve Catalina, change and clean her, and then bring her to Miren for feeding. At times Miren would sit in the rocking chair Miguel had built and nurse while cooing to the baby. Other times she might just double the pillows behind her head and sit up in bed to nurse. Miguel then would wedge his pillow behind him, too, and regardless of the hour and the darkness and how soon he might have to head up into the forest, he watched the sublime connection.

'*Astokilo*, go to sleep, you don't have to be awake for this,' she always said to Miguel. 'There's not much you can do to help this process, you know.'

But he always waited until Catalina was finished and had been patted on Miren's shoulder before taking her back to her cradle. He would kiss her head and smell her feathery hair and the breath of milk she sleepily exhaled. Then he would return to bed, kiss his wife – who often was already back to sleep – and thank her for feeding their baby girl.

In the evenings, Miguel and Miren sat beside each other and babbled at Catalina. After all, there had never been such a child, so intelligent and beautiful and well behaved. Why had no one told them of the wonders of parenthood? 'Did you see how she grasped my thumb?' one would say. 'That must be a sign of early advancement. Here, watch how her eyes follow my face when I move from side to side. And that smile . . . she will break hearts once she sprouts teeth.'

Miren worked with Catalina on her dance steps before she was able to support her own head. Holding Catalina in the hammock of her skirt, Miren would put her hands out so that Catalina could grasp her thumbs. Miren raised her daughter's arms over her head and moved them in a gentle rhythm.

'This is how you do a *jota*,' she said. She then took the baby's bare feet and kissed the tender arches until Catalina emitted a giggle that sounded like tiny bells. She wiggled her feet as if quick-stepping to a tune.

'You, my dear girl, will be the finest dancer in Guernica one day soon.'

When Catalina saw Miguel over her mother's shoulder, she began frog-kicking furiously, excited by the sight of him.

'Isn't that always the case?' Miren said in baby tones. 'Papa is for fun; Mama is for food.'

'But we'll let Mama be responsible for the dance lessons,' Miguel said, also assuming the high pitch of excitement he used to delight his daughter.

The parents soaked in the image of their baby girl, the dark, clear colouring, the wispy black hair and dark almond eyes that were already starting to resemble her mother's.

It started with Josu Letemendi, a neighbour who helped Alaia Aldecoa gather the scents for her soaps. He enjoyed her company so much that he often chopped wood, stoked the fire, heated the water, and cleaned up. They chatted casually about a number of topics when they walked the fields or as he measured out portions of ingredients for her soap mixtures.

Josu had never been a handsome boy, with a large head bracketed by perpendicular ears. He received little attention from girls at school or at any *erromeria*. He found himself more at ease around Alaia than he ever had been with the girls of the village, even though she was infinitely more beautiful and exotic.

At times in the cottage it became easier for Josu to simply put a hand on each of Alaia's shoulders and direct her to a jar or container holding a specific ingredient she needed. Alaia found herself anticipating those touches. Josu positioned her in front of the milk and a saucepan one afternoon. Instead of feeling out for her ingredients, Alaia backed up slightly, slowly, so that her back touched his chest. The bow knot of her apron tie made contact just below his waist. In a moment, he pulled her in, closer, until her hair touched his face.

'Er . . .' Josu asked permission with a tentative syllable.

'Yes,' Alaia said.

The soaps went unattended for many days.

Within six months, though, Josu was called to Bilbao to work in the *taberna* of an uncle. He would return to Guernica several days a month to see family and also to help Alaia with her projects, but both knew the distance would keep the relationship from advancing beyond what it had been, a time of joyful discovery.

It was then that Mr Zubiri stepped in and began helping Alaia, and he, too, soon provided her with a physical outlet that carried no expectations other than touch and secrecy. It was different with the patient and grateful Mr Zubiri. But it was still fulfilling for Alaia and certainly a highlight for the widower. In time, a man who sometimes brought her eggs initiated similar attention.

Alaia became well attuned to the delicacy and timing of human contact. Men were appreciative, and their groaned approval caused her to become more inventive and eager. The partner made little difference to her, and the man's appearance certainly did not affect her. Her visitors learned that the enterprise was not a social function; she had little patience with explanations, commentary, and complaints about former relationships, politics, or the status of crops. She was not available to hear confessions or offer absolution. She accepted trade, services, chickens, eggs, bread, wine, firewood, or supplies for her soaps.

In a gossipy town that prized fidelity, hers was not a volume business, but there were a few regulars. Alaia's clientele consisted mostly of widowers, inquisitive strays, and unmarried young men whose thoughts were dictated by flowing sap. Alaia's arts were largely wasted on the latter, as it was her practice to wash them with warm water and one of her special soaps beforehand, an activity that many times cured the problem spurring the visit in the first place.

If some of the more devout in town had heard of Alaia Aldecoa's activities, they might easily have gathered and burned her out of her home, blindness be damned. But most practised the more fundamental orthodoxy of pragmatism. Had this been a girl with a full complement of God's gifts, she would have been reviled, perhaps stoned in the market by the women in town.

It was this matter of need that made her different. If not honourable, Alaia Aldecoa's position was viewed as excusably practical and was tolerated if not ignored by most of the community. As hints of her activities inevitably seeped into town, she was spoken of as the village soap-maker, rarely anything else. How could the chattering *amumak* ignore a prostitute in their village when a neighbour's flirtatious glance might trigger decades of hostility? Because Alaia Aldecoa, relinquished to a convent when her parents discovered she was blind, was one of God's needy children.

That she could support herself despite impairment was judged slightly more admirable in its enterprise than scornful in its immorality. She was unofficially shunned by many who knew the whispered secret, and they turned away without comment. But most rationalized that the girl was providing relief for widowers and for young men who might otherwise seek out and assault their unsuspecting daughters and granddaughters.

Another factor played into the community's forbearance: all knew that Justo Ansotegui held her in high regard and would tolerate no demeaning comments. All knew and respected Mariangeles Ansotegui without reserve. And Miren Ansotegui? She was as close to the sightless girl as a sister, and to say something harsh about Alaia would feel like impugning Miren. Few would consider that.

Alaia had no way of knowing how the village had shaped a consensus on her lifestyle, just as she did not fully understand how comforting to men was her lack of sight. It amounted to the gift of anonymity at a time when being unrecognized was a man's second priority. She knew who they were, most of them, at least. She could tell by their voices, having encountered them at times in the market. But there was never a name, never a discussion, sometimes no talk at all. A man might appear at her door with a plucked chicken, a clutch of eggs, a string of chorizos.

If the man wished to engage in conversation, she had several effective means of causing talk to abruptly cease.

With great ceremony, Justo Ansotegui uncorked the wine and poured small amounts for his wife, daughter, and son-in-law. As the wine burbled through the opening, Justo echoed its sound: 'Glug, glug, glug.' New glass. 'Glug, glug, glug.'

'This,' he announced as he wet a glass for himself, 'may be the last bottle of *txakoli* we see for some time. With the next bottle, we may celebrate the glorious defeat of the Falange pigs.'

'Don't call them pigs, Papa, that makes me think of food,' Miren said, drawing out 'food' as if she could savour the taste of the syllable. It had been months since a pig had been slaughtered in the neighbourhood, and Miren's cows had been sacrificed, one by one, over the previous years. This diet of limited protein created gaunt faces and stooped shoulders among even the town's most robust citizens.

They took tender sips of the clear, fruity wine to make it last.

Usually at this time, when the first flush of wine had moistened his throat, Justo began telling stories. But Miren did not give her father the chance to start a tale that might take an hour to finish before he finally linked it to an example of his own strength or mystical powers.

'Papa, Miguel is talking about joining the army and I want you to force him to give up the idea,' Miren said.

'He's a man and I would say you hold more sway over him than I do,' Justo said. 'And as for physical force, *kuttuna*, what good would it be if I returned to you a broken husband?'

'No, I don't *want* to join the army,' Miguel stressed, putting down his glass with unexpected force. 'I don't want to fight anybody. I want to be left alone, but I don't think they're going to let us.'

'Good man,' Justo said. 'I will not let that happen, either.'

'Don't start that, Papa, he's a father now,' Miren said, gesturing to Catalina, who was asleep in her pram. 'They're looking for unmarried men to fight now.'

'Don't kid yourself, they'll take whoever they can get,' Mariangeles said. 'I want both of you to promise not to do anything stupid.'

'Have we ever done anything stupid?' Justo objected.

'You are men,' Mariangeles said.

All four nodded.

'Papa, Miguel is thinking about trading some work for a rifle; I told him it will only get him in trouble,' Miren said.

Justo agreed with that point. 'I had a bad experience with a rifle one time.'

'That's the same thing Miguel says about berets,' Miren said.

'No, son, you don't need a rifle, and I don't need a rifle,' Justo said, clenching his hands as if strangling a thin-necked Fascist. 'If anyone sets foot on Errotabarri I won't need a weapon.'

'That's probably what Roberto Mezo believed, too,' Mariangeles said.

Miren had heard the reports of atrocities and that there were dangers and threats, but she was helpless to comprehend them. These things happened, but not to her, not here. She was too embarrassed to say this, but she felt that if she could just talk to Franco, sit down with him, she could straighten this all out. She could make him see the importance of stopping the war, especially the fighting against the Basques. She could convince him. He would see her as a human being who deserved to be left unharmed. She could teach him a *jota*.

'We've never invaded anyone else's territory,' Miren said with an expectation of fairness.

'Xabier has studied these things and told me that when the Romans came, we tolerated them because they built bridges,' Justo said. 'We let them stay for a while, build some roads, and then watched them leave when they lost interest.'

'Could the same thing happen with Franco?' Miren asked. 'Could he just come in without fighting and nothing would change?' All knew that was not the approach the rebels had taken elsewhere.

Mariangeles saw a clearer reality: 'These aren't Romans, these are Spaniards, and like it or not, we are in Spain, at least as they see it. Franco's made it clear he wants to be rid of the Basques.'

Justo grew defensive. 'We've always fought in the woods and the mountains and outsmarted everyone who invaded until whatever it was they wanted from us was not nearly worth the inconvenience of being stabbed in their sleep or being shoved off a mountain trail.'

'Franco is the devil,' Mariangeles continued. 'I heard at the market that he had his own cousin executed on the first day of the revolt. And most of the Guardias have fallen in with the rebels now, too. Stopping the Fascists in Spain is something that we might manage. But with the Germans and Italians joining them, and nobody acting very interested in helping us, it's different; you can't stab an aeroplane in its sleep.'

Miguel felt a surge of anger mixed with stubbornness. He began to understand what Dodo had tried to tell him years before, that there would come a time to fight. 'Are we supposed to just let them walk in and take over?'

'Some people around here won't merely stand for it, they'll welcome it,' Mariangeles reminded him. 'There're Falange in town, you know it. They think if they support Franco it's the best way to protect themselves. Who do you think turned in Mezo? Most of the priests in Spain are behind Franco. He has the support of the Vatican in Rome.'

Miren was stunned. 'The Church wants Franco to win?'

'Xabier said that's true; it's coming all the way from Rome,' Justo said. 'But many of the Basque priests are ignoring the Vatican and supporting the Republican army.'

The four turned their attention to their glasses as Justo poured the last of the wine equally.

Justo raised his glass in a toast to signal the end of the discussion.

'Let us recall one of my favourite sayings,' he said. 'Neither a tyrant nor a slave . . . a free man I was born, a free man I will die.'

They touched the rims of their wineglasses, which rang delicately inside Errotabarri.

CHAPTER 13

Miguel objected to the tradition because it felt like an act of desecration. But Justo insisted, with Mariangeles and Miren acting as willing conspirators. Catalina was to have her ears pierced, just as Miren had at her age.

Among the many genetic advantages of being Basque, Justo reminded them, was the presence of gloriously pendant earlobes. The ancients would pierce the tiny lobes of baby girls and adorn them with ornamentation as a declaration of their Basque purity. Never bashful about trumpeting a perceived superiority, they developed a dismissive label for outsiders: 'the Stumpy-Ears'. So Mariangeles and her sisters had their ears pierced when they still were in the cradle, and so did Miren. As much as Miren wanted to abide by the custom, she knew she could not perform the operation, leaving the task to Amuma Mariangeles, an experienced hand in the matter.

They gathered at Errotabarri for the ceremony, and Miren laid Catalina on the table, where she wiggled and babbled and stretched her arms up, clenching and re-clenching her tiny fingers, trying to instruct these large oblivious beings that she'd rather be held. The process was as traditional as the deed. A small sewing needle, threaded with fine silk, was seared by fire. A wedge of raw potato was cut so that it would fit behind the baby's earlobe to provide resistance. The baby was held by her arms and head to keep her steady; the lobe was penetrated and the thread of silk was left to prevent the hole from healing over. Every day, a drop or two of olive oil was dribbled onto the thread as lubricant, and it was pulled back and forth to keep the passage open until it was healed enough that tiny hoops or posts could be inserted.

'Miguel, these are the baby earrings that both Miren and I wore,' Mariangeles said, taking from a box the tiny silver *lauburuak* that were affixed to thread-thin studs.

Although outnumbered four to one, the writhing Catalina was easily their equal. Justo held her head but was more concerned with petting her fine dark hair; Miguel held her arms but was afraid of bruising her if he asserted his strength; Miren held her legs, but whenever Catalina thrust them, Miren's resistance only provided leverage for her to scoot towards Justo at the head of the table.

'Goodness, you'd think we were butchering a ram; this is a little baby,' Mariangeles chided.

They continued their passive restraint but affected greater stridence by assuming stern expressions. Mariangeles pressed on anyway. When the hot needle penetrated Catalina's left ear she squealed but did not wrestle too fiercely, and the thread hung in place as Mariangeles dabbed away drops of blood. Catalina's subdued sobbing lulled them into false confidence, and Justo, Miguel, and Miren were unprepared for Catalina's adrenalized struggle when the needle began its second penetration. She wrestled her head inside Justo's tender grasp and blood flowed.

'Damn it!' It was the first curse anyone had heard from Mariangeles.

Mariangeles attempted to staunch the blood with her skirt as Catalina's howls mortified her parents. When Catalina calmed enough to allow examination, it was clear that her jerking away had caused the needle to rip a notch in her earlobe.

'Will that heal? Will she be all right?' Miren asked frantically.

'She'll be fine; it will heal up, I think,' Mariangeles answered. 'We can try again a little higher up in a few months.'

Exhausted, Catalina whimpered and sobbed on the table and outstretched her arms in the direction of Miren. Mariangeles, feeling deep guilt and the fear that her granddaughter might forever hold her responsible, handed the baby to Miren.

The silent discomfiture in the room was broken only by the sounds of the sniffling Catalina until Miguel began laughing, slowly at first, and then more loudly. The others stared him down.

'Miguel,' Miren said sharply.

'My God,' Miguel said. 'Look at her, our perfect little baby girl is going to go through life looking just like her *aitxitxia* Justo!'

Justo fingered the frayed edges of his right ear and had no hope of containing the smile that bunched up his cheeks so hard that his eyes squinted.

Jean-Claude Artola told Dodo that the associate he needed to meet would be at a place on Rue de la République, the Pub du Corsaire (Bar of the Privateers). He knew that St-Jean-de-Luz was famed not only as a port for the storied Basque whalers but as the den of some of the greediest cut-throat pirates and privateers to sail since the seventeenth century. He entered the door and found himself in the dark-oak belly of a corsair's ship. Golden lantern light puddled amid the shadows. Stout knees attached the false futtocks to the upper deck. In the middle, the mainmast extended down to the keel. The bar ran perpendicular to the beam, up the port side to the middle of the ship. He could almost feel the swell of the seas.

'I'm home,' he announced to no one.

A few tables and booths were clustered near the 'bow', and Dodo sat at the fore end of the bar. A woman sitting with friends soon rose to leave; her dog had been sleeping at her feet.

'*Allez, Déjeuner,*' she said to the small bristle-furred dog as she neared Dodo.

Déjeuner? Lunch. He grasped the amusing implication.

'You must have been eating in Spain recently,' Dodo said to her. With a broad belt cinching the waist of her skirt below a loose shirt, the woman seemed to match the decor. She could have trodden the foredeck with the corsairs, Dodo thought. She flashed across his mind in images of impish larceny and feminine roguishness. This was a woman, he was certain, with whom a man could raise infinite amounts of hell.

Within a minute, he discovered that she was Renée Labourd, the woman he had been told to contact. Within weeks, they were companions, attracted mostly by their own qualities in each other. To Dodo, Renée carried a hint of the wild. To Renée, Dodo displayed, in the most interesting ways, the spirit of her father.

Sensing his potential, Renée began schooling Dodo in the crepuscular arts, the '*travail de la nuit*' that had served as her family's business for generations. Her father and mother operated a small auberge on the road outside Sare. The town, just south-east of St-Jean-de-Luz, was situated near so many mountain passes along the Spanish border that it was considered the capital of the *contrebandiers* who exploited a thriving unsanctioned import–export trade. For several generations, the Labourd family had let rooms, with mountain views from each shuttered and flower-boxed window, and served exquisite French-Basque cuisine to locals and guests. But their real job always had been ferrying goods across the border.

After hearing from Dodo the accounts of his first few disastrous nights in the mountains, Renée instructed him in both the practice and the philosophy of the business. The creative avoidance of unlawful taxes, unfair tariffs, and absurd embargoes carried no negative connotations among those who lived there, she stressed. The border didn't belong there; it was not recognized by those in residence on either side because their families pre-dated its random scribble across the maps.

Renée's parents had used her as a decoy or an appealing little diversion since childhood, letting her charm the Guardias or gendarmes with a dance or a song or a story as Mère and Père slipped past them with anything smaller than an elephant carrying a piano. Some nights it was as simple as carrying packs of French wine and cheese, other times as tricky as herding a string of horses up the steep passes.

After having dropped their delivery one night, Dodo and Renée strolled hand in hand through the French checkpoint like lovers enjoying the moonlight. As they were cleared to pass, the border guards were roused to investigate suspicious activity up a nearby gulley. Dodo and Renée stood and watched as the two guards gathered their weapons and headed off into the darkness. Slipping into the unattended guardhouse, they pocketed whatever blank paperwork they could find for future use, collected the small cache of spare ammunition, and made love on the captain's desk.

Miguel stepped lightly, heel to toe, and crouched in the cover of weeds when he neared the stream. There were fish to be had, but it was no longer a matter of recreation. Now it was about fending off hunger. So, like nearly everything else in their lives, it was more serious and harder work. But on this day, he took six trout from a stream he hadn't fished in some time. Two would serve as dinner, two would be a nice gift to Mendiola to supplement his family's meal, and one would brighten the evening of the widow Uberaga next door, leaving one to spare.

'Miren, you should take a fish to Alaia's,' he suggested. 'I don't know how much help she's getting from Zubiri these days. It might be a nice surprise.'

Miren appreciated her husband's thoughtfulness, and as soon as they finished eating she walked to Alaia's cottage, hoping to get the trout to her before she prepared her evening meal. Miren had never heard Alaia complain, but the scarcity of food had to affect her at least as much as anybody in town. Selling bars of soap inexpensively at the market could not provide much for her to live on.

As Miren slipped through the door, she called out, 'Alaia, look what Miguel brought home for—'

She could not actually see Alaia as she entered, only a pale, furrowed rump cresting and plunging.

'Uuugggg.' It was old man Zubiri, whom she did not recognize until her shout caused him to dismount in a panic and snatch up the overalls that were gathered at his ankles. Having not bothered to remove his boots for the experience, all Zubiri had to do was regain his feet, pull up his overalls, and fly past Miren through the door she had left open. His beret had been firmly in place the entire time.

Miren said nothing. She stood frozen, holding the fish.

Alaia sat up on the bed, inhaled deeply, and readied for Miren's inevitable inquest. But her friend was stunned mute.

'Miren?'

Miren was paralysed by two revelations: someone as old as Zubiri still had sex, and her friend, now standing nude by her bed, was so beautiful that it caused her to stare. Her figure was lush, so pleasingly arched and dimensional, and her nipples were as round and deeply brown as chestnuts.

'Miren . . . oh.' Alaia sensed her embarrassment and retrieved her grey cotton dress, calmly felt the collar edge for the opening that would identify which was the front, and then slipped it over her head.

'Miren?' she said, straightening the dress.

Miren recaptured enough composure to place the fish on the table.

'Here is a fish I brought,' she said. 'I can help you fry it if you're hungry.'

'Say it, Miren.'

'Alaia, how could you be in love with old man Zubiri?'

Alaia's outburst of laughter shocked Miren again.

'I'm not in love with Zubiri,' she said. 'We're more like business partners.'

'Then why were . . . and . . . that didn't look like business.'

'He helps out with food; he brings me the things I need for soaps, and milk, and wood for the stove,' Alaia said.

'And you?'

'I help him with things he's needed for a long time.'

Miren wondered how she could trade herself for things that she would have gladly supplied. If Alaia needed help or food, all she had

160

to do was ask. Miguel would cut and stack firewood for her. Her father and mother would help. She didn't have to resort to this.

'Miren, it's not just Zubiri. There are a few others, too, and I'm not going to tell you who they are, because they expect me to keep this private. Some of them, in fact, don't want to believe that I know who they are.'

'You have *many* business partners?'

'Miren, I know what I'm doing. I don't have to make excuses, but I will remind you that I was in that convent for eighteen years. I grew up with dozens of nuns.'

Miren mumbled something beneath her breath that Alaia could not hear.

'Miren . . . I'm a big girl. I do it because I want to. If you have worries about me, thank you, but save them.'

Miren was new to intimacy herself and was certain that she was more naive than prudish. Yes, if Alaia cared to know, she enjoyed the contact, too, so much so that she thought about it much of the day when Miguel worked. But that was different.

'Even with an old man?' Miren asked. 'Do you enjoy that?'

'It's still closeness,' Alaia explained. 'It meets a need for him, and I can promise you, as much as you might not believe it, considering the love you have with Miguel, it helps me, too.'

'Do you do this with anybody?'

'I don't ask questions because I don't want them asking questions of me either,' Alaia said. 'I know who they are. I hear them in the market; I can recognize most of them, although they like to think that I can't. If I know it's a married man who shows up at the door, I act as if he is here to buy soap and tell him that I only sell it at the market on Mondays. But I don't sit here judging them, either. I don't have room for that.'

Miren was flushed; the smells, the stream muttering, the unsettling realization that her best friend was . . . what? What do you even call it?

'I hope I didn't scare him off for good,' Miren said. 'I'd hate to be responsible for the failing of your business. You might have to work to get more good customers.'

'I think he'll come back,' Alaia speculated. 'I just have to start remembering to bolt the door when I have a guest. I think that will provide enough security for him. I would ask that when you see Mr Zubiri in town you try not to point at him. I don't want any hints of anything to get back over those convent walls.'

Miren remembered Alaia's inability to have children, which sated some of the practical elements of her curiosity. How does word of mouth spread if she's scrupulously confidential? How does she avoid more than one arriving at a time? Does she have a schedule? Does she sell them soap afterward? She struggled to turn aside her curiosity, and she remembered her uncle Xabier's words once when she asked him to explain the shaky character of someone in town.

'Well, we are here to witness, not to judge,' Miren said to Alaia, tentatively echoing Xabier.

'Good girl,' Alaia said. 'I don't expect you to understand, I just hope you would trust me.'

'I have to tell you, Alaia . . . I just bore witness to images I may never be rid of.'

'What . . . not a handsome vision?'

Miren didn't say it – she felt too hurt to try to be clever – but she believed it was the first time she envied Alaia's absence of sight.

The priest slid back the panel on the grated port that provided the confessor plausible anonymity.

'Welcome, my child,' he said, feeling a bit ridiculous greeting a man in his early forties that way. But it was protocol.

'Forgive me, Father, for I have sinned,' a voice pronounced in the customary low and serious tones the situation demanded. 'It has been a week since the last time I got drunk with my priest.'

'That will cost you ten Our Fathers and another bottle for the priest. But for our new president, the penance will be waived.'

At times, if Xabier could not be found in the rectory when he sought his private counsel, Aguirre would slip into a confessional and talk to his unofficial adviser. That position of confidence had become more important in recent months. In a move to assure their assistance in the fight against the rebels, the embattled Republican government had granted nationhood to the Basques. As expected, Aguirre was named president, and he swore his oath of office in Guernica in an intentionally understated ceremony. No one saw benefit in announcing the event to prospective Francoist assassins, who would not have been pleased with his message that day.

'Humble before God, standing on Basque soil, in remembrance of Basque ancestors, under the tree of Guernica, I swear faithfully to fulfil my commission,' Aguirre said before presenting his statement on the war.

'We stand against this rebel movement, which is subversive of the legitimate authority and hostile to public will, because we are forced to by our profoundly Christian principles,' he said. 'We believe Christ does not preach the bayonet, the bomb, or the high explosive. Until Fascism is defeated, Basque nationalism will remain at its post.'

In a time when informants and spies and political opponents might shadow someone in Aguirre's position, the meetings with Father Xabier in a back confessional, half obscured by a concrete column, offered welcomed privacy.

'Bad news,' Aguirre announced softly.

'Has there been any other kind?'

'Workers and farmers were trying to defend Badajoz against Franco's rebels, and doing a surprisingly good job of it,' Aguirre said. 'But the African troops fighting with the rebels were so upset by the resistance that they drove them all into the bull ring, and machine-gunned every one of them.'

'Damn them,' Xabier said, forgetting his location.

Aguirre paused. 'Four thousand dead.'

'Dear God. In the name of the Church, of course,' Xabier added sarcastically.

'Of course. Pious Franco.'

Hard-heeled footsteps neared and paused. Aguirre and the priest sat silently.

The footsteps moved on, and Xabier now whispered so close to the grating that he could smell the tobacco on Aguirre's breath. 'It's not a matter of piety. The Church is a broker of power, so he's waving the banner of Catholicism. I'm not surprised he's trying to exploit it; I'm surprised the Church is falling for it.'

'Does the Vatican really understand what he's doing here?'

'That's the war I'm fighting: the Roman front,' Xabier said. 'The bishops of Vitoria and Pamplona broadcast a letter to condemn Basque Catholics who supported our cause, but, thankfully, the vicar-general rejected it. So we're again facing a split that could turn nasty.'

'Have you said anything to them, to the bishops?' Aguirre asked.

'All I am is an assistant parish priest; the prelates aren't going to tip their mitres just because I ask them to.'

'Would that lead to trouble for you from above?'

'Do you mean the Vatican or God?'

Aguirre laughed more loudly than he should have. They hushed and listened for footsteps.

Miren couldn't warn Miguel or alert her father, fearing both would revolt and physically restrain her. They would never understand the problems she faced, the trouble that was being caused, and how much pain she'd endured. She was certain that this was one crucial decision she had to make on her own and live with the consequences. She had no choice; she had to cut her hair.

It dangled into problem areas when she leaned over to change Catalina. And whenever the baby came up onto her shoulders to be patted to sleep, she would grab tiny fistfuls and attempt to pull herself up by it. The pain jolted Miren to the roots. Besides, to waste time in vain pursuits like maintaining it was inexcusable. Mariangeles understood and was surprised it had taken Miren this long to reach the decision. She offered to cut it.

'You're married, you have a good and understanding husband,'

Mariangeles reminded her when Miren grew skittish at the sight of the shears. 'You will be as beautiful to him with short hair. He might feel as if it's a new wife for a while.'

'He'd better not,' Miren objected. 'I just wonder if I should have asked him about it first.'

'Too late now,' Mariangeles said, snipping off a foot and a half of plait in one clean cut.

'There you go . . . feel like you've lost weight?' she asked.

'And taller,' Miren said as she retrieved the hair and moved to discard it.

'Wait, I've got an idea for that.' Mariangeles took another small ribbon and tied the severed end so that the plait was secure on both ends and would not unravel. She then clipped and straightened the edges of the remaining mane and shaped it around her daughter's face. Miren looked the part of a mature and lovely young matron.

When Miguel came down from the hills that evening, Miren rushed to him, lifting the ends of her hair to the side of her head in a quick display. She twirled so the hair flew, stopped to face him again, and unleashed her most winning smile.

'I like it,' Miguel said. 'I liked it long. I like it short. I like it.'

'I was afraid you'd be angry,' Miren said, relieved. 'I thought you might be done with me until it grew back.'

'It's different now,' Miguel said. 'We were young and now we're parents. Things are different. It looks wonderful. Even better. Easier to take care of.'

She feared her father would be less understanding. When Miren was young and her hair was too long and full for her little arms to manage, she would lie on the kitchen table with her head over the edge so that her hair hung nearly to the floor. Justo would sit in the chair, brush out the tangles, and plait the mass, all the while kidding her that he felt as if he were currying a picador's mount. Even in her teens, she would enter the main room in her sleeping gown and deliver the brush and hair-tie to her father: 'Papa, would you do my hair?' He never passed up the opportunity.

When she and Miguel walked to Errotabarri that night, Catalina asleep in the stern of her pram, Miren knew she would have a critical audience.

'*Jinko*, girl! What have you done?' Justo shouted on her arrival.

'Papa, Catalina kept pulling my hair out and it hurt and I had to cut it.'

'It was beautiful; I loved your hair,' Justo said, immediately nostalgic. 'Did you have to?'

'I did, Papa, but I have a present that I hope will make you happy and help you forgive me.'

Miren offered her father a small rectangular box that Miguel had made for her to hold her few chains and earrings. It was now topped by a ribbon and a bow. Justo opened it as if it was Christmas and started laughing.

'Thank you,' he said. 'This is perfect.'

He took from the box the lengthy plait of her hair.

'Thank you for saving this for me,' he said. 'I'm touched. I'm surprised Miguel would surrender this.'

'I have the rest of the hair, the head beneath it, and the woman who grew it all,' Miguel said. 'This part belongs with you. From what I hear, you've invested time in cultivating its growth.'

Justo retrieved a hammer and a nail and attached the plait to the mantelpiece. 'I'll keep it in a place of honour,' he said.

CHAPTER 14

Lieutenant Colonel Wolfram von Richthofen of the Luftwaffe discovered that even those Spaniards with a passion for revolution treated war as if it was something to be played at between a leisurely breakfast and a lengthy siesta. They were occasionally fierce but chronically inefficient. They were capable of killing but not of planning. They understood rage but not urgency.

He had not given up the diplomatic service in Rome to become allied with a nation of bumbling procrastinators who had old-world notions of warfare. Besides, they constantly wanted to kiss him on the cheek and ask of his relationship to the famed 'Baron Rojo', as if he hadn't heard enough of that.

Von Richthofen had no interest in Spain's internal conflicts, except to the extent that Franco's invitation to participate created an opportunity, a low-risk testing ground. As always, he would be a diligent officer regardless of the circumstances or the nature of the allies. Still, he had made himself comfortable upon arrival. It could be reconciled as yet another means of reinforcing his status among his men. His suite on the top floor of the Fronton Hotel near the airfield in Vitoria was symbolic of his rank.

The name of his command was ridiculous, he thought, but his airmen liked the sound of 'Condor Legion', and they loved the new, experimental bombers at the airfields in Vitoria and Burgos. His men took particular pride in the legion's emblem near the nose of their planes, comprised of a graphic condor, whose body was a blood-red bomb with swept-back white wings, emblazoned on a death-black circle. They did not seem to be bothered by the reality that condors were scavengers who lived off carrion.

Another comfort for von Richthofen had been shipped to Spain by the Führer himself: a new Mercedes-Benz roadster. When duties called for him to meet staff in Burgos, von Richthofen drove it like a fighter, flying low and fast across the winding roads, covering the seventy-five miles in less than an hour.

He rose before dawn each day, examined the bedside photo of his wife, and performed a series of callisthenics: press-ups, stretches, running in place. His commander, Göring, was detestably porcine, which further spurred von Richthofen to maintain his condition. He was forty-one and fit as his youngest pilots. He was not merely an officer but a military weapon himself, and he understood that such things required daily maintenance to operate smoothly.

Miren agonized for more than a week, weighing whether she should tell Miguel her discovery about Alaia and whether a lack of disclosure amounted to a betrayal in a marriage. She decided to test him, to dance around the subject delicately as they slipped into bed.

'When I took the trout to Alaia's—'

'Was she alone or with a guest?' Miguel interjected.

Miren paused for several breaths, trying to calm her heartbeat.

'With a guest?' she asked.

'Maybe she wasn't alone; maybe somebody else was there helping her with something, or giving her something she needed.'

'You know, don't you?'

'Yes.'

'How?'

'Whispers in town.'

'What did you say?'

'I told the man I would hear no more, from him or anybody else.'

'Why didn't you tell me?'

'Because I didn't know if it was true, and I didn't want to pass it on if it was just evil gossip.'

'Well?'

Miguel took time with this, because he had struggled to sort through the implications.

'I love you; nothing will ever change that,' he said.

She squinted in fear of the next sentence.

'But this is a problem—'

'Miguel, she has so little in her life.'

'She has your friendship; I would think that's something to protect. She has a reputation, like anybody else. What she does affects you.'

Quiet.

'It's not about me, Miguel.'

'It is about you, and us, more than you think. It's about all of us.'

Quiet.

'So is it what people think and what they might say in town that bothers you, then?'

'My mother always told us that the most important thing we have is our name.'

'Miguel, I don't understand it; I'm more shocked than you are,' Miren said, reaching to him, petting his nearer arm. 'I don't like it either. I was upset, too. I don't know why. I know she had nobody for so many years that she is trying to find some closeness.'

'Closeness you can get from one man,' Miguel said, for the first time raising his voice. 'You get other things from many men.'

She took her hand off his arm and rolled to face the wall.

'I've thought about this,' Miguel continued. 'I thought about just demanding that you not see her. But I hoped you would make that decision on your own. I know I'm going to keep my distance. I don't think she should come here.'

He could feel the bed shake from Miren's crying.

'*Kuttuna*, if this was some other woman, I would never say a word,' he said, rolling to touch her back. She jerked away. 'If it were some other blind woman, I might even admire her in some way. It's not. It's your best friend; it's the girl – woman – you spend your time with. Yes, it *is* about how it looks. And it's about Catalina. Yes, it's about me, too. I'm angry that I have to talk like this to you when it's something that should have nothing to do with us. My job is to protect you and Catalina. And I'm going to do it.'

'Are you saying I have to choose?'

'I'm not saying that.'

She stayed silent as she played that comment back in her mind. Did he stress the word 'not' or the word 'saying'? Did he mean that he was not going to force the matter with her? Or did he mean that he expected her to stop seeing Alaia without his having to demand it?

Miguel turned and stared at the wall in the opposite direction. He was angry at Alaia, he was angry at Miren. And he was angry at himself, because he knew he could never tell her that it wasn't coincidental that he sent her to Alaia's that evening with a fish in her hands.

'El Director,' Picasso said to the gathering at a back table in a Left Bank cafe. 'You may call me El Director.' They laughed, but Picasso gave no hint of self-mockery.

He had lived in Paris for more than thirty years but never sought French citizenship. Spain was his home, in his mind and his art. But nothing had caused him to adopt a side in the country's chaos, even when Franco rose in revolt against the Republic, until a simple letter pulled him into Spain's complex politics. The position offered him was titular and meaningless – Director of the Museo del Prado – but of considerable significance emotionally. He couldn't calculate how many hours he had spent memorizing the masterpieces of Goya and Velázquez and El Greco while studying at the Prado as a teenager.

He accepted the directorship, which did not require him to return to Spain. It became an unexpectedly functional role within two months when Falange rebels encircled Madrid. Shells from Heinkel bombers and artillery struck and damaged the museum. Hand-to-hand combat left bodies beneath the plane trees lining Paseo del Prado in front of the museum. The scenes of devastation on the street were hardly less disturbing than the Bosch triptych *The Garden of Earthly Delights*, which Picasso had devoured for hours there as a student.

The museum was closed to the public as madrileños dealt with more pressing matters than the appreciation of art. The Prado staff removed the paintings from the upper floors and stacked the pieces in rooms encased by sandbags. In fierce fighting, loyalist troops managed to fend off the assault on Madrid while members of the government fled for Valencia. When Picasso heard this, he demanded that the masterpieces of the Prado be evacuated. From Paris, he organized the transfer of hundreds of paintings to Valencia.

El Director discovered that he was no longer a non-political observer of events in Spain. Rebels slaughtered countrymen and threatened masterpieces. This moved Picasso as both an artist and a Spaniard, and it made him susceptible to an invitation that soon arrived. He was asked to provide art for the Spanish Pavilion at the World's Fair to open in Paris the following summer. If he would complete a mural, it would be used as the pavilion's signature piece.

Picasso had never painted anything of that size, considered the notion garish, and did not appreciate the concept of an artist's being commissioned in such a manner. As much as he now supported the Republican cause and despised the way Franco was burying his sword in the neck of Spain, he feared that he would be expected to produce something that was more a political statement than a work of art. Art sprang from the gut, not from assignment, he said.

But there was much to consider. In response to the invitation, El Director promised only that he would give the matter thought, as it would do no harm to wait and see if a suitable subject arose.

Miren struggled to recognize some of the townspeople she'd known all her life. Going hungry had caused them to shrink from the inside, leaving them wearing their skin like old clothes that no longer fitted. The crowd in the ration queue was mostly women, as few men had the patience to pass the numbing hours there, and most who did were widowers or half of elderly couples who needed all four shaky hands to transport the few precious packages of food.

Talk was limited to those near to each other in the queue, and the tone was low. Get this many people together two years ago and there would have been a dance, Miren thought. Now they scarcely speak. Still, she smiled and greeted everyone she saw, trying to enquire about their families and businesses. But she knew she could no longer say, 'Good to see you, you're looking well.' They weren't looking well. Or 'Your chorizos are wonderful this year.' There were no chorizos. But smiling cost nothing and carried no demands.

Although most had seen Catalina in town many times, Miren still thought it worthwhile to introduce her, believing that a few moments with a cheerful little one could benefit everyone. Cat could pull herself up and stand at the edge of her pram, greeting all who neared with an extended arm. It drew people to her. 'I'd like my daughter to meet you,' Miren would say. Not 'I want you to see my daughter.' She made it sound as if seeing them was a privilege her daughter would remember until she was grown. It was a small distinction, but Miren felt it brought a few words of respect to days now filled with indignities.

Depending on stores, the ration card allowed the purchase of small sacks of chickpeas and rice, a little sugar, perhaps a hundred grams of bread, and either a bottle of olive oil or tomato sauce.

Two women in the queue in front of Miren were mothers of girls who had danced in her group. 'It is not as bad here as it is in Bilbao,' one said to Miren. 'We still can get things from the farms and the Monday markets. In Bilbao, with all the refugees and no farms around, there's nothing but what you can get from queuing.'

'Yes, we're lucky,' Miren said.

The women would not go that far.

After a few moments of quiet, Miren heard Catalina speak a sentence in her own language and pull herself up.

'What's her name?' a girl asked, having approached the pram.

172

'Hello . . . this is Catalina.'

The girl, perhaps eight, in a long cotton skirt and faded white scarf, stepped slowly towards Catalina, careful not to make it seem as if she was trying to push forward in the queue.

'What happened to her ear?'

Miren told her the story.

'Mine were pierced when I was a baby, too,' the girl said, turning an ear up towards Miren for inspection.

'Mine too,' Miren said, leaning over in a similar display.

The girl's mother was home with 'the babies', she explained. 'I'm big enough to get the rations now.'

She smiled at Miren and went back to a clap-hands game with Catalina, singing a soft chorus that caused the little one to laugh and rock the sturdy pram. It made the time pass, and Catalina's giggling lightened the solemn trudge forward.

Miren brought a bag to hold the packages and bottles, which she arranged in the bow of Catalina's pram after handing over her ration card. The girl behind her collected her bread, beans, and rice, holding them up with the hem of her skirt. But when she was handed the slippery bottle of olive oil, it shot through her hand and crashed on the stones.

As she screamed, the wrapped sacks of rice and beans fell from her skirt, along with the bread, until everything was scattered around the broken bottle. Miren turned at the sound of the glass breaking and picked up the other foods to keep them from being wrecked in the oil spill.

'My mother . . . ' the girl cried to Miren. 'My mother.'

'It's all right,' Miren said softly. 'Here, we'll take care of this.'

'My mother . . . the oil . . . ' she grieved.

Miren emptied her rations into the pram from the bag she'd brought to hold them. She gave it to the girl to carry what was left of her packages.

Calmer, slightly, the girl still shook against flowing tears and a running nose.

'Thank you,' she said. 'My mother . . .'

'Be careful now,' Miren told her, pushing the pram towards home.

As she put the bags of rice and beans into the bag, the girl saw a corked bottle of olive oil inside.

'Wait!' she yelled after Miren, who waved back and continued.

Miren had worried about the strain with Miguel for the past week, since their talk of Alaia. Now she wondered how he'd react when she told him that she had dropped their olive oil for the week on the stones of the square.

Although effective, the rebel blockade of the major Biscayan ports could not completely choke off the shuttling of guns and food into Spain and the evacuation of refugees to France. Across the border in St-Jean-de-Luz, Dodo Navarro cultivated sympathetic contacts to donate grain, potatoes, and other food supplies, while the two *patroiak* had no trouble finding people eager to get out of Spain ahead of the Fascist army. José María Navarro and Josepe Ansotegui would off-load the goods in Lekeitio at times, or challenge the rebel blockade and sail up the Nervión River to the edge of Bilbao, where the influx of refugees had made the problem of starvation among the locals a contagion.

For a time, rebel gunboats rarely stopped to inspect the smaller fishing boats from the Lekeitio fleet. But they were more insistent now as the smugglers' inbound cargo changed from food to arms and ammunition.

Josepe Ansotegui devised an effective means of veiling the contraband. The boats would arrive at barren coves near St-Jean-de-Luz or other nearby ports, where Dodo and his friends would load the bags of potatoes or grain, or boxes of rifles and ammunition, into the hold. As they fished their way back across the Bay of Biscay towards the blockade, Josepe and José María and their crews topped off the holds with anchovies or whatever happened to be filling their nets.

A few nets of anchovies or sardines served as an effective

disincentive to most inspectors who might stop their boats. A number of times the *Egun On* and the *Zaldun* were boarded for inspection, but neither the rebel navy nor their Guardia Civil allies would wade down into the hold to check beneath the day's catch.

If the special cargo of the day was human, the passengers were told to hold their noses and burrow under the fish. Many responded with a grunt of disgust, but when the boat was stopped by a rebel gunboat, they had no problem sliding under the reeking fish.

One guard, automatic weapon slung across his chest, ordered Josepe to open the hold. He peered down the hatch as Josepe and José María looked at each other, silently praying that the three refugees hidden there would be able to hold their breath and not move beneath the weight of the sardines.

The guard inhaled meekly, shuddered, and motioned for Josepe to shut the hatch.

'Stupid Baskos,' he said, walking towards his boat, which was lashed alongside them.

'Yes, we are just fishermen,' Josepe said.

'Ugly, too,' José María added.

'And we smell of fish,' Josepe continued as the guard stepped over the side.

'Poor us,' José María lamented.

CHAPTER 15

Justo entered his daughter's house as he entered most rooms, with an exclamation. In this case, it was a rumbling greeting to his grand-daughter on her first birthday.

'Cat-a-leeen-aaaa!'

Aboard her hobby-ram, she kicked and scooted in his direction so she could be picked up and pulled tight to his scratchy face. Her great joy was pulling the beret from his head and flinging it to the ground, and then grabbing great handfuls of his moustache and pulling it in all directions as her *aitxitxia* responded with groans of pain.

For her birthday, Miguel had made a little rocking chair and Miren had sewn red gingham pads for the back and seat. Miren had stashed sugar aside for weeks to bake a cake.

'Look what your *amuma* made for you,' Justo said, holding up a bag for Catalina to open. She pulled out the small white dress, looked briefly, tossed it in the air, and went back to work on her *aitxitxia's* moustache.

'Catalina . . . ' Miren scolded, picking up the dress, which Mariangeles had crocheted. 'It's beautiful, she'll love it.'

'Well, we have arranged an occasion when she can wear it soon,' Mariangeles said. 'Justo has talked to Arriola at the photo shop and he is going to take a family portrait of the three of you for her birthday. We'll both get copies.'

Miguel wore his black wedding suit; Miren could still fit in a black-and-white dress she'd made for herself before she was married. It was tighter in places since she'd had Catalina but still attractive. Catalina was certain she was the most special little girl, standing, wobbly, next to her mother, holding out the hem of her skirt to her sides, and then pulling it up over her head with a squeal.

'No, Cat,' Miren corrected her, pulling the skirt down.

'What do we do about the, er . . . ?' Miguel asked Miren, touching his right ear slightly.

Miren brushed Catalina's hair from a left parting over to the right, but she did not have nearly enough to cover it.

'A hat?' Miguel asked.

'Then we couldn't see her face. It's really not very big. It's such a small ear.'

When Miguel made whispered mention to Arriola of Catalina's ear notch, he nodded. This would not be a problem. He positioned Miren in a dark wooden high-backed chair, with Catalina sitting on her lap, facing to her right, towards Miguel, who was standing beside the chair.

'Watch the birdie,' Arriola said. Catalina turned her head slightly towards the camera as the flash went off, perfectly catching her face at a three-quarter angle, with the light reflecting off the tiny silver *lauburu* in her left ear.

Picasso hurled brushes and kicked newly stretched canvases and easels, storming across his studio. Franco's rebels had taken Málaga, where he was born, and after the bombing and artillery destroyed the buildings, they machine-gunned civilians. Enough. He announced to friends that he would create a project to sell in support of relief for the Republican cause.

The Dream and Lie of Franco, in essence a comic book, portrayed the Fascist leader as a buffoon, as a woman, and as a centaur being eviscerated by a bull. At times, he was drawn wearing a bishop's mitre, kneeling before the image of money.

To accompany the cartoon plates, Picasso spewed written images in a poem filled with such anger that it had no room for punctuation or syntax until he reached an artistic rhythm.

'. . . cries of children cries of women cries of birds cries of flowers cries of timbers . . .'

No, the artist could not return to Spain to fight. But he could raise money with his art. And he could let the world hear his rage.

Juan Legarreta collected the carpenters Teodoro Mendiola and Miguel Navarro and took them to the Taberna Vasca, near the marketplace, for a few glasses of Izarra, the liqueur that tasted of mint and left a person's lips tingling. Legarreta, chief of the volunteer fire department, needed help. The Germans had bombed Durango and the Guernica town council had charged him with the task of constructing shelters, *refugios*, where citizens could retreat in case of a similar attack.

Mendiola and Miguel had heard of the attack on munitions plants in Durango, but they knew nothing about the specific damage created by high explosives and had no clue how carpenters would go about constructing shelters to withstand such extreme demands. Besides, both had commissioned projects in the works, the pay from which might allow them to continue feeding their families.

'I know,' Legarreta nodded in sympathy. 'I'm not getting paid either. But some of the council think we need to build these things just in case. Some are certain that we have no cause to worry. Others are convinced that if we build shelters it'll just create a panic in the town.'

'Do they know something we don't know about the danger here?' Mendiola asked.

'I don't think they know much of anything,' Legarreta said, removing his beret and raking his fingers through his hair. 'You get a couple of old Carlists and some Republicans and mix them with some Monarchists and reds and sprinkle in a few would-be Fascists and an Anarchist or two, and what comes out of the room is guaranteed to make no sense. But it's better to have some protection than none, and if it gets some people thinking about potential danger, maybe that's not bad. I just don't see anything here they'd want to bomb.'

Mendiola and Miguel nodded. Even though it meant sacrifice, they were both committed to helping.

'And, Juan,' Mendiola pressed, 'do you have any advice on how we should tell our wives that we've been diverted to a project we really don't know how to build to protect against an attack that probably won't come, and for which we will receive no pay?'

Miguel had not considered the problem of explaining such things to a wife. He laughed at the response he imagined receiving from Miren. 'As soon as I tell Miren what we are doing, she'll insist on coming down to start sewing curtains and putting down rugs, promising to round up all her friends to make these the cosiest bomb shelters in all the Pays Basque.'

Legarreta and Mendiola had known her for many years and could imagine exactly those comments.

'You know, it might be easier to get her to recruit the construction crews,' Mendiola said.

Legarreta took them to the town hall and several of the more stoutly constructed residences, and he suggested reinforcing the basements with additional supports. Miguel quickly envisioned bolstering the connection of each column to the beams with knees akin to those used to attach ships' frames to the decks, and strapping joints with metal bands. Another freestanding shelter was to be constructed on Calle Santa María, between the town hall and the church, with the plan calling for a series of oak supports to uphold beams covered by layers of sandbags.

'I have no idea what it would take to protect people from a bomb; I just hope this is one building project that never gets tested,' Mendiola said.

'It won't,' Legarreta said, adding a chuckle as reassurance. Still, he harboured two deep concerns that he did not share. The council's

179

notion of what constituted a good shelter was a tightly enclosed area that would prevent penetration of bullets and bomb fragments. But that meant that there was little flow of air to these basement rooms. His second worry was more direct: he had ten lightly trained men in his volunteer fire department and one small fire engine, a serious issue in a town constructed mostly of wood.

Father Xabier understood why he'd been sent to Guernica when he came upon the refugees, belongings tied in ratty bundles, clustered in a shapeless mass in the courtyard in front of the train station. He watched ambulances arriving in staggered succession to disgorge their cargoes of broken soldiers at the temporary military hospital established at the Carmelite convent near the river.

When Xabier left Bilbao, the town was swollen with the wave of refugees that gets pushed out in front of an invading army. But the inflow of homeless to Guernica evoked a far more ominous sensation. Bilbao was defended to some extent; this was an unprotected valley flooded with human runoff.

When he arrived, he heard of break-ins and the rumour that retreating soldiers had breached the cloister and taken up positions in the Santa Clara convent on the hill. He looked at the rain clouds smudging the sky before twilight and saw no birds. Atop the Carmelite convent, movement caught his attention. Two dark, spectral figures revolved in an agonizingly slow dance. As he walked closer through the crowded street, he could distinguish the black robes and white wimples; they were nuns on the roof, with upraised binoculars, scanning the skies for intruders.

President Aguirre had tracked troop movements of the Republican forces, mostly Basques in this region, in the three weeks since the bombing of Durango. He knew his forces had battled well but been overpowered on successive fronts. They had withdrawn towards the protection of Bilbao, which required many of them to filter back through Guernica. Another battle line had to be established, to forestall rebel troops and earn time for the continuous attempts to strengthen the 'Iron Belt' fortifications of Bilbao.

Late in the week, Aguirre had visited Father Xabier's confessional. Xabier knew Aguirre had entered his box before he heard his voice; through the grating, he could smell him. He had always been a heavy smoker, but now the disquieted Aguirre was lighting one cigarette with the last embers of its predecessor and carried in his clothing a heavy film of tobacco.

'Are you smoking in the confessional?' Xabier asked.

'Forgive me, Father, for I have smoked.'

'Put it out; it's blasphemous.'

'I have already confessed to it; absolve me and let's move on,' Aguirre said.

They crossed themselves simultaneously.

'You'll never believe this . . .' Aguirre started, his voice more tense than the priest had ever heard. 'Our engineer, the great Captain Alejandro Goicoechea—'

'The designer of the Iron Belt?'

'Yes, that one,' Aguirre said. 'He's defected. To the rebels . . . took all the blueprints with him. Every detail. Every place where the ditches are narrow and the fence is unprotected.'

'God help us,' was all that Xabier could think to say. 'What now?'

'I need you to go home,' Aguirre said. 'I need you to arrange to speak at Mass, to warn them about what's going on, to tell them everything you can about the danger.'

'Me? Why not you?'

'They know you and they trust you. You're one of them. I'm sending others, advisers and counsellors, to towns in all directions.'

Xabier had no need to weigh the factors; he knew it was the right approach. Aguirre, kneeling in the confessional, detailed the grim threats constricting around them.

'Now do you see why I need you to tell them?'

Xabier, sensing a challenge greater than any he had imagined for himself as a student, sent word to the priest at Santa María in Guernica and began shaping his warnings.

He arrived at Errotabarri for dinner on Saturday evening, a starchy marriage of bread and chickpea soup. He waved off Mariangeles's apologies. His brother and his wife were gaunt.

'I want to warn you about what I'm going to have to say at Mass in the morning,' he said. 'It is going to shock people, but it's for their benefit. They need to know what might happen if things keep going as they are.'

'Won't the rebels go straight to Bilbao?' Mariangeles asked. 'There can't be anything in Guernica they could want.'

'Nobody knows,' Xabier answered between bites. 'Franco's troops are bloodthirsty for Basques, and the Germans are unpredictable. For Franco, there is more to this. Every one of us he can be rid of now will be one fewer to worry about when he's running Spain.'

'If our few troops retreat to Bilbao, then the rebels would just be able to walk in with no need to hurt anybody; isn't that a possibility?' Mariangeles asked, her voice inflecting upward.

'Anything is possible,' Xabier said. 'That could happen, or many could be hurt. There're no rules to this.'

Justo held a palm up towards Xabier; he had a point to make.

'They know the history of the town. They know what it means to us; they know it's the heart of our country. If they attack Guernica it would be a sacrilege – it would have the opposite effect of what they want.'

Xabier focused on Justo's face for a moment.

'Exactly,' Xabier said. 'They know the importance of this town.'

When the bells of Santa María made their call to mass, Xabier watched the pews fill with the people he'd known since he was a boy. Not a seat was empty, yet there was little sound beyond a few whispered greetings and pardons for jostling as parishioners slipped into their usual seats. When Xabier stepped to the altar, murmurs of recognition rippled in a wave from the front to the back. 'What could bring him back from Bilbao?' 'Did you know that Father Xabier was going to preach today?' 'He looks thin, don't you think?'

All rose.

'A reading from Psalm Thirty,' he said, opening his Bible at the purple cord that marked his page. ' "I praise you, Lord, for you raised me up and did not let my enemies rejoice over me." '

Solemnly, more slowly, he repeated the passage, stressing 'and did not let my enemies rejoice over me.'

He gestured for all to sit.

'Most of you know me and know my family,' Xabier said. 'And I hope that you will trust that I'm not here to frighten you into greater piety. President Aguirre himself asked me to come and speak to you. He wanted me to tell you that we are all facing danger as the war comes nearer. It is near enough that some of us should not even be here at Mass today. Some of us should be in the mountains and the fields fighting a threatening enemy. We should be preparing to protect our families, our loved ones, our property, our homeland.'

Parishioners stared forward.

'Men and women and children are being slaughtered by Nationalist rebels all over Spain,' Xabier continued. 'We have failed you by not telling you how dangerous this is. The rebels are killing in the name of God. And the Church, by its silence, would appear to be condoning this evil. I cannot be silent.'

Xabier scanned the front pews, trying to gauge the impact of his words. He wished to shock them into alertness but not scare them to the point that they could no longer absorb the message.

'I know a priest should stand here and tell you how wrong it is to take a life, that it is a mortal sin. But it is not a mortal sin to give your life in the protection of all that is important or for a cause that is just. To protect your family with your life is not a sin.'

A woman near the front gasped. The priest, who grew up worshipping in this church, who had known and provided clerical counsel to many in the town, had committed a stunning heresy.

'It is difficult to understand the savagery of this war,' he continued. 'I remind you of the trials of young St Agnes, who was violated and murdered. You must not let that happen to your children or your wives; defend all that is precious to you, even if it means giving your life or taking a life.'

Some sobbed openly now.

'I tell you this story only because you need to know the truth,' he said. 'There has been too little truth told. It is not a story of some ancient biblical atrocity. President Aguirre showed me a report of what happened recently to the parish priest at Eunari. The Moorish troops of the rebels arrived as he was reciting Mass.'

Xabier swallowed against his own emotions.

'They cut off his nose . . . and skewered it to his tongue; they sliced the ears from his head and left him to die, hanging from the bell tower. These troops, these murderers and defilers, are fighting for Franco only several valleys to the south. Your lives, your family, your country may depend on you leaving this place or fighting to defend it.'

Planning attacks involved mundane decisions regarding personnel, matériel, bomb loads, targets, and timing. But Wolfram von Richthofen, from warrior stock and a noble caste, was more than an accountant of ordnance, more than a stationmaster eyeing his watch to be certain his operation ran on schedule. Von Richthofen recognized a vehicle for virtuosity and creativity. Attacks were about planning, yes, but also about orchestration. Anyone can point an index finger to a crossroads on a map. But to counterplay the timpani bass of heavy explosives with the pizzicato of fighter guns is the province of a maestro.

Reconnaissance photos revealed Republican troops in retreat near the small town of Markina, with no anti-aircraft weapons to offer resistance. Von Richthofen ordered bomber squadrons to attack in twenty-minute waves, hyphenated with fighter assaults. After the initial bombs forced troops to flee on the open roads, the waiting fighters gunned them down there, and those who sought protection from the fighters under cover were then convenient targets for the next wave of bombers.

Casualty figures among the Republican loyalists, comprised mostly of Basque soldiers, were impossible to estimate as so many were scattered in clusters along the roadsides and in the hills. Some were blown apart by the five-hundred-pound bombs; others became torches when struck by the phosphorus incendiaries that flared pink when they burned flesh. Many more were gunned down by the fighter planes.

Von Richthofen mentally superimposed the reports from his pilots onto the map of Biscaya in front of him. The map sprang into three-dimensional relief as he visualized tiny columns of men in retreat, following the paths of least resistance, flowing like running water in predictable tributaries, collecting at a low point or being funnelled through a topographic sluice. The intersection of paths that caused Guernica to sprout into a town centuries earlier made it a collection basin for troops. If soldiers fled from the south or east towards the protection of what was left of Bilbao's Iron Belt, they would coagulate behind the one narrow passage, Guernica's Renteria Bridge over the slender Oka River.

'Do any of you know anything about Guernica?' he asked his countrymen.

All shook their heads.

Around the blue dot on the map that symbolized the historic village of Guernica, Lieutenant Colonel Wolfram von Richthofen drew a precise circle in yellow ink, marking the Condor Legion's next target.

The dancing was Miren's idea; she wanted to spend an evening as if there were no war, no Franco, no danger a few mountain passes away. Lights were strung in the trees at the Plaza Las Escuelas. The music echoed other times; the *txistu* and tambourine were lively, with a fiddle and accordion added. At times, Mendiola stepped in with the cross-cut saw that he made to hum eerily when he stroked it with a fiddle bow. Miren could never hear the music and stay seated, so she and Miguel danced several waltzes as friends watched over Catalina in her pram.

This was part of their agreement. After hearing Father Xabier's sermon, Miguel insisted that Miren and Catalina leave for Bilbao, which was being lightly bombed but was fortified and sure to be the safest long-term stronghold. Xabier made arrangements. She objected; she felt her place was with her husband, and she believed a family should not be splintered. Miguel convinced her that it would be best for them all, but Catalina particularly. He would stay and watch over their home, then join them in Bilbao if the Nationalist rebels arrived.

After leaving home that evening, the young couple felt awkward being out. They had seen the refugees and the agitated soldiers retreat into town, and to dance in their presence seemed insensitive. They agreed their stay would be brief. But the music overcame those thoughts, and the dancing caused them both to slip into a welcome fugue that softened all else.

Reasonably adept now, Miguel loved dancing with her, feeling a part of something special. He revelled in the memory of her shock at his dancing at their wedding. He would never be a confident dancer, but he could at least remain vertical. He felt the rhythm of the music and managed to connect it to his movements. He could not look at his wife's feet or the movement of her hips because it would disrupt his own tentative sense of timing. He focused on her face and on those eyes.

'Just one more,' Miguel said, taking Catalina from her pram. They held the little girl between them and they stepped slowly together.

'Papa is going to miss his little girl,' Miguel said, kissing Catalina on her cheek before tightly squeezing Miren. 'And his big girl.'

It was a slow waltz, with Mendiola's saw emitting weary sighs. Miren wept at the sound. This is twice in the past few weeks, Miguel realized, pulling her in even closer. She looked away and the lights became distorted stars, aligned in tree-shaped constellations. As they turned, all else revolved around their core; the confusion, disorder, hunger, war, and pain were somewhere else. Everything outside was blurred by her tears.

'It shouldn't be for long, *kuttuna*,' Miguel said, placing a kiss on her wet cheek. 'This will be over soon and we'll be back together.'

Miguel tried to place Catalina back in her pram, but she was sleepy and held on to her father's shirt. He kissed her again, and she relented. They walked home, arms around each other, amid the unsettling sight of desperate strangers in the town.

Miren would go to the market the following afternoon to lay in provisions for Miguel. He might be on his own awhile. She didn't want him to be alone and lonely and to be hungry as well. She knew how to stretch their money at the market and Miguel reluctantly agreed. On Tuesday morning his two girls would board the train for whatever safety they could find in Bilbao.

Wolfram von Richthofen settled into the cockpit of his roadster and piloted it south-west towards Burgos, using the hour of travel time to organize his thoughts. He would confer with the Nationalist military leaders over the next step towards Bilbao.

To the gathering of brass in Burgos, he outlined the plan for the Monday bombing of a town he knew to have no air defence and no military relevance other than his presumption that enemy forces might be knotted there behind a small bridge. Plans were now dependent on the weather reports from reconnaissance planes that would overfly Biscaya in the morning.

Von Richthofen wrote in his journal, 'Fear, which cannot be simulated in peaceful training of troops, is very important because it affects morale. Morale is more important in winning battles than weapons. Continuous, repeated, and concentrated air attacks have the most effect on the morale of the enemy.'

Downstairs, two pilots in the officers' lounge celebrated the day's sortie over Markina and unwound with doses of cognac.

'Heard where we're going tomorrow?'

'A place called Guernica.'

'Never heard of it.'

'Just another Spanish dump.'

PART 4
(26 April 1937)

CHAPTER 16

Miren slept without stirring, but Miguel hardly dozed, passing the heart of the night making plans while studying his wife's outline in the darkness. He feared there were still angles and shapes he had not yet memorized. He mentally sketched in the scenarios for the upcoming days and plotted the appropriate responses to each, with the protection of Miren and Catalina as the sole objective. He would take on any man or group of men who neared his home or threatened his family.

But he kept losing focus. (Her hair has more waves since it was cut, he thought, as if its weight had caused it to stretch and straighten, and it was now allowed to recoil and contract. Her plait used to rest across the pillow like a thick, dark cable. Now it is fuller and frames her face as she sleeps.)

If troops came to his home, he would fight – Nationalists, Germans, Italians, Moors, all of them, it didn't matter. (She breathes so easily she hardly makes a sound, and she's completely still except for her feet, which twitch at times, like a puppy running in its sleep.)

If forces approached before they left for Bilbao, he would take the girls into the mountains, having already scouted out caves and the thickest forests to protect them. But troops were said to be thirty miles away; even with steady advancement, they could not reach the outskirts of Guernica until the end of the week. (She always sleeps on her left side, facing Cat's crib, with both hands tucked up under her left cheek and her knees bent like a mitred right angle.)

Options covered, he concentrated on storing the images of Miren. She would be there only one more night. His throat tightened.

More than a year old, Catalina called for only one feed in the night; now, as she stirred in the predawn hours, Miguel retrieved her and took her to Miren.

'*Kuttuna*, she's ready,' he whispered, hoping to ease his wife into wakefulness. 'Miren . . .'

Without actually wakening, Miren moved her pillow behind her shoulders and sat up to create a basket with her arms to hold Catalina, who immediately went to work. She was a dainty diner; at times, when stopping to catch her breath, she would look up at her mother and smile in gratitude. Miren dozed, feeling the comfort of the milk release, the closeness of her daughter, and the relaxing sensation of Miguel rubbing the back of her neck in the dim night. She fell back into her peaceful sleep as soon as Catalina was full and taken away by Miguel. But as was often the case when Miguel took hold of her, Catalina began kicking and squirming, eager to play.

He placed her back in the crib while he went to stir the fire in the main room, where they could play without disturbing Miren.

'I shouldn't be doing this, you know,' he said directly into her face as she sat up on his leg. 'You'll think that it's time to play every night after feeding.'

'Ba-pa-ba-pa,' she replied.

'But you will be gone for a time and you won't remember this when we're back together.'

She offered no response except to reach towards his mouth and pull his upper lip towards his nose.

'Hey, you, ugh.' Prising her pincers off his mouth, Miguel held both her hands and gave her a pony ride. He was rewarded by a belch that would have made her grandfather Justo proud.

*

They agreed that Miguel would not work in the morning; he would walk into the hills in the afternoon once Miren and Catalina set off for the market. By evening, he'd have finished his logging and they would all meet at Errotabarri for dinner with Justo and Mariangeles before the Tuesday morning trip to Bilbao. They would settle into the temporary housing Father Xabier had arranged and wait for the future to sort itself out.

Still awake at dawn, Miguel left his sleeping wife and daughter in their beds and walked to the bakery on Calle Santa María in hopes of finding something other than grainy black bread for their breakfast. Strangers filled the streets, strangers who were hungry and upset, dirty and homeless.

At the bakery, where he saw nothing worth buying, he was told that there had been a break-in the night before, the first time they'd had such a problem. Some who sat in the bakery shopfront that morning, finding comfort there in their mutual uncertainty, told of hundreds of war-wounded who had been brought to the hospital at the Carmelite convent overnight. Men from the Loyola Battalion had been burned and disfigured by phosphorus bombs; others had lost limbs or bled to death before they could be treated by the few doctors available.

Surely, Miguel thought, these were tales from the alarmists, exaggerated like so many stories told in town. From more reliable mouths, he heard talk of cancelling the afternoon market and the pelota games scheduled for the evening. At the last moment, the council agreed that people would have too difficult a time making it through the week without the market, and it would be impossible to get word to the outlying farmers who were already herding stock towards town. And to cancel the pelota games might cause more alarm than necessary.

The news that all would proceed as normal settled Miguel as he trudged back home without the bread he'd sought.

Wolfram von Richthofen rose before dawn, executed his callisthenic ritual, and braced himself with a cool scrub-down and a close shave.

He brushed back his retreating hair and covered it with his forage cap, pulling it low and tight so that the German eagle on the front spread its wings directly between and only slightly above his eyes. Scanning the skies on his short drive to the airfield, he saw that the clarity overhead faded into a grey film over the mountains to the north.

The merest possibility of a weather-abort caused worries. Planes that sat on the ground did nothing to further the war. By nine thirty, the reconnaissance planes touched down at the Vitoria airfield and the technicians hurried inside to develop, fix, and print their film for the impatient von Richthofen. The reports were specific and encouraging: light clouds would move into the region until midday but were expected to blow through by afternoon, leaving conditions ideal.

Father Xabier faintly attended to a series of irrelevant matters in the Santa María presbytery, and when he found himself dusting the feet of Christ on a wall-hung crucifix, he finally conceded that his procrastination in returning to Bilbao was a matter of avoidance. He had no way of knowing whether reports of his inflammatory sermon had reached his superiors in Bilbao. He had not asked for approval before taking on the mission to Guernica for President Aguirre, which in itself could be viewed as a breach of protocol. He did not doubt that penalties or a defrocking were in the works already.

That Xabier, from his bed in the presbytery on Sunday night, could hear the dance music from Plaza Las Escuelas convinced him that his message had gone unheard. If the parishioners had fully comprehended the threat, there would have been no dancing but running to safety far from this valley; there would have been no music except for the steady hum of cartwheels on the road to Bilbao.

Had he known during the Sunday service that Republican forces were being bombed and strafed at Markina as he spoke, he would have stressed that fact in his sermon. Had he known that the makeshift hospital at the Carmelite convent would swell on Sunday night with the dying and disfigured, he would have urged the flock to go and look for themselves. To talk of blood is theoretical; to have them see it, step in it, smell it as it darkened into sticky puddles would have been infinitely more illustrative.

Instead, they danced. Were the hazards less immediate, he would have been amused at this display. If there was to be a dance then it was foolish to believe that anything would keep them from dancing. If there was to be a fight, they would fight – and *then* they would dance. None would argue that the circumstances were worthy of a battle to the death, but they obviously were not enough to cause them to forsake an evening of dancing.

Dominus vobiscum.

Xabier walked down Calle Santa María, past the eyesore *refugio* in the street, towards the train station. At the station plaza, he found hundreds aligned to buy tickets for passenger trains that were now running with sporadic unpredictability. As reluctant as he had been to return, biretta in hand, to face his superiors, he knew he could not put it off another day. He walked back to Santa María, where a young priest arranged for a car and driver to take him the twenty miles to Bilbao that afternoon. Soon enough, he thought.

Justo was conditioned to take a break from work at midday, even if the noon meals had grown sparse. June would bring the twenty-third anniversary of their marriage, and he still anticipated seeing Mariangeles over lunch even if their separation had been only the length of one morning.

He had been hoeing and weeding his early plantings, and when he came into the house he found Mariangeles mending a pair of his trousers that had been patched so many times that it was only her thread that sustained the thin fabric mosaic. Justo's disregard for his appearance always amused her. If she didn't notice that the seat of his trousers was split wide open and demand he surrender them for repairs, Justo might wear them for months that way.

'The sheep have never complained,' he always responded, even after all the sheep were gone. Mariangeles also had volunteered to bind a seam in a pair of trousers that Miguel had ripped while logging, a favour for her daughter, who was so busy with little Catalina.

'I am going to miss that little one,' Justo said, already wistful. 'Give her a big kiss from her *aitxitxia* when you see them at the market.'

'You can give it to her yourself; they're all coming up for dinner tonight for a last meal before they leave for Bilbao.'

'Do we have a few crusts of bread and crumbs of stale cheese that we have stolen from the mice that we can lay out for company?' he asked sarcastically. 'Or have we got lucky and are able to cook up the mice themselves?'

'Justo! We'll have some soup and some vegetables and bread, and we will have each other's company,' Mariangeles said, biting off the end of a thread before asking, 'Justo, do you think we should invite Miguel to stay here while they're gone?'

'He wouldn't be as lonely here,' Justo said. 'But if he didn't have work to do at his shop or in the woods, he would be going to Bilbao with them already. Besides, I think that if he stayed with us he'd feel he needed to help us with the jobs rather than do his own work.'

'We might be able to convince him that he'd be safer here than in town,' Mariangeles continued.

'If we tell him we think it's safer here, that would only convince him that there's real danger to his home and belongings, which would make him more determined not to leave,' Justo said, sitting at the table, examining the dried maize that Mariangeles had soaked and softened into a soup for his lunch. 'With all these strangers about, I'm sure he'll want to stay at home to protect their things.'

The image of rebels and Moorish mercenaries strolling through Guernica chilled them both. Was it possible they would come into the hills and farms to take what they wished? Would it come to fighting the intruders with *laiak* and hoes and scythes?

'Mari . . .' Justo said.

'Yes . . .'

'Would you consider going with Miren and Catalina? It might be good for all three of you to go. I know you'll be safe here, and we'd be here to protect each other, but you might be a help to Miren with Catalina.'

'Are you trying to be rid of me? We've never spent a night apart. My place is here, with you. Miren will be fine with Cat. She would feel the same way about staying with Miguel if it weren't for the little one.'

'She is still so young and Bilbao is a very large place that isn't always safe even in good times,' Justo said. 'I worry about her being alone with Catalina.'

'Justo, this isn't about Miren and you know it; you're worried about me being here,' she said. 'I think we both need to be at Errotabarri – together.'

'I am worried about this, Mari.'

Justo finished half the soup and offered the rest to his wife, saying he was filled to bursting. Mariangeles pushed the dish of soup back to her husband, hugged him around his shoulders as he sat, and kissed his prickly cheek.

Wolfram von Richthofen's intolerance of mistakes caused him to double-check the reconnaissance photos and intelligence information before entering the operations room.

An initial flyover by a single bomber would serve as bait to lure fire from anti-aircraft defences that could be spotted and eliminated. The vanguard plane would circle back and lead the bombers south through the valley. Fighter pilots were instructed that anything that moved on those roads could be assumed to be unfriendly and should be attacked.

Intelligence reports assured von Richthofen that Mount Oiz had been secured by General Mola's forces and would offer the perfect 'opera box' from which to view the bombing. The mountain rose to well over three thousand feet and was considered the bay window onto Biscaya. The locals claimed the mountain was the home of the most powerful divinity, Mari, who controlled the forces of thunder and wind. At times she assumed the shape of a white cloud or a rainbow, or was said to ride upon fireballs between the mountain peaks or drive through the sky on a chariot pulled by a team of snorting rams.

With an aide beside him, von Richthofen drove his Mercedes up the steep and twisting road on the west side of the mountain at attack speed. He wore his heavy watch coat, collar peeled up at the back, and woollen gloves.

Once parked, he lit a cigarette and admired the temperate afternoon. 'We could not have asked for better weather,' he said, taking a deep pull on his cigarette. He flipped the butt into a clump of heather, exhaled a white pennant of smoke, and scanned the scenic hills to the north.

Miguel played with Catalina all morning, pulling her hobby-ram gently around the room, taking corners slowly to be certain she would not get bucked off. Miren gathered and packed the necessities for the trip, wrestling with indecisiveness, placing an item in the bag only to remove it as she reconsidered its utility. What does one take when setting out to become a refugee? Every decision seemed a referendum on her faith in their return. I must remember to clean and put everything away, she told herself before realizing the absurdity of making her home orderly for a possible invasion.

While Miren fed and held Catalina, Miguel whittled down a forked oak branch he had cut a few days before. With a strip of rubber pared from the band of an old lathe turner, he created a catapult. After having dropped the tasty grouse, he had his eye out for other small game.

'Oh, this should be good,' Miren joked. 'The mighty hunter.'

'I am ready if attacked by rebel squirrels or rabbits,' he announced, testing the draw of the rubber and sighting in an imaginary target running past him.

'Why do I not believe you'll be able to shoot a rabbit?'

'I will if one sits still long enough and has enough patience for me to fire and reload as many times as it will take to hit him,' Miguel said. 'The squirrels are too fast, and they hide around the back of trees and laugh at me. I will admit that I would have trouble killing doves. I like them too much.'

'So I shouldn't bother trying to buy any meat at the market today, since we can assume you'll be killing enough game up in the hills?'

'As if there's any meat, or we could afford it – or we were brave enough to eat what they might be selling,' Miguel said.

'Meaning . . .'

'Mendiola told me a vendor gave him the new "translations" at the market these days: small dogs are now named rabbit, and large dogs are lamb. And seagulls—'

'No, don't . . .' Miren squinted uneasily as she awaited the grim translation.

'Turkey.'

'Miguel, you're starting to sound like my father,' Miren said.

'You watch, I'll come down from the mountain with something to add to the stewpot at Errotabarri tonight,' Miguel said. 'And your father will have reason to tell us stories of his great experiences killing game when he was young.'

Miren finished nursing and readied the pram.

'Don't worry about food,' Miguel said. 'I'm going to do fine, and I'm sure your mother is going to turn into a pest trying to take care of me. Has she considered going with you?'

'I haven't asked because I don't want her to think I need her,' Miren said. 'I really wouldn't mind her help and her company. I've never been to Bilbao. But if she's with us she'll feel guilty about being away from Papa. I know she believes she couldn't leave him on his own; he'd be walking around barefoot in shredded clothing.'

'Well, don't worry about me; I may have so much fresh game that I'll be able to take something to them every day,' Miguel said, drawing and releasing the rubber of his weapon, with one eye closed tightly to facilitate precise aiming.

With Catalina settled into the pram, Miren approached Miguel for a quick kiss before they set off.

'Be careful up there, *asto*,' she said, reaching around to pinch him on the bottom. 'Don't let any squirrels get you.'

'Miren,' Miguel said seriously, 'you be careful; there are a lot of strange people in town.'

They kissed again, and Miguel leaned in to nuzzle the sweet-smelling black hair on the crown of his daughter's head.

'Have you been washing her hair with Alaia's soap?'

'Of course, got to start her early, all the Navarro girls use it.'

Miren opened the door and manoeuvred the pram through.

The lead pilot checked his watch. As ordered, his wheels rolled at 3.45 p.m., and he eased the new Heinkel bomber off the runway. He headed north-east to a predetermined altitude above the village of Garay, where his squadron would rendezvous with the six Messerschmitt fighters that were to provide cover for his first wave of bombers. From Garay, they would fly north to the Bay of Biscay and the fishing village of Elantxobe, just up the coastline from Lekeitio. Over the bay, they would bank south and trace the path of the Mundaka Estuary and then the Oka River to Guernica. Von Richthofen had designed the circuitous route to avoid early detection.

As he adjusted his course to correct for a side wind, the pilot looked at the green hillsides and the transfiguring shadow of his plane, contracting into a tight cross as it climbed up the steep topography and broadening into a vague dark cloud as it reached the bottom of the valleys. There was a natural beauty in the countryside, the pilot thought, so like a mixture of the Alps and the Black Forest.

Trailing tightly meshed nets for anchovies off the shore of Elantxobe, the town that gave its name to the small fish, Josepe Ansotegui readied to finish an uneventful working day. He heard the planes first, grumbling angrily above the shore, and then watched them as they banked their wings directly above the *Egun On* and turned back inland.

Alaia Aldecoa considered going home. As she neared the edge of town, she grew uncomfortable with the dense traffic in the streets.

The crowd gave off a harsh sound and created an unsettling vibration that caused her stomach to tighten. Even on normal market days in the spring, when farmers from the hills and neighbouring towns joined the local shoppers, the crowds never generated such an ominous hum. The custom in the town, whenever one saw Alaia approaching on the path or street, was to ease away and make a greeting as she approached, which alerted her to their presence and helped her determine their position.

The walks and streets were too crowded for that now, and so many of those surging past did not know of Alaia or her disability. Many looked only at the ground in front of their feet, and she was jostled many times on her course to the market. She could smell the soldiers in the dirty woollen uniforms that had absorbed their sweat and blood. Many carried with them the more disturbing scents of phosphorus and fear. They did not bother to steer out of her path; in fact, some slid inside her radius of comfort, making the most of a chance to be near a shapely woman after months in the field. One knocked the bag off her shoulder as he passed, and as she tried to arrest its fall, her cane hit the soldier. Until the cane rose in his direction, he had not known she was blind. The victim's compatriots needled him for having been so helpless as to be clubbed by a blind girl. How would he ever hope to avoid Fascist bullets if he could be so easily struck by the cane of a sightless woman?

'It is busy today; I'm not used to such crowds,' Alaia explained to Miren and Mariangeles when she arrived at her booth.

'How can we help, dear?' Mariangeles asked.

'I'm fine; I don't really have much to sell, and I'm not sure how much people are interested in soaps today,' Alaia said, pulling out two bars separately wrapped for them. 'Here, these are for you.'

'Thank you,' Mariangeles said. 'Justo was asking me about the soap; he missed it.'

'I can't believe Papa would notice such things,' Miren said.

'He notices Alaia's soap.'

Alaia heard Catalina chatter in the pram and felt the edge of the bedding, cautiously sliding her hand down towards the little one. Catalina clutched Alaia's thumb and little finger and began pulling them as if milking a cow. She then pulled herself up and onto her feet at the edge of the pram. She'd be too big for it soon. Miren had already told Miguel to start working on a stroller and asked him to please make it smaller than an oxcart.

'Oh, she's getting strong,' Alaia said.

'She and I are leaving for Bilbao in the morning,' Miren said. 'We're going to the station to get our tickets.'

'Oh, Miren, when I walked past there, the queue was so long,' Mariangeles said. 'I don't want you and Catalina standing in it. You go finish your shopping and I'll get the tickets.'

'Thank you,' Miren said. 'If you truly wouldn't mind—'

'Of course I don't mind,' Mariangeles said, kissing her daughter on both cheeks and petting Catalina's head.

At the edge of the market, Miren held Catalina so she could touch the long, down-soft ears of the donkeys standing in their traces. She did it for Cat but also for herself, because she enjoyed being close to them again. Farmers used donkey carts to bring crates filled with chickens to market. Miren stroked the whiskered muzzles of the donkeys while Cat wobbled the ears back and forth. She showed Cat the chickens in their crates, remembering how many she had seen killed and plucked at Errotabarri, back before chickens were so precious. The caged birds were agitated, and their rustling against the wire caused a flurry of feathers to gather in white clusters beneath them on the ground.

Past the donkey carts were the pens where stockmen brought the powerful but genial oxen and the frighteningly large bulls. Miren did not take her close to the bulls but always stopped at the next pen, which held the constantly chewing sheep and the inquisitive goats with their jaundiced eyes.

From the outer edge of the marketplace, Miren could see the extent of the jostling crowd; people eager to get somewhere were mixed with an equal number who had no apparent destination. Perhaps half the booths were closed early, but there were still more people in the square than she had seen before. The man who sold the *barquillo* biscuits she always bought for Cat was gone already. A handwritten sign on the fronton announced that the pelota games were cancelled, and there would be no dance. No dance. People were leaving town.

Mariangeles had not exaggerated the size of the crowd in front of the station; she might be standing in the queue for hours. Although to call the milling mass a queue was to assign it more order than actually existed. She had never seen such a collection of afflicted souls. Some had started fires with scavenged wood and were cooking unrecognizable mixtures of found leavings. The steady motion and shuffling of shapeless groups seemed to create a friction, and with it a charge of electricity that felt combustible. She was glad that Miren was not there with Catalina. As crowded and chaotic as the marketplace had been, this was worse, and it had the feeling of a mob.

The bedraggled woman in front of Mariangeles, perhaps a few years older, dropped a paper wrapping out of her bag. As she struggled with her things, Mariangeles retrieved it for her.

'Thank you,' the woman said, after determining that Mariangeles was not trying to steal it from her. Her red-rimmed eyes flashed the look of weary suspicion that many in the plaza shared. 'It's our family Bible.'

'You would not want to lose that,' Mariangeles said solemnly.

'It has all our family names in it.'

'Where are you from?' Mariangeles asked with as much cheer as possible, hoping to prove herself unthreatening.

'Durango,' the woman said.

Mariangeles knew what that meant: rebel bombing. She hadn't the heart to probe further and waited for the woman to continue on her own. Now standing almost side by side, they both shuffled a few steps to remain in contact with the mass ahead.

'We had a haberdashery in town, but we were hit during the first attack,' the woman volunteered. 'My two daughters were grown and had moved to San Sebastián, so they were gone, thank heavens.'

Mariangeles nodded. 'You lost the shop?'

'Yes . . . and my husband.'

She stated it as a bloodless fact, like the final enumeration of misplaced possessions. The cumulative losses had emptied her over these weeks. When she said 'and my husband', she could have been saying 'and my chest of drawers'. All things lost had assumed secondary relevance to survival.

In that moment, this became Mariangeles's war, too. This haggard, diminished woman could be her. She could be the one who was homeless, with her life reduced to what she could carry and what she could not forget. She could be trying to find a way to live without her husband. How unspeakable could life become that a marriage, with its decades of shared moments, could be distilled into the dry comment, 'Yes . . . and my husband'? Mariangeles' shoulders shook. She sobbed with each harsh intake of breath. The woman put her hand on her sleeve, and Mariangeles clenched it desperately.

'I'm sorry; I'm so sorry,' she said, aware of the irony of her needing the woman's comfort. She'd never broken down like this before. She'd always considered herself so strong.

When Mariangeles composed herself, the woman supplied answers to all the questions that Mariangeles was too shaken to ask. Her husband was killed in the first raid on Durango. Their home had been on the second floor, above the shop, and the building collapsed in on itself when a bomb landed in the street. She escaped by having the fortunate timing of being in the back room collecting supplies. The blast knocked her down, but when she was able to stand and take stock, the shop was in pieces around her and her husband was buried beneath their belongings, which had fallen in on him. She sat with his body a full day, as no one ever stopped to help her lift off the weighty debris. As the rebels neared town, she realized there was nothing to hold her in Durango, and she stepped into a line of people shuffling north as if trailing a bell cow.

She was staggering and weepy for many days, moving only because the tide of others sucked her along with a steady undertow. As she grew hungrier, she cried less frequently and dwelled less on her losses. She wore the same apron she had on the day of the bombing, with the same list of goods she needed to restock in her front pocket. That was nearly a month ago, she said.

On Sunday, she had sold her wedding ring to a young soldier she met who was considering marriage to his girlfriend. Although it sold for only a small amount, it brought enough for her to afford a ticket to Bilbao.

'Have you thought of going to San Sebastián to stay with your children?' Mariangeles asked.

'They have their own troubles.'

The queue barely moved. Mariangeles felt her emotions surfacing again. She would tell Justo of this woman, and she would tell him that she had reconsidered their plan to stay. Maybe it would be best for all of them to leave Guernica, to go to Bilbao, to go to Lekeitio, maybe to even get Josepe to sail them to somewhere in France. She knew Justo would never want to leave Errotabarri, but Errotabarri would be there when they got back.

CHAPTER 17

The nuns on the convent roof spotted them first, reflecting a flash of light like the wings of distant cranes. The nuns rang their hand bells, as if the melodic tinkling could rouse the attention of a town dense with refugees. Santa María's bells then amplified the alert but created more confusion. They had already chimed 4 p.m., and this was not a call to Mass. Was it?

As the nuns followed it with their binoculars, the vanguard bomber slowed to accommodate visual inspection by the bomb aimer. By the time most people grasped the meaning of the bells, their ringing was muted by screaming engines overhead. A few ran for the *refugios*; some raced towards Santa María because it was the house of God. Others stood frozen.

But the plane dropped no bombs; instead it climbed and banked away. Those in the marketplace cheered. The devil was just taking a peek.

Mariangeles Ansotegui responded to the bells and the sight of the plane and the spreading chaos by remaining dedicated to her task: standing in the queue. Around her, refugees sought cover and screamed curses new to her. The woman in front of her was gone, her bag dropped where she had been standing. Mariangeles stooped to collect it; the family Bible was still there. She would hold it for safekeeping until the woman returned. She began thinking that the sight of the plane had been beneficial. Many had abandoned their places, allowing her to move forward a considerable distance. The bells continued to call out. She thought they must be saying that it was safe.

Miren and Catalina had left the stock pens and were sorting through the few ragged stalks and stems of vegetables available. She had seen nothing worth buying except some potatoes, but Miguel could make those stretch, especially if he managed to kill a rabbit or some squirrels as he had threatened. She smiled at the thought of him stalking game. He would be more likely to try to share his food with the rabbits and squirrels.

The bells of Santa María began to ring with an unexpected urgency. Miren looked towards the church for explanation. She heard the machine rumble to the north of the town and then saw it fly into her range of vision. 'Cat, look,' she said, pointing to the sky. Catalina looked only at the end of Miren's upraised arm. But her mother's voice was excited, and that was meaningful to her, causing her to kick and laugh in her pram. She pulled herself up at the edge to look out.

As the driver swung around a turn heading out of the valley towards Bilbao, Father Xabier saw a black, birdlike shadow speed down the hillside and across the road. From the side window he saw the aeroplane just as it banked behind a mountain. President Aguirre had shared with him the scarcity of Republican air presence, so Xabier knew this had to be German. He ordered the driver to find a wide spot in the road and turn back to Guernica. Perhaps this was a reconnaissance flyover, but he knew there could be panic in town.

The driver, who had been horrified by the priest's sermon the day before, was now more certain of the cleric's insanity. He pulled off the roadside before entering town and refused to go further, not bothering to shut the door as he abandoned the car and the priest and flopped into ankle-deep water in a drainage ditch to diminish himself as a target when the forces of the apocalypse stormed through Guernica.

Biretta perched on his head, with his pumping legs hidden beneath his full-length black cassock, Father Xabier appeared to be floating at high speed towards the centre of town. The powerful current of people fleeing in the opposite direction hardly slowed him. The vision of the priest in flight caused the crowd to part as he approached and congeal back into a solid mass in his wake. Some were certain they had witnessed a miracle, but they were not eager to stay and offer testimony towards his canonization. Recalling the crowds at the station, Father Xabier decided he would go there first, hoping to bring order to what he feared could become a dangerous stampede.

From the north, the rumbling returned and grew nearer and louder, causing the ground to vibrate. Mariangeles Ansotegui squinted up into the near-cloudless afternoon sky. Around her, those who had stayed in the queue sprinted off in all directions. A high-pitched whistle added an upper register to the sound of chaos in the plaza. Objects were falling from the plane, whistling and falling.

The first bomb exploded in the middle of the plaza. The bodies of several dozen people rose intact to varied elevations before sprouting like chrysanthemum blossoms.

Father Xabier had reached the edge of the plaza when he was knocked to the ground by the explosion. 'Dear God, it is happening. Make me strong. Make Your strength my strength,' he prayed aloud, repositioning the biretta that had been blown off his head.

The first deliverance of random death struck mostly women, including one refugee in a white apron with tired eyes who had tried to run away and a lovely woman standing in line, holding a stranger's family Bible, which was incinerated in midair by the heat of the explosion.

In a shed at the Mezos', focused on repairing tools, Justo Ansotegui heard church bells. But he paid attention to them only when he needed to know the time, or if it was Sunday morning and they announced their call to Mass. It must be four, he thought.

But they continued pealing, and he wondered why there would be a Mass on Monday afternoon. When the blasts sent shockwaves rippling up the valley and into the hills, Amaya Mezo knocked back the shed door and told him of the plane she had seen, and pointed to the dome of dust rising at the centre of town.

'No,' he said. 'No.'

Where was Mariangeles? Where were Miren and Catalina?

They were in town. A plane is dropping bombs in town.

As he ran from the shed, Justo picked up a *laia* for protection. It was time to fight.

It was almost a mile into town and he raced with his *laia* in front of him like a primitive avenger, shouting as he ran.

'Mari . . . Mari . . . Mari . . .'

And as he slowed from lack of breath, his shouts matched the two-syllable toll of the bells: 'Mar . . . ee . . . Mar . . . ee . . . Mar . . . ee.'

Up a nearby slope, Miguel's cross-cut saw hummed a jagged tune as it nibbled through the broad bole of an oak. He, too, heard the bells far below, muffled by distance, and paid no attention. In moments, though, he felt deep thuds through his feet, as when a tree falls. Waves of sound radiated up to him, and he turned to the valley. Dust and smoke had risen above the buildings.

Oh, dear God, an explosion, he thought. He ran, churning so fast downhill that he couldn't control his legs. He fell and rolled and rose and was running again in one motion, driven by instinct and the ringing of the bells.

When the explosions shook the earth only two streets away, Miren pulled the hood down on Catalina's pram to shield her ears. With the pram in front of her, she picked up speed heading not towards a *refugio*, as Miguel had instructed, but to the train station in search of her mother. Up Calle de la Estación, towards the smouldering plaza, she became a blur of motion.

Ahead were screams choking out from the veil of hanging dust. From behind came the sound of the bells.

Alaia Aldecoa heard the bomber before anyone noticed it; it caused windows to rattle violently in their casings. But there was no context to link it to alarm. Machines had flown over before; she had heard them. It seemed another ugly vibration in a day filled with them. But the threat became obvious when the bells began their impatient clangour and the crowd started to rush around her. No one thought to guide her to a *refugio* or explain the madness.

Her mind flashed on the sisters' story of the terrifying end of days. Just as they had predicted, the explosions sucked the air from her lungs while the ground bucked and rolled. Hell was powering up through the crust of the earth to swallow them. The brimstone smelled exactly as it had been described.

Her best chance was to stay in this spot; Miren would come back for her. But when the ground opened up, her instincts compelled her to run, something she had never done.

She began a flat-footed trot, as if trying to feel her way with her toes, arms stretched out in front like stiffened antennae. She had not picked up her cane.

The screams were coming from her right, so she ran to her left, off a kerb.

The sound in the sky had returned, only stronger, with greater vibration and more urgency. There were more machines.

The whistling was more intense. Within moments, there were more death screams.

With outstretched arms, she touched the facing of a building and followed its abrasive brick surface around a corner.

She ran again when she reached the street.

An explosion knocked her to the ground.

She ran again.

People knocked her down. She rose, was knocked down again.

She crawled below the spreading smoke. The town was on fire.

With the next explosion, Alaia Aldecoa disappeared.

Amaya Mezo, having chased her children into the house and watched Justo Ansotegui race into town, returned to her hillside field to make sense of the sounds and the panic below. Her eldest daughter disobeyed her order to stay inside, hoping to be there if she needed help. They saw the large planes come in successive wedges, with a number of smaller planes zipping in erratic paths, like swallows among flights of migrating geese.

One broke off from over the edge of town and dived at her as if intending to grind her up with its propellers.

Parallel lines of dust puffs raced towards them with the sound of rapid drumbeats. Her daughter ran at the sight, shouting at her mother to hide. But Amaya had no concept of the danger and stood yelling at the machine, waving at it to go away from her home and loved ones.

A bullet tore off her right shoulder. The pilot flew so close she could see his face looking down at her. He wore a leather hat, and his eyes were covered by round goggles that reflected the glare of the afternoon sun.

The visions came in flashes as Father Xabier sought places to do God's work. With staggered sprints and crouches, he had made his way towards the market as the second echelon of bombers struck.

He ran past the fire station, where a bomb had crushed the town's lone fire engine, killing the young stable boy and the massive dray horses in their stalls. The blood from the horses and the boy flowed together down the sloping entranceway into the gutter and down to the storm drain.

To his left, several incendiaries had landed in the temporary cattle pen, and a bull engulfed in blue-white flames bellowed and broke through the fence, rampaging into the crowd.

Sheep ignited and their wool burned black as they tried to butt their way out of the pens.

A large bomb had taken out several oxen and farmers, leaving

Xabier trying not to fall on their slippery remains.

Bullets from fighter planes whistled and thudded indifferently into humans and animals.

Everything burned.

A woman with three children huddled in the protection of a recessed doorway, and the priest stood as tall and wide as he could to shield them. When a lull in the bombing brought a sense of respite to their ringing ears, the family took off from behind the priest's skirts and ran down the middle of the street.

'Wait!' Xabier shouted.

They had covered less than twenty yards when a fighter plane raked the street with gunfire, cutting down three of the four in one burst. The surviving child, wounded herself, dived near her mother, screaming, trying to lift her up and make her run.

The fighters darted without pattern, chasing anyone in the open. Xabier's mind flashed on the image of sheepdogs racing back and forth, herding people to their deaths.

A street away, a cluster of incendiaries pierced the roof of the sweet factory and flared with heat as the thermite ignited the most com-bustible substance, the hair of the women working inside.

Another street away a group of teenage boys who had been playing near the pelota fronton sought shelter in the mouth of a concrete culvert. When a bomb exploded within yards of them, their flesh fused into an indistinguishable mass.

In the Residencia Calzada, a home for the elderly, a bomb vapor-ized many of the old men and women, along with the nuns there trying to help them limp to safety.

Seeing no other means of escape from the first floor of a burning building, a man leaped from a window, flailing his arms to put out the flames on the back of his white shirt, or perhaps hoping to fly.

In a basement *refugio*, two dozen corpses lay in a mosaic. They were untouched – no wounds, no blood – extinguished by the absence of air.

Hundreds clustered under the arched ceiling of the church of

Santa María, praying frantically before the holy statuary.

An incendiary bomb knifed through the roof and impaled the floor. The fire that could have incinerated everyone in the church never flared. The bomb did not ignite.

Miren stopped her search for Mariangeles out of fear for Catalina. Running up the street behind the bouncing pram, she was lost in her own town. The wheels of the pram kicked up cockerels' tails of dark fluid. She fought against the vortex of traffic created as the flow of people fleeing the station plaza swept into the equally misdirected flow of those frantic to leave the marketplace.

She could go faster with Catalina in her arms, but debris fell in hot gusts and stung Miren like hail. She'd almost been knocked down by the crowds, so Catalina was safer inside the pram. She kept speaking to her, though, telling her through the canvas canopy that everything was all right.

The rumbling bombers again muted the cries for help.

Miren choked on the concrete dust and on the heat and the smell. As she passed in front of the Hotel Julian, several young mothers herded a group of shrieking schoolchildren into the entryway.

Miren turned at the doorway to follow them, but a screaming whistle caused her to look into the smoky air as a bomb sliced through the middle of the small hotel. The explosion thrust a column of air through the funnel of the entryway, and within seconds, the hotel's concrete facing sloughed off, burying those in front of it beneath several tons of flaming rubble.

When the strafing fighters peeled away after others, Xabier knelt to inspect the small family that had been gunned down. The youngest, a girl of perhaps four, bled from her side but continued to tug at her mother as if to wake her from a nap.

Xabier pulled her away from her dead family and carried her to the nearest *refugio*. The door opened quickly, allowing him to squeeze inside a different level of hell.

Hundreds had wedged into a space meant for dozens, and as layers of incoming souls entered, they compressed those in the back.

Early arrivals, gagging on the superheated air, begged those in the front to leave the doors open for ventilation.

'Get us out,' a woman screamed.

But when they swung the double doors open, a percussion bomb landed just outside, and its violent intake of air sucked four people into the fireball. In shock, others tried closing the doors, but they were blocked by the lower part of a man's leg, still wearing a black espadrille.

At the back, in the dark, people licked the walls, trying to suck in condensation to fend off the steaming heat.

They stumbled and could feel with their feet in the darkness that they were now standing on the bodies of those who had collapsed.

At times, men or women overtaken by claustrophobia would scream wildly, crawling over others, clawing against flesh to clear their way to the front.

They would take their chances with the bombs and the fire rather than die from being trampled or smothered.

As calmly as he could, standing at the gate between two hells, with a little girl dying in his arms, Father Xabier offered prayers of absolution.

'Holy Mary, Mother of God, pray for us now and at the moment of our death . . .'

Wolfram von Richthofen and his aide, standing on the northern face of Mount Oiz, admired the precise waves of planes on their approach to the valley. But even from this vantage point, some ten miles south of Guernica, they were unable to see the village itself. A rising mass of smoke and dust from the explosions climbed above the hilltops, providing evidence that heavy damage was being inflicted. But von Richthofen could not see the destruction as clearly as he had hoped.

He discarded his cigarette and headed down the mountain for a quick drive back to Vitoria.

As the town emptied, Miguel rushed against the flow into the core of devastation. His instincts were to fight through the mayhem and get to the market.

They would be with Alaia, and all of them would have gone to the closest *refugio* in the middle of Calle Santa María, the one Miguel had shown her.

Why did he let her talk him into staying another day?

He would scold her when he saw her.

No, he wouldn't.

Bombs still fell from the chevrons of aeroplanes droning above the town. Smoke and dust rose, but Miguel barely noticed the explosions, and none of his impulses to run away from the destruction registered.

Near the market, Mrs Arana bent and keened over a mass of concrete and brick rubble that had once been a shop. She saw Miguel running in her direction and shouted, 'They're here, help them!'

Miguel threw himself on the pile. He could not know that he was streets from his family. He could not understand that this was futile, that the bodies beneath were neither alive nor his loved ones.

He thought of none of these possibilities. 'They're here,' he had heard.

Miguel lifted concrete, slab after slab, tossed aside broken bricks, and dug into glistening piles of shattered window glass with his bare hands.

Bombs fell and buildings ignited. He heard none of it.

Dig to find them. Dig to save them.

Miren. Miren and Cat.

He hoisted off more slabs and shards, which began to bite at him, and he could not lift them as well as he had. Even the smaller bricks became slippery and difficult to grasp.

There was no air to breathe.

The bombs fell and the ground shook and guns fired. He didn't hear them. He didn't hear Mrs Arana begging him to stop and to look at his hands.

He had no hands, he had no feeling; he would dig until he rescued them. He'd dig because he promised. He'd dig until he found them.

Until he was blown from the pile by an explosion.

Souls in shredded clothes, with gaping mouths and blank eyes, stumbled past Justo as the streets became smoking flues. He dropped his *laia* as he entered town, realizing his ancient tool would be useless against the aeroplanes he saw winging overhead.

Legarreta, the fireman, brought him to a halt by clasping his shoulders and speaking into his face. Justo wrestled against him, looking past him to places where his wife might have sought protection.

'People are still alive in parts of this building, Justo; you have to help me get them,' Legarreta explained with uncommon calmness, barely glancing away from Justo as a man crawled past using his arms to pull along his mangled legs.

'Have you seen Mariangeles or Miren?' Justo shouted as a bomb exploded a street away.

'No, Justo, I need you to help lift debris; we need manpower,' Legarreta said, his face soiled black as a sheep's. 'People are in here now.'

'Mariangeles and Miren?'

'I promise . . . I promise . . . I'll help you find them if you help me get these people.'

A bomb had fallen on a boarding house, but as it collapsed, the wooden joists and beams scattered in a way that allowed people to breathe but not escape. Legarreta knew that to go in and randomly hoist beams without cross-braces and supports would cause the structure to collapse on anyone who had survived.

But when Justo crawled in and discovered a young woman with her head turned around on her neck and bones protruding from her cornflower-blue dress, he could not respect Legarreta's urges of caution from just outside the building.

'Help me,' another woman called with a fading voice. She was deeper in the pile, wedged beneath a tangle of crossbeams, her face covered in dust that had caked onto the blood tributaries seeping from a head gash.

Justo recognized her; she was the baker's wife. The debris was strewn like puzzle pieces, and Justo's eyes moved upward from her trapped legs, tracing the pattern of load-bearing beams.

'Don't move anything yet, Justo, we've got to get in there and shore it—' Legarreta's voice was muted by a bomb blast that shook down more dust and larger pieces of wood.

'Help,' she called again, weaker, more urgent. 'Justo . . . help.'

An oak beam angling up from the pile was the key to her release. If he could prise that up even a few inches, it would raise the pile so she could pull herself free.

He was made for this, he told himself as he backed in under the beam and tested for footing and leverage.

Inflating himself mentally as he found purchase amid the tangle, Justo strained against the underside of the beam with his left shoulder, his head tilted far to the right, with his left arm wrapped around the upper side for grip.

He pushed against it lightly at first, as a test, and he sensed it budge.

I can do this, he thought. No one else can, but I can do this.

With a scream, he thrust his legs and his back and shoulder muscles upward; the beam groaned and lifted off the legs of the baker's wife, and the creaking from behind him was replaced by a grinding above. A joist lying across the angled beam broke free and slid towards Justo as if greased.

Justo never saw it ride down the beam with the weight of the building behind it, never slowing as it wrenched his arm off the top of the beam and left it hanging behind his head. He collapsed beneath the network of wood and concrete and bones.

The bodies lay in parts and Guernica burned. The attack had been going on for almost two hours by 6 p.m., but the Condor Legion's main bomber force was only now taking off. The largest squadron, almost two dozen Junkers, circled over the field at Vitoria before heading north.

Messerschmitt fighters joined them again for their duties of rounding up the strays fleeing to the fields and forests. More of the Heinkel bombers returned at 7 p.m. to complete the cycle of bomb–refuel–bomb. At seven thirty, more than three hours after the initial bomb fell, the airmen retired for the day.

The bells of Santa María tolled 8 p.m., ringing through smoke from the fires that consumed the town's buildings.

Bucket brigades stretching to the river were formed, and fire engines and crews from Bilbao arrived. But bombs had gouged out the water mains, leaving no pressure for their hoses and limiting their contribution to standing and watching the blazes. They joined the line of bucket-passers.

By the time the buckets advanced through dozens of hands, only small sloshes of water remained in each, and the fires flamed at such temperatures that the last man in the line could not stand near enough for the small splashes of water he threw to touch the crumbling buildings. Those near the flames saw the absurdity of the endeavour, but they knew it helped the others in the line feel as if they were putting up a fight, so they continued the charade until the fires had consumed all available fuel.

Father Xabier moved between clusters of the suffering, offering comfort, manning stretchers for the wounded, and joining in rescue efforts. All the while, he shouted, 'Justo!', searching for his brother and his family. He saw men respectfully aligning blackened figures, charred beyond identification. Others were engaged in the reconstruction of parts, attempting to find something, anything, that would help loved ones grieve the victims.

He saw the vagaries of the attack. Most of the town was destroyed or aflame, but on top of a pile of rubble sat a birthday cake that had somehow gone untouched although all who had gathered for the celebration that afternoon were dead. He saw young children, unscathed, racing and chasing others near the fragmented remains of their classmates. He saw on the hill that the Parliament somehow appeared unharmed, and, thank God, the tree of Guernica stood untouched.

In the timeless aftermath, he searched, bending to pray over the wounded and dead every several yards, but searching. And as he reached the station plaza, a train carrying rescue workers arrived from Bilbao. Xabier knew he had to tell President Aguirre of the atrocity. Aguirre might not be able to comprehend the enormity of this attack without the word of someone he trusted, someone who had seen it all in person. He decided he could come back to Guernica on the next train to continue searching after he reported to Aguirre.

Xabier boarded with many hundreds of stunned refugees, and the wounded, and the aged and the bloodied. He squeezed from car to car, looking for family. As they gained distance from Guernica, Xabier could see the red-amber glow of the burning town, and in his priest's mind he wondered if the night sky was filling with smoke from the raging fires or from the ascending souls of the needlessly dead.

The ground crews applauded as each plane was chocked and the flight crews descended. The pilots who had shuttled across northern Spain all afternoon and evening had returned to their fields in Burgos and Vitoria in a jubilant mood.

Following the initial debriefing, von Richthofen sent a quick message to his superiors: 'The concentrated air attack on Guernica was the greatest success.' Von Richthofen knew that war is impatient and impossible to appease; it allows little time for savouring a victory. Yet he was more than satisfied by the day's events. He had never expended more resources towards the destruction of a single target, and the town of Guernica had been levelled without a Condor casualty.

He had always been cautious in his reports to Berlin, knowing that it was better to be accurate and conservative with damage assessments than to earn a reputation among the brass as a breathless self-aggrandizer. But, yes, he was comfortable reporting that the day's events had been 'the greatest success'.

The crews celebrated through the night in the lounge of the Fronton Hotel, drinking and singing. Using their flattened hands like wings, the fighter pilots mimed the banks and dives they used to gun down fleeing peasants, making glottal *ack-ack-ack-ack* sounds to represent their gun bursts.

Von Richthofen had been right; the people had been like sheep, clustering together in predictable patterns, exposing themselves on bends in the road and at the edges of wooded areas, as if foliage would block machine-gun fire. He had taught them an art. There would be more difficult tests in the war to follow, but now they were learning their craft.

Von Richthofen chose not to join the celebrants, but rather took his nightly stroll among the planes at the airfield, conducting his customary inspection as he formulated the more detailed official report he would send to Berlin. This was a genesis moment, he felt. This had been unexpected, instantaneous, all-consuming, compellingly lethal, and without prejudice between military and civilian. Effective. Modern. The new war.

Of course, he could not be certain that Mola's ground forces would act appropriately and occupy the town quickly, before the Basques could physically regroup or emotionally recover from this bombing. The opposite had been his experience with these Spaniards; they would find reasons to delay their advancement and reduce the effectiveness of the entire campaign.

The next objective, he knew, would be Bilbao, and it would require a different approach, one demanding greater precision. Bilbao would be the final battle on the northern front, and the Basques would retreat there with all their remaining resources. It would take time to rout them out, although the naval blockade and a siege would undermine their determination. But how much of that could remain after the events of this day?

He entered through a side door and ascended the back steps of the hotel to avoid the partying in the lounge. In his suite, von Richthofen penned his official report to be sent to Berlin:

Guernica literally levelled to the ground. Attack carried out with 250-kilogram and incendiary bombs, about one third of the latter. When the first Junkers squadron arrived, there was smoke everywhere already (from the vanguard assault); nobody could identify the targets of roads, bridges, and suburbs, so they just dropped everything right into the centre. The 250s toppled houses and destroyed the water mains. The incendiaries now could spread and become effective. The material of the houses – tile roofs, wooden porches, and half-timbering – resulted in complete annihilation. Bomb craters can be seen in the streets. Simply terrific.

He did not explain why more airborne firepower than had been expended throughout the entire First World War was dedicated to destroying the lone target of military significance – the small Renteria Bridge. He also did not explain why the Renteria Bridge was not only still standing, but was untouched.

PART 5
(27 April 1937–May 1939)

CHAPTER 18

Father Xabier hurried to President Aguirre's office in Bilbao, arriving at 3 a.m. on Tuesday. His robes were stiffening with dried fluids, and he reeked of phosphorus and smoke and putrefying tissue. As he fought exhaustion, his hands quivered and his legs bounced.

'Good God,' Aguirre gasped, coming around his desk to embrace the priest and try to calm his palsy.

'I know . . . I'm sorry,' the priest said.

The military had briefed Aguirre, but he hadn't talked face to face yet with anyone who had been on the ground in Guernica.

'Go slowly,' Aguirre said. 'Tell me everything.'

Xabier sat in a hard-backed wooden chair and his legs shook so violently that the chair vibrated against the floor. He knew that Aguirre needed a dispassionate chronology, sparing sanguine details, but he had to pause and catch his breath as the recollections overtook him. What he had seen was stored as disconnected images, which were stacked in his mind like still photos. But as he reconstructed the day for Aguirre, his mind replayed it all as if it was a newsreel. Having to explain the avalanche of events forced him to crystallize those things that he had intentionally allowed to remain unfocused. It meant affixing words to it all.

Aguirre stopped him after only a few moments; he had been given summaries earlier. He needed a few immediate specifics from someone he trusted.

'Is there any chance the planes were not German?' he asked.

'Who else would they be?'

'Italians, maybe, maybe Nationalists.'

Xabier thought. Of course they were Germans, but there may have been Italians involved, too. 'A fireman showed me an unexploded incendiary on the street that had German eagle insignias all over it.'

'That's important; we can only imagine the lies Franco will use to explain all this. If there's ever been an argument against the Non-Intervention Pact, this is it. The world won't stand for this. There's still a chance to win this war if the French and British and Americans are shaken out of neutrality by this.'

'Politics!' Xabier yelled. 'Is this about politics?'

But before the sound of his shout had died in the room, he knew that yes, of course, it was about politics.

'I know . . . I know . . . I know, I'm sorry,' Aguirre said.

Xabier's mind turned back to his family after he had made his report: Are they safe? What can I tell them? Who is left to tell? He knew Aguirre had to take a larger view, how it affected all the Basques. He had family, too.

And of all the questions flying through his mind, Xabier voiced one: 'What do you want me to do?'

'You can tell the world everything you just told me.'

Aguirre moved behind his cluttered desk and began writing papers that would accommodate Father Xabier's quick transport out of Bilbao.

'I need you to get to Paris, to tell the press what happened,' the President said. 'I want an eyewitness, a priest in his frock, to tell the people the truth. Tell them what happened. Tell them who was responsible. Tell them everything. The sooner the better. Write your speech on the way and leave nothing out. I've heard your sermons, Father; go preach to the world.'

'All right, I can go later today; I've got to get cleaned up and changed.'

'Father,' Aguirre interrupted, 'don't.'

Xabier understood. 'Can you do one thing for me? Can you have somebody track down my family?'

Aguirre promised to do so and ushered him out. He needed to concentrate now on a crucial morning-radio response. The people had to be convinced that this was not the end. There was still a chance to save Bilbao, which was the main rebel goal in Biscaya anyway. They needed inspiration from their leader now. They needed reassurance. He was certain this attack wouldn't crush the Basque resolve but would reinforce it.

A few hours later on Radio Bilbao he announced:

German airmen in the service of the Spanish rebels have bombarded Guernica, burning the historic town that is held in such veneration by all Basques. They have sought to wound us in the most sensitive of our patriotic sentiments, once more making it clear what Euskadi may expect of those who do not hesitate to destroy us down to the very sanctuary that records the centuries of our liberty and democracy. The invading army must be warned that the Basques will respond to terrible violence in kind with unheard-of tenacity and heroism.

*

On a cool late-April afternoon, Pablo Picasso was taking a short walk through familiar territory. He headed south from his studio on Rue des Grands Augustins towards the bustling Boulevard St-Germain. He passed the ancient church of St-Germain-des-Prés as he strolled to the Café de Flore with his Afghan hound at his side.

A human-rights march stirred Paris that day and civic passion rose for the impending May Day parades. It is unlikely that many noticed a brief in the evening editions containing the first sketchy details of the Guernica bombing. Dora Maar, his muse of the moment, brought the papers with her to the cafe and intentionally inflamed Picasso with the accounts of atrocities in his native country.

'This,' Maar prodded, tapping at the paper, 'is the subject for your mural.' But there was so little information in the brief notice.

The next morning, as the artist pottered in his studio, Maar read to him the headlines that topped the more extensive reports in *L'Humanité*: 'Most horrible bombing of Spanish war' and 'Planes reduce city of Guernica to cinders'.

'Read more,' he demanded, pacing the studio.

Picasso heard only phrases as Dora read aloud from the *Times*: 'Guernica, the most ancient town of the Basques . . . destroyed by insurgent air raiders . . . fighters plunged low to machine-gun those who had taken refuge in the fields . . . unparalleled in military history . . . destruction of the cradle of the Basque race.'

She thumbed to an even more graphic report in another paper: '. . . a small hospital, wiped out with its forty-two wounded occupants . . . a bomb shelter in which over fifty women and children were trapped and burned alive . . .'

Picasso grabbed the stack of papers in front of Maar. Impossible. Other reports marginalized the damage. Some reports even suggested that Basque arsonists played a role in the destruction of their own spiritual home.

Picasso knew and admired many Basques. They were tougher than bark, he said, and natural defenders of their land. They would never set those fires or kill their own. They also wouldn't surrender, he told Maar.

Early on Thursday morning, Father Xabier Ansotegui reached the Gare de Lyon in Paris and met reporters eager for credible eyewitness accounts of Guernica's destruction. Reports from various sources in Spain were vastly conflicting, and the town was closed to outsiders.

The Basque priest stepped in front of the gathering, still unwashed and wretched. His hair was matted, his cassock had grown stiff in spots, and his gold crucifix was covered with dull-brown matter. He introduced himself as a native of Guernica who had grown up in the town and now lived in Bilbao. His credibility was unassailable.

He had shaped a presentation on the train but did not read from the outline, knowing it was better to speak as it came to him.

'It was one of those magnificently clear days, the sky soft and serene. The streets were busy with the traffic of market day.'

He spoke softly, and some reporters were still so shaken by his appearance that they were slow to begin taking notes.

'. . . Women, children, and old men were falling in heaps, like flies, and everywhere we saw lakes of blood.'

Xabier swallowed, looking into the eyes of reporters in the front row.

'. . . I saw an old peasant standing alone in a field; a machine-gun bullet had killed him . . . The sound of the explosions and of the crumbling houses cannot be imagined.'

Xabier explained the bombing patterns, the waves of planes that swept through the valley, the craters that carved up the town, and the manner in which the incendiaries turned the city into 'an enormous furnace'.

'. . . We were completely incapable of believing what we saw.'

Respectfully, reporters raised their hands and tried to steer the priest from his emotional account into specifics. They wanted to define the event with numbers. But Father Xabier Ansotegui was unable to.

'How many?' he was asked by a writer attempting to get an estimate of those killed.

'How many?' Xabier asked back. 'How many what? How many people? How many pieces? How many lives? How many children?'

How could he explain? His friend Aguirre knew the politics of numbers. But he felt it was like stacking bodies onto a scale to weigh the loss.

'When you see burned children laying in the street, charred . . . melted, you don't count them,' Xabier said. 'When you see a group of boys fused into a blackened mass, you don't take an inventory. How many died? How many? Death was infinite.'

*

In Friday's edition of *L'Humanité*, Picasso read the stories of the priest's moving speech. He could see the sky he had described.

He could feel the fear of the people and could hear the explosions.

In the paper that day was the first written statement from Basque president José Antonio Aguirre, calling upon the free world to help in the fight to save a small country soon to be overrun by Fascism. 'I ask today of the civilized world whether it will permit the extermination of a people whose first concerns always have been the defence of its liberty and democracy, which the tree of Guernica has symbolized for centuries.'

Images formed and splintered in Picasso's mind, with the classic symbols of Spain anchored in his consciousness, splayed by unseen torment. This would be his mural, his *Guernica*.

Miren turned to Miguel and kissed his neck behind his ear, lingering there long enough to give him a playful nip with her teeth. God, she smelled wonderful. It was so good to have her back. He had been so worried.

They sat at the transom of the *Egun On*. It felt strange for Miguel to be so comfortable on the water. But that's how it was with her, just like the first trip when he took her to meet his family in Lekeitio. Except she was older, of course, and her hair was bobbed. She was more lovely than ever.

'I tried to find you,' Miguel said.

'I know,' she said.

'I couldn't.'

'I know. Don't worry.'

The boat moved so smoothly through the waveless waters that Miguel had no trouble maintaining his focus on Miren, with her thick sable hair that absorbed the light and her wide sable eyes that gave off their own light.

'I missed you,' he said.

'I missed you, too.'

'Why did it take you so long to come back?'

'I had to find my way. There was so much confusion. There were so many . . .'

Miren looked out across the water at a flight of gulls.

'You look so well,' he said.

Miguel pulled her to him and lifted her onto his lap, smoothing out the layered skirts of her wedding dress to make it comfortable for her. He hugged her again tightly and breathed in the scent of her neck. They stood to waltz slowly on the deck, shifting without speaking.

Mariangeles, piloting the boat, turned to them and smiled . . . yes, yes, Miren, I taught him to dance. The boat began rocking with their steps, rolling harder as the music quickened, harder now, and the waves splashed over the gunwales on both sides. Miguel began feeling that tightening of his throat, as if he would soon be sick again.

'Where's Cat?' Miguel asked.

Miren sat with him and took Miguel's hand.

'Look,' she said. 'Look there.'

She pointed to a pair of lines that etched a parallel path, with another merging at an angle.

'Look there,' she said.

He looked. They looked like his father's hands.

'Keep looking.'

He stared more deeply at the lines.

A heavy teardrop landed there, between the two lines, and flowed towards his thumb, spreading like thick quicksilver.

'Keep looking,' she said.

He looked, but it wasn't a tear that had fallen. It was a caustic acid, and as it flowed, it began dissolving his flesh, eating into the meat of his hand, and causing the bones to crumble and fall to the deck.

'Miren!' he shouted.

But she was gone.

A bull blinded by fire had raged through the market before collapsing and dying on a flaming pile of wood that had been the coal-merchant's booth. The bull cooked there for a day, and as its internal gases heated, it expanded; the carcass swelled to twice its original size. When the bull exploded, it sounded like a bomb's echo, and Teodoro Mendiola was caught in a fountain of sizzling entrails and waste. He peeled off his jacket and wiped the mess from his eyes and mouth with disgust, and then he went back to work.

Along with most of the other men in Guernica who were not crippled by the attack, Mendiola fought fires, carried wounded to shelters and temporary hospitals, and sorted through scatterings of victims. After being assured that his family was safe, he worked for the next day and a half without stopping. His revulsion at the grisly task dulled with the hours, allowing him to continue a job for which none was prepared. While so many bodies were indistinguishable, at times he was jolted by a familiar face staring up at him when a wedge of concrete or a fallen beam had been repositioned. The instinctive response was to say, 'Hey, José,' as if greeting them. But after several hours, he knew that none who appeared in this way had survived, and the sight of a friend's face brought only more sadness to be stacked on top of that which he already could not carry.

At times, the rescuers were left to stare down into the jagged caverns of melted metal and splintered wood that had collapsed into the craters left by the heaviest bombs. They would see the back of a white dress, and a leg with a shoe and a leg without a shoe. They called out: 'Is anyone alive? Is anyone down there?' They would need heavy equipment to lift and untangle these warrens, and the woman in the white dress would have to be patient for another day.

The bodies they could recover were laid flat, shoulder to shoulder, with tarpaulins or cloth pulled up to their necks. Heads were left exposed to allow identification. The undead shuffled past, staring into the faces, praying to find loved ones and praying not to find loved ones.

Many of the unidentified had been hastily interred in mass graves, making an accurate casualty count and complete identification forever impossible. But the real work of clearing the debris had not yet started. From parts of town, structures that teetered at delicate angles finally collapsed, causing skittish rescuers to look up in fear that the planes had returned.

Across the street from what had been the Hotel Julian, Mendiola saw the burned shell of the stout wooden pram his friend Miguel Navarro had built for his daughter. He turned it upright, slowly. Scorched black and empty. He turned towards the hotel and almost tripped on the body of a child. No, it was several children. He could not tell how many.

He joined in with crews excavating the tons of concrete that had been a hotel. He was the one who found her. He still thought of her as Miren Ansotegui, Justo and Mariangeles's daughter, although he knew her better now as Miguel's wife. He forced his eyes closed and he concentrated. Memories flipped like pages in his mind. Miren dancing; Miren with her parents at the festivals; Miren on her wedding day; Miren dancing again. With as much respect as he could summon, he removed her body – she was so light – and laid it in the line with the others. He returned to the pile in search of Catalina. But there were so many children there, dozens from the school who had been taken to the hotel and had been caught in that doorway. They would never be identified.

The rains came then, helping the fire-fighters subdue most of the stubborn fires. At the point of collapse, Mendiola joined a small group of exhausted men who stumbled up the hill to one of the few places that had gone untouched by bombs and fire. They slumped to the ground and fell instantly asleep beneath the leafy shelter of the ancient oak tree.

He slashed his first sketches across blue paper, making them look as if they'd been done by a knife rather than a pencil. In these rages, the connection between the passion and the art was direct. A wounded horse took shape, followed by an enraged bull with a long-winged bird on its back. From a window, a woman leaned out and cast lamplight onto the scene.

233

On that first day, the primary elements of what would become the final composition assumed their places. There were puzzles to be solved, problems of angles and perspective, along with the addition of the hidden and the mysterious. But a horse, a bull, a fallen warrior, a mother with a dead child, and the woman holding the lamp were all there. These would be his cornerstone symbols, and they'd be offered in a stark vocabulary of black and white and greys. There would be foreground and background, shadows and light, and narrative, but no explanations.

His second day of work on the project was a long, frenzied repeat of the first. Exhausted and drained, the artist then put down his pencils to allow the newborn characters a rest after their difficult delivery.

CHAPTER 19

For the first time since Miguel renounced fishing in the sea, monsters attacked him in his sleep. In his dream, it was autumn; the alders along his favourite stream had turned yellow and the weather was cool. But the wood fires in the valley smelled of something harsh, like chemicals.

The trout hit his hook with surprising firmness and he pulled them in with a struggle, but when he attempted to unhook them, they bit into his hands with jagged teeth, like those of the small sharks they sometimes caught in the nets at home. Each chewed away at his hands, gnawing at his bones. He called to Justo but there was no reply. Then he heard his mother singing in the streets . . .

'For the love of God, arise!' Ah, it was time to get out of bed and head to Mass before joining Patroia and Dodo on the boat. But he could not arise.

Miguel Navarro had been struck by a flying brick from a nearby building that bounced off the rubble pile and caught him on the side of the head. Mrs Arana had dragged him off the mound of concrete and wood by herself. His head injury was not a concern – in fact, it was a blessing, as it halted his digging through the collapsed building. His fingers bled a great deal, but the loss of blood was not lethal. Of greater danger was sepsis from his injuries. For more than a day Miguel lay in a basement hallway of the Carmelite convent, his unconsciousness deafening him to the cries of the burns victims and the death gasps of those irreducibly broken. Many could not be saved by the few medical personnel and were too far gone to warrant the expenditure of anaesthetics, supplies of which were limited. Those doomed by blood loss or tissue damage were summarily patched and treated only with extreme unction in a back hall where the white-tile walls had been stained by blood.

Anonymous as the others coated in the dark grey stucco of blood and concrete dust, the young man with the mangled hands was a low priority for the few available surgeons and was allowed to float through his troubled unconsciousness for several days.

When the surgeon finally examined Miguel's hands, he saw where the skin and muscle fibre had been torn off and how far down the exposed bones were abraded. The patient was not burned; the fingers were not blown off by an explosion. This was like nothing he had seen.

'Anybody know what happened to this man?' he asked.

'He was digging through the concrete and glass trying to find his wife,' a nurse said.

The surgeon looked over his mask at the nurse and then up at the patient's face. 'He did this to himself?'

'He was trying to find his wife,' the nurse repeated.

'The fingers have more nerve endings than the genitals,' the surgeon told the nurse with clinical dryness.

With the bones shredded to the marrow, the chance of infection or embolism was high, as was the possibility that fragments could enter his circulatory system and create a fatal blockage.

The surgeon examined the man's face again. He was young; to amputate both hands would be to sentence him to a difficult life. He decided that the most damaged fingers, the first two of each hand, required amputation. For thumbs, he might be able to create crude stumps by stitching skin over the remaining bone. There was enough left there to allow him to pinch objects, if nothing more. The two outside fingers of each hand could be saved almost intact, and with the short thumbs, he'd at least have the capacity to grasp objects. The surgeon hoped that the man was not someone who built things with his hands.

Justo Ansotegui smelled his wife Mariangeles in bed beside him. He had loved that scent since she had begun getting the soap from Alaia Aldecoa. She smelled so much like when she came in from the meadows or after she cooked a meal at Errotabarri.

'Justo, Justo,' she said. He had to awaken soon, with so much to do, but if he lay there long enough he might arise to the smell of chorizos sizzling in a pan of fried eggs. Maybe she'd make green peppers for lunch and then lamb with her special mint jelly for dinner. But now he thought of the chorizos frying with eggs. He loved that smell only slightly less than that of Mariangeles's freshly scrubbed neck.

'Justo, Justo.' He rolled his head towards Mariangeles' scent and opened his eyes to look out a partially open window at a blooming tree outside.

'Justo, Justo.'

It was Xabier.

He looked again towards the fresh smell and realized he wasn't in his bedroom. And Mariangeles was not beside him. And his senses were dulled as if he'd been drunk at a feast day, and he wanted to do nothing but go back to bed and to sleep and to smell Mariangeles and the chorizos.

'Justo.'

Xabier kept tugging him away from Mariangeles. Spikes of light from a bare bulb overhead pained his eyes; the taste of ether burned the back of his throat.

'Justo.'

His brother leaned against the bed, wearing full vestments. Was he there to perform the last rites? He felt bad enough.

'What happened?'

'Justo, God bless you, you're going to be fine.'

'What happened?'

'You were trapped in a building.'

It was enough to trigger memories of the bombing, and the woman with the backward head, and the baker's wife. But no more.

'Justo, they had to amputate your arm, there was nothing they could do to save it,' Xabier said.

Justo looked to his left side. Although he felt his fingers, hand, and arm, and sent the mental instructions for them to wiggle and move, he saw nothing there beside him. It was gone. He gave the matter some thought.

'It wasn't my best arm,' Justo said.

Xabier nearly laughed.

'Does Mariangeles know about this?'

'Justo . . . I'm sorry . . .' Xabier knew there was no other way. 'She was killed by a bomb.'

Killed by a bomb. He had to keep asking, to be done with this.

'Miren?'

'Justo . . . I'm sorry . . .'

'Catalina?'

'Justo, there were so many little ones at the market . . . yes, gone.'

Justo rolled his head towards the window and looked out. He was sick. Xabier knelt to clean the mess.

He'd been such a fool to think that being strong would protect his family.

Xabier had returned from Paris immediately after meeting the press, and Aguirre's aides had already located Justo and compiled a report for him on his family's fate. As it turned out, Xabier had entered the station plaza in time to witness Mariangeles's death, although he had no idea she was in that first cluster of victims. Miren had been found and quickly identified because everyone in town knew her. He was assured that she died without suffering.

Legarreta told of Justo's foolish bravery. He lay for many hours trapped and bleeding, with his arm disarticulated behind his head from the weight of an oak beam. With the help of bilbaino firemen, Legarreta arranged a series of supports and braces and extracted victims and survivors.

'Where am I?' Justo asked after his brother finished cleaning the floor. He did not actually care where he was, but to speak and listen was a defence against thinking.

'In the hospital in Bilbao. They stabilized you in Guernica and put you under to make the trip here. There wasn't much they could do there and the doctors here had no choice but to amputate.'

Justo looked again at his left side, where the sheet lay flat.

'My ring?'

'I got it for you,' Xabier said. He had arrived from France on the morning of Justo's amputation. The surgeon asked if Xabier wished to bless his brother before the operation. He did, and when he dared examine the grotesquely twisted appendage, he saw purple flesh swollen around his wedding ring.

'Can you get his ring off?' Xabier asked the surgeon.

'I'd have to cut it and prise it off because the tissue is so swollen and damaged around it.'

'Don't do that,' Xabier said, bothered by the symbolism. 'After you remove the arm, could you then cut the finger to get at the ring?'

The surgeon nodded. 'He won't feel a thing.'

As Xabier waited for Justo's surgery to finish, he walked the crowded hallways and offered blessings to patients. After several hours, the surgeon appeared and presented Xabier with the ring, intact and freshly sterilized.

'Was the surgery a success?' Xabier asked.

'I think so, but it took twice as long as I expected,' the doctor said. 'I've never seen an arm like that. It was like sawing through a ham shank. But he should be fine. He should consider himself fortunate; that beam could have taken off his head. As it was, that injury would have killed most men.'

At his brother's bedside, Xabier took the ring from a pocket and put it on the third finger of Justo's right hand. No, he thought, I don't think Justo will consider himself fortunate.

When the canvas arrived and was stretched onto its frame, an odd happenstance surprised Picasso. The expansive studio had no problem accommodating the twenty-five-foot breadth of the canvas, but at nearly twelve feet high, it didn't fit vertically against a wall. Instead, Picasso had to wedge the frame against the rafters at a slight angle and keep it in position with a series of shims he whittled. He worried: would the angle alter the perspective?

Upon this tilted canvas, Picasso began transferring his pencil studies. The sketches on paper had grown from the vague geometry of the mural into detailed explorations of each component. A cartoonish horse came to life next to a mother with a dead baby draped over her arms, the baby's eyes open to display pinpoint pupils. The artist repeatedly sketched the horse, the woman, and a fallen warrior, sometimes in pencil, sometimes in paints.

The bull was turned and transmuted, assuming a thick face with giant nostrils and huge, muscular cheeks atop a pair of human lips. Across the prominent brow ridge spanned a tangled pair of eyebrows, thick as a Basque man's. Teardrops started appearing everywhere – teardrop nostrils, teardrop eyes – along with sharply conical tongues and ears.

With a thin brush and black ink, Picasso outlined the images on the canvas. He used a ladder or a long stick to hold his brushes for the upper reaches. With the sleeves of his white shirt rolled up to his elbows, cigarette in his left hand, Picasso crouched deeply to work on the lower reaches. His hair, combed from low on the right side to cover his balding crown, kept slipping out of place and falling across his forehead.

Alaia Aldecoa's blindness saved her life. As she stumbled away from the sounds of successive explosions, the earth opened and swallowed her. She had tumbled into a bomb crater several yards deep, a depression that protected her from the force of a bomb that would have vaporized her if she'd been at street level. Dazed and losing consciousness, bleeding from her fall, she lay balled up at the bottom of the crater until long after the attack. She awakened coughing, choking on the dust she had inhaled. Rescuers heard her at the bottom of the pit and carried her to an aid centre that had been set up outside the Carmelite convent.

The minor head wound and concussion she suffered in the fall served merciful narcotic purposes, numbing her to the sounds of the fires and collapsing buildings and the smells of incinerated beasts. When two nuns began to wash her wounds in cool water, she regained consciousness.

'What was that? What happened? Where—'

'There was an attack,' one nun answered. 'Be quiet, you've been injured.'

'My friend Miren; have you seen her? Is she all right? Miren Ansotegui.'

The sister wiping Alaia's face with the cloth subtly looked to the nun next to her. She shook her head slightly.

'We don't know yet, dear,' the first sister lied. 'You should rest now.'

Alaia gladly slipped away.

Several days later, a squad of nuns carried her across town to the Santa Clara convent, where her old friends once again took in an abandoned orphan.

With the two smallest fingers extruding from each bandaged hand, Miguel struggled to open the door at Errotabarri. The pain caused him to suck in deep breaths and pinch his eyes shut until they watered. People had been inside – wandering troops, perhaps, or maybe just hungry refugees – leaving a small mess. Nothing important to them had been taken or damaged. The floral apron was on its nail. Miren's dark plait hung from the corner of the mantel.

When he saw the hair, his chest constricted. He felt the exact outline of his heart, and the pain made it difficult to breathe. He could not look at it, but he could not take it down. He would have to decide what to do with it before Justo returned. It would be the first thing he would see. But would he be more hurt by its sight or by its absence? At some point they would discuss it. Or maybe they never would.

The maize drying on the crossbeams was gone; the medicinal herbs were gone. Another small meal for somebody. He went outside and around to the ground floor. There were no animals in the stalls, of course. There was a flash of grey and white in one corner, and Miguel saw a rabbit seeking shelter beneath a shock of rotted straw. He could kill it with his catapult . . . but he'd left that on the mountain when the bombing started. It was still up there with his cross-cut saw. I'll go and get them later, he thought, as if he could use either.

After leaving the hospital, Miguel first walked to his house to find that it had been gutted by fire, which caused the roof to collapse, leaving a stucco shell of scorched-black walls encasing a pile of shattered tiles. A few tools remained undamaged in his workshop, but the furniture, the things he had built for Cat . . . the bed . . . all were gone. Little more than the charred hinges and lock flap remained of the chest he had made as a wedding present to his wife. For Miren on their wedding day. Miren.

The painted horns of the hobby-ram were intact, but he could find little else.

In the streets, he saw others stumbling about just as he had, searching for things that no longer existed. All scanned the ground in front of them as they walked. At his feet, Miguel saw letters. So many letters and papers. And pieces of broken crockery. Somebody's cracked spectacles. Unmatched shoes. Shoes everywhere, but never in pairs. Splashes of colour among the grey. Splashes of colour on the paper. How could there have been so much paper? Did the bombers drop paper to feed the fires? Black water from the firemen pooled in low spots and smelled of wet ash. He saw a hair ribbon still knotted in a bow. And more paper, burned around the edges, soggy in the puddles.

The rebel troops were plentiful in the town, but there seemed to be no hostility or threat, and none made more than a casual gesture towards him. They could see that he was in no condition to offer resistance. His bandaged hands were pulled up in a protective pose near his chest, like the squirrels he used to see when they sat up on their hind legs in the woods. He unconsciously curled his torso over them to keep them from being jostled, leaving him to walk like an old man with a sagging spine. Miguel felt no anger towards the troops. He did not connect them with those who'd done the damage to the town and his family. They didn't drop the bombs. They looked as dour as most of the townspeople; they exuded no sense of victory. They wandered as aimlessly as the homeless; some of them were wounded and suffering as well.

When Miguel walked near people he knew, they exchanged nods, saying little or nothing. What was there to say? Who would benefit from an accounting of comparative grief? I lost a husband and two sons and a business and a leg. Oh, that is terrible; I lost a wife, a mother-in-law, two hands, a home . . . and a baby girl. A baby girl. Stop it, he told himself.

At first he wanted to find someone who could tell him what had happened to Miren and Catalina, where they had died and how. Were they buried or just gone? But when he saw what was left of the town, he recognized the pointlessness. Details would be more to carry. In his mind, they had just disappeared after leaving the house that afternoon. He would remember them as they were at that moment.

Before leaving the hospital, Miguel decided that he would stay in Guernica, at Errotabarri, and help Justo as much as he could. Since everyone in town knew Justo Ansotegui and had heard the story of him 'lifting an entire building to save the baker's wife', Miguel had been told of his condition soon after regaining consciousness. 'Surgeons had to use a cross-cut saw to amputate that giant arm,' they said.

At least Justo has accomplished something, he thought. It will add to his legend.

Going home to Lekeitio was an option to consider; his parents would nurse him and feed him. His little sisters would care for him. There would be fish to eat. But if he did, he would be the family victim, and he knew he could not tolerate that. Araitz would open every door for him, Irantzu would want to feed him. The Ansoteguis would be across the street, and they had known Miren . . . Miren . . . much longer than he had; they would understand his grief and they would be smotheringly solicitous. There would be reminders in Lekeitio, too.

Maybe he would go to America and start over there. Maybe he could find his old neighbour who'd gone there. Yes, there must be great demand for four-fingered carpenters in America, he thought. No, he would go nowhere else; grief is not a matter of geography. He needed to stay in Guernica. It would be the only place where he wasn't an outsider. We are all forged of the same alloy now, he thought.

But what he had known as Guernica was unrecognizable now. A deep crater occupied the plaza where they had danced. The streets were clogged with the debris workmen had stacked to be hauled away. He passed a man who had bought a chest of drawers from him for his wife.

What to say to him? What to say to anybody? Nothing.

He had made his way slowly to Errotabarri, looking only at the ground where his next step would fall, careful not to walk on the papers and the letters or the unmatched shoes. He had to get things for Justo's return and somehow scratch up something for them to eat. Together, they would try to heal. Perhaps together they had enough arms and fingers to sort through what remained of their lives.

As he walked towards Errotabarri, he tried to conjure Miren, but he couldn't. What would she say now? She could always read his mind and steal his thoughts. She did that from the start. What now? What would she say now? 'We're all right, *astokilo*; look out for my father,' and 'Take good care of Alaia now; she needs you.'

Is Alaia alive? he wondered. How could she be?

And what would Miren say about the plait? What would she want him to do?

Dodo heard of the attack from the fishermen at the harbour. Their report, exaggerated through progressive retelling, was that the town had been bombed to the ground, and those who were not blown up by the bombs were burned to death or machine-gunned. Dodo thought first of his brother's welfare and then of revenge. He urged his fishermen friends to set up a meeting with his father and Josepe Ansotegui as soon as possible. He knew of no other way to learn the truth of who had lived and who had not.

Within a day, a friend ferried him in a small skiff to a rendezvous with the *Egun On*. Josepe and José María had tried to reach Guernica when they heard of the bombing but found the road blocked, and it wasn't until Father Xabier contacted them that they learned what happened. They linked arms with Dodo and told him the news.

'I envied Miguel for his marriage to Miren,' Dodo said. 'No one deserved it more than he did. But I envied it. It seemed that he had everything that he had ever wanted.'

'He did, son,' José María said. 'He did. He had a wonderful little family.'

The past tense struck them all as they stood in a tight cluster on the deck of the bobbing boat.

'We don't really know yet how badly injured he is,' José María said. 'He lost some fingers trying to dig through the buildings for Miren and Catalina.'

'You'd have had to kill him to get him to stop digging, I know that,' Dodo said. 'Has he come home?'

'No, he wants to stay at Errotabarri and help Justo,' Josepe said.

Dodo squeezed them both, compressing the triangle, and moved towards his skiff.

'Tell him that as soon as he heals, if he wants to get away from Guernica, we can put him to work in the mountains here,' Dodo said as he prepared to slip back into the smaller boat.

'This will take some time, son,' José María said.

'Well, I know he's going to be upset,' Dodo said. 'And I'm sure I can work out some ways to help him cope with that.'

CHAPTER 20

For most of the previous day, the orphans had been shuttled on trains from Portugalete Station in Bilbao to the main docks at Santurce. By the morning, most of them had marched up the gangplank of the SS *Habana*, holding hands like paper-doll cutouts. An ageing single-stack passenger ship now converted to a troop transport, the *Habana* was moored at the quay of the port that served Bilbao, making it a target for the Condor Legion or Italian bombers serving the Nationalist rebels. That morning, rebel bombs fell into the river close enough to splash the *Habana*, but four thousand Basque children nonetheless were wedged on board and seemed thrilled to be leaving.

They were orphans of war dead or the children of the displaced, and they were in jeopardy in Bilbao. Some were babes in arms who had been taken aboard by the nurses and volunteers from the orphanages. Others were in their mid-teens. These tiny passengers had not eaten enough and had seen too much, a combination that would only grow worse with the effects of the blockade, continued bombing, and the anticipated rebel occupation. They had to be evacuated. Still hiding behind the shield of the Non-Intervention Pact, the British government reluctantly agreed to evacuate the dispossessed children. But only the children.

Before the *Habana* cast off, Aguirre and Father Xabier boarded, Aguirre to assure the children that they would be gone for only a short time and that this would be a great and memorable adventure, Xabier to bless their voyage and assure them that God was watching over them.

Aguirre came away revived by their happy faces and awed by their resilience. They had been bombed, starved, and uprooted and had endured the deaths of loved ones, but there was little apprehension and no apparent sadness. He told them to be proud of being Basques, because every Basque was proud of them. They cheered the man in the black suit, although few had any idea who he was.

'Do you believe they'll be gone for only a few months?' Xabier pressed his friend when they stepped down onto the quay.

'I know that if they stay here they may be dead in the next few months, or even days.'

'Along with the rest of us?'

'Maybe,' the President acknowledged through the smile he forced as he waved to the children looking down from the ship.

The children were too young to recognize the significance of having the *Habana* as their lifeboat. It had other qualities that were more immediately appreciated. It carried food. Many had teetered on the verge of starvation for months. They were fed eggs and meats and bread. They gorged themselves and hoarded as much as would fit into their pockets. The richness of the food and the vast amounts caused many of them to become ill. An early summer squall whipped up the waters in the Bay of Biscay, and very early on in what would become a turbulent forty-eight-hour passage, many grew seasick.

On the evening of the second day, the *Habana* dropped anchor off Fawley, near Southampton harbour, and was boarded by more doctors volunteering to give medical examinations to the children. Aside from the minor illnesses during the passage, the children were sound and in high spirits. From the deck, they saw the houses along the inlet decorated with flowers and fronted by immaculately tended gardens. It seemed a fantasy world, so apart from and beyond what they had known, and they repeatedly screamed, '*Viva Inglaterra!*' They docked the next morning to the musical accompaniment of a Salvation Army band. Because of their uniforms, the children called them the 'lady policemen'.

The reception camp featured a banner stretched above an earth pathway proclaiming it the Basque Children's Camp. A crop of five hundred circular tents, peaked by central pikes, had sprouted in the field. The children were bathed, given further examinations, and fed by a coalition of volunteers.

The following morning, the *Southern Daily Echo* presented an article headlined 'Sincere and hearty greeting': 'We appreciate the trials through which they must have passed in recent weeks and hope that there in the quiet green fields of Hampshire they will find rest, contentment and – more important still – peace.'

In contrast to their government's position, generous locals were glad to 'intervene'. These were children, after all, babies. Many received new clothes from Marks & Spencer and chocolate from Cadbury. Within months, they were sent not to the Basque Country for repatriation but to more permanent camps in Stoneham and Cambridge and Pampisford and dozens of other towns that supported Basque children's colonies. They continued their schoolwork and play and began the process of recovering from the things they had seen.

The civil war continued to plague their country, while England was peaceful, if uneasy. To send them back to Spain might be a death sentence, or at least an invitation to greater privation. The children assimilated quickly, except for those at a camp near an air base, where nurses and supervisors repeatedly had to promise them that the planes overhead would not drop bombs.

Father Xabier needed an informer. His accomplice was an old friend named Sister Incarnation. At four and a half feet tall, she weighed no more than a sack of feathers, was of indeterminate years between fifty and ninety, and was as well intended as any of the sainted martyrs memorialized in the statuary around the hospital. Sister Incarnation was a nurse's aide who also spent time at the Basilica de Begoña, where she would take patients seeking the comfort of an altar or a confessional. There she came to know Father Xabier, who so admired her energy that he once asked the sister if she ever stopped to rest.

'We little people don't need to sleep,' she told him. 'Did you ever see a hummingbird snoozing on a branch? We rest during blinks.'

After a succession of surgeries trimmed off his left arm up to the shoulder, Justo Ansotegui was transferred to a rehabilitation ward. When Xabier realized he couldn't visit him every day, he deputized Sister Incarnation to serve as his watchdog. Loving her spirit, Justo adopted her and began calling her 'Sister Inky'. She could have fitted in his pocket.

Wounded soldiers and civilians, amputees and burn patients at various stages of rehabilitation filled the wards. These were the victims expected to live, if they still cared to make the effort. The hospital had long been out of wooden legs, and orders for crutches and canes were running months behind. The war had strained the producers and suppliers of such things beyond their ability to capitalize.

In the meantime, Sister Incarnation helped the wounded to reclaim the parts of their lives that could be regained through adaptation. She taught those missing legs to operate crutches, to negotiate stairs, to adjust to their altered centre of gravity. She taught the tricks of one-armed existence to those in need: how to bathe and dress, how to use other parts of the body to pinch objects and serve as a second hand. She taught female arm-amputees how to thread a needle and sew. She instructed leg-amputee farmers to swing the scythe while propping up the limited side with both crutches. Balance and leverage, she preached. Balance and leverage. The world is filled with three-legged dogs and one-legged gulls, she claimed. If they can manage with the tiny brains God provided, then so can you.

To the burn patients, she offered suggestions on coping with pain and the reality of disfigurement. Hair from one side of the head could be brushed over the burned area on the other side of the face. Long sleeves, gloves, and hats could be worn quite inconspicuously. They needed to remember that the looks they received from people in the street were usually of curiosity, not bad intent or insult. If not, they were stupid people and their opinions didn't matter anyway.

In addition to the physical skills, Sister Incarnation sought to inject attitude into the diffident and spirit into those without. To those who required pushing, Sister Incarnation was a disciplinarian. To those who needed consideration, Sister Incarnation was patient and compassionate. And to those who sought sympathy, Sister Incarnation was deaf as a stump. She was not there to reward self-pity.

She had a ready answer to the complainers: 'Look around. Think of all the ones who have been carried out of here. Find the value in what remains. Balance and leverage, balance and leverage.'

She had no trouble staying aware of Justo's activities. With this nun who was a third of his size, Justo felt a kinship of power. Her energy was magnetic. And since the lack of an arm did not impede his mobility between surgeries, Justo became her shadow.

'He follows me around all day,' the sister reported to Xabier. 'He wants to carry things for me; he wants to lift things for me. He is so eager to prove that he's healthy and strong and whole. If he sees a job for a two-armed person, he jumps in and tries to prove he can do it himself with one. And he has started getting tough with other patients, pushing them. He threatened one with harm if he ever spoke back to me or didn't do exactly as I had taught. There was one wounded soldier I had to push hard who said he felt I was treating him like a Fascist. Justo almost killed him.'

'So he's creating a problem?'

'Well, I don't need an enforcer,' she said. 'And the doctors are getting weary of his trying to get them to arm-wrestle.'

Xabier was not surprised.

'He keeps asking me to punch him in the right arm so I can see how much he can take,' she added.

'So then we should presume that he's healed now and ready to go home?' Xabier asked.

'No, no, not at all, that's the problem,' the nun stressed. 'Doctors have done what they can with his arm, and he'll be ready for discharge soon. But he's been so busy convincing us all that he's healthy, he's never dealt with the loss of his arm. He tries to act as if he was born that way.'

'Sister, it isn't the loss of his arm that is the problem; I can guarantee you that,' Xabier said. 'Justo sees that as a challenge. What you see with him wanting to work and help heal others, even if he has to strangle them to do it, is exactly who he is. My fears aren't about the arm at all. What has he said about his family?'

'Not one word. He gets quiet and he goes dark at night. I've checked on him and I know he's acting as if he's asleep, but he rarely is. Father, the nurses and I realized that he's the only patient who has reached this point in rehabilitation who has not been begging to go home. By now, they're sick of us and ready to get back to their lives. He has not said a thing about his home or about wanting to *go* home. It seems as if he would be happy to just stay here and follow me around all day.'

'Has he been counselled on this?'

'Father, we were hoping that would be something for you to take over.'

'Me?'

'To be honest, the doctors are a little afraid of him,' Sister Incarnation said. 'Nobody wants to make him angry. When he goes dark, it's as if he can't even hear us talking to him. We know something is going on inside that mind, but we don't know what.'

The mural projected chaos, and in that regard it was perfectly at home in his work space. The artist, an inveterate hoarder, could scarcely walk through his studio without tripping on an African tribal mask, an ancient bronze cast, sculptures of his own or his friends', sketches of unfinished works, and priceless paintings by Matisse, Modigliani, Gris, and others strewn in this museum of clutter. Interspersed with the art was an abstract tumble of shoes, books, hats, unopened letters, empty wine bottles, and partially eaten meals.

Across the threshold of the mural was the detritus of his art, crumpled paint tubes and a carpet of flattened cigarette butts. The air was thick with the smell of smoke and paint, linseed oil, and Dora Maar's fruity perfume.

Picasso had repositioned his characters, with the bull, too late the saviour, curled in a protective pose around the woman with the dead baby. He'd used the image of the Minotaur in many works, but this was not the bull-man myth, this was an anatomically complete beast ready for the *corrida*.

He erased the dotted pupils of the baby's eyes, leaving a haunting emptiness. The warrior's upraised arm had dropped. The sunflower burst became an incandescent lamp casting jagged light spears onto the scene. Subtly, Picasso encased all the human and animal suffering, and the burning exterior of a building, inside a room with electric lighting, creating a diorama of grief. On the far right, he painted a door to this inside-out world, slightly ajar.

Through successive incarnations, he eliminated most of the blatant gore. Many of the studies and early figures featured bullet holes seeping black blood and body parts randomly scattered. He flirted with the idea of adding texture with collage techniques, attaching a cloth scarf to a woman's head. And he once taped a piece of paper, resembling a blood-red teardrop, to the mother's cheek, making it the only dot of colour in an achromatic scene. Too obvious. It is simple to make people uneasy, more difficult to make them think.

Guilt consumed the penitent at the confessional. She outlined for the priest the details, how she tucked a loaf of bread under her apron at the local market. It was not for her but for her children. That she had not eaten herself was of minor consequence, but to hear her children plead so pitiably was impossible to ignore.

'Yes, I stole,' she said. 'And for one afternoon the children had some stale bread in their stomachs. I am sorry to God. I am sorry to the baker. When the war is over, I will pay him back double. God understands, doesn't He?'

Father Xabier faced more of these stories each day, along with the parishioners' more difficult questions of how such a life could continue and how many prayers would go unanswered. They had lost parents to bombing or sisters to starvation, and, most often, husbands to artillery shells on the front as the circle of fighting cinched tighter around them.

They challenged Xabier to come up with excuses. But he found it impossible to be the interpreter of the inexplicable. To go by the book, Xabier would have had to remind the woman that difficult trials were a common biblical theme, and that strong people with deep faith survived and afterwards knew the reward of their virtue. But he said none of that as he looked through the screen at the emaciated face that made the still-young mother look ages older. Instead, he told her that she need feel no guilt over trying to feed her children. It was her most important job.

'Try to find ways other than stealing; remember, the baker has hungry children, too,' Father Xabier said, knowing she faced few options. 'Try to find a shelter. And have faith.'

'I will, Father.'

'Then go, my child,' he said, again feeling foolish wearing the paternal expression.

'Is there no penance, Father?'

Xabier knew the woman had been through enough without his imposition of further duties. But he also knew that she would not feel genuinely absolved without paying remittance.

'Yes, there is something: pray.'

'Pray? How many times?'

'As often as you can.'

'I am already doing that, Father.'

He loved and hated unveilings, the way they all would gasp even if they had no idea whether what they were seeing was art or rubbish. But this new one could not be veiled. It was too large. The room would be the veil. When his guests stepped through the door, they would step into the painting, into the room within the room.

The painting screamed, and they heard it immediately, but it took time for them to catch the whispers. They saw the fallen warrior before they detected a shadow flower next to his broken sword. They saw the bull before the broken-winged bird on the table in the dark background. The wound to the horse was noticed only after attention was drawn away from his pained muzzle. They stared and paced its length, making new discoveries as they moved from angle to angle.

Most were jolted by the work, by the mass and scope if nothing else. All hints of colour had been removed, leaving it starkly black and white, with muted greys. They needed many minutes to absorb the work, taking it in from far away to close, then left to right, and then back out to a full-frame perspective again. It took time to discover the motility: things hiding in shadows, features half-erased and progressive, growing and fading with movement.

The bull had turned now to display its puckered anus and pendulous testicles, and the nipples on the women resembled babies' dummies. On each visible palm a set of intersecting lines presumably foretold their common misfortune.

When it appeared at the Spanish Pavilion, some questioned the symbolism and meaning. He was told that some expected a more literal depiction of the bombing. He assured them that the message was clear.

One woman attempted an explanation of her reaction to the mural and could only say, 'It makes me feel as if somebody is cutting me to pieces.'

Asked how he expected the work to be viewed over time, Picasso would not commit. It would depend on whether or not it made a difference.

'If peace wins in the world,' he said, 'the war I have painted will be a thing of the past.'

President Aguirre alerted Father Xabier to his need for a conference at the rectory, which meant there would be no random arrival in the confessional. The rebel troops had almost surrounded Bilbao, with the road to Santander the only means of escape.

'How soon?' the priest asked.

'I was sitting at my desk last night with a few ministers, planning the evacuation, and the window exploded,' Aguirre told Xabier. 'Rebels on Monte Artxanda were close enough to take pot shots at us. Three bullets hit the desk and wall. One shattered a glass in front of me on my desk. They not only knew where we were, they were within rifle range of us.'

'They're that close now?' Xabier said, expressing alarm more than asking a question.

'Monte Pagasarri is falling this minute,' Aguirre said. 'We've got three battalions left, and they headed into the mountains with nothing but bolt-action rifles and grenades. I listened to them singing hymns in the trucks: "We are Basque soldiers; to liberate Euskadi, our blood is ready to be shed for her." ' Aguirre spoke the lyrics.

Xabier groaned in sympathy.

'We've shipped more than a hundred thousand refugees to France in the last two months,' Aguirre said, 'but there're still so many—'

'Friend,' Xabier said, stopping him, 'I wanted to tell you I admired the release of the rebel prisoners. I know it was hard, and it brought criticism, but it was the right thing to do.'

'I was afraid they'd be slaughtered out of vengeance before the rebels got here,' Aguirre said. 'I don't regret it. We got a ceasefire out of it for a few hours to accommodate their return to the rebel lines.'

'It's not something they would have done for us,' the priest said.

'We're not in the murder business. War is bad enough; murder is something different.'

'I'm the priest, but I've vilified the rebels far more than you ever have. Especially after what they did to Lorca.'

Rebels had captured the priest's favourite poet, and because they understood him to be homosexual, they shot him repeatedly in the rectum and finished him with a bullet to the head.

'I know,' Aguirre said. 'But there's been much for both sides to be ashamed of.'

'How long do we have before they march into Bilbao?'

'It depends on how eager they are. Right now, it's convenient for them to surround us and starve us. That achieves the same results with less ammunition.'

'What then?'

'Rather than have the troops fight to the last breath here, we're going to try to sneak out our last divisions to the front in Barcelona. There's nothing more we can do here, but our troops can still fight for the Republic there.'

'What about you?'

'That's why I'm here; we're leaving for Santander tonight,' Aguirre said. 'We discussed keeping the troops and the government here and fighting to the death, but the feeling is that our fate is already determined. We're going into exile.'

'I'm glad you're going, and I'm glad you came here before you left,' Xabier said. 'I will miss hearing your confessions.'

'I'll be back,' Aguirre protested. 'It may take a while, but we're trying to keep the government together so it doesn't have to be entirely rebuilt. We finally got our autonomy and that's worth coming back for. Besides, I've got to get back here to keep an eye on the radical priest of Begoña.'

'Go with God, my son,' Xabier said out of habit before amending his blessing to, 'Until later, my friend.'

Aguirre sneaked out of the rectory, but the scent of cigarettes lingered in his path.

That night, he and his family boarded a plane under heavy shelling at Santander airfield, lifting off the ground as rebel forces stormed the strip. In the coming months, the Aguirres would be chased across Europe, often wearing disguises. Several in his family would be shot and killed.

Knowing his return to Spain would mean a swift execution, Aguirre could not come home as long as Francisco Franco was dictator. José

Antonio Aguirre, the first Basque president, who took his oath of office beneath the sacred oak of Guernica, would never again see his country.

Franco's first act after the fall of Bilbao was to declare that speaking Euskara was illegal. Basques were told to 'speak Christian', and within two weeks, the Catholic hierarchy of Spain issued proclamations condemning Basque priests for having ignored 'the voice of the Church'.

CHAPTER 21

Miren called him in from the workshop in that frisky way that meant she had a job for him. He'd been lathing a table leg and he smelled of cypress shavings and sweat. 'What do you think of this colour?' she asked.

'*Kuttuna*, the paint's getting all over you,' Miguel said. 'You shouldn't paint in your wedding dress.'

'I thought the yellow was too bright in here,' she said. 'The black will be better, don't you think?'

'It's pretty dark . . . but it's different.'

'Exactly – it's different,' she said. Dots of paint freckled her face.

'I don't care what it looks like,' Miguel said. 'Do you need me to get the high parts?'

'No, I can reach.'

She put down her brush and they held each other, and at the sound of Mendiola's saw music, they danced.

'I ache for you,' he said.

She nodded.

He leaned down so his mouth was at her ear. 'I love you. I miss you.'

She whispered the same words to him.

'I looked for you,' he said.

'I know, *asto*, I know. Thank you. I knew you would.'

'I'm sorry we fought,' he said.

'We didn't fight,' she said, pulling back to look in his eyes.

'That wasn't ever about us. That was so small.'

'It was time we wasted.'

'Maybe not. We had things we needed to say and that was all it was. Every married couple has those things.'

They turned slowly to the music, moving like one connected body. Turning, turning, holding tightly.

They drifted and swayed. Closer.

'Thank you, Miguel,' Mariangeles said. Miren's mother?

She joined them dancing, holding them both. The same feel. The same smell.

'She misses dancing, too,' Miren said.

They turned, all three, and as the music slowed, the walls grew darker until they were entirely black.

More difficult for Father Xabier than addressing an elderly person as 'my child' was trying to become a father to his big brother. Being subservient to Justo, being his little brother, was the position he'd occupied longer than any other. To help him was tricky, to guide him impossible. Justo's physical progress had impressed the surgeons and nurses and Sister Incarnation. But each worried about his emotional withdrawal.

Xabier had written to Josepe in Lekeitio with updates on their brother. In the past, Josepe had occasionally sailed to Bilbao to visit Xabier at the basilica, but the blockades and the mining of the harbour made these trips impossible now. Xabier reasoned that Josepe would have the best advice on dealing with their brother because of his age and the fact that he had more in common with Justo than a celibate cleric. If nothing else, Josepe had known him a year longer. But his plea for advice elicited only a terse response:

Dear Xabier,

   Let me know if I can provide anything – absolutely anything – other than advice on how to deal with our brother. Maybe this is why Justo sent you to the seminary. Pay him back. Good luck.

   Josepe

Seeing no alternatives, the priest made a place for Justo at the Basilica de Begoña rectory. There, at least, he would have food and attention and be away from the hospital and doctors. Xabier could take care of him and keep him away from the rebels who had taken over the town. Xabier feared how Justo would act in their presence and knew there was little he could do about it if Justo decided to instigate a confrontation.

With parishioners, he spoke from a seat of power, and his advice might have been ignored, but it was at least superficially respected. Trying to tell his older brother how to respond to the tragedy in his life required a greater level of sensitivity. But he also knew that Justo would not tolerate his being less than entirely honest. He would demand frankness and reject coddling from his kid brother. But if Justo would not talk about Mariangeles and Miren, where was *his* honesty?

For several weeks, Justo woke before dawn and worked at the rectory, sweeping, dusting, picking up leaves in the grounds. 'I have to earn my keep,' he volunteered whenever anyone approached. 'I can help around here.'

That Justo had not stormed any of the rebels' garrisons relieved Xabier, who slept uneasily the first few nights his brother was in residence. Rebel soldiers had not ventured into the basilica, and Justo had not left the grounds, so there had been no chance for a clash. Instead, Justo attacked his adopted daily work at the basilica as he always had at Errotabarri.

He sat near the main door through every Mass, acting as an unofficial usher, jumping up to help the elderly to their seats whether they needed it or not. At times he would lift an older woman off the kneeler if she had hardened in place during a lengthy prayer. Afterwards, he picked up any mess between the pews and mopped up the floor near the door if it had been a rainy day. The basilica employed a caretaker, but he had the sense to be cautious around Justo.

Justo brightened when Sister Incarnation appeared, and he shouted a deep, 'Sister Inky!'

'Look how well I'm doing; ball up your fist and hit me,' he said to the tiny woman, leaning down to within her range in case she chose to accept his invitation.

'No, Justo, I don't strike patients, it doesn't look good,' she said.

'Yes, but look at me,' Justo pressed. 'Eh?'

'Yes, Justo, you are doing very well. Your brother tells me you are a great help around here.'

'I have to earn my keep,' he assured her. 'Watch this.'

Justo wielded the broom with one hand in a display of his adaptation.

'That's very good,' she said, as if to a child.

Sister Incarnation played along with Justo, agreeing that he certainly did seem physically sound. Decent nutrition and better rest had helped him regain his vigour. But she felt that the return of his external shell only made the hollowness inside him give off more of an echo.

'I think . . . I *believe* he is ready to start the hard work,' the nun told Xabier. 'I think if you wait much longer, the walls will be too strong to ever let you inside. He trusts you, Father, he's told me so many times how proud he is of you and what a wonderful priest and brother you are. If you trust your instincts with him, he might even help you along.'

Xabier felt comfortable relying on her sense of timing; she had worked for decades with those recovering from trauma. Over a late dinner, when the brothers were alone, Xabier voiced the first uncloaked question he'd dared to ask since Justo joined him.

'You're doing so well, Justo, have you thought about when it is you'd like to go back to Errotabarri?'

Xabier mistimed the question, as his brother had just taken a large bite of bread. He looked down, finishing his mouthful. Xabier watched as Justo's moustache undulated rhythmically.

'I was guilty of the sin of pride, brother,' he finally said. 'I thought myself a god among men, and the real God decided he needed to teach me the truth.'

'That was no sin, Justo. It was who you are, who you've always been. We made it through because of your strength. Your strength let us keep Errotabarri. Your strength helped you find Mariangeles. Your strength built your family. Your wife and your daughter, even you, were loved by almost everyone in town. These things were important.'

'Yes,' Justo said unconvincingly. 'But being shown to be a fool is a hard thing.'

'You're nobody's fool, Justo.'

'I'll tell you what a fool I was. After your sermon that frightened everyone, I went home and I spent the day and night honing my axe on the whetstone and sharpening the *laia*'s points with a file. I was a fool.'

'What can I say, Justo?' Xabier said. 'It isn't your fault, you have to know that. I can't tell you how to stop hurting. I can't help anybody with that, and that's what I feel is my greatest failure here; it makes me feel like a fool sometimes, too. But you have to find a way to deal with this other than pretending it didn't happen.'

'Oh, I know it happened,' Justo said. 'And I'm ready to deal with it in my way.'

Xabier feared where this was headed. 'Revenge will do nothing for Mari and Miren. If you kill a few Fascists, they'll soon kill you.'

'Why would you think I'd do such a thing?'

'You haven't thought of it?'

'Xabier, I don't think I ever told you about the night I met Miguel,' Justo said. 'He came to Errotabarri and that evening he told me that he thought our father was selfish.'

Xabier had not heard the story, and it surprised him.

'He did. He had the *pelotas* to sit in our house and say that to me on the day we met. He said that if Father had really loved our mother, he would not have grieved himself to death. The real love would have been for him to get over it, and live, and take better care of us.'

'I never thought of it in that way because we were all so young, Justo, but I think he's right. If a parishioner were in the same situation, I would give him that same advice.'

'He asked me to think what our mother would have said to our father, and he said he thought she would have asked him to grieve hard, yes, but then be strong and move on.'

'Justo, what do you think Mariangeles would want to say to you now?'

'I think she'd say, "Go ahead, Justo, grieve hard but then be strong . . ." ' Justo said, dropping his head.

'I think you need to listen to her, brother,' Xabier said, reaching for Justo's hand.

By autumn, most of the burned and gutted buildings had been cleared to make way for the town's reconstruction. Workmen bulldozed the concrete debris into the bomb craters, packed it down, and paved it over. Holes from bullets and shrapnel still pocked many of the standing structures, and most would be tuck-pointed to erase the evidence later. These were the scars most easily repaired.

For a carpenter, it should have been a profitable time. The council asked Mendiola to help supervise parts of the reconstruction. He questioned Miguel about helping, and Miguel remembered that the last time they joined in a civic endeavour, it was to build a *refugio*. What construction codes would be required now? Were they to replace the buildings in the same spots as if nothing had happened? Or would everything be new and different to avoid comparisons to all that had been?

Most of the work was done by forced-labour crews of captured Republican soldiers, many of them Basques, who were now compelled to rebuild the city they had been unable to protect in the first place. But the Francoists who now dominated the town council also hired locals for minimal pay. Miguel dodged recruitment by reminding them that many of his tools were lost or damaged. He could have just held up his hands as an obvious excuse, but he kept them in his pockets now. He had found a few small hand tools amid the debris of his house, and he also had discovered, rusting on the hillside above town, the cross-cut saw that he had dropped that afternoon. He decided he would starve before working beside the prison-labour force of men who might have been neighbours.

Miguel tested his capabilities with some light work at Errotabarri, mostly maintenance to the house and shed. He had not gone into the room where Miren had slept when she was growing up. He also had not killed and eaten the rabbit, and his restraint was rewarded by the appearance of several others, who established a colony in the basement. From somewhere a bony chicken arrived, too, as if sprung from an egg that had been dormant beneath the rotting straw. Perhaps this was the final chicken in all the Pays Basque, Miguel speculated. The Basque Country – could he even call it the Basque Country anymore?

He eased himself into his return to work, not because of the pain he still felt, but because there was a limit to what could be achieved at Errotabarri. Some volunteer corn popped up over the summer, and he mostly kept it as seed stock for the next year. Since there were no animals to feed, he let the grass grow untouched in hopes it would reseed itself and come back thicker.

He discovered that his favourite stream still had a few fish that would take worms and grubs, which made a satisfying meal when fried along with the wild mushrooms that still grew in the shaded ravines on the hillside. He relearned the skill of fishing through trial and error. Mostly he learned to adapt. He could awkwardly grasp the crosscut and bow saws, and the brace-and-bit drill. It was exhausting and inefficient but manageable if he took it slowly.

Miguel had no interest in spending more time than necessary in town. Falange soldiers were still about, and he could not even nod in their direction as he passed. Their force had thinned out since the first weeks after the attack, but there were still Fascists and the Guardia Civil in sufficient numbers to make him uncomfortable.

To walk through the town carried the risk of having to talk. And he found himself losing the knack. Ventures in public forced him to rise to the surface, while the rest of his time was spent at some subsurface level, lost in thought or dreaming. If he could stay away from people, his days were less complicated. Not easier, because it all felt like wading through a viscous twilight, but less complicated. For long stretches, he wouldn't realize his distance from consciousness until he tried to say something, to the squirrels or to the fish he'd caught, and was surprised by the words coming out in a coughing sound, as if dust and cobwebs had collected in his throat.

The day of his release from the hospital, he'd asked of Alaia's welfare. He'd been told that she'd been unharmed and the sisters were looking after her. To enquire further would have meant more talk, more time in town. He'd met his obligation.

It was better to just stay in the mountains and at the *baserri*. He could still fell a tree and swing an axe. It was much slower, but it was quiet work in the quiet hills, and the exhaustion dulled his mind. Until the point when fatigue would numb him, he was vulnerable to memories. How old would Catalina be right now? Would she be walking? Would she be using the bigger toys he'd made her? Would it be time for them to start another baby?

He'd empty his mind again and focus on the saw blade's hum, dropping tree after tree, until exhaustion rid him of memories. He repaid the occasional loan of Mendiola's mule with a portion of the timber he brought in, and he made enough money to stay alive, to buy some seeds for replanting, and to replace some of the tools that he found himself needing.

Alaia Aldecoa felt cloistered again as silence joined darkness as a constant in her life. She had so desperately sought to leave the convent and then spent so much energy convincing Miren that she needed to be independent. And now, back at her cabin, she had nothing but independence, and a life once empty somehow grew more empty.

There would be no more business partners, as Miren had labelled them. She was done with that. The closeness she'd wanted turned out to be something else. No one knocked on her door, and she would not have admitted them anyway. So many were gone now; so many were desperate for other things. She kept the hatchet that Zubiri had used for splitting her kindling. If soldiers arrived with bad intent, she would swing it in the direction of their sounds until she made contact or she was killed.

No one arrived to buy soaps, either, and the market had not been re-established.

She could tell from the way her dress hung slack that she'd grown stringy from lack of food. Zubiri continued to help as he could. He was alone and could share what subsistence he could scrape off his small *baserri*. He knew without discussion that their arrangement had changed. They were friends now, and he would help Alaia for that reason. They talked more, and that seemed important. He had managed to hide a goat in a shepherd's cabin in the mountains, which meant milk and cheese for them. He also kept bees, and he shared the honey with Alaia. It was a different closeness.

She thought of Miren often. She remembered the smell of breakfast at Errotabarri, and how Justo greeted them both with hugs and outrageous stories while Mariangeles was careful to make sure her needs were met. She remembered Miren and Mariangeles, and the way they were like two generations of the same person. And she thought of Miren when she went to sleep, recalling the nights in her bed, sharing private thoughts and wrestling.

Alaia no longer needed to recognize the time of day. She slept when she wished and for as long as she could. There was only waking and sleeping now, and in her solitary darkness there was little difference between the two.

Why go to town? So much had changed and she had no one to

show her the ways in which the new streets bent around the new construction. So she stayed at home and survived without purpose. At times she worked on her soaps, even though there was no market in which to sell them. She gathered herbs in the meadows for scents and for making tea, and she collected greens to boil and eat.

She found herself thinking of Miguel and how enormous was his loss. It had been a perfect family. But he had almost two years with Miren. He had Justo and his family. She had only soap and thoughts, and she felt that was slender excuse for a life. But she also had a small, worn rag doll that had become more important to her than she could have imagined.

The herringbone pattern of the wood made the floor of the Basilica de Begoña seem to rise on the lengthy path from the entrance to the altar. Sister Incarnation helped a woman on crutches all the way to the front pew, taught her how to genuflect in her new condition, and then retreated to give privacy to her prayers. At the back of the main nave, she found Justo Ansotegui, who had been watching her.

'You look well, Justo,' she whispered.

'Thank you.' Justo gestured for her to sit. 'I need to apologize to you, Sister. I was dishonest with you. I've talked with my brother Xabier and we've straightened out a few things.'

'Dishonest about what, Justo?'

'About my family, about my life, about what was going through my mind,' he said. 'I didn't believe I could talk about it without breaking down, without being weak. I didn't want you to see that in me.'

She patted his knee.

'By not telling you about my wife and daughter I kept you from knowing them,' he said. 'And it's important to me that you understand who they were.'

'Justo, people have to find different ways,' she said. 'That takes time; that's not being dishonest. You just weren't ready.'

'Sister, my wife and daughter were my life,' he said. 'I know you hear that all the time. The only thing I could do was convince myself they were alive somewhere and I was going to see them again. So, yes, I was dishonest with you and I was probably being dishonest with myself. I apologize. For as hard as you worked with me, you deserved better than that.'

'Justo, I knew your family,' she said. 'Father Xabier told me everything. I just couldn't talk about them until you were ready. I knew when it was time that you would tell Father Xabier how you felt and he would be the one to help you through this.'

They sat quietly for a moment, watching the altar candles flicker and reflect off the stone columns as parishioners branched off to the side chapels for prayers. It was a busy place, but solemn.

'I wanted to tell you that I'm going home soon,' Justo said. 'I hope you will keep watch on that brother of mine. We have a family problem of thinking we can save the world.'

'Justo, that's almost exactly what he told me about you,' she said. Both laughed loudly enough for some in prayer to turn to scowl, easing back around when they saw that a nun was involved.

'I worry how he makes everyone's problems his own; he invites their suffering,' Justo said.

'Don't worry for him, that's what makes him such a fine priest,' the nun said. 'He told me that you were the one who saw that in him.'

'Sister, I just wanted to get him out of the house.'

'Justo,' she said harshly, 'you are in the house of God; you should not lie here.'

From her pocket, she retrieved a small green cloth medallion connected to a string to be worn around the neck, emblazoned with the likeness of the Virgin Mary and the inscription 'Immaculate heart of Mary, pray for us now and at the hour of our death'.

'Justo, I want you to wear this scapular.'

'Thank you, Sister, I will.'

'You never know when you might need help from the Mother of God.'

'True enough.'

He spread the supportive cord of the small medallion to

accommodate its passage over his head, slipped it down around his neck, and tucked it inside his shirt.

Both rose, dipped deeply as they stepped into the aisle, and crossed themselves. Sister Incarnation checked that her patient in the front pew was still bent in prayer and then walked towards the entrance with Justo.

'Justo, I've never had a patient like you,' she said.

'Is that a compliment?'

'I think it is, yes,' she said with her small birdcall laugh. 'I want you to do what your brother says. Listen to him. You are a good man and there are not enough of those to go around these days.'

'Sister, I promise you I'll do my best to be myself again.'

'Good, Justo,' she said. 'Because I would not want to have to get tough with you.'

The tiny nun moved in closer, as if to hug him. Instead, she reached up to her full height and punched him on the right shoulder.

Fishing was the best part now, on the hillsides in the afternoon with the coolness of the stream beneath the alders. Neither shouted when a fish was caught, although it meant more to them now. But an instinctual response surfaced whenever the line was pulled hard by one taking the bait. The connection seemed so different to Miguel from winching in hundreds in a net.

When they first returned to the stream, Miguel knew not to ask Justo whether he needed help baiting his hook. Even with just two fingers and part of a thumb on each hand, Miguel was quicker at some things than Justo. Baiting a hook was one. After mutilating dozens of grubs and worms while trying different ways of stabbing them with the hook, Justo arrived at a method that disgusted Miguel, although it did not surprise him. When he found a fat grub under a rotting log or downed branch, Justo would pop it into his mouth. With his teeth and lips pinching it in place, he brought the hook up to his mouth and threaded it through the plump body. Once he hooked his own lip, causing him to howl. Often Miguel would see blood or worm guts on Justo's moustache and found he had to turn away.

'What?' Justo asked when Miguel groaned at the vision.

'Nothing.'

'The taste is not that bad, Miguel. It is not worse than some of the things we have been eating and calling dinner. If we don't catch anything today, it might just *be* our dinner.'

But there remained scattered fish to be caught. Unhooking them was somewhat less disgusting, although hardly artful. Justo would lay the fish on the ground, step on it with his left foot, and yank the hook out with his right hand. Sometimes the string broke or the hook bent or the fish's lip ripped off with the hook. The weight of his foot smashed the fish soft, leaving it with a mealy texture. But no one was choosy.

Miguel was slightly more deft, but a number of times, as he tried to unhook the fish, it would flop out of his hands and land back in the stream.

'We're a fine pair,' Justo said.

'We are,' Miguel said. 'One hand and, what, maybe nine fingers between us.'

'And three ears,' Justo added. 'Do you have all your toes?'

Yes, Justo's ear. Miguel had not expected to have so much trouble with Justo's ear. When Father Xabier sent word to Errotabarri that he was bringing Justo home, Miguel did what he could to prepare, cleaning the house and restoring order as he remembered it. He wanted to have a meal prepared, too. Miguel had gone to the Mezos' when he returned to see if there was any help he could provide, but the home was empty. He knew that Roberto was likely still in jail somewhere, but he had not heard of the fate of Amaya and the seven children. When he walked up to their *baserri*, he saw in the garden a mound of earth bearing a cross of scrap wood. In charcoal writing across the horizontal board was the word *Ama*. Mother.

What happened to the children was another of the many mysteries. Miguel looked through the house to be certain there was none left to help. And when he saw no one, he looked for anything that might help him survive. No food was visible, but to his surprise, he discovered a bottle of wine in a drawer in the kitchen.

He saved it for the meal to celebrate Justo's return. One of the rabbits in the downstairs stalls was sacrificed. Miguel had a fire burning and dinner cooking when the Ansotegui brothers arrived.

It was an immediate disaster. Justo saw Miren's plait and broke down. Miguel saw Justo's ear and thought instantly of Catalina. They sobbed in the same rhythm as they hugged, and Xabier put his arms around both and recited prayers. He hoped it would calm them and that maybe it would call down spiritual assistance, but mostly he prayed because he could think of nothing else to say.

Xabier saw the wine on the table and broke from their embrace to pour three glasses. There was no toast, no *osasuna*. And there was very little talking. Miguel stepped to the hearth to remove the pot simmering with rabbit and a few vegetables he had collected to make a stew. Justo rose to help, looking at the apron hanging from the nail.

When it was time for bed, all three slept in the main room. When he had just come out of the hospital, Miguel had brought in a small, ratty cot from the lambing shed, and he had been sleeping on that. He offered that to Father Xabier, who saw no benefit in arguing over it. Miguel and Justo slept seated in the two padded chairs.

Xabier visited Santa María church the next morning before returning to Bilbao, subtly urging his friends and colleagues to keep their eyes on his brother. In Xabier's absence, Justo and Miguel were left to find their paths around each other's grief.

Renée Labourd's parents, Santi and Claudine, were still spry and clever enough for the work. But they had taken fewer jobs as the civil war in Spain caused the border guards to be supplemented by Franco's military forces, who were quicker to perform impromptu executions for sport. The contraband was more precious now, as Basque, Catalan, and Republican refugees sought ways to seep across the border into the relative peace of France. But the boundary was decreasingly permeable and the Labourds were recognizable as frequent crossers.

Mostly it was Renée's operation now, Renée's and her new partner Eduardo Navarro's. Eduardo had overcome his disastrous apprenticeship to discover an innate talent.

'Papa, you'd be so proud of Dodo; he's coming up with new ideas,' Renée said at dinner.

'Tell us, son,' Santi Labourd said. 'We are not too old to learn.'

'No . . . you are the heroes of the mountains,' Dodo protested. 'I'm new to all this. If I have any advantage it's that I have a better idea how the Spanish guards think. You French Basques try to use logic on them, but your logic doesn't apply.'

'How so?' Santi asked.

'Spanish guards are predictable,' Dodo said. 'If it is a hot day, you may be certain that the shaded areas will be fully staffed and impeccably guarded. You are mostly free to do as you please out in the sunshine. If it's rainy, they will be vigilant in their attention to all covered areas. If it's cold, they will surround the stove and protect it with their entire force. So you can out-think them and outwork them. They'll cluster in the easiest paths, where they assume you will pass. In their minds, it's inconceivable that anybody would walk along a steep, rocky trail when a gentle path is available.'

'What about in town?' Claudine Labourd asked.

'I think you manipulate their perception; people are led by what they see, and you can make them believe just about whatever you want them to.'

'Yes?'

Renée laughed. 'Let me tell them,' she demanded. 'He invented the illusion of the baguette,' she said. 'It's so simple and it never fails. You may have a sack spilling over with pistols and ammunition, but if you have a loaf of bread sticking out of the top, you're nothing more than somebody out shopping.'

'I just noticed how many people on this side of the border walk around with bread, and how I never suspect them of anything other than being hungry,' Dodo said. 'It's the cheapest disguise you can use.'

'And it's edible,' Renée said. 'Tell him about the sheep bells; my father will love this one.'

Dodo grinned. 'We had tried to get some packages through several of our favourite passes but checkpoints had been set up,' he said. 'The last chance we had that night was to try to get past the guardhouse at one of the ports that is popular with herders moving between grazing lands.'

'How did you manage?'

'With sheep bells,' Renée broke in.

'It was cold and raining a little, so I suspected the guards in the shack would be patrolling their stove,' Dodo said. 'I borrowed a few neck bells from a friend's flock. We walked slowly up to the shack, rattling the bells every few steps as if we were grazing, and nobody ever looked out.'

To Justo, Miguel was guilty of unforgivable courtesy; to Miguel, Justo was cruel in his unrelenting thoughtfulness. It was as uncomfortable as a formal dance between two strangers. One could not attempt the simplest task without the other wondering if an offer of help would be an insult.

Except for the subdued joy they shared fishing, it became easier for them to avoid each other's company. Justo went to the new market once it was re-established, just to hear others talk. Miguel would stay in the hills even after his logging was done. Justo eventually took to sleeping in Miren's old bed, and Miguel remained on the camp bed in the main room.

Both were habitual early risers, but Miguel generally heated weak tea and was gone before Justo left his room for the morning. Justo worked at Errotabarri, trying to grow enough to sustain them but not so much that it would cause others to think there was something worth confiscating. Miguel and Justo instinctively knew that the less contact they had with the plunderers, the better were their chances of staying out of prison.

The two generally reconvened in the evening for an unsatisfying dinner of whatever they had been able to forage, kill, or purchase with Miguel's small income from logging. After several months, even the conspicuous courtesy faded, and days would sometimes pass when all that was said between them was 'Good night, Miguel' and 'Good night, Justo.'

A knock on the door one night after dinner brought a change.

'Justo . . . Miguel . . . it's Alaia,' they heard from outside. 'Are you at home? Can I come in?'

They rushed to the door. Justo pulled it open the first part of the way, and Miguel then helped push it fully aside. Alaia had found her way to Errotabarri with her cane, having remembered the path.

'Have you eaten? We have some food left – if you want to call it that,' Justo offered.

'I've eaten already,' she said. 'I don't really eat that much anymore. Not like those huge meals Mariangeles and Miren used to make, with the lamb and asparagus and peppers.'

'You did have a fine appetite,' Justo recalled. 'Mariangeles loved feeding you because you took such joy in eating everything. You wouldn't even speak because you didn't want to waste time talking when you could be eating.'

'Miren used to make fun of me all the time, but while she was busy gabbing away with her stories, I was putting away all that good food,' Alaia said as Miguel guided her to a chair at the table. 'And that flan, oh, God, that flan.'

'That flan,' Justo and Miguel added in harmony. 'Ohhh.'

Alaia had been at Errotabarri only a few moments, and the names 'Mariangeles' and 'Miren' had been spoken for the first time in the months since Miguel and Justo had returned. While talking to Alaia, there was little discomfort. She somehow buffered the connection between them; they could not say the words to each other but were able to talk about their loves and even remember pleasant stories about them when she raised the topic.

'You gave me those wonderful bear hugs,' Alaia said, holding out her arms in Justo's direction. Justo closed in and encircled her as completely as he could with his right arm. She pulled him close.

'Justo, I hope you don't mind, I brought something for you,' Alaia said, placing a small wrapped package on the table. 'If you don't want it, I understand. I just thought it might be something you two might like to have around the house.'

Justo knew what it was at the sight of it. He unwrapped the waxed paper and removed one of perhaps half a dozen bars of soap.

'It's their blend,' Alaia said, although she was sure that Justo and Miguel would recognize the scent. 'The ingredients aren't as easy to get anymore, but I won't make it for anyone else.'

Justo handed a bar to Miguel. Both held the soaps to their nose for a moment, inhaling deeply and staring at the young woman who had brought the scent of life back into their house.

CHAPTER 22

The sign over the main door of the derelict rectory read 'Welcome, *niños.*' The thousands of displaced Basque children who had spent a year in the temporary Southampton camp were being redistributed across the British countryside in smaller groups, including the one here at Pampisford. As the government had not relented in its stance against providing support to the orphans, local citizens were recruited to help via a series of flyers and announcements in the newspapers. Those of a charitable nature began arriving to prepare for the children.

Annie Bingham, a timorous young woman with short red hair and a constellation of freckles across her nose and cheeks, wanted to help however she could. She was among more than a dozen volunteers working to clean and refurbish the building. By the time Annie entered the cold, dusty rectory, it was throbbing with the rhythm of hammers and the melody of saws. Because it burned like a beacon near the ceiling, she noticed the hair of a young man up a tall ladder. It curled out from under a painter's cap. Where hers was more copper, his was flame. The young man belonging to the hair edged nearer the top rung of a ladder while fastening rods for curtains.

'Blast.' The red-haired young man dropped a bracket that clanked with an echo against the hardwood flooring. Annie stepped to the base of the ladder, retrieved the bracket, and tossed it back to the young man so he didn't have to make a full descent. It took her three tries to get it close enough that it didn't threaten to knock him off his perch or fall well below his reach.

'Thanks, Red,' he said.

She nodded and smiled.

Charles Swan finished screwing in the bracket and climbed down to introduce himself.

'My friends call me Charley,' he said, offering a hand after wiping it clean on his trousers.

'Annie Bingham,' she said, shaking the hand. 'Of Pampisford.'

'And what brings you to this holy hovel?'

'I should say that it's out of my charitable nature, and it is, in a way, but actually I hope to be an instructor of Spanish one day.'

He smiled.

'I thought I could help out with the little ones and practise my language at the same time. I came today to see how things were coming along here.'

'*Maravilloso*,' Charley said.

'*Usted habla bien.*'

'*Yo no hablo tan bien como usted.*'

'And you?' she asked, holding her palm up to gesture at all the work in progress.

'I've just finished my first year reading engineering at Cambridge, but I'm going to take some time off to learn to fly,' he said. 'A friend at school told me about what was going on here and I offered to help them get the project off the ground.'

'Fly what?'

'Whatever they're willing to teach me,' he said. 'I want to learn to fly something.'

'Who? The RAF?'

'They're looking for young men with an engineering background.'

Or with good vision and a pulse, she thought. 'What if there's war?' she asked.

Charley had considered the possibility, of course.

'I've always been interested in the science of it more than anything else, since I was little,' he told her. 'That's the biggest attraction for me.'

'How a plane gets in the air?'

'And stays there.' He chuckled.

They shared brief biographies, and when volunteers arrived with a pot of hot soup and several plates of cold sandwiches, they sat side by side on a bench, with vapours from the cups of soup rising in front of them.

'Will you be coming back once the building is ready and the children arrive?' Annie asked, her glasses fogged slightly.

'I hope to,' he said, although he had not previously considered it. He had planned to return to his parents' home in London for those few months before starting reserve flight training in Cambridge. 'If I can work it out, I'd love to help these children.'

'I would, too,' Annie said.

'Would you mind if I came by to see you from time to time?' Charley asked.

Annie Bingham had done nothing to attract the boys at school. But here was one who knew what he wanted. Besides, she liked his hair.

She tapped her tin cup to his to toast the possibility.

Justo began disappearing. Now Miguel would awaken early and discover Justo was already gone for the day. Mendiola told Miguel several times that he had seen Justo in town, just walking or quietly sitting on benches on side streets at odd times.

But rather than making him more distant, Justo's sporadic disappearances made him more purposeful. He had regained some vigour and was more engaged when he was at home. He was still subdued much of the day and was never as boastful and brash as he'd been, but he was going about his work at Errotabarri with more energy.

'You have to get out more, Miguel,' Justo said one day. Miguel could not have been more surprised if Justo had suggested he join the Guardia Civil.

'Get out more?'

'Yes, get out more. Get out of this house. Find some projects, something to keep you busy.'

'I'm out of the house from before dawn until after dark,' Miguel reminded him. 'I'm working.'

'Here, smell this,' Justo said, handing Miguel a bar of soap from his pocket, as if that would explain his renewed vitality.

'Yes, I smell it,' he said. 'I can't go anywhere around here without smelling it.' And when he smelled it, he thought those thoughts, the ones he already had enough trouble controlling. He wanted to tell Justo, Maybe it's comforting to you, but it's killing me; everywhere I go in this house, finding those soaps, smelling that smell, thinking about where her neck met her shoulder, how it smelled after she washed Catalina. To Miguel, it was just another reason to be gone from Errotabarri.

On one of his visits, Father Xabier noted Justo's improved attitude. He complimented his brother on his well-being. He said he would be sure to give Sister Incarnation a good report.

'Is he up to something?' Xabier asked Miguel when Justo was outside.

'He's still quiet, but he keeps on the move; that's made a difference for him,' Miguel said. 'I haven't heard that he's spending time with people in town, but he's at least working here and getting out. It seems to help.'

'And you, how are you doing, Miguel?'

'I do my work.'

'Have you visited Miren's friend Alaia?' the priest asked.

'She came here once, but that's all I've seen of her.'

'Should I go and see her, Miguel? I know that Miren would want somebody to look in on her.'

The new Guernica town council took on a vastly different composition and mission after the bombing. The old supporters of the Republic and Basque nationalism were exiled or in work camps, replaced by men new to the town or those with the talent for political malleability and situational loyalty.

Angel Garmendia had been so vague in his political posture over the years that he had never allowed himself to be categorized by party or beliefs. The sometime Carlist and occasional Basque loyalist was now a firm pro-Franco member of the new council. Like most converts, Garmendia was keen to prove the strength of his conviction. He led the council to declare that several of the businesses that remained standing in Guernica would need to be compulsorily surrendered to pro-Franco businessmen for the good of the reconstruction.

'The future strength of our town depends on our association with the Nationalists,' Garmendia said before the gathered council, having ceased calling Franco's forces 'rebels' or 'Falange'.

Garmendia enjoyed his expanding influence in town, and in the cafes at night, over wine, he would conduct desultory seminars on the wonders of the new Franco government, if, of course, his audience was not too filled with disgruntled loyalists or scarred bombing victims.

Rules regarding the dumping of industrial waste in the river needed to be relaxed, Garmendia preached. In these times, it was important to make it easy for businesses to thrive. Confiscation of certain businesses was crucial, too, to rid the country of the leftists and reds who spurred the problems in the first place. Those were the people who invited socialism into the country with their concerns for so-called workers' rights.

Garmendia consumed a great deal of wine one night during such a discourse. He stumbled on the threshold of the cafe as he set off alone in the darkness.

It surprised no one, then, when word travelled the following day that he had met a tragic end. Garmendia, of the town council, who had so many ideas for the new Guernica that he loved to share, had fallen over the side of the Renteria Bridge and drowned.

Since many had witnessed his public intoxication, no further investigation was needed when he was found dead on the rocks slightly downstream of the bridge. Angel Garmendia had not been known as a particularly devout man, however, which made it curious that he was found with a green scapular hanging from his broken neck. *Pray for us now and at the hour of our death*, it read.

The children came from social-welfare homes in Bilbao. Many had lost their fathers in the war or their mothers in the bombing. They awed Annie Bingham with their sense of unity and spirit. She could not imagine the things they had seen, and yet they remained happy and playful. They had jokes about the Fascist bombers over Bilbao, particularly the 'Milk Man', who visited early each morning. They told Annie of the Basque air force, which consisted of a single plane so underpowered that the children would race it with their bicycles as it struggled to take off.

Annie wondered how natives of a warm country would adapt to the rainy cool of East Anglia. When she asked, they voiced a unanimous love for the weather. An older child explained it. 'The bombers could not fly on rainy days,' he said. 'The clouds made it safe to play outside. We love rainy days.'

How different Annie's life had been from what they had experienced. It was all so quiet. Her town was quiet; her parents were quiet; her house was quiet. In the evenings, the three would sometimes tune in the wireless to hear news and shows. But often they sat in their parlour at the front of the house, her mother working on embroidery, her father reading the paper, Annie focused on her studies, with the passage of time marked and stressed by the hypnotic ticking of the large Westminster mantel clock. She could scarcely imagine, from this peaceful background, how little ones learned to cope with the effects of regularly falling bombs.

Yet that was how they had developed the complaisance Annie so admired. The food there was plentiful but rather bland. No complaints; it wasn't chickpeas or rotting sardines. The loose iron headboards of the beds squeaked. No complaints; they had mattresses and blankets with no lice or hungry bedbugs. The boys played pelota or football in the boggy courtyard. No complaints; bombs did not interrupt their games. The girls gathered to dance in the narrow hallways and squealed when muddy boys chased them. No complaints; it was not the Guardia or the Falange. When the littlest ones cried at night, an older child would join them in bed for comfort. No complaints; they were family.

Helping the small group of nurses and teachers who had accompanied the orphans, Annie cooked and cleaned and sought to maintain order among the energetic children. She got down on the floor with the little ones, counselled the older ones, and stood as a continual amazement to all of them in one regard: her hair. The dark-haired and olive-skinned Basques had never seen such hair or freckles. They gave her the name Rojo, which they shouted in unison when they saw her, making her feel as if she had been adopted into their overflowing family. Annie left her home eagerly every morning because she knew she'd be greeted at the colony with several dozen hugs and kisses from the appreciative children.

Sometimes she brought her budgie, Edgar, in his cage.

When seeing Edgar for the first time, many of the children twirled their thumbs and index fingers in front of their mouths as if nibbling on an a tiny, invisible drumstick.

From the day she purchased Edgar, Annie had assaulted him with a stream of 'Pretty bird . . . pretty bird . . . pretty bird' in a nasal birdlike tone, trying to teach him the phrase as he perched in his cage in the family parlour. In two years, the remedial budgie had responded to Annie's rote recitation only by producing a clacking sound with his beak. Because Annie said 'pretty bird' so often, the children assumed that Pretty Bird was his name and shouted it each time he visited.

Edgar's only response was, 'Docka, docka.'

Annie Bingham looked forward to her days at the children's home for another reason. Charles Swan had decided to stay in Cambridge and take summer classes rather than go home to London, as he had planned, to spend the time with his parents before beginning active service. He often arrived at the end of her day to walk her home or take her to dinner in small neighbourhood cafes. They drew looks from the locals, these two with the pale skin and bright hair, taking their tea while conversing in rudimentary Spanish. Very unusual Spaniards, it was decided.

But most people in town knew they were helping with the Basque children, which was considered a good deed. Besides, they were young and were drunk on infatuation, so they were expected to be strange.

Miguel knew Josepe Ansotegui from his earliest memories and considered him a man of high integrity. Since he was young, he had heard Josepe talk about his big brother, Justo Ansotegui of Guernica, as if he were a giant, the strongest man with the most beautiful wife. When he finally met Justo at Errotabarri, he was intimidated but a little disappointed that he was not towering. He was stout and immensely powerful, but Miguel was as tall as Justo.

As he came to know Justo, he understood why Josepe and Xabier held him in such regard. If anything, since his injury, Justo impressed Miguel more. He still sought to accomplish more than any man with two arms, and he filled his days with jobs even if the state of the *baserri* didn't require as much work. It was Justo's resolve that most astonished him. Although they still rarely mentioned Mariangeles and Miren, and never Catalina, Justo stowed his grief somewhere it couldn't seep into everything else. It was this that Miguel wanted to tell Josepe when he visited Errotabarri.

Josepe Ansotegui made rare visits to Guernica, but this time was special, as he brought a supply of salt cod, enough to make meals for several weeks.

'You remember how it's cooked, don't you?' he asked Miguel.

Miguel had seen his mother go through the lengthy desalination process a number of times, and he could practically smell the *bacalao* already.

'I wish you could stay a few days and have some with us,' Miguel said, knowing it was unlikely.

'Oh, my little brother has more fish to catch,' Justo said.

'It's not as difficult as running a *baserri*, but there is enough to keep me going,' Josepe said.

'Tell him, Miguel, tell him about the fish we catch; some of them are this big,' Justo prompted, attempting to make the gesture but realizing he couldn't with one arm.

Miguel held the remainders of his two hands no more than six inches apart, causing Josepe to laugh.

Miguel was fascinated by how Josepe, perhaps the most influential man in Lekeitio, assumed the role of little brother when around Justo. The pattern of their relationship had not changed in forty years. Miguel was envious of Justo's having both his brothers within range for occasional visits. And he wondered how his life would be different if he had gone to France with Dodo, or if he had stayed in Lekeitio. But he would not have changed his decision to come to Guernica.

'I have to get going,' Josepe said, embracing his brother. 'Enjoy the fish. Walk with me, Miguel, I want to tell you of your family.'

He didn't have news of the Navarros, though; he wanted to hear more of his brother. 'Is he doing as well as he seems?'

'He still has his moments, and he gets distant, but he's stronger than any of us could have known,' Miguel said.

Josepe saw that. The surprise of the trip, though, had been the sight of Miguel, who no longer seemed a young man to Josepe. Miguel kept both hands in his pockets, which made his shoulders slump and bend forward like those of a much older man. Josepe would have imagined the younger person to be more resilient and that it would be Justo who would be more diminished now. But Miguel looked worn down, smaller.

'And you?' Josepe asked. 'What can I tell your father?'

'I'm getting along; Justo's helped,' Miguel said, uncomfortable with the subject. 'Have you seen Dodo?'

'I see him, yes,' Josepe said. 'Your father and I see him regularly.'

'Still in business together?'

'In a way, yes.'

'Are you all staying safe?'

'We're all still alive, so that means we're being safe enough. With Dodo, of course, it's rarely a question of being safe. Safety is not his strength. But he seems to be making better decisions. He has some good helpers who have taught him a great deal. One is very special to him.'

'Really?'

'Yes, very clever,' Josepe said with a wink that Miguel could not interpret.

Miguel waited for more information, but when Josepe paused, he knew better than to press the matter.

'I have one more question; I meant to ask Justo, but I didn't want to make him angry. What is that smell?'

'He carries soap in his pocket,' Miguel answered. 'It's the kind that Mariangeles and Miren used to use. It makes him feel better.'

'What do you think about it?'

'It works for him.'

Josepe would never make light of his brother. And in truth, the smell represented a vast improvement. He just couldn't imagine it was easy for Miguel to smell his wife every time Justo walked past.

Miren danced just for him this night, in the bedroom of their house, spinning so quickly to the music that her skirts flew in a wild orbit and the red fabric shredded into strips that flickered like satin flames.

Oh, God. He groaned without opening his mouth.

'What's the matter . . . Do you miss me?' she asked with a flirtatious smile, spinning again so that her tattered skirt parted at the side. 'I've missed you, too.'

She spun several more times as she moved closer, to the foot of the bed, and then stepped up onto the chest he'd built to store her precious things.

The music slowed and the accordion notes dovetailed with Mendiola's aching bow until all settled into a metered hum and sigh, hum and sigh.

Miguel had never seen Miren move this way, swaying more than dancing, shifting more than stepping, moving her hips as if urging a horse into a slow canter.

The ribbons of her slippers now wound a path up her slender calves to tie below her knees. She was taller, and her face gave off light like the first night he saw her.

It was warm, suddenly warm.

'I love this dance,' Miguel said.

'Alaia taught it to me,' Miren said, her long hair a telltale of the breeze blowing the purple-red rosebay willowherb blooms that suddenly sprouted around her. 'She told me you'd like it.'

Alaia, yes, Alaia. The problem with Alaia.

'I'm sorry we argued,' Miguel said.

'I am too, *astokilo*,' she said.

'It wasn't about us.'

'It wasn't important.'

Miren swayed with the blooming stalks.

'I tried to find you,' Miguel said.

'I know you did. I knew you would. You love me.'

Miguel smiled. He watched her hips now, focusing on them, then feeling them move next to his. Touching him. Holding him.

But the hand that clutched him was incomplete, withered, and pained, and it couldn't grip. And he woke and never wanted to sleep again.

The science came easily. The physics of flight moved Charley Swan. He breezed through the study of meteorology and advanced navigation and through com classes, learning methods of communication ranging from Morse code to advanced wireless.

Fortunately, as a fledgling pilot, he did not have to undergo the challenging physical indoctrination of soldiers. He'd been an academic, never exhibiting aptitude for football or the stick-and-ball demands of cricket. Piloting, though, required a kind of physical prowess that was more a function of dexterity than coordination. It was clear from the beginning that Charley Swan had it.

His first experience of flight came in a de Havilland Tiger Moth. Trainees were allowed to take over the stick and rudder bar for attempts at level flight for several hours before they were eased into take-offs and landings. A plane at cruising altitude was a forgiving environment, the instructors stressed; it was when the craft became tangent to the earth that obstacles arose. 'There're fewer things to bump into up here,' Charley was told. Within five air hours, he was ready to try a take-off, and only a few outings later he was allowed to handle a landing. He bounced in the first time, short-ended the second one, and from the third landing on, he delicately tiptoed back to the ground.

'Most of the lads yank about on the stick like they're trying to strangle a snake,' his instructor told him. 'It has to be more gentle, like milking a mother mouse.'

Swan's classmates were a gathering of British, Australians, and Canadians, all bright, young, and lured by the romance of flight. At night, when they flew ground sorties to the local pubs, Charley Swan was off to Pampisford before his mates began circling. They started intentionally exaggerated rumours about Swan's secret love life on the outskirts of town.

Only a fraction of Swan's classmates would advance through training. Some were academic washouts, others never grew comfortable with the delicacy of flight and chronically over-flew the plane. Most of those left quietly at night, with only their empty bed as an explanation.

The new commander of the local Guardia Civil, Julio Menoria, had always fostered a narrow view of citizens' rights in Spain, particularly in the Pays Basque, where the locals were chronically unable to grasp the futility of their quest for autonomy. If they were fortunate enough to be located in part of Spain, with its proud tradition, why would they ever wish to have a country of their own?

With Franco's Salamanca government in control, Menoria's distaste for the Basques could be openly expressed, and he expanded his powers to include search, seizure, confiscation of property, and recreational torture whenever necessary to promote and protect the new government.

His résumé had been bolstered by the arrest of the Basque poet/journalist Lauaxeta, whose words were silenced by a firing squad. It was a notable achievement for Menoria, one of which he bragged about at times over wine.

The officer tended his duties early each morning and worked until mid-evening, when he left to take his dinner. The path from his office to the cafe where he ate each night was cluttered with scaffolding and piles of supplies to be used in rebuilding the town. Bomb craters remained, and other holes were being excavated for new foundations.

Perhaps focused on his plans for the next day's work, Menoria apparently failed to see a warning sign and fell into a hole that was being dug to repair the damaged water main. It was a small hole, but it was deep, and Menoria's body wasn't discovered for several days, not until workers noticed an unpleasant smell.

Julio Menoria was a Catholic, but he must have been more devout than his officers had believed, since he was discovered to have a scapular of the Immaculate Heart of Mary around his neck when he was discovered.

Eager to attribute coincidences or the inexplicable to the forces of God, the devil, fairies, or spirits, those in town began assigning responsibility for the recent events to a powerful avenging spirit.

'It is the Virgin Mary,' Mendiola told Miguel one day at the sawmill. 'They both wore the symbol of the Immaculate Heart of Mary. Do you really think that is a coincidence?'

'Isn't it possible that they just wore the scapulars?' Miguel asked. 'Maybe Franco orders it.'

'Each of them dying from an accident?' Mendiola asked. 'Each wearing the scapular? That is the work of the True Spirit.'

'Miracles? Why here?'

'She is killing Fascists because they dropped the bombs on her church, Santa María,' Mendiola said. 'You see, Santa *María*. You may not have heard of what happened at the church with . . . with everything else that was going on, Miguel, but a firebomb dropped right through the roof only to stick in the floor. It didn't explode, Miguel. Many say that they saw the Holy Mother's image in the dust floating down from the roof.'

'Have the priests said anything about the scapulars?'

'They are not about to deny such an obvious message; after all, the pews are filled, and many candles are being lit these days.'

'Has anyone mentioned this theory to the members of the town council?'

'Some have tried,' Mendiola said, shaking his head. 'But after this second death, they are becoming harder to find.'

CHAPTER 23

Annie Bingham, Charley Swan, and Mrs Esther Bingham watched as Mr Harry Bingham delicately tuned the wireless. Each reflexively extended their right hand with fingers bent around an invisible dial, helping to make the final adjustment to capture the purest signal. Edgar exercised, flying between the open door of his cage on the mantel and Annie's shoulder. It had been an important day for the British, particularly those whose collection of loved ones included someone in the services, and they were eager to hear the historic announcement.

At flight school that afternoon, news spread of Neville Chamberlain's return to Heston Airport from the Munich meeting with the German Chancellor, Adolf Hitler, the Italian dictator, Benito Mussolini, and the French Prime Minister, Édouard Daladier. Charley had been informed of Chamberlain's pronouncements of peace second-hand, through several of the radio men working in their windowless hut. The Sudetenland was to be ceded back to Germany. Hitler would be satisfied, and a war that could engulf the Continent had been avoided.

'Just like the Spanish,' Annie objected. 'We didn't know them, so it didn't matter what happened to them. Well, Mr Chamberlain, I know them now. We should have done something to help them.'

Her parents and Charley, surprised by her passion on the matter, were unable to respond. Charley hoped that the evening broadcast would temper Annie's anxiety. From the steps of No. 10 Downing Street, Chamberlain's voice filled the Binghams' parlour.

'We, the German Führer and Chancellor, and the British Prime Minister, are agreed in recognizing that the question of Anglo-German relations is of the first importance for our two countries and for Europe. We regard the agreement as symbolic of the desire of our two peoples never to go to war with one another again.'

The broadcast picked up the cheers of the gathered crowd as someone in attendance shouted, 'Hip, hip, hooray for Mr Chamberlain!'

'We are determined to continue our efforts to remove possible sources of difference and thus to contribute to the peace of Europe.'

Charley and Mr Bingham joined the cheers on the wireless.

More casually, no longer reading from his prepared statement, Chamberlain continued. 'My good friends, for the second time in our history, a British prime minister has returned from Germany bringing peace with honour. I believe it is peace for our time. Now . . . go home and get a nice, quiet sleep.'

The four in the Bingham parlour exhaled. The Prime Minister assured them of peace and bade them a quiet sleep.

Annie and Charley removed the tea service and cups from the parlour, buying private time for closeness in the kitchen. As directed by Chamberlain, Mr and Mrs Bingham nodded off in their chairs, breathing in time to the ticking mantel clock upon which Edgar now perched, fast asleep himself.

Emilio Sanchez held no aspirations of political power in the service of Franco. A squad leader in a garrison in the south of Spain, he had joined Franco's rebellion because it appeared he would be shot if he acted otherwise. Politics and deep beliefs were not a factor, since he had neither. He had merely followed the path of least resistance that day. The most fanatical of the rebel officers pointed weapons wildly and fired without much provocation, so it would have been foolish to protest. Such was the birth of many indifferent rebels.

As commandant of the forced-labour unit in Guernica, Emilio Sanchez now appreciated his job. He was delighted to hold a position that gave him authority without pressing responsibility on him. There was little oversight because none of his superiors cared about the speed or quality of the reconstruction. The implied mandate was keep them at work, feed them as little as possible, and don't come around asking for more resources. If they die, get new ones. If they protest, shoot them. If more food is needed for the guards, confiscate it from the locals.

He was now the law, and the rules were his to make and amend as required. He had no moral problems with the spoils-of-war theory. His side won. He was surprised, in fact, given the nature of the times, that his uniform was getting tighter. He was gaining weight.

Officers in his unit had commandeered a small undamaged house at the edge of town for their headquarters. Sanchez's office was in the largest room at the back, off a porch where one could enjoy a view of the pleasant neighbouring hillsides. At times, in the evenings, he would retreat to a chair on the porch with a bottle of confiscated wine, have a smoke, and look out on the pastoral setting and unwind from the day.

One evening his reflection ended abruptly. He was discovered the following morning by his aides, who noted immediately that there was nothing accidental about his death. His chest had been run through by the two-tined Basque hoe, the *laia*, with such force that he had been pinned to the wall. Blood drained in parallel paths down the front of his uniform. Hanging from the *laia* handle was a green scapular of the Virgin Mary, swinging in the morning breeze.

Charles Swan brooded over his secret. Before the holidays he was to be sent to Norwich for training on the Blenheim bomber. Even as his mates clustered to congratulate him, he fretted over Annie's reaction. He decided to present her with the news at a time when he sensed she was at her most understanding. It just never arrived, and he had held the news for a fortnight.

She went on with such enthusiasm about the children that whenever Charley met her after work he never had the chance to tell her. Annie instructed the children in conversational English. At times, she took small groups to markets, where they could use their new language skills. They often went to a nearby park on sunny days, where keeping track of the boisterous children challenged her energy, if not her patience.

When Charley arrived at the end of her shift, she buried him in all the trivialities of her day. How could he listen to her happy ramblings for half an hour and then break in and unload important news on her?

They spent almost every evening together in a tentative courtship. It took weeks before they held hands and a month before they were seen walking arm in arm in the village. They visited the cinema once a week, where, in the darkness, they interlaced freckled fingers until they cramped. After clenching and stretching his hand and drying his palm on his trouser leg, Charley sought out her small fist once again, and they would smile at each other.

But on a mild late-autumn afternoon, Charley reached the point where further silence would be inexcusable. He would arrive as she finished for the day, they would walk together across a nearby park, and he would tell her of his move. Having rehearsed his speech, Charley Swan stepped into chaos. Children's screams echoed through the old rectory.

A child had opened Edgar's cage. The bird circled the room once and alighted on the sill of an open window. The *niños* shouted, 'Pretty bird! . . . Pretty bird!' Annie ran towards him, holding an index finger horizontally in the air, creating a perch that always attracted Edgar whenever he flew around the parlour. Edgar looked at the screaming mob and made a hasty exit without so much as a 'docka, docka' for a farewell.

Annie Bingham could not blame the children, or Edgar. And she contained her emotions until Charley walked her out of the rectory.

Sniffles led to sobs and then to tears. Charley produced a handkerchief and hugged her to his chest. He kissed the top of her knitted hat, and then her forehead, and then her moist cheeks. Annie hugged back until the energy of their closeness overwhelmed her sense of loss. Charley took Edgar's empty cage from her, and they held hands as they walked slowly through the park. It was not an appropriate time, Charley decided, to tell her that he would be gone soon as well.

After the Immaculate Mother sent three Fascists to their graves, she changed her tactics. The message had been sent, the point had been made; those who had taken part in the destruction of this historic town were vulnerable to death at the hands of a vengeful spirit.

Guernica town-council member Angel Garmendia drowned in the river, Guardia Civil head Julio Menoria was found dead in a hole, and forced-labour commander Emilio Sanchez found himself skewered by a farm implement. All were discovered with Immaculate Heart of Mary scapulars.

Townspeople knew this to be the work of a divine avenger. No mortal person could bring about the demise of three of the most heinous individuals in the town without a trace. The scapulars said it all. Miracles happen. They heard about them all the time at Mass. What better place for her appearance? The Mother of God sees all, they said; they agreed that she was there, and it was very clear that she was in a sour mood.

Further convincing the populace that this was the work of Mother Mary was that she was not unendingly vengeful. After her initial thinning of the Falange herd, the curious deaths ended. But the messages continued.

Not more than a few weeks passed before certain individuals began receiving reminders, which added to the growing mythology. One morning, when a Guardia commander headed off to work, he discovered a green medallion hanging on his front door. He retreated to his bedroom for three days.

A council member opened the desk drawer in his office and found a scapular lying there, with the inscription facing him: *Pray for us now and at the hour of our death*. He had an immediate physical response and then resigned his position.

Amid his customary daily dispatches, the commander of the local army garrison found an envelope with no name or address. With his letter opener, which resembled a small sabre, he sliced through the envelope to reveal a religious pendant.

The threatening visits quickly became public knowledge in the small and gossipy village, fomenting greater fear and suspicion among the oppressors, as well as considerable satisfaction among the locals. At a time when the people of the village found little cause for happiness, the news that a protective deity had so frightened a pipsqueak Francoist that he had wet himself in his office was enough to cause the day to brighten immeasurably.

The queue waiting to see the painting snaked down Whitechapel High Street, with forward motion limited to a few small steps between long pauses. Except when plotting his plan to propose to Annie Bingham, Charley Swan had been focused on the specific physical and mental mechanics of piloting the Blenheim bomber.

After two weeks of holiday, even as he headed towards an art exhibit, his mind flashed to the varied demands of flying. He walked around corners as if banking hard; he felt the wind direction and calculated how its velocity would affect his airspeed. His months in training changed him. But he had not changed more than Annie, who had inexplicably blossomed during his absence. He could not help but think of her as an engine that now idled at a higher RPM.

The daily exposure to the Basque children energized her. Sucked into the social squall created by several dozen children, Annie found no time for stifled comments or reserved expressions. Charley noticed the difference when he returned to Pampisford to start their holiday trip to London. He discovered an assertive woman in place of the sheepish girl he had left a few months before.

She greeted him with a shout of 'Red!' a lengthy double-armed embrace, and a kiss on the lips, followed by a withdrawal for inspection and then another forceful kiss. Although they had written every day since Charley left for his RAF base, Annie still chattered the entire train journey to London, telling Charley of the children and her excitement over spending the holidays with his family.

If anything, Charley edged in the other direction, as he now carried more thoughts that needed to be withheld. With 'Blens', learning to fly was no longer about physics and geometry; it was the study and practice of dropping bombs. No one could confuse it with anything but war and killing the enemy. The reality of war's peril caused him to plot his next waypoint. He wanted to marry Annie before bombs dropped and bullets flew.

He proposed on Christmas Eve after Mass. Annie shouted yes before Charley could open the ring box, and she cried on his shoulder for several minutes. They decided that an early summer marriage would be appropriate, but the location and exact date would be vulnerable to the dictates of the RAF.

Before the presentation of the ring, Charley camouflaged his most important mission with another thoughtful gift: a new budgie. It was young, blue and yellow, and Charley had already named it Blennie. It delighted Annie.

'Maybe I can get Blennie to actually say a few things,' she said.

'You should try to keep his cage in your room where you could talk to him all the time,' Charley suggested.

'But Mother and Father enjoy a bird in the parlour,' she countered.

A week after their engagement, Annie decided she wanted to attend an exhibition at the Whitechapel Gallery, where Picasso's mural *Guernica* was to be on display.

'Some of my children are from the town,' she explained.

Charley had heard nothing of the painting and agreed to go so he could enjoy Annie's company. Once inside the gallery, they understood why the queue had moved so haltingly: people were reluctant to give up their place in front of the giant mural.

Annie anticipated the painting being a gory display. Instead, she found an almost cartoonish depiction in black and white. And when they looked more deeply, they heard the soundless screams and the bellow of the horse, and they felt the heat coming off the jagged white disc of light. They stood transfixed until the nudging of those behind them caused them to shuffle ahead. And then they were out through the half-open door and onto the street. Changed.

'Could that be us?' she asked Charley, pulling him close.

Charley held her. If he spoke, he might have answered, 'Of course it could be. It could happen to any of us. You have no idea how short a flight it is across the English Channel or the kind of weapons the Germans developed while they were flying in Spain.'

But aside from holding his comment, Charley Swan also fought against a realization he hadn't allowed himself to fully consider: at some point he might be the one dropping the bombs that devastated a village.

Miguel enjoyed the mindless exertion of felling and logging trees, being lulled by the sound of the cross-cut saw as he pushed and pulled, sometimes becoming so lost in thought that he was surprised when the tree fell in front of him. It all took much longer than before, but time was not much of a consideration in his life.

The higher elevations of the woods, where he could be alone with the squirrels and doves, provided a less pressured environment than did the town and even Errotabarri. The trees sought no explanations. They exuded the scent of pitch and sap, and they spat out the fresh wood chips that flew into his hair and down the front of his shirt. The work consumed the energy that might otherwise have been exploited by his mind. It was a welcome exhaustion, and after a day's sawing he slept through most of the nightmares and all of the dreams.

Today he had a less cumbersome load on the downhill trip. Alaia Aldecoa had asked him to gather any scented flora he might find while in the forests. Miguel appreciated the diversion, and he found enough flowers to fill a small basket that he carried along with his saw, axe, and water bottle.

On his way up the edge of the rill, he saw that her cottage was almost indistinct from the trees clutching at it now. Miguel thought he might come back someday to scale the roof and cut the branches that seemed to embrace her home. Since the night Alaia had brought soap to Errotabarri, Miguel had seen her only briefly in town. What could he say? What should he say? Should he tell her how Miren had made excuses for her? How she had been loyal to her without question? That now, more than two years after her death, Miren still spoke well of her in his dreams?

She expected his knock and turned from her washbasin once he entered. She sensed his location and walked directly to him, placing a hand on each cheek.

Freshly washed, she smelled of a lilac soap.

'I'm here, Miguel,' she said, putting her arms around him.

He inhaled until his lungs could hold no more; he heard the stream humming outside, and he breathed deeply again of her skin. He was exhausted from the day of work, diminished by two years of grief, eroded by constant incomprehensible thoughts. And here were the smells, different but still wonderful, and the sounds, and the forgotten touch. They were four unseeing eyes, four uneasy hands, and they made love to the same tender memory.

'I haven't—'

'I know,' Alaia said. 'I haven't . . .'

Miguel closed his eyes again, and Alaia could feel his breathing catch and buck erratically. He cried without sound, as if he could keep it from her.

'I know, Miguel, I know.' She petted his hair.

This wasn't Miren and he knew it. There was no confusion. This was different; this was urgency and memory.

'Tell me, say it, you can share it with me,' she said, still stroking his hair.

'Justo and I can't talk . . . nothing . . . nothing,' he said. 'We remind each other of them.'

Alaia held him tighter. 'Tell me, tell it to me.'

'We both see that plait hanging on the mantel every day,' Miguel said.

She cried with him, and he buried his head in the pillow of her hair. The stream hummed and the day dimmed into evening before they could pull apart and speak again. It became easier in the dark. They talked of Miren, and a reservoir of thoughts flooded the room. Miguel reminded Alaia of his wife's energy and her grace and exuberance. Alaia spoke of her voice and her warmth and her caring. They told the stories of how they had met Miren and recounted their favourite times with her. They talked of Mariangeles and her wisdom. Together, they were able to talk of them without being overwhelmed.

Neither mentioned Catalina. There was a threshold.

They talked through the evening and most of the night, then slept in the cradle of each other's arms beneath the quilt Mariangeles had sewn for Alaia. Neither spoke as Miguel readied to leave in the morning, both sifting through the meaning of what they'd done.

'Miguel,' she said. 'Before . . . I should tell you why—'

'No,' he stopped her.

'I—'

'No.' More forcefully the second time.

Another moment passed without words. Alaia pulled open a drawer in the small cabinet at her bedside.

'Miguel, come here, please,' she said. 'I have something to show you.'

Alaia placed in his hands a doll made from an old worn sock. She had one more story to tell him.

PART 6
(1940)

CHAPTER 24

Eduardo Navarro possessed neither the language skills nor the heartlessness to translate the Latin message etched onto the church's clock tower. The Polish refugee, referred to only as 'Monsieur', had pointed out the phrase to his wife, who was spoken of only as 'Madame'. The man was well into his sixties and paunchy, with the bearing of a person from whom much had been taken. What remained of him was a sloping midsection and a proud insistence on protecting his wife, who had also been reduced by their trials.

Monsieur had shed the haughty residue that sometimes lingers in wealthy men after the money and its power are exhausted. But he continued to make a show of assisting his struggling wife as he limped along himself, clutching this token of masculine dignity as if it was the final family heirloom. And when Dodo or Renée offered instructions, Monsieur repeated the signals to his wife, to signify his approval of the plan.

The walk from St-Jean-de-Luz to Ciboure and then Urrugne, through a passage trellised by plane trees, was the simplest part of the journey. But the couple, already badly faded, needed a rest across from Urrugne's ancient Church of St Vincent. After long drinks of water from the *bota* and many wheezed inhalations, Monsieur gestured towards the inscription below the clock on the tower.

Vulnerant omnes
Ultima necat.

It spoke an unpleasant truth bluntly expressed: 'Every hour wounds, the last kills.' Dodo saw no need to act out the translation.

Left to their own judgement, neither Dodo nor Renée Labourd would have found worthy risk in smuggling this Jewish couple into nominally neutral Spain, where they could be shuttled further along towards England or America.

Since the Nazi occupation of France, the heavy patrolling of the border with Spain had all but choked off the easier routes of passage. When the smuggling of refugees was merely a matter of sneaking past the indifferent Spanish or French border guards, reasonably safe options had been plentiful. They could time their movements between shift changes at a bridge passing from Béhobie into Irun, or they could load the refugees onto a boat piloted by Dodo's father and take the short ride from Hendaye or St-Jean-de-Luz into any port in Spain.

But the Nazis viewed the evasion of subversives as a specific insult and operated random patrols at the river, installed unblinking guards at checkpoints, and planted a network of informers in each border town. Now boats in all harbours faced extensive searches, and those in open waters were stopped and inspected with greater enthusiasm.

Captured refugees were shipped to concentration camps, often accompanied by the locals who had provided their passage and protection. If resistance was met? Well, bullets were plentiful, and sometimes paperwork was less demanding when subjects were shot in the process of 'escape'.

When word reached Renée of the Jewish couple's impending arrival, she and Dodo were doubtful. This would be the frailest cargo they'd ever handled. But the refugees had migrated through France on a series of local trains, spending as little time as possible exposed on the platform, trying to tiptoe along the narrow path between effective stealth and conspicuous skulking. They had shown papers half a dozen times, and their altered documents passed casual inspection. They travelled as a pair with a shepherd who stayed at a safe distance, ready to step in as a concerned third party if the couple was detained.

For Renée and Dodo, smuggling humans was much easier than smuggling other commodities. Food, alcohol, weapons, and ammunition were heavy and obvious. Humans transported themselves to some extent. But they also could talk when it was most dangerous, they could fall and break bones, and they could drown. If a pallet of rifles was dropped in the river, no life was lost. Refugees? A different matter.

'What must they have been through already to get this far?' Renée asked Dodo.

'Lost everything . . . they surely have lost everything, family, home . . . everything,' Dodo said as the two inflamed their strongest bond: mutual indignation.

'I'm not sure they can make it, and where does that leave us?'

'I'm mostly sure they can*not* make it,' Dodo said, adding a playful smirk. 'Let's try.'

When the couple struggled to descend from the train at the St-Jean-de-Luz/Ciboure station, Renée released a fatalistic groan in Dodo's direction. And now, only hours into a plodding escape, the couple appeared unable to go on. After a year of living off scraps while hiding in basements and attics, and then being trundled on and off trains and through a succession of safe houses, they neared collapse.

It was already late evening and their best chance was to get to Béhobie and the edge of the Bidassoa River in the darkest part of the night. The hope was that they could row them across in a friend's boat during a gap between patrols. If not, they'd have to swim and/or wade into Spain, and these two were of questionable buoyancy. The trip across the slippery rocks was tricky for Dodo and Renée; for a pair in their sixties, drained of strength, it would border on impossible.

The couple needed a few more minutes' rest in Urrugne, so Dodo and Renée used the time for final reminders. They had dressed Monsieur in a sheepskin coat with a beret and espadrilles. He looked authentic but ridiculous. She was in a long black skirt and woollen cap. Uncomfortable and unnatural. They had already instructed the couple never to speak. Dodo and Renée would be their grandchildren taking them for a walk through the woods, a nonsensical notion at two or three a.m. But if detained, the old couple were not to speak. If questioned, they were instructed to cup an ear and say one word: 'Eh?'

As a refresher, Renée stood in front of Monsieur and officiously acted the part of a guard, holding an invisible rifle at his chest.

'*Papiers!*' she said.

'Eh?' Monsieur responded, not only bending his ear towards Renée but also squinting hard, as if the failure to see accompanied his deafness.

Renée repeated the process with Madame, who was slow to understand and issued a resentful flurry of Polish comments. Renée pulled the trigger on her pretend rifle and, with a percussive lip movement, went, 'Bop.'

Madame understood this and corrected herself. 'Eh?'

'*Très bien,*' Renée mumbled, and turned. It was time to press on. The sun eased into the Bay of Biscay and they had another five or six miles of surreptitious walking to reach the preferred point to ford the river. It took five hours rather than the anticipated two. Several cars passed on the road below them, perhaps carrying Nazis, although the darkness made identification impossible.

Dodo and Renée had used this route without detection a number of times before the Nazi occupation. The river was slower this close to the mouth but wider, with less chance of concealment. Across the Bidassoa was a series of safe houses where Basque connections would feed the couple before shuffling them down the line.

They reached a patch of alders near the riverbank at almost dawn, with the option of rowing now eliminated. The Nazis had begun using a small fleet of shallow-draft skiffs, and they had helped the Spanish guards install floodlights that could be directed at the most appealing spots for river crossing.

'*Pas bon,*' Renée whispered.

Their hopes for good fortune on this mission, slim as they were initially, had further receded. The best option was to head back, bivouac in the closest safe house, and reconsider other paths. Perhaps they could try it again the next night, get a better start on it and walk further upstream.

Renée pantomimed a retreat to the couple.

Monsieur shook his head violently. Madame did not understand the forces at play, but her husband's anger registered and she unleashed a series of inhaled sobs. He lifted his wife to her feet and pulled her from the brush towards the rocky shore.

Dodo stepped in more forcefully as lights scanned the river, spreading ribbons of silver crêpe across the rippled water. 'You've got to stop,' he barked with as much authority as he could without screaming above the river sounds.

'*Arrête!*' he yelled, assuming the Polish man would be more likely to understand French than Spanish or Basque.

Monsieur turned and indignantly wrestled his arm from Dodo's grasp, wading into the water with Madame in tow. Dodo came at him again, and in his haste, he tumbled on the slippery rocks.

'*Arrête!*' he yelled from his back.

Monsieur, now knee-deep and slogging forward with his wife clutching his jacket, turned towards Dodo and cupped his hand to his ear, miming deafness. 'Eh?'

Within two more steps, the woman had wrapped both arms around her husband's neck, causing them both to lose balance and slip into the water. The river was shallow enough that they could have easily stood, but they bobbed together on the surface, appearing almost relaxed as they floated off. Dodo raced after them along the shore. When they crossed a slice of illuminated water, he saw that they were not even trying to swim, just holding on to each other.

307

They were found next to each other on the shore near Hondarribia the next day. They had died in Spain.

As friends failed to return from missions and the fire from anti-aircraft guns and Messerschmitts stitched vents in his Blenheim, Charley Swan no longer saw a disconnection between his flying and the results of his bombing. He understood the processes of war by the time he landed after his first mission. This was no longer about the physics of flying objects. Charley was at war, and he strongly believed in the British cause. The Blitz on London had spared his family, and his wife was unscathed in the Cambridge area. But through the letters from his family and from Annie, he could feel what it must have been like to sweat out two months of consecutive nights of ruinous German bombing.

Annie never complained in her letters. She tried to include updates on the family and highlights from her daily life.

. . . Speaking of Blennie, you're not going to believe it, but after more than a year of my saying 'pretty bird' to him, he has started speaking. Does he say 'Pretty bird'? No, he says, 'Docka, docka,' just like Edgar. Can you believe that? I won't take him to the children's home because I'm afraid he'll meet the same fate Edgar did. Of course, if he escaped, Blennie might fly away and find Edgar somewhere where they could sit around and say 'docka' to each other. Silly bird.

Silly bird, indeed, Charley thought. At times, he would carry Annie's letters with him on missions to read again while waiting to taxi or during the quiet moments of the Channel crossing, but the Blenheim was so cramped he began giving himself the lone luxury of carrying the one 'family' photo of himself and Annie, with Blennie in his cage on her lap. There was not much time to focus on anything other than business once he was strapped in, anyway. He was responsible for two others in the craft, not to mention the potential devastation of a misplaced bomb load or what might happen if he was a tick slow in sensing the threat of fighters.

The Blenheims were already being phased out. They were slow and cumbersome, and susceptible to enemy fighters because they had no hope of outrunning them. The yoke blocked his view of some of the instruments, and other instruments on the panel were stacked so high in front of him it was impossible to see the runway as he neared the point of touchdown. But they had good range, and that allowed him to fly deep into the Continent.

His crew praised him (cautiously, out of superstition) for his capacity to anticipate the attacks of German fighters. They had little hope of evading their dives, but he seemed to have a knack for dipping or banking slightly to reduce the bomber's profile to enemy pilots. It kept them from absorbing the worst of the attack.

No mission was without damage, and the times were few when Charley landed without a 'dent or two', as he put it, in the wing or tail or fuselage. But as other planes fell from the sky or returned in pieces, Charley Swan's was always relatively easy to patch up and make ready for the next mission. His crew called it a gift. Charley didn't call it anything.

It was Renée's idea that Dodo should coax his brother into the mountains. Dodo's invitation forced Miguel to confront his need to get away from Guernica. He worried that leaving Errotabarri was abandoning Justo. Together, they were a collection of broken parts that, in most cases, was functional. Miguel had assumed that two damaged hands helped replace one lost arm in the piecemeal assemblage.

Miguel told Justo of his intention to turn down Dodo's invitation, as if it was a courtesy, an unspoken payment of a debt.

'Don't be stupid, go and help your brother. I'm fine here.'

To prove his claim, Justo dropped to his knees, leaned forward on his right hand, and did ten press-ups.

'Come on, sit on my shoulders and add more weight,' Justo demanded.

Miguel declined. Justo was right. There were now a few sheep and a small patch of vegetables to tend; even a man with one arm had little trouble managing them. He was rarely there anyway.

But what were his responsibilities to Alaia Aldecoa? What did their night together change? She could count on Zubiri to help, he presumed. Justo could look in on her, too. If Justo knew of her activities he had never commented and had shown no bad feelings towards her. She was part of the family, Justo always said.

But if forced to assess his reasons for making the move, the distancing from Alaia would be the first. After that night, Miguel had been careful about his visits, keeping them brief and impersonal. The one evening had surprised them both and seemed somehow excusable. A second would have been more than happenstance.

Renée made him comfortable in St-Jean-de-Luz from the first moment. While trying to brag about his brother's skilful adaptation to the ways of the *travailleurs de la nuit*, Renée inadvertently diverted Miguel's concentration by serving him foods with scents and flavours that caused him to focus intently on his plate. He listened, to a degree, while he inhaled a plate of red peppers stuffed with cod. He grew less attentive when the fillet of salmon with white asparagus arrived, and he almost completely tuned out when Renée presented the *gâteau Basque* for which her family had gained some regional renown.

'Good,' Miguel said when he finished. The residents of Guernica were living on old sardines, chickpeas, and bread fashioned of sawdust. This was food he'd never had even in the best times. As he suctioned up the plate of *piquillo* peppers, Renée explained that there were hardships in St-Jean-de-Luz and in France, too, but those in their business developed sources to supply almost anything.

They didn't have to go far for anything, either, as many of their business meetings took place downstairs at the Pub du Corsaire. Once Dodo had sanctioned the bar and discovered that it was Renée's primary haunt, he found a cheap room on the top floor. His rent was offset by various procurements he arranged for the bar's owner. Yes, after a few mishaps in the mountains, he had learned the ways of trafficking goods from Renée and her family. And then he started inventing methods of his own.

'Dodo was made for this job,' Renée told the distracted Miguel.

'That's not what your father said,' Dodo objected. 'He claimed I was too big and not ordinary enough.'

The best smugglers, Santi Labourd told Dodo, were so nondescript as to be nearly invisible. They were unnoticed background, insignificant scenery. They needed to be strong enough to carry loads and tireless enough to walk the mountains all night, but small enough to remain nimble and fit through passages in brush and boulders that might challenge a hare.

'Maybe you weren't the perfect physical design, but mentally? You have it; even Father says so,' Renée said with pride, placing another basket of bread on the table, as Miguel had eaten most of the first loaf and was still intent on sopping up the abundant sauces.

'At the start, his experience and connections on the water were most important to us,' Renée continued. 'For a while, we traded services and surplus goods for grain and whatever food we could collect, and then we got it to your father, who shipped it to Biscaya. We then moved on to weapons and equipment.'

Miguel looked up from his plate at Dodo. He had no idea the *patroia* was so involved.

'Discreet, eh?' Dodo said.

'There was a small mention, but I didn't know how far it had gone.'

'Not so much anymore,' Renée said, putting her plate, still coloured with sauces, on the floor for Déjeuner to lick clean. 'He'd still be working with us if he had his way, but it has got too dangerous to use the boats much now. Still, when the cargo is merely information, he's extremely valuable.'

'Information?' Miguel asked, distracted by the sight of a dog licking up the remnants of the dinner.

'Deployments, the movement of men, defences, that sort of thing,' Dodo said. 'Patrols can inspect boats as much as they wish, but if the important cargo is in the head of the *patroia*, it can't be detected or confiscated.'

'Then what?'

'Then maybe he sails to Bilbao to off-load the catch . . .'

'And?'

Dodo knew the next link in the network would jolt Miguel. 'Then the most natural thing in the world might be for the *patroia* to visit his new favourite priest, Father Xabier, and then it might be equally natural for the good Father to hear the confession of men who are, let's say, of British heritage, perhaps working at the consulate, who might be able to pass along portions of his divine message.'

Miguel shook his head numbly, still several steps behind Dodo. 'How do you get such information?'

'How does he get anything?' Renée laughed. 'He's clever.'

'We have a network of helpers – sympathizers, Resistance,' Dodo said. 'Sometimes it's a barmaid overhearing drunken Nazis, or an officer who is trying to impress her; sometimes it's a maid at a hotel where an officer is staying while on leave who manages to go through his papers after making the bed. Sometimes there is information in a letter home from a soldier that happens to get opened at the post. You'd be amazed by the bits and pieces we can pick up.'

'*Patroia?*' Miguel asked, still trying to process the information.

'Yes, yes, Miguel,' Dodo said. 'And now we're working with a Belgian group that is relocating RAF airmen who have been shot down, working to get them back to England. They're very brave. They pick up the crews, sew them up if they have to, hide them, forge papers that are good enough to get them through Paris and down here. Then we move them across the border into Spain. Once they're across the river, helpers take them down the line to the consulate in Bilbao, where they arrange to get them on a boat out of Lisbon or Gibraltar.'

The German occupation had changed so many elements of their work. The gatherings at Dodo's apartment stopped as the inner circle was pulled tighter for security reasons. The chance to add a trustworthy blood relative like Miguel felt like a blessing – but also a serious responsibility. Despite being older, Dodo had seen Miguel as an equal as early as their teen years because of Miguel's physical and emotional maturity. In some ways, Miguel was the wise older brother. This, though, was Dodo's world, and although he knew Miguel could take care of himself, he wanted to do everything possible to keep his brother from suffering more pain.

'All this is why Papa is so proud of him now,' Renée said, turning to Miguel. 'Even if he is too big and a bit conspicuous, he never tires and he always seems to find a way.'

Dodo accepted the compliment with a lengthy kiss. Miguel looked puzzled.

'He was quick to learn the paths and the signals we've used forever,' she said. 'Stacking stones or notching bark. And he worked out a perfectly natural identifier of our "brotherhood" – the beret. All smugglers wear berets. It does not mean everyone in a beret is a smuggler, but he's certainly no guard and he's no patrolman. He might be someone who has turned informer, true, but Spanish guards and Nazis will never wear them.'

'So,' Dodo interjected, 'you'll have to start wearing one again.'

'I haven't worn one since we were fishing together,' Miguel objected.

'I know, but you'll start again and get used to it or one of our friends might decide to drop a rock on you in the mountains one night.'

Dodo called the dog to his side and placed him on his lap.

'We've put Déjeuner to work, too,' Dodo said, petting the strange little beast, the obvious product of a series of crossbreed liaisons. 'If I'm walking in public with a flier, another healthy young man, then it's suspicious. They might wonder: if these two aren't in the services in some capacity, then maybe they're Resistance. If Renée and a young man have a dog on a leash, they're merely enjoying each other's company and getting a little exercise for *le petit chien*. And Déjeuner is the perfect little dog of the Resistance.'

'Oh?'

'Yes, he pretends all the while he knows nothing of the charade.'

Dodo laughed. 'There're other things: walking with a limp is good, too, or bent over with a bad back. The crippled are not likely to be carrying illegal goods over mountain passes. There's a human sympathy that takes over.'

'At least it does with the French and Spanish,' Renée said. 'You can't count on it with the Nazis.'

'What about bad hands?' Miguel asked.

A calm overtook Charles Swan. He felt as if he had broken free from hell's torments and was ascending peacefully to heaven. Except that he was headed in the other direction, floating to earth through the sublime tranquillity that attends the end of chaos. A flock of Messerschmitts had caught him in a frantic fire-fight and his Blenheim had broken apart as metal screamed around him like the death howl of a giant mechanical animal.

He now floated in a flawless sky without a sound except for the pulse hammering in his ears. Silence. Sudden silence, he thought, oddly flashing on his favourite readings from Lewis Carroll's Alice story when he was young.

> *Anon, to sudden silence won,*
> *In fancy they pursue*
> *The dream-child moving through a land*
> *Of wonders wild and new,*
> *In friendly chat with bird or beast –*
> *And half believe it true.*

He had never quoted that verse for Annie, his bird-talker, and he decided he would have to tell it to her when he returned home. Annie, yes. Home. The place that isn't war. Of course, there was no place that wasn't war anymore. But it was at least life alongside war. Life and Annie. He scanned downward for the first time. There was no sign of his plane or his squadron or the gnat-like fighters that had arrived in a lethal, buzzing cluster.

The mission was nothing out of the ordinary; they were to bomb troop positions and tank formations in southern Belgium. But fighter defence was heavier than Charley had seen, and half the group had been shot down or forced to turn back before his Blenheim was set upon. The first wave must have put out his dorsal turret, as he couldn't hear return fire. He dipped from the second wave, but the instincts that allowed him to react to the threat of one attack caused him to bank slightly into direct fire from another pair of fighters on the other side, and he could hear bullets bite the metal skin of the fuselage. It took only the span of several racing heartbeats for the plane to disintegrate. He signalled for his crew to bail out, but both the bomb aimer and gunner had been killed in their positions, and when the craft started spiralling, he knew he'd never maintain flight.

As the earth eased up towards him, he took a quick inventory. His crew was dead. Nothing he could do about that. Fisher was single, the son of a vicar (a Fisher of men, they kidded), but Maplestone had a wife in Dover. He would have to contact their families at some point, he thought, hoping that he would arrive on their doorsteps and tell them in person rather than them having to learn the news through an impersonal post.

The air collecting in the parachute caused the cords to whisper. He wasn't going home tonight. Fisher and Maplestone certainly weren't. The crews that made it back tonight would say nice things about them, raise a toast, and then make jokes to relieve the pain. They all had done it, trying to create distance between themselves and the friends that had died last month and last week and yesterday. There wasn't time to grieve or you'd never take off again. You could remember them all later, after the war, all at once, and for a long time.

Focus, Charley, focus. Below was a pastoral land overrun by the enemy. He had no weapon, no survival kit, no food or water. A knife, a map, and a picture of Annie and Blennie. Trying to calculate the drift caused by the wind, he pulled at the cords of his parachute to guide himself closer to a small cluster of trees. It would either give him quick cover or break his back if he got caught up in a limb. He floated in just short, though, and when he collided with the ground, a jolt of pain caused him to make another entry in his mental inventory.

A German bullet had gouged a deep furrow through his right thigh.

CHAPTER 25

The march up the River Nivelle valley in his brother's wake gave Miguel the clarity of mind to order his thoughts. Dodo had been uncharacteristically quiet, having learned the value of silence when exposed in public. The path to Sare had been rutted by footfalls since medieval times, and it followed a gentle grade through fallow pastures and shady woods. They had no reason to skulk on a more sheltered route because they were merely two men on a walk, carrying no contraband and having no subversive intent. This was orientation.

'Sare is the hub of our business,' Dodo said, 'with spokes of trails heading towards the border up every small watershed. Sometimes we arrange for herders to cause a disturbance in one pass to draw attention while we go through another.'

'Do we have to go up there?' Miguel asked, gesturing with his head towards the peak of La Rhune, rising into a cloud cap above them.

'Only as a last resort. Don't worry, you'll get enough terrain to get that heart pumping.'

After lunch with Renée's parents – more delicious peppers and sauces, roast chicken, and cake – Miguel's lessons in the ways of the smugglers continued as Dodo led the way towards the border.

'You look good in your beret,' Dodo said.

'Makes me feel like vomiting.'

'No, no . . . no seasickness up here,' Dodo said, and after a pause, he added, 'I'm glad you're here, Miguel. We need your help. We're getting more British airmen coming down; we need to keep Renée in town and off the trails as much as possible, and we need to keep me out of town equally as much. She's so good at getting everybody off trains and into safe houses; it's more important than having her hiking around in the hills. Nazis look at her and their first thoughts are not of the Resistance.'

'How do I help?'

'I lead and you follow,' Dodo said. 'Sometimes we'll have one guest and sometimes as many as four or five. I want you to be the trailer, keeping everybody up to speed and watching for patrols coming up from behind – mostly shepherding the stragglers.'

'I think I'm up to that.'

'The one thing I had to learn first was to slow down,' Dodo said. 'As much as I wanted to race, this is a matter of pace and timing and of staying together. Anybody who's in a hurry draws attention. Nature doesn't rush; we have to move steadily.'

Dodo led Miguel up the east side of La Rhune, following a rill that cut a small wedge into the hillside.

'You'll want to follow the water,' Dodo explained. 'It's found the best path for centuries, and there's normally better cover there. But the brush is sometimes thicker. If it's a good, dark night without patrols, getting out at the edge of the trees and brush is not a bad risk if it helps you make up time. If the moon and patrols are out, stay covered or stay home.'

'But you'll be there leading all the time, right?'

'I hope so,' Dodo said. 'But you never know. Here's where it gets tricky.' Dodo led him out into an exposed meadow that took up the better portion of the eastern ridgeline. Granite boulders cluttered the slope, looking like sun-bleached skulls of long-dead giants, turning it into a walker's nightmare.

'It's hard to tell from here, but there are paths through the rocks,' Dodo said, gesturing with a sweeping hand. 'Which is good for us and bad for them. I'll show you the signs and the markings. Always,

always stay on the paths, and make sure the guests do, too. Getting off the path means a broken ankle or leg – or maybe worse, depending on how you fall or trip.'

'And we're going to be going through here in the dark?' Miguel asked.

'Dark . . . darker than you can believe – and sometimes wet, too,' Dodo said. 'Our safest times are when it's darkest, which means cloudy nights, which means rain sometimes. The rocks get slippery in the rain, and if you slip on a boulder up here, you might tumble all the way down to Sare.'

Dodo laughed. Miguel did not. He looked down. The wrinkled valley, of varying hues of green in the afternoon sunlight, made him think of being in the hills above Guernica, and of fishing with Justo, and of logging with Mendiola's mule. And at the moment he had that thought, he heard his mule whiffle.

'Meet the noble *pottok*,' Dodo said, pointing across a meadow at a group of the sturdy little Basque ponies that have run wild in the Pyrenees for generations. 'The old-timers used them quite a bit when the loads were heavy. The night workers have a great love for them. They work hard, never complain, are sure-footed, and they have the delightful ability to fart whenever border guards are near.'

A group of six, including a foal, grazed, oblivious to the presence of humans. The newborn romped around its mother with abandon, and Miguel wished he could simply stop to watch.

'I first met some alone on the mountain one night, and they had me convinced they were mountain bears about to kill me,' Dodo said.

Even with the daylight and his brother to follow, Miguel found it difficult to stay on the trail and not be diverted into a cul-de-sac of boulders. Without explanation, Dodo led him off the ridge and into a forest of beech trees, which seemed like a city park to Miguel, with no undergrowth to entangle them or boulders to trip on. It was beautiful and cool, and a small white butterfly bobbed ahead of him along the path. A flock of sheep appeared along the trail, with their muffled bells and melancholy bleats sounding like an ambling chorus.

A shepherd stepped out from behind a tree, Miguel never having noticed his presence.

'*Ami,*' the shepherd said, addressing Dodo as 'friend'.

'Eh, *ami,*' Dodo returned.

'New herder?' the man asked. He was dressed exactly as Dodo, carrying a *makila*, with a *bota* slung across his chest.

'*Oui*, my brother,' Dodo said. Names were not used. 'He is going to help tend the flock. Are there others about?'

'No, quiet,' the man answered. 'But it is early.'

They nodded to each other and the man locked eyes with Miguel, held an index finger under his right eye, and winked. It was to say, Welcome to the brotherhood, my friend, but if you see me outside these hills, I am a stranger to you.

After clearing another ridge and dropping into a glade, Dodo stopped to show Miguel a small boulder-covered cave in which they cached bottles of Izarra and tins of cheese. They could hide inside if necessary.

'There's a cave we spent the night in once that winds back into the hills for half a mile,' Dodo said. 'It's been there since the cavemen shared it with bears. Our guests were not very happy with the chirping of thousands of bats hanging from the roof. To keep their minds off that, we told them stories about how the spirit of Mari and the *lamiak* lived in there, and how for so many years the witches held meetings in there until they were burned at the stake.'

As usual, Miguel never knew how much of Dodo's commentary to believe, but he hoped that spending the night in a bat-filled cave would not be a part of his new job.

'Are there fish in here?' Miguel asked as they walked parallel to a stream.

'The best fishing is up in the forest of Iraty, I'm told,' Dodo said. 'Since when do you care about fishing? I thought you despised fishing.'

'I like it when I'm not in a boat – fishing in rivers and streams,' Miguel explained. 'Maybe some time when we're not working we can go to the Iraty and I can show you how to fish in streams.'

'What do you know about it?'

'Justo taught me.'

'How is Justo?' Dodo asked, his first direct question about Guernica and those living there.

'Still strong,' Miguel said.

'Even with one arm?'

'The number of arms has nothing to do with it.'

Dodo let the subject hang as they started to descend a ridge. 'We're in Spain now,' he said. 'Down there's the Bidassoa. The river is always the biggest problem. The Spanish guards mostly sit on their arses on the south side and wait for us to come to them.'

'The river?'

'It cuts a gorge west of Vera, closer to the source, with steep slopes and a strong current,' Dodo said, laying out the terrain and pointing to the forest below them. 'As it gets towards Irun, it widens and slows, depending on the time of year and volume of flow. It's easier to cross below, and that's why there're guardhouses down there at every bend in the river.'

'How do we cross?'

'We row in a boat that a farmer leaves for us, or we wade, or we swim,' Dodo said. 'Probably wade and swim now, since a boat is too obvious these days.'

'Dodo?'

'What?'

Miguel held up his partial hands. 'I don't know if I can swim anymore.'

Dodo hadn't considered that. He thought of challenging his brother to a rematch of the Loop but remained quiet.

Aside from his solitary walks through town in the early morning and late night, and his work trying to keep Errotabarri from falling apart, Justo spent much of his time in Bilbao, a short train journey away. He enjoyed helping his brother at the Basilica de Begoña and visiting

Sister Incarnation at the hospital. He owed much to these two, and it felt good to get closer to his baby brother and to the nun he so admired.

Sister Inky humoured Justo by allowing him to act as her enforcer with stubborn patients. Assisting his little brother, Father Xabier, was more difficult. Now that Justo was back on his feet, the priest felt that it no longer seemed appropriate for him to go around sweeping up the rectory and doing work in the grounds.

In truth, Xabier had become a visible political figure, as his connection to exiled President José Antonio Aguirre had made him a target of some scrutiny for Franco's security and intelligence forces. Xabier knew he was being watched and he feared this might endanger his brother. It would have been better if their meetings were less obvious for a while. But he so enjoyed Justo's presence that he could think of no tactful way to discourage his visits.

Justo was not surprised that Xabier had grown increasingly political. He had become known as a force in the Basque consciousness, an anti-Fascist voice when so many had been silenced. As assiduously as Xabier kept his pulpit free of politics, many parishioners still sought his opinions on the state of the Basque Country, Biscaya, and Spain. Most frequently, he was asked, 'Have you heard from Aguirre?'

'No, no, no,' he said. 'Why would a great man want to talk to me?'

But he had heard from Aguirre, who had followed a dangerous path across Europe, at times barely escaping Gestapo agents on his heels. His sister Encarna was shot dead by Germans while their family was in Belgium.

When Aguirre needed a sense of the political climate or news on the ground at home, he got word to Xabier. It was not as simple anymore as turning up at the back confessional at the basilica, but such things were still possible.

Xabier knew without question that Justo would have loved to be involved. But Justo surely was incapable of stealth. He had the bravery to meet a battalion head-on if needed, but to be sneaky? That wasn't him.

'Justo, it is so thoughtful of you to come and help, but there is really no need,' Xabier said. 'I know you have so much to do at home and I hate to take you from your work.'

'It is not a problem, Your Excellency,' Justo said. 'I get my work done well enough, and our family home is recuperating well.'

'Of course, of course. Justo, I have to just come out and tell you this, then. It might not be good for you to be seen with me a great deal at this point.'

'Little brother, I have to tell you that it might not be good for you to be seen with me at this point,' Justo countered.

In spite of his serious intent, Xabier laughed. 'I mean it; I'm considered a political figure now, and other priests all over the country have been imprisoned or killed – you know that. I worry they might try to get to me by attacking you if you become too visible.'

'Me?' Justo raised his deep voice, holding in the air the broom he had been carrying. 'I can be the essence of discretion. I can be a whiff of smoke. I am a thought, a memory. I can come and go unseen.'

Xabier laughed harder. 'You see?'

'We will discuss this at some other time, Your Eminence,' Justo said, taking the broom to a cupboard. 'I'm going to see Sister Inky now.'

Justo walked down the hill towards the river to the hospital and spent the afternoon helping the tiny nun with her convalescents.

'I enjoy seeing you, Justo,' she said. 'You're one of our success stories. It does the patients good to see how well you have learned to adapt.'

Justo followed Sister Incarnation's tone with her patients; those in need of nurturing benefited from his patience and good nature. Those needing to be jolted from their self-pity were frightened into action by the forceful man.

'Anything I can do to help, Sister,' he said.

'You're helping enough, Justo,' she said. 'You're spreading a good message and being a good example.'

*

Well, this is some progress, Annie Bingham decided: now I have two jobs that don't pay. The small stipend for her work with the Basque children had run out. Their numbers had dwindled by half anyway, as some had been repatriated and some adopted. Many of the older ones had just grown up and, in large part as a result of Annie's teachings, were able to join the community on their own.

Even without pay, she continued helping those remaining; they felt like family. And now, having joined the Women's Voluntary Service, Annie Bingham was spending her nights bundled up at her station, manning her searchlight. She thought that her eyesight might be an issue when she volunteered for the job, but the recruiter seemed only too delighted to welcome her in any capacity. Night work would not interfere with the children's aid, and she didn't need much income, anyway, as she lived with her parents.

She wanted to write to Charley with the details of her new job and how she was contributing to the war effort, how she practised by training the light on seagulls and tracked the poor confused birds through the sky with the high-powered beam. But she was warned that her placement was considered a secret and she should tell no one.

To the children at the home, though, she felt comfortable offering the vague suggestion that she was involved with anti-aircraft defences. The children had gone several years without worrying about death by bombing. When they arrived in England, they had been assured – promised, actually – that they were forever safe. But the Germans had followed these children to Great Britain, and they once again found themselves shuttled off in the night to shelters. At least their friend Annie would defend them.

And for her new husband, she physically suffered. She could not believe there was an actual pain of separation. After the marriage, they had decided to live with her parents since Charley would be gone soon anyway. They would start their lives together, in their own home, when he returned. To keep her looking forward and staying optimistic, Charley asked her to start scouting out prospective flats. No one knew how things would be changed by then, but she wanted to be prepared as best she could for his arrival . . . whenever that might be. Would either of them go back to school? Would they have an income? Would they start a family immediately?

That would be good. Yes, that would be a fine thing to do. She didn't need more waiting.

There wasn't much time for idle wanderings, though. She slept from dawn until seven a.m., when she headed to the rectory to spend the day with the children. As soon as the skies grew dark, she was in her place on a ridge at the edge of town, waiting for any radio word that enemy bombers were entering the eastern quadrant.

Pedalling her bike home one morning as the sky became tinted pink, she turned the corner towards her house and saw a black car at her door. Men were there to see her.

Justo Ansotegui approached. Alaia Aldecoa could smell him; no one else carried that combined scent of farm and sweat and soap.

'*Kaixo*, Alaia, it's Justo Ansotegui,' he said. Yes, she knew. He introduced himself this way every week. It was a courtesy, as he assumed that her blindness kept her from sensing his approach.

'Would you like more of your soap?'

'Yes, I would like a bar of the Miren blend,' he said.

She removed from a sack the two bars that she made and put aside for him every week. He tried to pay and she rejected his coin. Justo moved on to visit other booths, as was his habit these days at the new market, which now was located closer to the river. He tried to act like the Justo from before the bombing more than three years ago, but she could sense the deep sadness that surrounded him, as it did so many others in town. Even when he talked of small things and tried to be light, there was a heaviness in his voice. It was not much, but she heard it.

As Justo moved on, she could hear the matrons chattering and the men playing *mus* at the cafe, and a man squeezing and fingering his accordion beneath the awning in the corner. She knew that much of the talk in the village was of Justo, speculating whether he, with his soap bubbles sometimes seeping through his pocket and his strange wanderings around the town, had lost his mind as his father had. Still, he seemed otherwise normal. He'd had his sufferings, not unlike everybody else. But he was dealing with them in his way. He would visit, buy a few potatoes, and then disappear down a side street on his curious rounds.

He's doing better than I am, Alaia thought. The making of soaps was far from stimulating. Mostly she did it for Justo. Otherwise she would not have left her cottage and would have had little reason for venturing to town alone. Except for one strange reconnection.

Sister Terese at the Santa Clara convent contacted her with an invitation. The sisters needed soap. No one had been able to replace Alaia in these years, and many of the nuns had mentioned it. They had not complained, of course, as it would have seemed a frivolous request. But Sister Terese had worried for Alaia. She knew that her cousin, Mariangeles Ansotegui, and Mariangeles's daughter, Miren, had been important to Alaia. Where was her support now in their absence?

Alaia found an unexpected comfort in the convent, going back inside the walls when she delivered soaps for the devout sisters. They seemed content with their lives, so certain of their direction, so insulated from uncontrollable outside forces. It was sheltered and orderly there, and they cared about her. Except for brief and somewhat uncomfortable moments with Justo at the market, when she tried to lift his spirits, the time spent visiting the sisters was the only human connection she felt.

Miguel's breaking away had been painfully executed. As he had on the occasion of his brief visits, he brought her a fish one afternoon. After placing it on her table, he announced his intention to go to France to live and work with his brother.

'What about Justo?' she asked, meaning, What about me?

'He'll be better without me around as a reminder,' Miguel said, speaking of Justo but meaning Alaia.

'No, he won't,' she blurted.

But Miguel was gone before she could say what she really thought.

CHAPTER 26

Intelligence from the Continent warned RAF pilots that German patrols sought downed airmen with the energy of children questing for Easter eggs. There was ceremonial joy in the hunt, and they looked in every bush and hollowed tree trunk, and beneath every leaf pile and haystack. After Charley Swan hit the ground and made a brief examination of the source of the blood on his trousers, he rolled and buried his parachute and burrowed into a thick hedgerow.

Throughout the late afternoon and evening, he listened to patrols on the roads stopping to inspect the fields and at times coming so close he could hear their barking dogs. He pulled himself up tightly into the brambles and tried so hard to stay still that his legs cramped and quivered. But the dogs never sniffed him out.

Several hours after dark, a watchful farmer retrieved Charley and ferried him back to a barn in a wheelbarrow that squeaked under his weight. He sensed the ridiculousness of this, but he asked no questions; the farmer had arrived with water, a piece of bread, and a way out of the thorn bushes. That alone made him worthy of trust. It took only a moment to see that a piece of metal had gouged out a segment of the meat of his outer thigh on its way through, which would end up being somewhat unattractive in the future but was little more than a nuisance at the moment. His blood loss was not life-threatening, and if infection could be avoided, he would be able to fly again after a period of recuperation.

A doctor risked his practice and his life to come out to the barn and clean the wound, stitch the jagged edges, and apply an antibiotic. A Belgian couple in town risked their home and their lives by taking him in, caching him in the attic, and sharing their rations with him until he could regain his strength. After a month of hiding and resting, Charley Swan would be placed in a conduit created by scores of Belgians and French, who would risk their lives to get him back to England.

The day he arrived in the attic, exhaustion overtook him. He slept for most of three days, awakening only for treatment and food, which he consumed with groggy appreciation. Oddly, being shot down had brought him peace, and when he arose, he was rested and ready to prepare for his escape.

His handlers coached him on the protocol of subtlety. They identified the areas of greatest danger and schooled him on means of avoiding confrontation. But as someone with an active mind and a new reservoir of energy, passing each day quietly in an attic tested his patience. He had no option, though, as the Gestapo conducted random searches of houses in most towns. And who knew who might be scanning the windows of the houses in the neighbourhood? So he remained prone most of the day, watching the path of the light through the dirty window as it crept around the walls and floor, casting changing patterns across the room like a very slow, colourless kaleidoscope.

Flies convened on the windowsill to die, and a mouse negotiated the inner wall with sprints and halts. Charley listened to planes overhead, trying to detect their direction (Ours or theirs? he wondered, tempted to look out but too disciplined to risk it). He traced the sound of the lorries that passed on the street, anxious until each passed. From the vents, the scent of boiled cabbage rose.

He created puzzles in his mind to stay alert. He thought through his daily flight checks and flew mental missions, setting flaps, adjusting the throttles, tilting the rudder bar, pulling back on the yoke. He would be ready to fly again as soon as he returned. To keep his muscles loose, Charley stretched and exercised on the floor for hours, lying on his back, making dust angels on the hardwood, and turning onto his stomach, attempting a dry breaststroke move.

At night when no moonlight slipped into the attic he walked laps and did knee bends to strengthen his leg. Anticipating a passage through Gibraltar, he worked at remembering his Spanish, conducting conversations in his mind.

But mostly he thought of Annie. One of his first questions was whether notification could be sent home to assure her of his wellbeing. He was told that they would mention it to airmen ready to pass down the line and see if they could get the message to her. But there was already too much on the minds of these evaders, and such information might be more of a liability to the system if it was pressured out of them in the face of the Gestapo. So nothing was said. The wife would just be all the more surprised when he turned up on the doorstep, they reasoned, and she'd not be doubly upset if his escape went awry and she had to hear he'd been killed a second time.

Healed sufficiently to stand the journey and now able to walk without a limp, Charley learned the plan. Outfitted in cotton trousers, a denim shirt, and a light jacket, he was to act as if he was a student going south on holiday. His handler, a woman he would meet only on the day of his departure, would keep a safe distance as they travelled to Paris, changed trains for Bordeaux, and transferred again to a smaller line for the southern points of Dax, Bayonne, Biarritz, and St-Jean-de-Luz.

Charley learned some French in his month of recuperation but was unable to fully express his thanks to those who housed him. He spoke a few words and finally hugged them both. They understood.

'Bonne chance,' the man said to him. 'Bombardez les allemands.'

Charley understood. *Good luck, and as soon as possible come back and bomb the Nazis.*

Previous escape attempts had taught the operators of the pipeline that the places of greatest vulnerability were station platforms, where passengers could be funnelled through checkpoints and suspicious individuals could be culled randomly as they filed past. The Gare de Lyon in Paris, particularly, proved a tricky bottleneck.

Charley felt so prepared for the journey and confident of its success that he fell asleep on the trip to Paris. But when he stepped down from the train, he understood the problem. A row of German soldiers blocked the passage from the platform to the main concourse as a pair of Gestapo agents sitting at a table examined identity papers. The long queue of passengers implied that this was not a casual search.

Odd, he thought; he had been fighting Germans for more than a year and these were the first he had actually seen. But now was the time for analysing the options, and he had to be careful not to scan his surroundings too obviously. He turned to re-board the train for an attempt at exiting the other side, but as he looked in the window, he saw soldiers with automatic weapons making a sweep of the cars. Stay calm, he told himself. The handler would know what to do. He would shuffle along in the queue and hope his papers withstood inspection. Be calm. Breathe. Relax.

'*Pardonnez-moi*,' he heard. '*Pardon*.'

The cluster of impatient passengers parted to make way for an overloaded baggage cart pulled by a man too old for the task. The teetering load appeared ready to spill as the two-wheeled cart rolled over uneven concrete.

Charley took a shot at a French word. '*Assistez?*' he said, pointing to the load.

'*Ah, oui!*' the old man said. As the man bent down to set the cart on its uprights, his blue porter's cap fell off. Charley repositioned the bags, picked up the man's hat, and placed it on his own head. He winked at the man and nodded at him to proceed. He walked along behind the cart with his hands steadying the wobbly load.

The line of soldiers with automatic weapons remained shoulder to shoulder as the baggage cart neared.

'*Pardonnez*,' the old man shouted under the strain of a heavy load.

The soldiers looked him over, up and down, and parted. Charley focused on balancing the bags without looking up as they passed the line.

'Halt!' one shouted. The old baggage handler and Charley froze in place.

An officer slid his weapon down off his shoulder and approached. He looked Charley in the face. Charley looked directly into his eyes, focusing on his pupils. The officer moved towards the load and repositioned a few bags to be certain no one was hiding in the pile. Satisfied the cart was clear, he gestured for the old man to move on.

'*Merci, monsieur,*' the man said when they reached the baggage room. He gestured for the return of his hat.

'*Merci beaucoup,*' Charley said, handing him the cap. He turned back out onto the concourse, examined the departure list, and strolled like a student on holiday towards the train for Bordeaux.

Something had to be done about the hair. At a time when inconspicuousness meant survival, nobody wanted to risk passing off a pilot with hair the colour of a warning flare as a Basque shepherd in the mountains.

Renée Labourd met Charley Swan at the St-Jean-de-Luz/Ciboure station as if he was a boyfriend home from school. Past a pair of Nazi soldiers, she cleaved to him, leading him down a side street to the Pub du Corsaire and up the back stairs to Dodo's apartment.

As she entered the room with Charley, Renée pointed immediately to the hair. 'Meet our newest shepherd,' she said sarcastically.

'I don't think we have a beret big enough to cover that,' Dodo said. 'We'd have better luck pretending he's one of the sheep.'

'Coal dust might do it, but that would wash off in the rain or in the river,' Renée said.

'The stain I used on furniture was stubborn; that would surely work,' Miguel added.

'Do you have any?' Renée asked.

'In Guernica. Sorry.'

331

'I'll get some dye,' Renée said.

These irregular tasks, requiring scavenging in town, had become part of Renée's responsibilities as their small group had developed an efficient division of duties. She could find hair dye without causing suspicion. Dodo could not. She could buy men's clothes of various sizes as gifts, whereas it would seem strange if Dodo stumbled through it. She could pick up a young man at the station and it would look like the start of a romantic liaison, whereas Dodo meeting him would seem the roots of a conspiracy.

In his short time in the mountains, Miguel had fitted in without a missed step. His experiences logging in the hills above Guernica prepared him for the night work along the border. He could walk all night, keeping his mouth closed and his eyes alert. More important, their small band could have added no one equally trustworthy.

Whatever limitations Miguel's hands were in his other pursuits, they were not a factor in guiding escaping airmen to the Spanish frontier. Dodo noted without comment that he appeared to be walking taller now, too, looking about him rather than at the ground in front of him.

The exertion and the danger energized Miguel but were not nearly as regenerative of his spirit as was the sense of revenge. Every pilot to make it back to England was one who could drop more bombs on the Nazis. It was not a Christian thought, but he found he could live with that guilt until his next confession. The idea of confession triggered another of the mental connections that took him on a predictable path: from Father Xabier to Xabier's brother Justo and back to Justo's daughter, Miren, again. Miren and sadness. Back to work, to find something that wouldn't lead in that direction. But everything brought him back.

Renée, Dodo, and Miguel had now successfully relocated more than a dozen airmen since the Nazi occupation of France. It had not been without narrow escapes, a great deal of improvisation, and the adaptation of routes almost literally in midstream. Several times they were forced to reverse course and quick-march up other passes. One night was spent in a cave with a few uneasy airmen. Once they piloted a drifting log across the Bidassoa, with only their heads above water on the dark side of the log as searchlights scanned and several target-practice shots ripped into the wood. Holding on to underwater branches, they waded across more easily than they could have without the stabilizing assistance of the floating log.

For some time, the Spanish guards took greater interest in the smugglers than in the refugees or fleeing pilots. The Spanish were considered neutral, as far as the war and its participants were concerned, but they had always been watchdogs – if occasionally indolent ones – against the unlawful transportation of goods and illegal entrance into their country.

Still, the Nazis had leverage on Franco, and the Gestapo had begun training – and intimidating – the guards responsible for manning the borders. An arrangement called for the Spanish to detain anyone caught fleeing France so they could be shipped to Germany for processing. As a consequence, the *évadés*, as the French called the escapees, were no longer guaranteed freedom once in Spain. And the Spanish, with new orders, were eager not to agitate the imperious Nazis.

But since the loss of the Polish refugees there had been no fatalities at the border for their group, an impressive record given the increased presence of the Nazis. The allure of the beaches and the pleasant nature of the towns along the Côte Basque caused the Germans to grow fond of furloughs in places like Biarritz and St-Jean-de-Luz in France, and San Sebastián in Spain. So Dodo's little corps had to deal with heightened pressure not only in the woods and mountains but also in the towns, where so many off-duty Nazis were sniffing about for women and pastries.

And into this difficult circumstance came a British flier with hair that shouted, '*Achtung, verboten!*'

'Fine, get some hair dye,' Dodo said to Renée.

'What do we do about that skin?' she asked.

'I guess we just have to get him dirty,' Dodo said.

German officers favoured the Labourds' inn near Sare. At dinner they frequently ordered several portions of *gâteau Basque*, never wondering about the source of the eggs and sugar and other rationed ingredients.

'I would crap in it,' Santi Labourd joked, 'except they'd think it was prune filling and order more than I could supply.'

For each officer who stayed, a small tariff was charged that did not appear on their bill. After Mrs Claudine Labourd ushered them out for housekeeping, she thumbed through the pockets of tunics and satchels for information, loose buttons, extra insignias – anything that might be taken without notice.

At times, she'd find a pocket holding three cigars, one of which she would take to sell to the same officer the next day after he noticed he was running low. 'Ah, you have my favourite brand, what luck,' he would inevitably claim, doubling her tip.

Although fully arrived at round-hipped matronhood, she still understood the value of flirting with the officers and hinted at the great delights she would share if only she was twenty years younger. Some were brazen enough to say that they didn't mind her age and asked her to their rooms anyway. She would act astonished by the officer's manliness as she squeezed his upper arm, toss off an excessively trilled '*Formidable*,' and reject the invitation by citing a 'woman's problem'. The officer would nod knowingly, without a clue in the world what it could be. He also had no notion that her pockets held identity papers that could be reworked into acceptable forgeries, a hundred francs in military currency, a collar insignia, a photo of the Führer, German stamps off his correspondence, and his spare campaign cap.

Because of the possibility of stumbling onto Nazis on leave, Dodo's approach to the small hotel was always tentative. Renée had decided to go as far as Sare this trip, walking ahead with Charley along the path as Dodo and Miguel trailed well behind and off the path. The only two visible were the lovers walking along the valley floor, arm in arm, sharing quiet time. Nothing could be more natural.

When Renée discovered no Nazis in residence that evening at the Labourds', the group entered for a large midday meal of lamb and vegetables, along with a vintage Bordeaux.

'The perfect wine, Papa,' Renée complimented him.

'Ah, it was going into Spain one night and a few bottles managed to get misplaced along the way,' he explained with mock dismay.

The plan was to try to sleep until well after sunset so they would be rested for the five- to six-hour walk. As usual, Dodo joined Renée in her old room, a proposition the Labourds found acceptable. The two lived together in the town, worked together, and loved each other; why bother with formalities? Besides, they admired Dodo and deemed him a more than suitable mate for their spirited daughter. 'Get it while you're young,' Santi always said to Claudine. 'Every one you pass up is one you don't get later,' he added before she slapped his shoulder.

Miguel and the black-haired Charley went to the back of the inn to sample the comfort of the barn loft. Charley's damaged leg caused no problems during the six-mile walk to Sare. With his 'new' hair, cotton trousers, woollen shepherd's waistcoat, rope-soled espadrilles, and beret, he was a plausible Basque, even with the oddly speckled face.

What more than adequately countered that liability was Charles Swan's fluency in Spanish. It allowed easy conversation among them all, particularly with Miguel that evening. It also meant that he could understand and respond appropriately if confrontation arose along the border.

The Labourds' barn housed a mule, two domesticated *pottoks* that were veterans of many midnight passages, and more than a dozen sheep. As was the case with the other special guests who had passed through, Miguel and Charley were billeted in the hay loft, and the mice were generally accommodating enough to nibble only on visitors' leather shoelaces and nothing more valuable. With the stacks of dried meadow cat's tail, the manger of oats, and the sheep, it smelled of Errotabarri to Miguel. Sheep, Errotabarri, Justo, Mariangeles, Miren.

Although he knew how important a few hours of rest would be to him later, Charley couldn't relax and constantly stretched and tested his leg. It had been a month and a half since he'd been shot down. The realization that he was now only a few hours away from a neutral country made it feel as if he was almost home.

Miguel shared little with the airmen. He couldn't understand most of them, and besides, nobody knew who might end up talking to guards down the line. If anyone were captured, ignorance would be an asset to all. But he was lonely, too. They passed between them a bottle of Bordeaux that Santi had given them.

'The biggest problem,' Charley said as they stretched out in the loft, 'is that my wife probably thinks I'm dead. I don't think there's any way for her to know that I've been taken in and nursed.'

Miguel shook his head, a gesture of sympathy.

'We've been married less than two years,' Charley explained. 'She has red hair, too.'

'Any little red-haired *niños*?' Miguel asked.

'Not yet,' he said. 'How about you, any family?'

'Yes. I have family.'

Charley continued with a few chuckles. 'I don't know about your wife, but mine is silly.' He pulled his photo from a pocket. Talking about her made her feel closer.

'A bird?' Miguel asked when he saw the photo.

'His name is Blennie – he's a budgie, one of those little birds that talk.'

'Your bird talks?'

'They just mimic sounds that they hear,' Charley explained. 'Annie is always trying to get it to say "pretty bird".'

'It says "pretty bird"?'

'No, all it says is "docka, docka".'

'Docka, docka?'

'That's the silly part; this is the second bird she's had that only says "docka, docka". She keeps repeating "pretty bird" to them, but she always puts the cage on the mantel near a very loud clock. All day

336

long the bird hears that clock ticking. Docka, docka, docka, docka. So that's what they learn to say, and she hasn't a clue why.'

Charley's explanation warranted a smile and then a chuckle, perhaps. But even that hint of humour broke through some inner wall for them both, and as they remembered how to laugh, it gained momentum until they had to bury their faces in their crossed arms to muffle the noise. The sound alarmed the *pottoks*, who shifted and stirred below, but Miguel couldn't stop. Charley's pink face flushed brighter as he was further amused by Miguel's response.

'Why don't you tell her?' Miguel asked once he regained control.

'Because I'm afraid it will make her feel foolish.'

Miguel looked at the picture, at the woman whose eyes were magnified by her glasses and at the vacant eyes of the bird, and he laughed again. 'Docka, docka,' he said.

'Docka, docka,' Charley replied, setting off another cascade of laughter.

Miguel handed the photo back.

'What about yours?' Charley asked.

'She's a dancer,' he said.

Miguel pulled from his shirt pocket the photo of his family on Catalina's first birthday. Justo knew that Miguel's picture had burned when his house was destroyed. Before Miguel left for the mountains, Justo had given him the copy that he had leaning on the mantel at Errotabarri.

'Oh, they're beautiful,' Charley said. He had not seen a more striking family. 'Your girls are gorgeous . . . perfect.'

'Not quite perfect,' Miguel said without thought, caught up in the high spirits.

'Why not?'

Miguel, still chuckling, hesitated.

'Why not?' Charley asked again.

Yes, why not? Miguel thought. He'd never see this stranger, this flier, again.

He explained why Catalina was not looking directly at the camera.

'We were hiding her ear,' he said. 'Four of us tried to hold her still while she got that ear pierced, and she broke loose and ripped out a part of her ear.'

He laughed at the recollection of the four of them unwilling to restrain the squirming little girl.

'That's a pretty earring in the left one, though,' Charley said.

'That's the *lauburu*, the Basque emblem.'

The Basque emblem? Charley had assumed that Renée, Dodo, and Miguel were French and Spanish and hadn't had the occasion to think of them as Basques. He'd been with them less than a day and no one had mentioned it, as they'd been busy planning the details of the escape.

'My wife knows many Basque children,' Charley explained, excited by the connection. 'Many, many Basque children.'

Miguel could not imagine why.

'There were thousands of children shipped to England during your civil war. My wife loves them and has been helping them out at a home. She's learning to speak Basque, at least a little. What town are you from?'

'Guernica,' Miguel said.

'Guernica?' Good God, Charley thought. Should he tell him he had seen the painting? Would he even know that there is a painting?

'Were you there . . . then?' Charley asked.

'Yes, we were there.'

'Your family?'

'Yes, they're gone.'

Charley closed his eyes. He had noticed the deformity of Miguel's hands but had made no assumptions; these days, it could have been caused by any of war's by-products. He thought back to the images in the painting and could remember the screaming woman holding the baby with the empty eyes. He hoped Miguel would never see it.

The flier focused more deeply on the picture he held and was not sure what to say.

'They are beautiful,' he said.

338

They kept talking in that loft, in the growing darkness, as protection from silence. The pilot told of the feeling of flight and how afraid his wife had been of him going to war. Miguel talked of his failure as a fisherman and how he could only imagine how sick he would get in an aeroplane if he had so much trouble on a boat.

He tried to explain what it was like to watch Miren dance, and he told the absurd story of Vanka, which caused Charley to laugh again and to pat him on the shoulder.

And when it grew dangerously quiet again, Charley added the only words he could: 'I'm sorry.'

Miguel had spoken of things to this stranger that he had not been able to say to Justo or Dodo or his father. They were all too close; they had their own suffering, and he could not expect them to carry his as well. It took this stranger to coax from him the words for such things.

'I was in the hills . . . I couldn't reach them,' he said. 'I was told that the first bombs killed her mother, and Miren, my wife, was buried by a building that collapsed later.'

'And the little one?'

Miguel's voice caught, but he had to say this now, while he could. 'There was nothing . . .'

'And your hands?'

'It happened as I tried to find them,' he said.

Silence.

Miguel's wife could have been Annie. The baby could have been theirs. Miguel's life could have been his. It still could.

'I have to get back,' Charley said. The statement was unrelated, but Miguel understood.

The loft darkened and the soft sounds of bedded stock below calmed them, but neither slept. Within a few hours, Charley would be closer to his own family, and he began organizing in his mind all the things he wanted to tell Annie.

The order came down an unusual chain of command. Sister Terese told the priests at Santa María that when Alaia Aldecoa came to the convent she looked weak, as if she hadn't been eating well. A priest at Santa María got word to Father Xabier in Bilbao that she was starving.

'You should take her in; it is the charitable thing to do,' Xabier said when Justo visited the basilica that week. 'You know how much she meant to everybody. We can't allow this to happen. We can't turn our backs.'

Justo couldn't deny that she had been like a member of his family, and he cared very much for her well-being. But taking her in at Errotabarri?

'Can't I just take food to her? Help her around her house?'

'It might be that she can get enough food but just isn't taking care of herself. She probably needs someone to look after her.'

'What about Terese at the convent, or Marie-Luis up in Lumo?'

'Justo, should that girl be put back in the convent? Or have to go live with someone she doesn't know?'

'But it's just me there, you know,' he said.

'What? Do you care how it looks?' Xabier challenged.

Justo thought. He'd heard the whispers in town before the bombing, but nothing since. Should that matter?

'Since when do you care how anything looks?' Xabier asked.

'I don't know, Xabier,' Justo said. 'I need to be free to get out. I do missionary work.'

Xabier could not be certain what that was about but could not see how a blind girl would get in Justo's way. He'd agreed to raise the topic only partly out of Christian charity for the girl, anyway. He felt that having someone else around Errotabarri, someone Justo liked, someone who knew Mariangeles and Miren, would force him to grow roots at home rather than spending his days and nights wandering about. The connection to his father seemed too obvious to ignore.

'Justo, look,' Xabier said. 'I know you always suspect I've got some kind of motive. I'm not saying she needs to come in and replace your daughter, and I'm certainly not saying she needs to come in and replace your wife. I'm just saying she's been a dear friend who may have nowhere better to go right now. That's all. She needs help.'

Justo walked to the cupboard and removed a broom to start sweeping the rectory. Xabier's instinct was to stop him, but Justo needed time, and he had decided to sweep as he thought. It would be uncomfortable having her there, perhaps, but that would pass. And no, he didn't care what anybody in town had to say. In fact, that was almost a good reason to do it, to get the tongues wagging. But at Errotabarri? He had a duty to Errotabarri. It would be better to take her in when Miguel came back. That would make more sense. But would Miguel come back?

Justo opened the back door and swept out the dust he'd collected, which was his method now that he could not coordinate a broom and dustpan with one arm.

'Let me ask you this, Xabier,' he said, replacing the broom. 'What does Alaia think of it?'

Xabier stopped and thought back through the chain of information as it arrived to him. Actually, as far as he could recall, no one had asked her.

Charley slipped, muttered, and smelled an odour.

'*Pottok* crap,' Dodo whispered after a quick sniff. 'It's everywhere.'

Telling Charley to watch his step would have been futile as they felt their way through a tunnel of night. They moved well together in the darkness, through the uneven boulder fields and up the brambled rills. Above, they skirted the tree line at the mountain pass that would funnel them into Spain. For the short descent along this path, they would be across the border. But to work their way towards Irun and the coast, they had to veer west across the invisible boundary again and ford the Bidassoa where it served as a very tangible barrier.

Once they crossed the river and hiked down to Irun, Miguel and Dodo would place Charley with helpers prepared to drive him to San Sebastián. From there, with the greatest danger behind him, Charley would board a train to Bilbao, where further plans would be finalized at the British consulate.

With Charley easily keeping pace and Miguel alert against followers, Dodo led them through a little-used pass and started traversing a side-slope to the west. They stopped once for water, a few splashes of Izarra that had been cached in a cairn near the pass, and some bread that Dodo carried in his pack.

'To calm the stormy seas,' Dodo whispered to Miguel as he tossed the first small piece off towards the rocks. Miguel nodded. It was a time to respect all superstitions.

Miguel stiffened, motioning for Charley and Dodo to be still. All held their breath. Within a few moments, Dodo heard the muffled bell, too. A herd was bedded down somewhere nearby and a bell ram had repositioned.

'Sheep,' Dodo whispered. 'It's OK.'

Charley hadn't heard a thing; in fact, he'd barely heard Dodo speak. He hadn't been aware of it until now, but it was apparent that the hours near his Blenheim engines had damaged his hearing.

They moved on. This route, it seemed, had been a good decision, and the extra walking to the east of the area that had been most heavily patrolled had been worth the effort. But the real test always came at the river, and Dodo had planned to cross some six or seven miles upstream of Béhobie. There the slope was gentle and protected by woods on the French side, and although there were guard stations at intervals on the Spanish shore, bends in the river created gaps in the lines of sight at some places.

Since no German patrols had been seen and they were still well protected by the night, Dodo hoped to have time to probe the north bank to find the best combination of cover from Spanish spotlights alongside the most manageable water.

The width of the river was not as grave a concern to him as the speed of the current and depth of the water. Although the river rocks were slippery and unstable, if the men were able to maintain their footing, it was much easier to wade a greater distance than to have to swim in the current even a short way.

Now creeping with frequent long pauses as they reached the flat terrain created by the flood basin, they passed directly across the river from a large guardhouse. From that position, the three-sided porch commanded an arc of river that bent in a crescent of several hundred yards. Spotlights made a deliberate scan of the water and the three dropped flat.

Ahead, the river curved back away from the guardhouse, and Dodo indicated the crossing point. Charley had tired now, and his right leg throbbed from the exertion. The weeks of inactivity in the attic had drained him of stamina. The sight of the water re-energized him, though, and when Dodo stopped and gestured towards the river, Charley realized that he was no more than thirty yards from Spain.

Dodo evaluated the terrain. A gently sloping rock shore extended out of the forest on the French side. As the river, over centuries, had eroded rocks on the outside of the arc and accumulated detritus on the inside, it had cut deeper towards the opposite shore. The bank was steeper on that side and thick with wild roses and horsetails. It would be a difficult climb, but at least it was sheltered from sight.

Dodo pulled them together and they knelt in a three-sided pack, arms on each other's shoulders.

'It won't do any good to follow too closely; you'll have to pick your own way in the same general direction,' Dodo told Charley. 'Take small steps. Feel for the next rock with your feet before you change your weight. Try to stay as low in the water as you can. You'll naturally angle downstream with the current. That's fine, but try not to go too far around that bend. We'll gather once we all get up the other slope.'

Charley listened hard and felt as he had when he first began soloing in the Tiger Moth, so excited that it seemed almost possible to fly without the plane. He slotted the information in his organized mind: small steps, feel each rock. Stay low. You can do this.

'Same order . . . go slowly,' Dodo said. 'Wait until I get near that large rock in the middle and then start.'

Dodo was soundless, his rope-soled shoes conforming to the surface of the tumbled rocks along the shore as he kept his eyes turned towards the guardhouse upstream. As Dodo slipped into the river,

Charley watched his pace and his path, and saw how the current grabbed at his trouser legs and how he moved slowly and half-bowed at the waist, as all little boys had learned to do while trying to sneak up on a friend in the playground. The extruding rock near the middle and slightly downstream was the limit of clear vision in the darkness, and when Dodo faded from sight, Charley stepped out exactly as he'd been instructed.

The current was stronger than he had expected, and it nearly sucked him off the slippery rocks when he was only ankle-deep. Small steps . . . smaller steps, he thought. He envisioned flying against a strong crosswind and banked his body upstream to try to counter his drift. By the time he was waist-deep, Charley knew his right leg was losing strength against the drag of the current. Every time he lifted his left leg to inch forward, the right threatened to surrender and release him to the river.

His analytical mind sought a better method: short steps with the left leg, long ones with the right, turn upstream and shuffle sideways with the strongest leg doing most of the support. Several times he slipped forward onto his hands, with the water deep enough for his head to go under before he could get upright and regain balance. The dunks into the cold rushing water stole his breath, and he gasped when he surfaced, dizzy now from the exertion and lack of air, and from the pain shooting up his right leg.

The Spanish spotlight broke its cycle of regular scanning and turned its beam in their direction. Miguel, ready to enter the water, backed slowly into the trees, waiting for the light to pass.

Nearing the opposite bank, Dodo heard barking from the downstream arc, on the French shore. The curve of the river that shielded them from the Spanish exposed them on the French side. The barking could be a shepherd's dog or one belonging to a farmer. But it could be a German patrol.

Dodo waved Charley back, but he was weak against the current, and his path had already taken him downstream. He fell into an unseen pool, and when he surfaced, splashing and spluttering, search lanterns stretched wrinkled streamers across the river. They scanned the darkness just as the tentacles of anti-aircraft lights had groped the skies for his plane during night bombing runs.

Charley went under again, and Miguel broke from the shore.

Stumbling as far as he could into the current, he dived on the run as he had so many times in Lekeitio while racing Dodo. He kicked and clawed at the water, but his hands cut through it without effect. He could not cup the water and pull at it to power himself.

'I'll get him,' Dodo shouted to Miguel. 'Get yourself across.'

Having been trained in survival techniques, Charley didn't panic and tried to guide himself to the south shore by kicking and paddling as he bobbed.

Miguel flutter-kicked towards the large rock, where he could collect his balance and his breath as the noise of Charley and Dodo pulled the scanning lights into focus on them. Several other dogs had joined in an escalating chorus of howls.

Dodo caught up to Charley, and both righted themselves as they floated almost even with the position of the patrols but within mere yards of the Spanish shore. As Charley scrambled up the bank through the thick bushes, Dodo stopped on the rocky southern shore and turned back upstream to help Miguel.

Bullets sprayed at the water, pinging off the rocks. A row of splashes raced up the river towards Dodo as he began to swim. And then he was gone, dragged under by the current.

With the lights and attention focused on Dodo, Miguel kicked himself to the shore upstream. He scrambled up the slope, gathered Charley down the shore, and climbed up the path above the bank in search of Dodo, hoping to find him already on the shore and prepared to join them. But he hadn't surfaced. He wasn't along the bank or the path.

The weapons fire alerted the Spanish guards, and patrols set out on both sides of the river now. Miguel and Charley stopped searching for Dodo and covered themselves. They made short advances and then hid for long periods, once ducking into a notch in the rocks while guards searched within mere paces of them. Dodo was gone downriver – shot or drowned. There was nothing Miguel could do except take over and get the pilot to Irun as planned. As well as Charley had kept up on the taxing path from Sare, his resources were exhausted by the river crossing. He limped badly.

They needed to stay unseen, but they also had to gain distance to the west. With halting progress, they sneaked along the edge of a road that occupied the first plateau of land above the riverbank all the way to Irun. Motor patrols cruised past at irregular intervals, rarely separated by more than five minutes. Some stopped and combed the riverside in small squads, often firing into the brush when movement was detected.

To cross the road and advance on the other side would provide level ground but no cover. It left them to fight through the undergrowth and washouts along the edges of the slope down to the river and hope a patrol didn't stop exactly where they hid at that moment.

'We're going nowhere like this,' Miguel told Charley. 'And if we're out here when it gets light, they'll have no trouble spotting us.'

Charley, out of breath, nodded.

'Let's hide and rest until a patrol passes, then pick up as much ground as we can on the road until we hear the engines again and then duck into the brush.'

Charley nodded again, willing but doubtful. And when the first lorry passed, Charley advanced no more than ten paces along the road before falling.

'I'm sorry,' he said. 'Just go. I'll find my way.'

Miguel saw lights on the road coming from the west and dragged Charley into a tangle of undergrowth. Unable to grasp his jacket and pull him, Miguel had to throw both arms around his chest and lift.

'I don't think I can keep going now; if we rest awhile I'll be better . . . just a few minutes.'

'We don't have the time,' Miguel said with enough force for Charley to understand.

The lorry sputtered past, and while the exhaust fumes still clouded the air along the roadside, Miguel rose again.

'Stand up,' he demanded. Charley complied, wobbly in the attempt.

Miguel dipped his shoulder to Charley's waist, folded him over his back, and lifted. With the flier on his shoulder, Miguel clamped his arms around the back of Charley's knees and set off on a staggering run along the roadside.

Within a few minutes, another droning engine was heard, and Miguel and his cargo dipped into the brush. Charley protested the second time Miguel moved to lift him, but he knew they were making progress. He trusted Miguel's strength and his judgement. The cycles of hiding and running continued until Charley simply could no longer stand to be lifted.

Shortly before dawn, they found concealment among a tangle of fallen beeches and collapsed. They'd made no more than two miles from their crossing point.

The fish returned to gnaw on Miguel's hands; the old octopus from his bed in Lekeitio wound around his legs and squeezed them so they ached. After a long while, the fish began laughing at him, spreading their huge lips to expose their rows of pointed teeth. Laughing. Laughing. And then talking.

Arise, the fish yelled at him. Arise. At a sharp jab to his chest, Miguel opened his eyes.

A Guardia Civil officer, in his patent-leather tricorne hat and cape, held a rifle at his chest. He laughed and made an exaggerated snoring sound.

Snoring? Miguel looked at Charley, who was being roused by another guard. They shook their heads, seeing the futility of escape. How would he ever tell anyone that after the trip through the mountains and the crossing of the river and the loss of his brother, they had been captured because they had been heard snoring in the bushes?

CHAPTER 27

Miguel thought as quickly as he was able and claimed that they were a pair of shepherds who had been lost and disoriented in the night, who started trying to swim across the river when they heard dogs chasing after them. Was there some problem? Was there some law against sleeping near the river? That was legal in France. If there was a fine, they'd gladly pay it, even though they were just shepherds who needed to sleep like anybody else.

The Spanish guards didn't care if they were Charles de Gaulle and Marshal Pétain; they would be confined in the Irun jail for two days, until Monday morning, when the Germans across the border would be notified. If the Germans had no need for them, they'd be taken before a local judge. If the Germans wanted them handed over, well, what happened after that was nothing they cared to know about.

Guards shoved them in the back of an aged lorry with a stubborn transmission, and they jerked and bucked to Irun. The old stone jail there hid dirt-floored cells in the basement. Before stretching out on the floor, Miguel and Charley removed from their pockets the still-wet photos of their families and laid them flat on a dry rock ledge at the back of the cell. Side by side. Neither had been ruined, but the backing was soggy and the corners were more frayed than they had been.

'What now?' Charley asked, removing his borrowed beret and

running a hand through his black hair.

'We wait. See if they believe us. If we go before a judge you can just tell them who you are and demand to see someone from the British consulate.'

'Is that possible?'

'If they get here before the Germans, yes.'

'I could be free?'

'Yes . . . maybe . . . the Spanish aren't at war with you.'

'What about you?'

Miguel had known of captured helpers who had been shipped away, presumably to concentration camps. Others who had been found guilty of minor violations had been added to the rolls of forced-labour conscripts.

'Maybe the consul gets me free, too,' he said. He saw no point in elaborating on his future for Charley. He might as well be left to envision the best possible outcome.

The day, a Saturday, was surprisingly pleasant for Charley. His fatigue and the possibility of a release to the consul allowed him to rest and sleep well.

If he had to face time in a Spanish prison, Miguel could deal with it. What was left to give up? But the loss of Dodo broke his spirit. Maybe he had made it downstream and away from the patrols, or maybe he had been captured and was in a jail somewhere else. But the way he disappeared did not suggest it.

The months in St-Jean-de-Luz and in the mountains with Dodo had been healing for him. Dodo, with his enthusiasm and infectious playfulness, had helped him gain distance from Guernica. They'd been drunk together again. They'd talked of Lekeitio and family, and even of the future. Miguel wanted to stay with them awhile, to see the thing out to the end, to help in the war, to be with his brother, whom he liked more than ever. With maturity, and his relationship with Renée, Dodo had shed the contentiousness that had sometimes made him difficult. Dodo had discovered his place, and he had been happier than Miguel had ever seen him.

Now? Who knew? Would Renée want him to stay? Why would she? Why would she want to be around someone who was such a magnet for bad fortune? All had gone well with Dodo until he got there, Miguel realized.

'We used to swim to an island outside our harbour,' he told Charley, feeling the need to speak of Dodo. 'Dodo would do anything to win. You've never seen anybody like him.'

'I saw him get us across the mountains and the river,' Charley said.

'Nobody had a greater hatred for injustice, even when we were little. He was always trying to take on a bully. He always had more passion about whatever he was doing than anybody else. Even if it was work, or fishing, or drinking . . . or chasing girls. There's no one like him.'

He started laughing, interrupting his serious monologue. 'It would drive you crazy sometimes,' he said. 'If the fishing was bad one day, he would try to convince you it was caused by the politics of the Spanish government. If a pretty girl looked in his direction, he was certain she was dying for his love. If she didn't want him, it was because she was a member of the wrong party.'

Charley smiled at Miguel's stories. With no siblings, he'd never experienced that kind of relationship. Maybe that was good, he thought; it saved him the pain that Miguel now suffered.

'Keep on,' Charley said. 'Tell me more about him.'

'Well, it was never boring,' Miguel said, starting another story. 'Life was a game to him . . .'

A few minutes after eight on Sunday morning, the phone at the jailer's desk echoed through the main-floor office. The sergeant of the guards, in charge of the lightly manned Sunday shift, was called to the phone.

A few indecipherable words leaped at him from the receiver, sounding like the growl of a mean dog. Ah, a German officer, he deduced. Then, in perfect Spanish, the officer began a lengthy excoriation of the guard.

'*Sí* . . . *sí* . . . ah . . . *sí*,' he tried to interject. He placed the handset down gently. 'Shit.'

Gathering himself, the sergeant resumed his air of authority before entering the cell of the new prisoners.

He descended the cellar and opened the door, and with an underling at his side, he roused the prisoners. The sergeant could not have weighed more than Annie, Charley thought. He had an arrow-point hairline and a sapling neck that did not touch the circumference of his buttoned collar at any point. He assumed a theatrical stance with his feet apart and his hands on his hips.

'*Señores*, we have just heard from our friends in the Gestapo,' the sergeant said. 'They have identified you as a famed Basque smuggler known as "the Claw", and his escaping *anglais* flier. They have demanded you be given over to their custody for shipment to concentration camps. Details will arrive within the hour. Make yourselves ready.'

He slammed the iron door and loudly turned the key in the lock.

The Claw? Miguel thought.

'They even know who we are,' Charley marvelled. 'Is there an informer?'

Miguel nodded. Apparently, but who?

Shortly after he returned to his office and applied more oil to his hair, the sergeant walked to the front door to await the instructions he was warned were forthcoming. A black car with a red swastika pennant on each front bumper skidded in the dirt in front of the small jail. A soldier in a forage cap was out of the back door before the car had stopped moving. He raced up the stairs, nearly striking the sergeant in the face with his Nazi salute, and handed over a sealed document. By the time the sergeant looked up from the envelope, the car had sped away.

Under the eagle-and-swastika letterhead, the typed document read:

The two prisoners captured at the border are to be readied for
transport to San Sebastián, where they will be processed and
shipped to Berlin. You will deliver them into my custody at Irun
train station. To reduce our profile at the station and eliminate the
chances of their compatriots making an escape attempt, I will meet
you on the platform for the train to San Sebastián at 13:00h.
Purchase three tickets for the trip and deliver the prisoners shortly
before the train is to depart. We can tolerate no mistakes.
Heil Hitler,
Major Wilhelm von Schnurr, SS

The sergeant roused his two guards and arranged the timetable for
the detail. They were to clean their weapons and polish their boots.
There would be no blunders, he warned them. They would leave
immediately after taking their lunch, and they should plan on being
back in time for their Sunday siesta.

As inconspicuously as possible, Charles Swan examined the station,
considering the geometry of the elements – the travellers, the guards,
the exits, the benches – as if they were pieces on a game board,
searching for a means of escape. While he considered clever ploys,
Miguel sized up the two guards, wondering about the possibility of
overpowering them and disappearing off into the clusters of locals.
The Sunday afternoon crowds were their best asset. Surely none of
the civilians in the station would move to halt anyone trying to escape
from the Guardia Civil. The sergeant personally led the small detail
and there were only two guards. The prisoners were not shackled or
cuffed, as that would be too conspicuous, but the guards' two
automatic rifles served as a convincing tether.

Miguel acted as if he was stumbling and bumped one of the guards
to gain their focus, hoping to give Charley the opportunity to run if
he saw an opening. But a rifle was turned to his face, and Charley
froze. The crowds moved out of their way, not seeing the point in
becoming involved.

As no practical means of flight surfaced, the two were led onto the platform with less than five minutes remaining before the departure time. Perhaps the train would offer an escape route, depending on how many would be guarding them.

The SS agent on the platform could not have been more obvious to the sergeant of the guards. He wore a black leather overcoat that fell to his knees; the collar was pulled high so that it almost touched his black fedora with its brim pulled low.

The agent approached the guards as if they wouldn't otherwise have been able to pick him out from among the civilians now moving to board the train. He opened his coat to retrieve his identification and in the process revealed to the prisoners a highly polished black Walther holster over his right hip. The leather holder for his papers was snapped open for the sergeant of the guard, who examined the picture of the agent wearing the same threatening outfit. The guard offered a clumsy Nazi salute.

'Idiot . . . I'm trying not to attract attention,' the agent growled.

'*Perdone*,' he whispered back, looking around the platform.

The agent pulled back his coat once again to remind them of his weapon and led Miguel by the arm.

'Do you need help?' the sergeant asked. 'Can you handle them by yourself?'

'Why would you think I'm alone, stupid?' The agent dismissed him with a glare and accepted the three tickets. Miguel and Charley were led onto the train only moments before its gentle forward motion caused the couplings to clank successively down its length.

Charley's mind filled with options now, as he saw only one armed agent guarding both of them. He assumed the agent was flanked by other undercover guards, as he suggested, but if they could overpower him maybe they could jump from the train. Surely they would have to make the move before the agent met with others in San Sebastián.

With his coat open so he could keep his hand on his holster, the agent led the two to a carriage that was not yet filled and motioned for them to sit across from him in a pair of facing bench seats.

'I'm glad you're well,' Miguel said to the agent.

The agent tilted his head up and removed his hat. Charley inhaled loudly. It was Dodo.

'What?' Charley started elbowing Miguel and leaned across and hugged Dodo. 'How?' He laughed so loudly it echoed above the rolling of the train.

'Once they started getting close with those bullets, I decided I'd be less of a target underwater and I swam as far as I could that way,' Dodo explained. 'When I found a spot downstream, I got out and collected some friends in Béhobie, who talked to some friends in Irun, who discovered you were captured.'

'Where did you get the Gestapo gear?' Charley asked.

'What Gestapo gear?' Dodo laughed. 'Anybody can wear a leather coat and dark hat.'

'What about the pistol?' Miguel asked.

'What pistol?'

'I saw it, the guards saw it.'

'No,' Dodo clarified. 'They saw a shiny leather holster.' He took off his coat and flipped open the flap of the empty holster.

'We sent a letter to the guards that was typed on paper Renée's mother stole from an officer. The car belongs to a helper in town. We even put a couple of swastika flags on the wings. The Nazis gave them to Renée's mother when she asked for a couple she could put up at the hotel to dress the place up and make it more homely for the officers.'

'This is unbelievable,' Charley marvelled. 'You're brilliant.'

'That's not the best part,' Dodo said, grinning at his deviousness and eager to tell Santi Labourd about this.

'The best part?'

'Yes; the Spanish guards paid for our tickets.'

'To the Claw,' Dodo said, raising his glass in his apartment.

'The Claw!' Renée said, adding her toast and moving in to embrace Miguel and kiss him on the cheeks.

354

'All right, all right,' Miguel said, tipping his beret. 'The real credit goes to Major von Schnurr here. I'd be in a prison right now if I hadn't been rescued by the Gestapo.'

'I'll accept that,' Dodo said, clicking his heels and lifting his arm in a Nazi salute. 'I looked good in black, didn't I? They never seemed to wonder why I spoke Spanish so well. Or why Major von Schnurr looked so similar to the soldier who delivered the instructions.'

'All Gestapo look alike,' Renée said. 'It is a fact.'

'All they saw was the outfit,' Dodo said. 'All they heard was the tone of voice. They're afraid to look too long at the Gestapo.'

'Mother will be happy to know that her Nazi collection was put to good use,' Renée said. 'She's been gathering these things for months.'

After the difficult river crossing, Charley Swan needed to rest for a few days at a safe house in San Sebastián before he could be driven to Bilbao. The friends who had supplied the black 'Gestapo staff car' in Irun had shuttled Dodo and Miguel back into France in a small skiff. The brothers had been back in St-Jean-de-Luz a day now. Renée prepared the celebration dinner. They could hear the patrons drinking and singing downstairs at the Pub du Corsaire – their bar – which Dodo now proclaimed unfit due to an infestation of German soldiers.

'So, Miguel, Dodo told us about getting you out but not how they caught you,' Renée said. 'If you don't mind . . .'

'I'd rather eat now,' he said, taking a large bite of salmon and then one of bread to fill his mouth.

'They both fell asleep and the Guardia heard them snoring along the roadside,' Dodo offered. 'We're lucky that the notorious Claw didn't knock on the front door at a guardhouse and ask for a room for the night.'

'Easy, Dodo, or I'll tell him all about your first trip across the mountains with the champagne,' Renée teased.

'Fair enough,' Dodo said. 'I'm kidding, anyway. He saved the flier's life; he was incredible. I wasn't at all afraid the Guardia would catch on to me at the station. I was worried that Miguel would recognize me and start calling Major von Schnurr "Dodo", and maybe slap me on the back or give me a big hug in front of the Guardia. But he kept his mouth shut and went along with it all. Very impressive.'

Miguel grinned and winked; he couldn't tell Dodo how close he'd come to doing exactly that.

'Maybe I'll turn into a master smuggler after all,' Miguel said. 'What's next?'

Dodo looked at Renée, who cleared the plates and began washing them with her back turned.

'Miguel, I think that might be a problem, for a while, at least,' Dodo said.

'What? Why? We did well. We got him through. I'm not much of a swimmer now, but I'm getting better in the mountains.'

'Yes, we did get him through, but I think the famed Claw might have too high a profile to risk going into the mountains anymore,' Dodo said.

'It was only the Spanish guards who saw me, and they thought they shipped us off with the Gestapo,' Miguel argued. 'They're not clever enough to follow up on it, are they?'

'What if they are?' Dodo said. 'We have to assume they contacted the Gestapo about you *before* we called them. I can imagine the sergeant in Irun had a major surprise when the real Gestapo arrived on Monday morning to get the two of you.'

'But they didn't know who we were,' Miguel said.

Dodo gestured towards his hands. 'I think he'll be able to supply a fairly accurate description.'

'I can keep my hands in my pockets,' Miguel said, louder than he intended.

Dodo wouldn't say this if he knew how important it all was to him, Miguel thought. The threat of the Gestapo and the guards, and of being caught or shot, consumed his attention during every passage. The concentration left no time to make all those connections in his mind. He needed this; he needed to continue more than Dodo could understand.

'It's not just you, Miguel,' Dodo stressed. 'And it's not just us. We're in a group of hundreds of people from Belgium on down. There's Renée, her family, the airmen. We can't take the risk.'

Miguel knew his brother had thought this through. This wasn't the daredevil Dodo anymore. He was being clever. But Miguel couldn't imagine anything he could do that was more important.

'So, what now? What's left for the Claw?'

Renée finished at the sink and joined them again, putting her hand on Miguel's shoulder.

'Go back to Spain,' Dodo said.

Miguel flashed on an alternative. 'I can help on the boats.'

'There's a risk of being seen there, too,' Dodo said. 'Not to mention your seasickness. I think you'd best go back to Errotabarri and become invisible for a while. We can let everything settle down and see what we can do with you in a few months.'

Miguel took another drink of wine. It was blood-red and rich. He took another drink and broke off another piece of bread from the basket. They were right. He had become a liability. He would endanger the entire system. He would miss it. He would miss Dodo and Renée. Almost as much, he would miss the food.

Patroia and Josepe Ansotegui anchored at a small inlet near Ciboure the next night. Miguel rode back to Spain in the hold of the *Egun On*, waist-deep in anchovies, prepared to hold his breath and dive beneath them if the boat was detained. He was dropped off at the same high-tide pier from which he'd made his first walk into Guernica on a Christmas morning before his life had become so wonderful and so terrible.

By the time he boarded a British-bound ship in Gibraltar, Charley Swan's wound had reopened slightly and become infected. It had taken a week to get to Bilbao and then down the length of Spain in a car driven by a man from the British consulate. There were roadblocks and inspections along the way, but the diplomatic papers opened all doors. He had been fed and tended to, but he had not rested, still anxious over the final leg of the trip, which would be through exposed waters back to England. He was stitched and cleaned and medicated by doctors during the passage, and when he arrived at Southampton he was sent home for two months of recovery. He would visit the homes of his crewmen's families first, but then he would heal.

The consul in Bilbao had sent word to Annie and to Charley's parents of his health and whereabouts. All had lived under the assumption that he was alive and in hiding and had never mentioned any of the other possibilities. Annie had spent a week with his parents in London after they heard he'd gone missing, and they had grown close through the shared anxiety. She wrote to them each week thereafter, sharing positive thoughts and feeling as if it sustained and strengthened her connection to Charley. Now his parents planned to visit them after Charley returned to Pampisford and had time to settle in.

Annie started working on his welcome-home surprise the day after she heard he'd reached Spain. She found lodgings for them down the street from her parents' home. In the three weeks it took him to reach England, she furnished it the best she could, given the scarcity of goods. She purchased a used wooden-frame double bed and some chipped cookware, and she co-opted some of her mother's older crockery. It was only two rooms with a bathroom at the end of the hall, but it would be more than enough for them. And Blennie was positioned in a spot near the radiator, which tended to clank noisily as pockets of air passed through.

They took a taxi from the station towards her parents' home but stopped a street away, and Annie told Charley to get out. She walked him slowly to the first floor, extracted her key, and opened the door. He had expected to be housed for the two months in Annie's room at her parents' house and was delighted by the idea of their own place, of any size.

'Until they rang up and told me you were alive, I never really thought otherwise,' Annie told him later. 'The time I was most worried was after they told us you were alive. I was afraid your ship would be torpedoed or bombed, or you'd be sick.'

After the first day or two of excitement, Charley was driven to bed by exhaustion and slept for much of the following week. When he arose, he pronounced himself fit and eager to get on with his life. They visited her parents, sometimes ate meals with them, and Charley told everyone of the brave people who had saved him. But mostly Charley and Annie spent their time together in their new home, making plans.

After a simple dinner one night, Annie laid out a few icebreaking thoughts on a proposal. They had talked of children and a family in those hours of gentle negotiations before their marriage. Both wanted children. As she awaited his return, she had decided that she wanted to start their family immediately.

'Dear, some of the children from the home have grown up and moved out,' she told Charley.

'That's wonderful,' he said, imagining them old enough to find their way on their own. It had been four years, and those who were teens were certainly ready for independence.

'And some have gone back to Spain, to rejoin whatever was left of their families, although that's surely going to be a hard life, at least for a while,' she said, moving towards the sink with the dinner plates. 'Some of the ones without parents have been adopted by English couples.'

With that comment, he understood where she was headed. She wanted to adopt a Basque orphan. He thought of Miguel and Dodo and Renée, and the Labourds, and the pleasant children they'd known at the rectory.

'Let's do it,' he said, trying to be calm against his growing enthusiasm for the idea. 'Let's do it now.'

The dishes were forgotten as she encircled him with a hug that nearly caused his chair to tip over backwards.

'I've been thinking about it,' she said. 'And I don't think I could pick one over the others here; it would feel like I had a favourite all along, and the others would be disappointed. They're already like family. If I can't take them all, I can't take one.'

Charley understood her point and suggested they try to find one of the younger children, who would be with them for a longer time and not ready for its own independence so soon.

From a dresser drawer, Annie produced a folder. It held the names of the hundreds still in camps and homes across Britain, with sketchy biographies and descriptions of each. That night, over tea, they searched through the lists.

They worked through the youngest first, some as small as five and six.

'This is harder than I could imagine,' Charley said.

'I think we'll just know,' Annie said.

They put small ticks beside a few of the names as they read through the lists from all the camps. In the register of those at Stoneham, Charley found her.

'Angelina'.
Real name unknown.
Brought to Bilbao from Guernica by a refugee after bombing.
Parents killed.
Identifying marks: Missing part of right ear. Silver *lauburu* earring in left ear.

'Annie, my God, Annie!' Charley shouted before falling silent.

'Pleased to meet you,' the little girl said in English, extending her hand for a shake.

She hesitated a moment, then dropped her bag and skipped a few steps towards the grinning man they said was her father. She raised her arms, warning him that she was coming in for a hug. She was tall and leggy, with pale bony knees peeking out between her skirt and white roll-down stockings.

The man with one arm closed in on them.

'I'm your *aitxitxia*, Justo,' he said. She did not remember him either. Miguel put her down, but the little girl continued to hold his hand, not questioning how it came to be damaged so.

If the party at Errotabarri overwhelmed her, she didn't show it. She had dealt with the entire process with less anxiety than anyone else from the start. When the couple with the red hair arrived at Stoneham, she was not in the least shocked to hear that she had a family in Spain that would be eager to have her back. She had always felt that somebody was there for her and they'd someday get around to finding her. In the meantime, she had bounced between camps and shelters and homes enough times to be comfortable with the process. She had adapted to new friends and new 'family' for as long as she could remember and accepted it as the norm.

She had never been told she was an orphan, not directly. She'd been labelled a 'displaced person' all along. She interpreted that as meaning a 'misplaced' person, picturing herself as having been temporarily put in the wrong spot, and assumed she would at some point be discovered and returned. When the red-haired couple arrived, she first thought they must be her parents. She rushed to them with hugs, which they accepted without complaint.

After Charley and Annie confirmed her identity, they cabled the British consulate in Bilbao. Father Xabier was informed by his friends there, and he drove to Guernica to tell Miguel and Justo in person.

Miguel had been back from France for little more than a month, and he and Justo were coexisting more easily. There still was no serious talk between them, nothing that would cause them to voice the heaviest thoughts they continued to carry. But the passing conversations flowed without strain. Neither realized how much he'd missed the other until Miguel returned. He gave Justo no specifics about the drama at the border, and Justo told him nothing about his own diversions. Justo told him he smelled of fish and Miguel volleyed that Justo smelled like women's soap. They both laughed, but Justo did not tell him that he had invited the soap-maker to live with them at Errotabarri. He would mention that in time. This was a time for the two of them to settle into the partnership of running the *baserri*.

Until Xabier arrived.

Xabier shoved through the door one evening, breathless, face pink, and ordered them to sit, saying he had 'important and wonderful news'.

'Catalina is alive,' he said. 'One of Miguel's new friends from the border found her in England and matched her to the description Miguel gave him. She's safe and she's healthy and she wants to come home.'

Justo assaulted him with questions through tears, and Miguel sat speechless, dizzy, wondering how such a thing could be possible, fearful that it was a mistake. It had to be a mistake . . . how had she survived? How could she have ended up in England? How could a flier he'd known for only a few days find his daughter? He had said he knew of children from Biscaya, true, and he'd seen her picture. But that was – what? – four years old.

'Did they check her ear?' Justo asked. 'They could tell by the ear.'

'Yes, there's a notch in her right ear and there was a silver *lauburu* in her left,' Xabier said. 'And she was found in Guernica that day, and she was the right age . . . it's her . . . it *is* her . . . there's no doubt. She's on a ship already.'

Xabier relayed all that he'd been told, everything they'd been able to re-create of her path. A frightened refugee had picked her off a rubble pile and taken her to Bilbao on the night train. Somebody else dropped her at an orphanage. Since no one knew her name, the *anglais* eventually called her Angelina.

Angelina. Somehow the name caused Miguel to connect and to believe it was her after all. He had never once pictured her dead, he'd never imagined what had happened. His mind couldn't shape it. He thought of her every day, but only that she was gone, disappeared, suspended somewhere at the age when he'd last seen her. But now . . . . Angelina. It was a name they should have given her from the start; it would have been a better tribute to her *amuma*, Mariangeles, and to Justo's mother, Angeles. Angelina. Little angel. It was perfect.

'We should call her that,' Miguel said. 'If that's what she's used to. There'll be enough other changes for her.'

'We should . . . Angelina,' Justo said, trying it out. 'An-gel-*eee*-na.'

Shaken, dazed, the two readied Miren's old room. The following day, word was sent to the rest of the family, and all were invited to a party at Errotabarri on the day of her arrival.

All the Navarros from Lekeitio came. Father Xabier brought Sister Incarnation with him from Bilbao, along with the little guest of honour, whom they collected at the Santurce docks. Justo invited Alaia and escorted her to Errotabarri that morning. She brought a gift for Angelina – the rag doll that Miren had given her. José María brought fish, and Xabier supplied several bottles of wine, making the sign of the cross in self-absolution for diverting spirits intended for future communions.

'God understands,' he announced.

The baker's wife, who had lost both legs to the bombing but had her life saved by Justo, sent up a double-layer cake that read *Ongi etorri.*

Welcome.

Justo and Miguel kept her between them, not wanting to miss a word. They provided lengthy introductions to everyone there, filling in the details of their relationship to her. By the afternoon, she was greeting everyone with '*kaixo*' rather than 'hello' or 'pleased to meet you'.

She had sailed on a British ship through waters thick with German U-boats, spent a night at the Basilica de Begoña rectory, and taken the train to Guernica. She had greeted dozens of new friends, and she hadn't slowed, enjoying, more than anything, being the focus of attention.

'What do you think of it here so far?' José María asked her.

'I like it very much,' she said. 'I like not having to worry about the Germans bombing us here. Germans bomb people all the time in England. We were always afraid of that. It feels safer here.'

Miguel and Justo looked at each other, and then at Xabier.

Angelina was placed at the head of the table they'd set up under the fruit trees. The seat was too low, and she had to raise her elbows to rest them on the surface.

'I'll make you a new chair your size,' Miguel told her.

'A chair for me?' she asked. 'I'd like that, *eskerrik asko.*'

By sunset, after everyone had a chance to talk separately with her and she finally tired, guests made their goodbyes; she hugged and kissed them all, sure to use as many of their names as she could remember. Justo and Miguel did not leave her side until they put her to bed in her mother's old room, clutching her mother's doll around its threadbare neck.

A half-bottle of Xabier's wine remained on the kitchen table. Justo poured two full cups.

'*Osasuna.*' They touched glasses.

'What will she need first?' Miguel asked.

'We have to get some little dresses for her.'

'We'll take her to Mrs Arana.'

'First thing.'

'School?'

'Is she old enough?'

'I don't think she needs to start school yet, but I'll check with somebody,' Miguel said. 'I think we should wait anyway. I don't want her gone yet.'

Justo agreed.

'She's so clever,' Miguel said.

'Of course she is,' Justo announced.

'We need to find some other little girls she can play with.'

'We'll have a party for them here.'

Justo poured the last of the wine and they drank in silence. They both were busy planning for the next day, and the day after that.

Verbal skirmishes broke out a thousand times in a hundred cafes each day. The German soldiers who occupied Paris acted as if they were on a grand holiday. Small acts of resistance sustained some of the Parisians – overcharging the occupiers for weak café au lait or spitting in the soufflé. More often, the outrage over their defencelessness against the superior forces was merely displayed through nasty looks and the occasional smart remark in a language that the invaders could not understand.

'*Vous êtes un cochon*,' said with a smile, might sound like a pleasant greeting to a German, if it was accompanied by a bow of mock obeisance. The German soldiers were under orders to not provoke or incite the citizens, so little damage ever came from sparks of spoken conflict.

Pablo Picasso, the most famous painter in the world, with a distinctive and recognizable appearance in Paris, was often identified and approached in the Left Bank cafes that he frequented near his studio.

The natives were accustomed to Picasso and his artist friends, who had gathered for decades in these cafes. But for the German soldiers who had any concept of contemporary celebrity, to see or sit next to Picasso was a development that would warrant mention in the next note home to the relatives or girlfriend.

As with many young men of military mien, the German soldiers might have understood little of painting, but they had no doubt heard of Picasso. It was the fame of his art, not his art, that impressed them. Some took pride in the way that the noted painter sneered in their direction; it would make a good story at the *biergarten*. '*Liebchen*, the old man Picasso made nasty glances at me today at the cafe Les Deux Magots. He had a thin dog and a young woman.'

One officer who considered himself culturally advanced approached the artist as he sipped his coffee at a table beneath the green pavement awning. The officer held a reproduction of the mural *Guernica*, barely larger than postcard size.

'Pardon me,' he said, holding the card out. 'You did this, didn't you?'

Picasso put his cup delicately onto its saucer, turned to the picture and then to the officer, and responded, 'No. You did.'

EPILOGUE
(Guernica, 1940)

Children play in the square near the new market. So many have been born after the bombing that it feels to Justo Ansotegui as if the town is being reseeded by God. At some point, thankfully, they will out-number those who were here before.

With each trip to town comes reminders of it all. The new buildings and streets are the least of it. They probably would have come in time anyway, and their presence obscures the civic scars. But the people left in town are more difficult to repair than buildings.

Justo sees them, the old women who try to shop while leaning on wooden crutches; the old friend who appears to wear a harlequin's mask, with one side of his face as it was and the other scarred and hairless from burns; another whose skin sloughs off, leaving his arms looking like the fraying bark of the plane tree.

Do they see him that same way, as a fraction of what he was? Is he too defined by what he lost? It doesn't matter what they see now. There is now much he wishes to accomplish.

The *mus* players continue to harass each other vigorously, and the *amumak* gather to sort through the limited foodstuffs, most of which they cannot afford anyway. It is simply a reason to gather themselves to talk.

Justo Ansotegui does not bother to announce himself to Alaia Aldecoa anymore when he approaches her booth. She lives at Errotabarri now, along with Justo and Miguel and Angelina, and makes all the soap they could ever need, so much so that the house smells of little else, so much so that Justo no longer hoards precious bars in his pocket during the day.

Miguel and Justo convinced Alaia that it made no sense for her to live at her cottage when all would benefit from her company. She was not Miren and she was not Mariangeles, but she was plaited into their family nonetheless. She helped them heal, like a bandage on a wound. She is important to Angelina, too. The two sleep in Miren's old room now and talk every night before they fall asleep.

They are as complete as this group can be. Justo learned from Miguel that if you lose someone you love, you need to redistribute your feelings rather than surrender them. You give them to whoever is left, and the rest you turn towards something that will keep you moving forward.

The political oppression is worse than ever. Having won his bloody mandate, Franco has further outlawed all things Basque. There are no dances on Sundays, no Basque flags allowed, and the language is aggressively forbidden, although they often get together in quiet places and exchange the words like smugglers trading contraband in the mountains.

Though, in the right surroundings, some of the old activities are possible. The four wander into the mountains; Justo and Miguel fish for trout, and Angelina plays and helps Alaia gather her meadow flowers and herbs. Alaia allows Angelina to guide her by the hand as she chatters in a language that melds the three she knows as well as any little girl could.

Angelina walks between Justo and Miguel to the market now, holding a hand of each. She stops to let them get ahead of her, and then she runs forward and swings in the air as they lift her. It makes her feel as if she's flying. They buy her an apple if she wants, or a *barquillo* biscuit. She enjoys standing behind the booth with Alaia, greeting the people who come to buy soap, talking to them, asking them about their day, getting to know them.

They work together at home with their few sheep and the small garden. The best times are in the evenings. After dinner at Errotabarri, Miguel teaches Angelina to dance. He is trying to pass along what he learned from Miren and Mariangeles. He stumbles and it makes everyone laugh, especially Angelina, who already is moving with an easy rhythm. At times, she tells Miguel what he is doing wrong, and he tries to correct it.

Someday this will change, Justo tells them. They don't speak of politics much anymore. But Justo contends that Franco can't stay in power forever. He had lied to the world, and the world believed him because it was convenient to do so. Franco will afflict their lives for a while, but the Basques have always endured, Justo brags.

If nothing else, they will outlast him, as they had the Romans and the others who had come to their lands over the centuries. Franco had promised to use whatever means necessary, but the oak tree on the hill still stands. Errotabarri went unharmed. And Franco cannot see them dancing at night, laughing by the light of the hearth.

AUTHOR'S NOTE

Readers of historical fiction face the challenge of separating the fiction from the history, especially when the two are often melded. Most of the historical 'characters' in this book are obvious. Picasso, Franco, Manfred and Wolfram von Richthofen, and President José Antonio Aguirre are real figures whose actions in this book have been fictionalized based on historical accounts.

Some actions by the fictional Father Xabier Ansotegui parallel those of Alberto de Onaindía, canon of Valladolid. Onaindía was an adviser to Aguirre who witnessed the bombing and was sent to Paris afterwards to tell the world about it. The British educator and politician Leah Manning spearheaded the evacuation of Basque children from Bilbao to camps and colonies in Great Britain, as was depicted in this novel. Brave resistance fighters in Belgium, France, and Spain helped lead Allied airmen to safety through what was known as 'the Comet Line'. Basque smugglers, most notably Florentino Goikoetxea, risked their lives to get these airmen to safety across the Pyrenees early in the Second World War.

The Spanish Civil War was one of the world's great tragedies, with savageries on all sides and a casualty total that may never be known. I tried not to tax the reader with elaborations on the complex and volatile politics at work at the time – especially the strange and sometimes shifting alliances, parties, and labels – but rather to establish a general context of the poverty, oppression, instability, and disenfranchisement that common citizens would have felt.

There are many faces to any tragedy, and this was told from the perspective of the Basques, who were famously staunch in the defence of their land. Historians have disputed the death toll from the bombing of Guernica, but the act nonetheless remains at the taproot of the assaults against civilian populations that the world still grieves on an all too regular basis.

ACKNOWLEDGEMENTS

I owe the deepest appreciation to the entire Murelaga family for introducing me to the Basque culture, from Justo and Angeles down through the generations to Josephine and then to Kathy Boling. They taught me about the Basques' fierce dedication to their families and heritage. And from them I first heard of the horrors of Guernica. Kathy, particularly, lived much of this book, which I will forever remember with gratitude.

Credit and much appreciation goes to InkWell Management's Kim Witherspoon, Susan Hobson, and Julie Schilder, who was the first person in the world of publishing to embrace this lengthy manuscript from a first-time novelist. Thank you as well to those at Bloomsbury USA, particularly Karen Rinaldi, Lindsay Sagnette, Kathy Belden, Michael O'Connor, Laura Keefe, copy editor Aja Pollock, and proofreader Nancy Inglis. Charlotte (Charlie) Greig at Picador UK served as an unwavering editor and friend throughout. I greatly appreciate the hard work and dedication of all those at Picador, especially Ellen Wood and Nicholas Blake.

Dr Xabier Irujo at the University of Nevada Center for Basque Studies provided expert editing regarding the Basque language and culture, while Ander Egia, Victor Arostegi in Lekeitio, and Emilia Basterechea of Guernica supplied invaluable oral history and translations from Biscaya.

I want to thank all my family, whose influence extends not just to this book but to everything I do. My two most important 'sources' carrying Basque blood are my daughter, Laurel, and son, Jake, who teach me valuable lessons every day. I am continually inspired by their spirit, and I am driven by their love and respect.

Novelists/friends Jess Walter and Jim Lynch gave me the best lessons in fiction writing when they critiqued my first two drafts.

Other critical reads and valuable support were supplied by my friends and colleagues Dale Phelps, Dale Grummert, and Mike Sando.

As a piece of historical fiction, *Guernica* was a product of considerable research. I am greatly indebted to the authors of the works mentioned in the following bibliography. Of particular value was the brilliant research of Gordon Thomas and Max Morgan Witts for the book *Guernica: The Crucible of World War II* (Stein and Day, 1975), which helped me construct a historical context for these fictional characters. No less valuable was Mark Kurlansky's *The Basque History of the World* (Walker, 1999), which is a must-read for anyone, but especially anyone who appreciated this novel. Joseph Eiguren's entertaining stories of growing up in Lekeitio (particularly a Christmas Eve conflict with the Guardia Civil) in his memoir *Kashpar* (Basque Museum, 1988) helped me understand the atmosphere and political climate of the region at the time.

Perhaps the best sense of the time and tragedy can be gained by a visit to the Guernica Peace Museum (www.peacemuseum-guernica.org). Picasso's mural remains on display at Madrid's Museo Reina Sofía.

Valuable background, history, and inspiration also were provided by these fine works:

José Antonio Aguirre, *Escape Via Berlin*, Macmillan, 1945

Adrian Bell, *Only for Three Months: The Basque Children in Exile*, Mousehold Press, 1996

Robert P. Clark, *The Basques: The Franco Years and Beyond*, University of Nevada Press, 1979

Peter Eisner, *The Freedom Line*, William Morrow, 2004